The
Powers
of
Charlotte

OTHER BOOKS BY JANE LAZARRE

The Mother Knot (Beacon Press)
On Loving Men (Dial Press)
Some Kind of Innocence (Dial Press)

The
Powers
of
Charlotte

Jane Lazarre

The Crossing Press, Freedom, CA 95019

ACKNOWLEDGEMENTS

I would like to thank the MacDowell Colony, where this book was begun; Kate Dunn, for her sympathetic and thoughtful editing; special gratitude to Rebecca Kavalers for helping me proofread; and especially, Wendy Weil, whose encouragement and commitment enabled me to persevere. I am indebted in innumerable ways to Gloria Friedman, who was always ready with the gift of clarity.

Library of Congress Cataloging-in-Publication Data

Lazarre, Jane.
    The powers of Charlotte.

    I. Title.
PS3562.A975P69   1987   813'.54   87-15736
ISBN 0-89594-249-6

Some of the paintings by Charlotte Cohen which are described in this novel—the *Horizons* and the *Coffin-Boats*—are taken from the actual paintings and sculptures of Emily Lazarre.

This book is for my sister, Emily.
And my niece, Sarah.

And in memory of Arthur Birnkrant who
advised me to write a real story.

Always (it was in her nature, or in her sex, she did not know which) before she exchanged the fluidity of life for the concentration of painting she had a few moments of nakedness when she seemed like an unborn soul, a soul reft of body, hesitating on some windy pinnacle and exposed without protection to . . . all the blasts of doubt. Why then did she do it? She looked at the canvas lightly scored with running lines. It would be hung in the servants' bedrooms. It would be rolled up and stuffed under a sofa. What was the good of doing it then . . . .

Virginia Woolf, *To The Lighthouse*

Life, however, was yet in my possession; with all its requirements, and pains, and responsibilities. The burden must be carried; the want provided for; the suffering endured: the responsibility fulfilled. I set out.

Charlotte Bronte, *Jane Eyre*

Book One

Rebel Girl

Charlotte was a very emotional girl. Disturbed, some said. Unreliable. A colossal temper, her aunt complained. Too serious, cautioned Uncle Buck.

Her very first year of life was filled with confusion, hastily made decisions with irreversible consequences, shufflings back and forth between two houses. One house was dark, quiet, somber, and Charlotte slept in a large oak crib of the most modern design. The second house was nearly hysterical, filled with dozens of faces that took turns appearing over the yellowed wicker laundry basket in which she slept nestled in the corner of a brightly lit, noisy kitchen.

Ever after Charlotte was to retain an intense relationship to sound. Music, the sound of leaves rustling, voices spoken, overheard and imagined, intrusive sounds and gentle, nourishing sounds and frightening, shrill sounds—all would have an indelible impact upon her from her days as a toddler until she was grown.

A receptive child, some called her. Sensitive. Overly sensitive, warned Uncle Buck. Perhaps his criticism was mixed with guilt. Her special relationship to sound had developed, obvious to them all, in the wicker laundry basket that was in Buck's house.

Isaac Cohen had been nicknamed Buck by his brother George. "I'm not calling you Izzy," George had told his austerely handsome older brother. "Izzy is an old man nodding in a corner chair. You're a young buck in the forest leading the other deer to safety. I'll call you Buck. And as for you, Dr. Friedman," he had said, turning to his new love whose name was Miriam and who had recently graduated from medical school—"you are not a *bitter sea,* but simply a *sea*—wild, passionate and strong. Mara should be your name."

Both names had stuck, a testimony to the power of George's claim on their consciousness. He was the sort of man, according to family legend, who made you feel as if just where you happened to be was the center of the universe—a man of swinging moods, alternately expansive and depleted by chronic, confusing rage. Mara had fallen in love with him during one of his highs, so the story went. She adopted the name he had given her, and offering the financial support that would enable him to write plays, which he had recently decided were his life's work, she rented a large apartment, reserved the best room for his study, decorated it tastefully and kept it clean. (George's moods, Aunt Rose said, provided the darkness or the increasingly occasional light.) The study was in the dark, somber, orderly house—the one Charlotte remembered only as an aroma, somewhere between hyacinths and furniture polish, thick, sumptuous, nauseating. She didn't remember her parents' faces, having seen them last when she was not quite six months old. But she imagined them surrounded by dark colors, lit up with amber light before golden beige walls, like the old brown photographs belonging to Aunt Rose, Buck's wife and Charlotte's adoptive mother.

They never explained why Aunt Rose had adopted her and Buck had not. Why she had to call Aunt Rose "Mama," as her cousins did, but was allowed to call Uncle Buck "Uncle Buck." By the time she was six, she refused anyway and referred to them both in their proper kinship status. This was not for lack of love. Buck and Rose were good to her. But always, from the time she ventured forth from her playpen and began to walk, which was when she was eight months old, Charlotte had a passion for clarity. Her very first effort that afternoon when she toddled across the wide, worn rug was to squat and make tidy piles of all the objects on the floor: one pile of old paper clips pinched in a hurry off manuscripts which overflowed a corner table; one pile of dark copper pennies dropped heedlessly and used for toys by the family cat; one pile of dust balls gathered together by Charlotte's fat

2

fingers from under the old red velvet chair and the patched gray corduroy couch. When Aunt Rose began cleaning up the mess, gathering dust, pennies and clips into a blue dustpan, Charlotte threw one of the irrepressible temper tantrums for which she was to become famous.

She never saw her parents again after those early, amber, aromatic days. Killed in Spain, she was told when, at four, she asked where they were. And this phrase, "Killed in Spain," was uttered with such resonance of tone, such raised eyebrows of respect, that even Charlotte, normally a disrespectful child, said nothing more about the subject for years. She did notice, however, a slight turn of sarcasm in Aunt Rose's raised eyebrow, but a stern look from Uncle Buck returned it to its ordinary uncommunicative position.

The first house disappeared with her parents. The oak crib disappeared. And when the wicker basket became too small for her, Charlotte was transferred to a white crib with fluffy pink lambs on it and someone else's name printed on the side. *Oscar,* it said in gold painted letters. No one in Buck's busy house ever had the chance to paint them over. What was the difference, they reasoned—Charlotte couldn't read. And she may never have found out had not her older cousin, Lynda, who was just beginning to read, begun calling her Oscar, which she continued to do on and off until Charlotte was well into her teens.

Many people lived in Buck's apartment. They came and went, moved in and out unpredictably. Some just came to dinner and then disappeared until the next evening. Some slept over regularly on couches and rugs. There was an old, pink couch in the large kitchen which always seemed to have someone sleeping on it. But there were only eight people who had permanent rooms and Charlotte thought of them as the people who really lived in the rambling apartment on the corner of 106th Street and Riverside Drive.

There was Uncle Buck's and Aunt Rose's room—the largest, sunniest space in the house—and what Charlotte always remembered about it were white chiffon curtains and small round end tables piled high with books. "Half the battle is won in piling the books up in the order to be read," Uncle Buck would say

3

modestly to anyone who remarked on the seemingly limitless extent of his knowledge about everything under the sun. On top of the topmost book were lined between two and twenty cigarettes smoked down to the filter. Buck hated the sight of crushed cigarettes in ash trays and hated the reminder of his obsessive habit. Lining them up like little white buildings and monuments along the ground of his books relaxed him. And only at the end of the week, on cleaning day, would Aunt Rose appear with a paper bag and swipe them all in, making room for the new tiny skyline to begin on Monday morning.

There was a second bedroom, across the hall from the first, for Andre and Jacob, the actual sons. And way at the other end of the apartment, through the large kitchen, was the bedroom for Lynda and Hannah George, the actual daughters, and for Charlotte, the adopted one. The room was crowded with three single beds, three desks and dressers, milk cartons full of toys and paints, three book cases painted royal blue and one overstuffed easy chair. But two large casement windows faced the enclosed garden behind the building which was always cooled by the overlapping shadows of many overgrown trees, always empty and always quiet. When Charlotte wanted to escape from the activity and noise of her home, that is where she would go. If the hour was too late, or the weather too cold, she would open the window wide and lean out, allowing the top half of her body to grow cold or wet, or letting her long brown hair be blown by the wind that often grew wild in that enclosed square of city space. Usually, when she leaned out the window this way, Charlotte would think about her parents, George (for whom Hannah George was named) and Mara. She would imagine her father, handsome in his brown army uniform, valiantly fighting the fascists until his heroic death; her mother, sacrificing professional security (a clinician of great promise, a girl of great beauty for whom beauty had not been enough) and leaving her newborn baby, going to join her husband to heal the wounded loyalist heroes at the front. Imagining them in war-torn Madrid, making their way over the dark Pyrenees, defending Barcelona, Charlotte would bring herself to tears, respect mixed with agonizing loss, holding her fist in her mouth so no one would hear. To increase the intensity of her sobs, because of the relief

4

they brought, she would repeat the words: Barcelona; Pyrenees; Madrid; until she felt her heart would break. Occasionally she wondered, but why did they leave me? until anger threatened where respect had been. But that was what was so wonderful about the wind and the way it blew through the narrow garden, pushing bad thoughts away.

Charlotte would remain for hours, half her body inside the apartment, half of it out, until someone, usually Aunt Rose, would find her and call her to come back in before she caught her death of cold. But Charlotte would rarely obey and generally had to be told at least five times.

"Why do you have to be told everything ten times?" Aunt Rose would shout at her, pulling Charlotte back into the room.

"Five," Charlotte would answer. "It was only five."

She began hanging out the window or disappearing into the garden for hours when she was about six. All the years before she merely stared a great deal, trying to make sense of the confusion around her. There was the mystery of why her mother had left her in the first place, which was always explained with the words, *She went to Spain,* in tones so reverent that Charlotte did not dare ask any more questions.

There was Lynda always calling her Oscar. "Why do you call me that?" Charlotte shouted at her older cousin one day. "My name is Charlotte. Isn't it?" "That's what it said on your crib so it must be your name," answered the arrogant Lynda. "So I guess that means I was born a boy," she told Lynda, hands on narrow hips, chin pointed to the ceiling, "a prince, or a king even, and wicked witches turned me into a girl." Lynda ignored her, which eventually caused Charlotte to capitulate, responding as readily to "Oscar" as to "Charlotte."

There was Aunt Mathilda, the younger sister of Uncle Buck and George, who came to dinner almost every night. She was a scary-looking person with long gray hair falling well below her shoulders and parted in the middle so that when she looked down it closed, like a fuzzy curtain, over her face. Her skin was marked by crevices from a childhood bout with smallpox, and she always wore long, tent-like dresses in bright colors. "Mathilda is an artist," Aunt Rose would sigh whenever Charlotte asked about her other

5

aunt's extravagant appearance. Charlotte, who already knew this because Mathilda's unappealing portraits, each a thickly layered rendition of her own face, were scattered all over the house, accepted the connection between being an artist and being slightly insane, a connection she would find both hindering and strengthening in years to come. But the strangest thing about Mathilda, from Charlotte's point of view, was that she always called Charlotte "Mara-I-mean-Charlotte." She almost never got the name right on the first try. She would fly into the house, as if on the wings of her orange or red or bright green dress, and say to Charlotte in a passionate whisper, "Mara darling."

"I'm Charlotte," Charlotte would explain uncertainly.

"Oh Charlotte darling," Mathilda would shout. "I am sorry, Sweetheart. You look so like your mother. I thought you were she."

Relief from all this confusion came during moments of simple pleasure: sitting on a high stool in the kitchen on an afternoon when the apartment was miraculously empty and watching Aunt Rose bake corn muffins or apple pie, humming a sad song from the old country; or sitting on Uncle Buck's lap on a late Sunday morning while he read her the funnies, *Mary Worth* or *Nancy and Sluggo,* the other children, his real children, gathered in a circle on the floor; or lying in bed at night, planning her dreams.

Each night before she fell asleep, Charlotte imagined herself in a large, round, well-lit room. A magical queen would come to her and point to the paintings on the walls, each of which represented a common dream of Charlotte's. There was the one in which Mara returned and took Charlotte back with her to Spain. There was the terrible one of Aunt Mathilda riding a large, angry dragon who crouched in the corner of the elevator. And there was the one about riding in a small cart, pulled at a fast pace by a snarling wolf, splintering into fragments as it sped down the road. Charlotte said to the queen: "Any dream at all, but not that one." She pointed to the painting of the wolf-cart dream and the queen, nodding royally, made the painting disappear with a confident wave of her wand.

If, after this ritual, sleep still wouldn't come, Charlotte had one last thing to do, a technique she reserved only for emergencies when no matter how wrong something might be it could still be considered necessary. She'd heard the philosophy explained by Uncle Buck and his friends when discussing world politics and the inevitable excesses of revolution. "It was wrong by absolute standards," said Buck's friend Leon as Charlotte listened carefully from her dark room where she was supposed to be asleep. "But it was necessary considering the requirements of the situation." He was referring to the execution of traitors in the Soviet Union.

Charlotte knew it was wrong to pull her pants down and touch herself there, but on some nights sleep took so long to come that she would begin to sweat until she thought she'd go crazy. So she turned over, put her hand underneath her belly and made up a story. Usually it was about someone she had encountered in a book or a comic strip—Wonder Woman, or Brenda Starr, or Nancy from *Nancy and Sluggo*—going to the doctor. As the doctor put the thermometer in or swabbed tense buttocks with alcohol for a shot, Charlotte almost lost track of where she was in a guilty swoon of pleasure, a powerful loss of control, and her fingers inched down from her belly to her silky wet vagina. Momentarily a soft tingling pressure down there would release her from possession by the bad thoughts. Within seconds after this ritual, used only in emergencies when it was admittedly wrong but absolutely necessary, Charlotte would be asleep.

At secret moments like these, Charlotte began to distinguish herself from Oscar, from Aunt Mathilda calling her Mara, from Uncle Buck's affectionate but continuous criticisms (too emotional, overly sensitive, he would mutter as he passed her room and saw her staring into space) from Aunt Rose's confusing status as her aunt by marriage and her adoptive mother. The life inside her own head would separate her from it all.

And there was one other time when Charlotte was able to achieve that wonderful clarity (others called it singlemindedness) that she so passionately and faithfully craved. It was every Friday night when she had her weekly talk with the other Rose.

The other Rose had lost all her family in a terrible fire. She was a writer, Charlotte found out before long, and she was treated with great respect by everyone in the house, a respect which was concretized by the fact that of all the visitors who came and went, the other Rose was the only one with her own room—a small rectangular space at the back of the apartment which was filled with dozens of plants.

No one ever spoke about why the other Rose had come to live with them, or where the other Rose's other home was. But every Friday night she left them to return, Uncle Buck explained, to her other home. Charlotte paid very little attention to the mystery of why the other Rose lived in two places. She was just thankful every Monday morning when the other Rose reappeared. And on Friday evenings, from the time she was six until the time she was about twelve, Charlotte tried to stretch out the time before Otharose (as the children called her) left by sitting on the toilet seat and asking as many questions as she could think of while the older woman tried to get her face made up and fixed to leave.

"Why are you so brown?" Charlotte asked, reaching a pale finger over to caress the dark cheek.

Otharose gave a snorting kind of laugh and said, "Oh Lord, mmmm," as she covered her dark skin with a powder of a lighter shade of brown, making her skin look as if a sparkling pink dust had fallen on it. Next Otharose painted dark purple onto her wide rounded lips.

"Why do you use such dark purple?" Charlotte asked moving

8

from a seated position on the toilet to her knees and leaning over
so far in order to watch that her own face appeared in the mirror
next to Otharose's.

"Lord, girl, get down. How can I see?" Otharose exclaimed.
And the obedient Charlotte (Otharose was the only person whom
Charlotte consistently obeyed) sat back down on her haunches
and repeated,

"But why?"

"Because I'm dark, so I use dark lipstick," Otharose replied.

Charlotte never failed to notice how dark Otharose was since
she often held hands with her and saw her own small light fingers
stripe dramatically between Otharose's nearly black ones. She
wondered at the vast array of colors people came in, but by the
time Charlotte was six she was always thinking about colors, trying to paint great splotches of watercolor designs in order to attach
color to all the sounds which constantly irritated, frightened or
thrilled her. She attached no social significance to the variations
in human skin color until she was nearly seven, about the time
she started staring out the window.

It was a Tuesday morning and Otharose had just disappeared
into her room, locking the door against all intrusion until evening. Charlotte was waiting for Lynda and Andre so that the three
older ones could walk Jacob and Hannah George the two blocks
to school, when she turned to Uncle Buck and asked, "Why is
Otharose brown?"

Looking up from his morning paper he took his round,
rimless glasses off his bony nose, arched his back slightly and
slowly buttoned his navy blue woolen vest right up to the top
where it formed an upside-down triangular pocket for his dark
red tie. Staring into the eyes of his attentive niece, he said with
great seriousness, "There are no differences between people,
Charlotte. We are all the same. You know that."

"But Otharose isn't the same as us," insisted Charlotte.

"She certainly is the same as us," Uncle Buck rebuked her
in an angry tone. "Rose is a Negro. But she has the same red blood
coursing through her veins. She has the same beating heart." He
thumped his chest. "The same right to dignity. You must always
respect her, Charlotte. She is a writer."

9

Charlotte had no idea what a Negro was or why it made your skin a rich shade of mahogany brown. She never doubted that red blood coursed through Otharose's veins since she had seen the woman prick her finger with sewing needles or cut herself on a kitchen knife. Then Otharose would mutter, "shoot," and squeeze the crimson liquid in a narrow stream onto her dark brown hand, spilling it in small drops on the stark white porcelain of the sink. Charlotte had made a picture of one such occasion. Brown, white and red in wide lines stretching over each other, mixing into beige at the borders. She certainly respected Otharose. And she had learned to practically shrink with veneration at the word, writer. It meant: an explainer, a record keeper, one who understands. Uncle Buck would say to the children, "Shhhh, she's writing," as another parent might say, she's praying. Or some new visitor would appear in the house and appropriate one of the rooms for days at a time, usually the boys' room, and Jacob and Andre would be moved in temporarily with the girls.

"What's he doing in my room?" Andre would shout. Uncle Buck would reply, his eyes cast heavenward, "He is writing." And Andre would march off to the large living room window, ease himself onto the fire escape and, for the next two hours, strum a loud guitar which he learned to play when he was nine and never after seemed to put down. In between the songs he would yell *shit, fuck, bitch,* loud enough for everyone to hear, and Uncle Buck and Aunt Rose, intimidated by their talented and angry older son, would look at each other silently, Uncle Buck shaking his head in dumbfounded consternation, and Aunt Rose, Charlotte always thought, looking at her husband as if he were the one at fault.

"What do you write?" Charlotte asked once, sitting on her toilet-seat perch, watching a dark blue chiffon scarf being tied around Otharose's neck and tucked between the lapels of a white nylon blouse.

"I write stories sometimes. And a few poems. Mostly I write letters," said Otharose.

"Oh!" shrieked Charlotte, who loved to write letters. "Who do you write to?"

"I write letters to the dead," Otharose replied, brushing back

10

her thick, wiry hair and beginning to divide it into a dozen tight braids.

Charlotte was quiet for a few minutes. Her attention, fully captured by this incomprehensible morbidity, was focused on some future letter she might write to Mara and George. "But why? If they're dead they can't read them," she declared. "Can they?"

"I write not to communicate with them," said Otharose flatly. "But to defeat Death who tries to get me every day."

The words echoed like chapel bells through the long tunnel-like, white-tiled bathroom. Charlotte thought she could see the sound swirling around the small room in the wake of the stormy air.

"But why does Death want you so much?" she finally whispered, worried that Otharose would suddenly terminate this fascinating conversation.

Otharose, having finished the last of twelve, evenly spaced braids, looked at herself in the mirror and picked up her spongy powder puff. "He don't want me, Baby. Ole Man Death got my babies and my husband. It's I wants him."

Charlotte pictured Ole Man Death, gray and ominous green, clutching Otharose's family in one hand, reaching for her with the other. She pictured Otharose writing desperately, obsessively, for if she stopped for even a minute she would be vulnerable to the icy grasp. She watched silently as Otharose wiped the orange puff, its bottom half colored darkly with salmony brown, over her wide forehead, across her prominent cheekbones, around to her pointed chin, up again and down in a neat slide over her broad nose.

By the time Charlotte emerged from her trance, question time was over. This was signaled by Otharose pulling her black wool hat down over her braids, blotting her lips against each other until the dark face had only a thin line for a mouth, then opening her lips again—a purple flower widening in the sun.

"See you Monday, Sugar." She bent close to Charlotte's face, smiling broadly, exuding the thick perfume of pink powder dust.

"But don't forget to write to Ole Man Death tomorrow and Sunday," Charlotte suddenly thought to remind Otharose, "or else he might get you before you come back."

11

"Shoot, girl," Otharose snorted, taking Charlotte's chin in her long hand. "I got to come back. I got to come back to you. Cause I love you best in all the world."

Otharose had said this before, and it agitated Charlotte with tantalizing guilt. *Better than Lynda and Hannah George. Better than Jacob and Andre.*

("We don't love anyone best. There are no favorites here," Uncle Buck assured them all periodically.)

"Why do you love me best?" Charlotte asked wickedly. She felt she was on the trail of a moment of clarity, the very sort she so insatiably craved. "Why do you love me best?" she demanded again as the woman, a warm, dark and quiet shadow softening the light, looked deeply into her eyes.

"Because you need me the most. You're gonna have big troubles some day," Otharose answered with slow emphasis on the *big*.

"But why?" Charlotte persisted, determined to have the revelation of her inevitable fate without delay.

"Oh, it's a secret, a real secret, Charlotte. I'll tell you when you're sixteen," Otharose promised and stood up straight. No amount of pleading could make her change her mind. And having added that ultimate mystery to the others, Otharose kissed Charlotte on the mouth and repeated, "I'll see you Monday, Sugar, now be a good girl."

Charlotte nodded her head up and down to this injunction with the very best and most honest intentions — to control her temper by counting to ten as Uncle Buck advised, to refrain from arguing with Aunt Rose over everything, to resist the impulse to squeeze Hannah George's fair skin until it blotched red when the younger cousin broke her crayons or mimicked everything she said, to pick up her soiled clothes and toys at the end of the day. She swore to herself every Friday night as she looked into Otharose's dark fragrant face to be a good girl. But she was rarely successful. And in the yawning gap between her strongly felt intentions and her constantly paltry results she was, on top of being unable to make sense of the world around her, confronted with her humiliating inability to control even herself.

12

Bright red blood floated on the surface of the water then spread into a circle of diluted pink. Charlotte stared at the stain in the crotch of her underpants. Described variously by friends and relatives as "the curse," "her friend," "her time"—the thing itself was here. She called Aunt Rose who placed a soft white napkin between her legs. When she walked out of the bathroom, feeling as if the entire world must know, Uncle Buck was standing with his hands behind his back staring out the window. He heard her step and turned to face her with tears in his eyes. "Your mother would have been very proud of you today," he said, clasping her to his bony chest. Charlotte remained stiff in his arms, her cheek pressed uncomfortably against his thick woolen tie.

"For goodness sakes, Buck. You're cutting off the child's air," Aunt Rose shouted from the kitchen. Charlotte looked at her aunt gratefully and, holding her thighs close together, fearful that the cotton pad would slip out of her underpants and fall down her leg, she walked, in as dignified a manner as was possible under the circumstances, to her room. Just before she closed the door she heard Buck's disgruntled whisper—"What do you want, Rose, that I should never mention her name?"

Charlotte left the door opened a crack, enough to hear whatever else might be said. But all she heard was Aunt Rose bustling around the kitchen and then Buck's voice again in a different tone —"Rosela." After a few moments of silence she slipped down the hall and peeked into the kitchen where Rose and Buck were locked in a passionate embrace. Charlotte had never seen them kiss that way before.

She pondered the mysteries for years and, whenever she did, that afternoon would eventually come to mind. She would see Aunt Rose and Uncle Buck kissing; she would hear Uncle Buck apologize for mentioning Mara; she would hear the softness in his voice when he said "your mother," and see his watery eyes as he pressed her to his scratchy tie. It was a clue, Charlotte decided. She added it to her mental collection of clues which brought her no closer to solving the mysteries, only confirmed her view, over the years, that they did in fact exist. Increasingly, she eavesdropped. She became adept at pretending to read while actually fully concentrated on a conversation taking place in an adjoining room. She asked apparently innocent questions for her own private ends. "Tell me a story about my mother," she would say to Uncle Buck, and never take her eyes away from his face, waiting for a sign of discomfort. If he became uncomfortable under her scrutiny and found an excuse to leave the room, Charlotte slapped her knee knowingly. "Mmm, hmmm," she muttered to herself, "another clue." Once she ruffled through Aunt Rose's desk when no one was home, but found only birth certificates, recipes, recent letters from people Charlotte didn't know. One thing she knew — Uncle Buck had a special feeling for her, and it didn't make Aunt Rose entirely happy. There were times when Charlotte hated Aunt Rose, for her interference, for the way she enforced silence in the house about so many things, for the way Uncle Buck deferred to her. And she couldn't connect those feelings to the other one she had when she recalled Aunt Rose bending over the toilet holding the white cotton in her knuckly fingers, placing it between Charlotte's thighs. Her palm held it there for a minute while Charlotte handed her the pins. She pulled up Charlotte's underpants and whispered, *ketzeleh* — little kitten, and hugged her close to her large, soft breast.

Despite persistent and creative snooping, Charlotte got no closer to a solution to the mysteries than she did to getting the secret out of Otharose whom she badgered mercilessly whenever she got the chance. "When you're sixteen," Otharose would croon, and Charlotte had to learn to be content with acquiring the more ordinary information of childhood.

14

In the spring of her fourteenth year, the weather was unusually warm. Charlotte would always remember that April—its weather, its events, its colors—because it was the beginning of a time in her life that would not end until she was seventeen.

In the silent backyard heat drifted in an irresistible breeze sweeping through the branches of the tightly packed trees. Charlotte sat on a white stone bench under a maple tree which was just beginning to bud, a large drawing pad across her knees. She warmed her winter-pale fingers as she watched them move the charcoal across the page creating an image of themselves. She was drawing a picture of her hands drawing.

Perhaps if she had not been sunk so deeply in reverie, her attention so focused that any sudden noise would have jolted her annoyingly into the unmanageable world of daily life, she might not have become so enraged at Lynda who shouted out the window at the top of her lungs,

"Oscar! Dinner!"

By the time Charlotte grabbed her pencils, which had gone flying out of her hands at the sudden intrusion, clutched her pad under her arm and stormed upstairs to the apartment, Lynda was already in the bathroom washing her hands.

Charlotte had a well-earned reputation in the family for clumsiness. Andre called her the family destroyer and made the sound of a jet plane diving and crashing whenever she spilled her milk, broke a dish or bumped into the corner of the dining room table. When she stomped into the bathroom, she misjudged the distance of the familiar space and crashed into Lynda whose eyes were hidden by the towel she was using to wipe her face, and who raised her head with such force that she bumped into the overhanging glass shelf on which Aunt Rose kept her collection of hand creams, toilet waters and small perfumed soaps. The shelf toppled sideways and several bottles slid off the downward slope, falling into the sink where they shattered, emitting a sickeningly sweet aroma.

"Jesus H. Christ," Lynda muttered, an epithet which she had learned in the seventh grade from her best friend Kathleen O'Mally and had remained attached to ever since. "Can't you ever be careful, Charlotte?"

15

"How come you only call me Charlotte when you're being an asshole?"

"Don't you know any other word besides asshole?" Lynda snapped and began picking small slivers of glass out of the sink in stoic martyrdom as Aunt Rose entered the room, glaring.

"Don't touch the glass!" she ordered her daughter. Lynda continued to lift small pieces from the sink and drop them into the toilet.

"I said do not touch the glass!" Rose grabbed her daughter's arm and pointed her in the direction of the kitchen. Lynda and Rose were alike, people said—competent realists. But their similarities of spirit and talent were subsumed in an endlessly re-enacted conflict of equally powerful wills.

"Of course. Yell at me," Lynda shouted. "She's the one who made the mess. But of course. Yell at me."

"Don't use that sarcasm on me, young lady."

"Fine," said Lynda sarcastically, and left the room.

Charlotte slunk into the corner between the bathtub rim and the dirty clothes bin, clutched her drawing pad to her chest and murmured, "What an asshole."

"And you can watch your language, Miss," Aunt Rose sighed, but her scolding lacked energy which caused Charlotte to feel as if she didn't matter much at all. Silently, Rose gathered glass into a mound of white tissue and flushed it down the toilet.

At the dinner table Charlotte placed her drawing pad, which she had not thought to put away, flat across her knees, spread her paper napkin on top of it and waited with the others for the dinner to be served. Jacob and Hannah George arrived together and took their places to the left of Buck who spoke in whispers to Aunt Mathilda about something which was obviously important.

"What'd you do now, Jet Plane," Andre quipped, smiling at his cousin as he poured himself a large glass of milk.

Otharose said, "Oh hush, boy," and winked at Charlotte. But Andre, who was Charlotte's favorite, was the only one in the family who could tease her without hurting her infamously raw feelings.

Lynda flounced into her chair next to Charlotte and silently mouthed—I hate you. Charlotte was about to respond, her lips already forming the word asshole, when Uncle Buck, apparently

16

oblivious to the commotion around him, looked at his family, smiled sadly and announced in a solemn tone, "Why don't we all begin to eat before I tell you the disturbing news."

"Jesus H. Christ," muttered Lynda.

"Kindly do not use that expression, Lynda," Uncle Buck lectured the daughter with whom he enjoyed the most untroubled relationship of anyone in the family.

"Well, Pop, whatayou expect when you start with that announcement? How're we supposed to eat?" Andre dropped his knife and fork onto the old oak table.

Otharose stared at Andre, but Charlotte couldn't tell if she were going to reprimand him or take him in her arms. Picking at her food, she worried about Uncle Buck's news. Soon she abandoned the noodle and chopped meat casserole and put her hands in her lap, where she folded and refolded the corners of her drawing until the tiny triangular segments came off in her hands.

"Eat," Buck commanded, and tossed the heel of the rye bread over to her, her favorite piece.

"Buck!" Rose exploded. "Throwing bread? This is a lesson for children?"

"Please! I can't stand to be in the middle of another fight!" Charlotte insisted with such energy that she knocked over her water glass; the liquid spilled over the table in a fast stream into Uncle Buck's lap.

"Rrrrrmmmm, bbbbbccchhhh, wham, argh!! Jet Plane crashes again!"

"Calm down, Charlotte," instructed Uncle Buck as if she alone were the author of the chaos. He dumped a huge wad of paper napkins onto the stream of water and left it there to sop up the various tributaries, a spongy, dripping white dam.

They all ate quietly for several minutes. Buck shoveled the noodle and meat mixture into his mouth with a swift fork, made a small pile of crumbs with a torn-off piece of bread, pushed the pile onto the bread and ate it quickly, ripping his napkin from his belt and wiping his lips before he was done chewing. The children watched anxiously. If Buck were eating like this, the news must be bad. Aunt Rose and Otharose made frequent eye contact over their plates, but Otharose continued to eat in her usual

17

painstaking manner. Aunt Rose hardly touched her food. Charlotte turned her back to her uncle and noticed a jagged edge of white napkin that remained stuck to his belt and hung vertically, parallel to his fly.

Andre snarled between heaping spoonfuls and three tall glasses of milk. At fourteen, he was as tall as his father. His shoulders were narrow and there was a crevice in his breast bone that caused his chest to appear sunken in the middle like a shallow empty bowl. Buck's body had the same structural flaw; there was nothing wrong with either of them, but their chests looked hollowed out, as if there had been some terrible accident. Andre's tight, thin tee shirt curved inward where the crevice was. Still, Charlotte thought he was the handsomest boy she had ever seen, especially when his hair was long and fell in dark unruly curls over his forehead and ears. Andre finished the last crumb on his plate, shoveling food in, a cruel parody of his father, then, looking across the table with dark, furious eyes he said, "We're done eating, Pop. Whenever you decide to let us in on the secret." Some unchewed chopped meat escaped from his mouth onto his chin, and he slapped it off with the back of his hand.

Uncle Buck leaned back in his chair and hooked his thumbs into his tiny vest pockets with a glance at Mathilda. "So," he said.

"So?" Aunt Rose whispered nervously.

"So what!!?" Andre slammed the table with his fist so hard his plate jumped.

"Wait. He's telling you." Aunt Mathilda looked adoringly at her brother, a second lieutenant supporting her chief.

Buck pushed his round, rimless glasses up the ridge of his curved nose. "As you all know," he proceeded, "we live in turbulent times."

"I don't believe this," squeaked Andre, nearly hysterical with frustration. Charlotte was in complete sympathy with him but before she could speak Lynda did.

"Andre, will you please let Pop tell it his way?"

Andre glowered at his sister, but Buck looked at Lynda with such sorrowful, grateful eyes that Charlotte felt her powerful identification with Andre slip out of place, and she reached over to take Uncle Buck's hand. His tears, therefore, seemed to be for his

18

niece as he stroked her cheek with his wide palm, though it was his daughter's remark that had engendered them.

"I just can't stand you," Lynda whispered, and Charlotte, feeling she had betrayed Andre and won an unjust victory over Lynda, dropped her hand from her uncle's and lowered her eyes. She straightened her pad over her knees as Uncle Buck began to speak again, and she began to draw. She drew with haste, compulsively. It eased the sharp pain wiring down her back as she listened.

"You all know there has been great tension at the university since the McCarthy statements and subsequent witch hunts."

Charlotte modeled the rounded edge of the fingers she had drawn that afternoon. She retraced the delicate line of the thumbnail and shaded lightly downward to the curve of the palm. She knew as soon as she heard Uncle Buck sounding like a history teacher that he had been fired. She didn't know exactly how she knew. It was that other part of her—it felt like another girl, or maybe a boy, who came out when she was drawing, who suddenly knew things. She looked over at Aunt Rose for a sign, an interpretation of the disaster.

"Last month," Buck continued, "my colleague, Joe Moskowitz of the Physics Department, was fired, and the power of this maniacal, paranoid fascist is growing, not lessening."

Andre looked appealingly at his mother. "Isaac," she spoke quietly. She almost never called Buck by his actual name. Two long strands of graying black hair, parted neatly in the middle and wound into a braided bun that looked like a crocheted pillow to Charlotte, fell over her forehead; she pushed them behind her ears. "Issac," she repeated. "We do not need a lesson in current events. Tell us for goodness sakes what happened." "I have been fired," he said at last and brought his open palms down on the table, a slow-motion movement with no accompanying sound.

Rose looked into her husband's small blue eyes as if she were trying to will him to fortitude, to hope. She had been a bookkeeper when she first met Isaac Cohen; but with four children and a niece adopted under, to say the least, upsetting circumstances, it had been necessary to give full time to running the household—especially with Rose Moore living with them and helping out only occasionally.

19

"I have a sellable skill," she announced the most admired possession anyone could claim. "I am a bookkeeper," she reminded them all. Her cheeks colored as she spoke. She looked youthful suddenly. The children relaxed a bit. "I will find something," she told her husband. Only as an afterthought did she respond to the other part of the catastrophe, "until you are rehired — or find another position," she added too late. Buck already appeared wounded by her priorities.

Andre stood up without a word and left the table. Grabbing his guitar from the living room couch, he climbed through the window to the fire escape.

Otharose said, "Lord have mercy." And Buck responded, regaining composure, "For once I would have to agree with that sentiment, Rose. I might even, under the circumstances, welcome the help of my daughter's personal deity, Jesus H. Christ."

This remark caused Lynda to smile adoringly at her father, Aunt Rose to begin tapping the table rhythmically with her fingers, calculating, and Charlotte to tear her drawing off her pad so violently that it ripped into halves. Suddenly Mathilda stood up and, spreading her green-draped arms, she addressed them all in a voice purposefully shaken with emotion.

"We shall not despair," she said. "Something — we know not what — will come up if we remain open to possibility." To which Aunt Rose impolitely snorted and got up to help Otharose who had begun stacking the dinner dishes on the white formica counter that stood between the large table and the sink. Charlotte saw Andre through the living room window, sitting with his back to them, his head resting on his knees, his posture suggesting such misery that all feeling in her was suddenly obliterated by her love for her cousin. Contradictions, ambiguities, clarity dispersed before the power of this attachment, her fears for him, her need to save him from something.

"Why do you have to be a Communist?" she loudly accused her uncle, because she knew this is what Andre would have said.

Aunt Rose's reprimand silenced her — "Charlotte." Just that word, her name, as if by itself a warning of chaos.

"Your parents gave their lives for the cause," Mathilda added in the reverent tone Charlotte had come to despise.

20

"Well why did *they* have to be?" she shouted.

"Personally, I think it's dumb," said Jacob who, at ten, already demonstrated little patience with his father's ideals. "You can't save the world," he said with a shrug.

"You don't know what you're talking about, Jacob, so shut up!" Lynda pushed his shoulder roughly. Hannah George, crying quietly, began to help her mother and Otharose with the dishes.

"Leave the boy alone," Uncle Buck admonished his eldest daughter. "Jacob is entitled to his opinion." But Jacob had gone into his room.

"Well, I think Pop is a hero," Charlotte heard Lynda say as she stormed away from the table to join Andre on the fire escape. "And I am more than willing to quit school and get a job."

Buck patted her curly head. "You'll finish high school," he said gently. "You have only one year to go." Looking knowingly at his wife whose ability to manage during hard times he had depended on for years, he added, "Something will come up."

In the early evening, cars moved only occasionally down the side street that faced the front of the apartment, and Charlotte and Andre played the old taxi game. It was a simple, foolish game from their early childhood that even Hannah and Jacob were too old to enjoy. But that evening it provided relief. They watched the corner as the cars turned onto their street from the crowded avenue and waited to see who could spot the yellow cabs first in the darkening twilight.

"Taxi!" Andrew pointed to the corner just as Charlotte saw the cab stop, discharge its passenger and turn on its roof light. They looked at each other, nostalgic and confused, and Charlotte took her cousin's hand. After a few minutes he reached for his guitar. The sound of his gentle strum was immensely soothing to Charlotte. She brought her knees up to her chest and laid her face on them as she watched Andre's face soften with his song. His long fingers moved swiftly across the frets; even when he played a bar chord there was no buzz. He sang an old Irish ballad he had learned from his best friend Brian Sullivan, one of the frequent in-and-out boarders in their home. It was a bittersweet song Brian's father had learned as a child.

21

If you ever go across the seas to Ireland,
Then maybe at the closing of your days
You will sit beside the turf fires in the cabin
And watch the sun go down o'er Galway Bay.

For the breezes blowin' o'er the seas to Ireland
Are perfumed by the heather as they blow,
And the women in the uplands pickin' praities
Speak a language that the strangers do not know.

During the last phrase, he and Charlotte always wept. He finished with a coda of carefully picked melody and banged the side of the guitar with his fist.

"I'm no good, Charlotte," he whispered.

"Andre, Andre," she put her arm around him and, leaned her head against his bony shoulder. "You are good. You're the best."

"Then why do I hate him?" Charlotte had no idea why Andre thought he hated his father. She knew only that it wasn't true. She could see his pride in Buck's lectures and explanations which sparked Andre's interest in justice. But Andre's approach was anarchistic, at times even fanatical, and so his father's inclination toward abstraction seemed to indicate a dedication to an absolute concept rather than to the victims his concept promised to redeem.

"I hate George and Mara too at times," Charlotte confessed. "I hate them for leaving me for some stupid idea."

"At least your parents sacrificed themselves for their beliefs," Andre answered.

"They also sacrificed me for their beliefs," Charlotte said.

Andre looked down at his dirty white sneakers and pulled up his stretched-out, cream-colored sweat socks. "My father talks talks talks. Really he's a weakling. My mother runs everything. You watch. Without his precious students going gaga over him every day, he's gonna become a drunk or something. He's in big trouble."

"Oh you don't know, Andre. He may come through heroically."

"Bullshit," Andre said. "He's a goner now. You, Hannah, Lynda — you're the survivors around here. Like Otharose. You and Hannah are strong. And Lynda's too mean to go under."

"What about Jacob?" Charlotte couldn't help asking. Mysteries were irresistible to her, even an unproven clairvoyance her idea of amazing grace.

"Jacob just ambles along. Ever notice how fast he changes the subject whenever anything upsetting comes up? He just goes off and plays with his blocks or works on a puzzle. Ask him what he's thinking and it's always the same—I'm wondering where to put the next block." He imitated his little brother's voice so perfectly that they both smiled with affection for Jacob whom neither of them knew very well.

"As for me," Andre said gaily, "I plan to die young, Charlotte, and then you'll have to carry on for both of us."

"What about Otharose?" Charlotte muttered into his arm, ignoring the last frightening prediction and legacy she had heard many times before.

"Her and her fucking letters," Andre said with surprising animosity. "She'll just keep writing it all down until she buries all of us in the fire she'll probably start so she can relive the deaths of her family. I honestly don't think she cares about anything except those fucking letters."

Charlotte began to cry softly. She didn't know if it was fear of Andre's sudden explosive rage at someone as wonderful and exciting as Otharose, anguish for Uncle Buck whose destiny Andre had predicted in such dire terms, or if it were that other Charlotte crying, because she had ripped the drawing she had been so pleased with, because she hated Mara and George right then for leaving her with so much confusion. But of one thing she was sure—she feared that power-hungry, angry Charlotte. She preferred to think she cried out of concern for Buck and Andre and Otharose's babies who had died so young. She preferred it when she felt weak and scared, not angry and rebellious, caring more for her drawings than about other people's feelings. She started humming, an old union song that Buck used to sing to them when they were small, about a miner who is killed by the bosses. Andre began to strum the melody on his guitar while they sang the words, *I dreamed I saw Joe Hill last night / alive as you and me. / Said I but Joe, you're ten years dead / I never died said he.* They sang through all the fourteen verses, an apology for their doubts. *The copper bosses killed you Joe / They shot you Joe, said*

I. / Said Joe what they forgot to kill / Went on to organize. They sang it slowly with harmony. When they were done they felt stronger, they felt cleansed. Soon Aunt Rose leaned out the window. "Come in now, it's getting cold."

On the cleared kitchen table were two plates of hot cinnamon raisin cakes with butter melting in the middle, and two white and pink flowered cups of honey-sweetened tea. The house was quiet. Mathilda had fallen asleep on the old couch in the darkened living room. No one else was around.

Rose put her hand on her son's shoulder and said, "Andre, when you've eaten, go and apologize to your father. He needs you right now."

"You were angry at him too, Mama," Andre said weakly.

"Yes," Rose acknowledged, bending over to kiss her son's hair. "He drives me crazy sometimes. But he's a good man, Andre. He provides. He cares. And he's not so strong as you think."

Andre hunched his shoulders high and tense, smirked once and shoved the warm cake into his mouth. Then he drained his tea.

"Go to bed, *ketzaleh*," Rose said to Charlotte, and for once she instantly obeyed.

Mara's eyes were dark gray, like the ocean on a cloudy morning. Her nose was straight and long, pointing to a wide mouth, too wide for her face. Sharp creases around her mouth made her look older than she was. But the length of nose and chin was offset by the width of her mouth and the broadness of her cheekbones so that the overall effect was one of balance, solidity, strength. Straight dark hair fell in even bangs over the flat plane of her forehead. Her skin was burned a ruddy brown by the Mediterranean sun.

George's eyes were gentler, a pale blue. His hair was blonder than Uncle Buck's, his mouth softer than his wife's. Their features reflected Charlotte's belief that it was Mara's determination that had led them to Spain though it was George who wore the soldier's cap. Grays, blues, tawny browns dominated their portrait. Only in the background had Charlotte used oranges and reds, gunfire that demolished the city around them. A child's arm floated grotesquely in the upper right-hand corner, just above Mara's sable-colored hair.

She put her brush down, wiped her fingers on the old white shirt of Andre's she used as a painting smock and stared at the canvas propped on her desk, now turned into an easel. The desk was next to the window facing the back yard, and Charlotte let in the autumn air which cooled her burning cheeks. It was dark. She had lost time. Checking her watch, she was amazed to discover it was well past eleven o'clock. The house was quiet, the room empty. Lynda was sleeping over at Kathleen's and Hannah George, unable to stand the smell of oil paint, had dragged her torn stuffed dog, her eyeless one-armed doll, and the raggedy remnant of the baby blanket she still could not sleep without into her brothers' room and crawled in with Jacob. Charlotte felt very much alone.

Looking back at her painting, she was relieved of anxiety by the observation that a suggestion of yellow ocher at Mara's temple would give a pleasing balance to George's hair. She added a swift stroke. Then, smearing a pallet knife in gray, she added a thick mass to the amputated arm which, she now realized, looked just like the lost arm of Hannah George's doll. The arm seemed to be decomposing a bit at the torn-off elbow, but it was pleasing to the eye if looked at only as color—a carrying over to the background of the facial tones. Charlotte stepped back and smiled at the gray-shadowed arm. She resisted the urge to paint tear-shaped drops of crimson blood trickling off the stump. She was pleased.

She spread her legs wide and bent over to touch the floor. Her back stretched with pleasant relief. She grabbed her right ankle with both hands and counted to ten. Then she moved to her left ankle and counted again. Her hair—a redder brown than Mara's—hung over her eyes, and she shook it back when she resumed a standing position. She turned around to the mirror to undress.

As soon as she was naked Charlotte knew that painting had been the right thing to do that evening. She had begun at seven o'clock, and now the evening was gone. It was time to go to sleep. Fear of sinking into a seductive, inactive melancholy had caused Charlotte to set up her oils and close her door against intrusion. She feared lying around all night on the bed, the rushing of her thoughts unbroken by a fight with Lynda; or wandering into the living room where the little kids and Aunt Rose would be watching the new television set Rose had bought, against her husband's wishes, with her first paycheck; or spending the evening on the chilly fire escape with Andre and Brian, smoking Marlboros, listening to lonely ballads and bitter words.

Charlotte had learned to fear aimlessness as the first stage of her worst mood, when she would become obsessed with images of Mara and George in the act of leaving or dying and yet be unable to draw or even sketch on her pad. At the same time she would become nervous almost to distraction over swiftly concocted theories as to the nature of Otharose's secret about her destiny. Next she would become confused about her feelings, confused about whether or not she ever wanted to draw again, confused about her direction on the street. Once she had become confused about what season of the year it was. And, as she had repeatedly tried to convince Andre who spent many evenings prone on his bed staring at the ceiling, it all started with aimlessness, too many hours of inactivity. But she had fought the urge. It was eleven o'clock, and she had finished her painting.

Adding to her happiness was the fact that Uncle Buck was engaged in an animated conversation with his old friend Leon who was staying with them while writing an article for a Chicago magazine. Leon was, according to Buck, a staunch party man—the man, in fact, who had originally recruited Buck and George as members years before. This meant, Charlotte knew, that while they were all members or at least sympathizers, Leon was an uncritical follower of whatever directives came from the top. But Buck liked his passion and his infatuation with the children, with whom he was patient and attentive.

It was the first time in months that Buck had energy for anything beyond his own despair. Each morning he rose at seven, as he had done for the twenty years he worked at the university. He dressed in his blue or brown three-piece suit. He attached his gold pocket watch to his belt hook, set the dial by the kitchen clock, and put it in his pocket. From his narrow top drawer he took a white handkerchief, which was folded in thirds and then in thirds again. (Charlotte knew, because when it was her week to iron she had insisted that Aunt Rose teach her to fold the handkerchiefs the way Buck preferred.) The only outward sign of his depression was the fact that he wore the same tie every single day. It was soiled, and getting ragged.

"Try this one for a change." Aunt Rose had attempted a light tone as she handed him a dark red one with white dots.

"What for?" he told her irritably. "So the cop on the corner will be impressed?"

He combed his silky hair with his skinny black comb and,

after two cups of coffee with a piece of rye bread and herring, he left the house. No one knew exactly where he went, but he never returned until dinner time.

"Job hunting. What then?" he would say when, to make conversation at dinner, Lynda or Aunt Rose would ask where he'd been.

Buck's spirit, faded in the inactive summer, was extinguished in the unproductive fall. No school would hire him, not even high schools. Finally, he had given up on teaching and answered any want ad he could find. He remembered some of his printing skills (he had worked as a printer while attending college). Certainly he could still handle a counter in a drug store. (His father had managed a drug store when he was growing up.) But nothing came through. Dinners had become quiet, uncomfortable times. Charlotte, Hannah George and Lynda bumped into each other in their eagerness to clear the table. Anything to get away.

The arrival of Leon was the occasion of Buck's first genuine joy since April. They walked through the neighborhood discussing housing problems for the poor, the influx of Hispanics into the city, the multiple layoffs in universities in the arts, the general catastrophe of McCarthyism. But even the alarming nature of the subject did nothing to diminish Buck's enthusiasm. Leon's investigations of defendants on trial for their political beliefs gave context and meaning to Buck's personal sorrows. Energy lent grace and swiftness to his movements. His eyes lit up in the evening when Leon came home for dinner filled with experience gathered in the course of his interviews that day. Rose could stimulate no such light with stories of her bookkeeping job in a fabrics company where she had revolutionized an inefficient system in a week. Even the green and dark blue silk remnant she brought home to use for new living room drapes seemed only to intensify Buck's mood of enervated fatigue. He left his dinner on his plate uneaten. He sighed.

The very Friday evening that she had brought home the remnant, Rose began work on the drapes, hemming and gathering and pleating with Otharose's help, while Charlotte, Hannah and Andre held the pins and threaded needles. Otharose went to her other home at midnight, but Rose continued until she finished,

28

at five o'clock the next morning. When Buck walked into the living room, dim in the newly created greenish blue light, Aunt Rose opened the drapes dramatically, an artist revealing her masterpiece, and she pulled the sash around the opened curtains with a flourish. But her husband retrieved his *Times* from the coffee table as if nothing special had happened, and he withdrew to the kitchen. Charlotte, who had run out of her room when she heard Buck's footsteps, anticipating the return of his magnetic smile, felt very angry in her aunt's behalf. Rose finished adjusting the drapes silently. But Charlotte banged her fist down on the table so that Buck's coffee cup jumped off the saucer and spilled, and she shouted into his face, *God help us and Jesus too!* It was a phrase she heard frequently from Otharose. Buck looked around at his wife with a quizzical stare, his hands held out in astonishment. Aunt Rose turned her back and began spooning corn muffin mix into a baking pan.

With Leon in the house, Buck seemed to be himself again. Charlotte hadn't even been tempted to eavesdrop on their conversation, which she ordinarily would do, furious to be left out, always eager for an inadvertently revealed secret. (Aunt Rose had shown her how to eavesdrop efficiently. You held the open side of a glass up to the wall and put your ear against the bottom. A funnel was made for the sound. Echos and muffled noise suddenly became voice, clear speech, just as if you were sitting in the same room. Charlotte had once caught her aunt listening in this way to Lynda and her friend Kathleen. Rose had handed her niece the glass to illustrate the technique and without any other explanation or excuse she had walked away.)

Charlotte felt hopeful about everything at the thought of Uncle Buck's happiness. She had been pleased to spend the evening alone and ignorant, painting the seventh portrait of Mara and George.

She liked her body, she thought as she gazed at her rounded breasts and slim neck in the mirror. She didn't know why one thing led to the other, but it had happened enough times to be indisputable. When she painted with the sort of attention that made her lose time, she liked her body afterward. When Charlotte liked her body, she masturbated to one of a long series of constantly embellished fantasies. As she looked at her breasts and her thickening brown pubic hair which in the last six months had edged—as Lynda's did—over her vagina to the very tips of her thighs, one of these fantasies began unfolding in her mind. She grabbed her nightgown and put it under her pillow so she could slip it on later, turned off the light and, deeply inhaling the strong smell of oil paint which permeated the room, she lay down on her stomach, pulled the red flowered quilt over herself and, clinging to the realness of the images which now filled the whole of her consciousness, closed her eyes and began.

The story developed in much the same way as it had ever since Charlotte could remember. Movie stars, or lately television actresses, had replaced comic book characters. Sometimes a stranger on the street whose skirt was especially tight, or whose breasts were unusually large, would find her way into Charlotte's extensive erotic repertoire. Occasionally, she would dare to use someone she knew. The woman with the familiar face would be dressed in a long, revealing black gown, and Charlotte would know that even more revealing lace underwear lay beneath the gown waiting to be removed by a commanding, sensual prince. Or the woman, clad only in a hospital sheet, would be stretched out on an examination table while a handsome and commanding doctor would remove the sheet and probe the woman's body in an exploration that was far more sensuous than medical.

Charlotte planned outfits, characters, scenes. She sometimes became so obsessed with her secret sexual life that she walked the streets looking for faces to use. Afterwards, she would lock herself in the dark bathroom (if the bedroom were unavailable to privacy), lie down on the furry blue mat and prepare for the building, shameful arousal. A major requirement for maximum pleasure (just as with her painting, Charlotte realized) was the intensity of focus—that absolutely nothing intrude on her consciousness to mitigate the blazing reality of the scene. But focusing this intensely, Charlotte could neither pace her arousal nor sustain the climax. "Spread your legs," the doctor or prince would say and, before commanding finger connected with pulsating flesh, Charlotte would come, her attention irredeemably dispersed, her frustration at being unable to finish her story outweighing the

30

gratification of the physical release.

Charlotte didn't use the word, "come," when she was four-teen. She called the tiny, rhythmic percussion of liquid emitted into her palm "the beating." It was many years later that she began to suspect her fantasies had a self-denigrating quality which gave her name for orgasm a certain irony. The women in Charlotte's fantasies were always naked or half-clad, wildly excited, nearly unconscious with rapturous satisfaction. The men were always dressed, self-possessed and in control. And yet, Charlotte would think much later in her life, (because now she never wondered about the fantasy's meaning) the men could also be seen as mere servicers of the woman's pleasure—witnesses, tools of her erotic demand.

On the night after she finished the seventh portrait of Mara and George, with the animated sounds of Buck's and Leon's con-versation drifting in from the kitchen where they were having a midnight snack, Charlotte had planned a doctor story. It was an especially daring plan. Only the successful completion of the painting (she didn't mind feeling wicked after she had painted well) had provided her with the recklessness to try. The doctor in the story was Uncle Buck's friend Aaron who had gone to medical school with Mara. Aaron had thick black hair and wistful eyes. He was Charlotte's favorite of Buck's friends, partly because he had almost become an artist and was constantly sketching. It was he, in fact, who had first taught Charlotte how to shade a face to give the eyes depth and the nose a third dimension.

Several nights before, Aaron had mistakenly entered while Charlotte luxuriated in a bubble bath. Most of the bubbles had melted and her breasts were completely exposed. Aaron had neither blushed nor clumsily withdrew, as any of the older men Charlotte knew would have done. He glanced at her small breasts floating like twin balloons in the water, looked straight into her eyes and said, "I beg your pardon, Madam." He remained one more moment in the doorway, then gracefully, unhurriedly withdrew.

Charlotte had never used anyone so close to her before. In fact, the man's face was generally vague, his identity less impor-tant than the woman's. It was risky to use a friend of Uncle Buck's, and Charlotte was intensely aroused.

Aaron, dressed in his white doctor's coat, asked Charlotte's math teacher, Miss Sipinelli, to take off her clothes and lie down on the table. When she was ready, he reached a commanding hand over to unwrap the sheet, never taking his eyes from her own. He pulled the top part of the sheet open so that she was covered only to her waist. Miss Sipinelli sighed and arched her back. Aaron moved his glance from her eyes to her large breasts and as he began to fondle them he asked doctorly things in a humorous tone. "Does this hurt? How does this feel?"

As the sheet began to slip below Miss Sipinelli's belly and Aaron's fingers traced a line from naval to the tip of lush pubic hair, as Charlotte's thighs tensed in nearly unbearable pleasure and her own finger moved toward her moist and erect clitoris, an astonishing thing happened that threatened to collapse her focus. It was ridiculous more than astonishing, really. An old fantasy from her earlier childhood suddenly imposed itself on this wonderful new creation. The scene was the same—a doctor's office, an examining table, white-tiled walls. But the sensuous seduction dreamed up by Charlotte's adolescent mind was gone, and the patient was on her stomach getting a shot. Then the patient was not Miss Sipinelli but Nancy from the comic strip Uncle Buck used to read to her while she sat on his lap, and the doctor, in snappy white coat with a stethoscope hanging from his neck, was Sluggo, the stubby little sticks on his head quivering with excitement as he extended a fat hand to caress Nancy's behind.

Charlotte was very irritated at the invasion of her childish imagery. She turned her head and focused again, thankfully with no trouble recreating the mood. Aaron was back, looking the way he had looked in the bathroom that day. Miss Sipinelli was back, the sheet hung about her ankles now. "Spread your legs," said Aaron. And just as Miss Sipinelli did, moaning with pleaure as Aaron penetrated the fleshy walls, just as Charlotte began to feel the beating which was stronger and more extended than ever before, Miss Sipinelli's face disappeared again and turned into Charlotte's very own.

Once Otharose had caught Charlotte masturbating and told her that if she kept jugging herself up there she wouldn't be able to have children some day. Once Charlotte had asked Aunt Rose if she ever touched herself there and Aunt Rose had sent her to her room. But neither time had she felt as exposed as she did now, lying on her back with her thin white gown back on, watching the portrait of Mara and George turn from dark gray to black as the curtains opened in the night breeze and then flattened against the window again.

It had been herself all along then. Not Nancy and Sluggo. Not Miss Sipinelli. Not the blond lady from the drugstore down the street. Herself. This revelation would have frightened her had it not excited her so much. Dozens of new fantasies suddenly suggested themselves. Innumerable casting possibilities. Her real doctor, Doctor Mandlebaum (and imagine when she went to see him again, knowing what she knew!) her English teacher, Mr. Sarienhoff; even Andre's friend Brian whom Charlotte had secretly loved for one entire year.

Herself. The beating had never been so strong. The liquid never so plentiful. Charlotte placed a hand firmly over each breast and wondered if after the thrill of the completed painting had faded again she would be able to maintain the courage to explore her new fantasies as far as she possibly could. A whole new world beckoned, one in which old masks would be discarded, new pleasures offered, where new powers waited for her to possess them for better or worse.

Perhaps it was this arrogant mood, which lasted for several days, that caused Charlotte to argue with Uncle Buck in a way she greatly regretted later but which, along with the completion of the seventh portrait and the sexual revelation, taught Charlotte something so important about herself she could not completely regret even the pain she had caused her beloved Uncle Buck.

One evening later that week, Charlotte stood very close to the wall between the living room and Buck's and Rose's room with the bottom of a glass pressed close to her ear. Lynda kept watch for Aunt Rose as she waited her turn with the glass.

"Give it to me now," she whispered. Charlotte gave it up reluctantly, although so far she had heard nothing interesting from Buck or from Leon, who was leaving the following day.

Anxiety that Uncle Buck would be even worse once Leon left

had been the excuse the girls used for their eavesdropping. They wanted to hear if he were assuring Leon that he was recovered or begging him to stay.

"Here. You'd better listen, Oscar," Lynda chuckled, handing the glass back. "They're talking about you."

Blood rushed to Charlotte's cheeks — maybe her secret was being told. She placed her ear flat against the glass and felt the familiar focus suck her into its core. Lynda, the blue green drapes, the old couch disappeared. The green and white wallpaper on which Charlotte loved to watch the design change from parallel lines to squares as she closed first one eye, then the other, faded and blurred. The muffled sounds clarified into the words: "a reporter, or a photographer. Like you. Something socially useful. Something which will pay the bills." It was Buck's voice and there was a pause during which she knew he was inhaling smoke from his Chesterfield.

"Charlotte may be too imaginative for that, Buck." Leon's voice was harder to hear. "She has a lot of George in her. I don't see much of Mara's realism."

(The words embedded themselves in Charlotte's brain. Later that night she would think of them, smirking at the irony of her temperamental similarity to George.)

"Charlotte has a passion for painting. It would be wrong to discourage it. I mean it." Leon must have gotten up and walked toward the wall because his voice became suddenly clear. It was Buck's voice that sounded muffled now, but Charlotte could just make out his infuriating words.

"Charlotte has a passion for passion," he said. And, too quickly for Charlotte to get rid of the glass in her hand, the door creaked open and the two men emerged from the room. Blushing, she put the glass to her lips as if she were draining a drink. Lynda swept up a magazine from the coffee table and began leafing through pages. But the girls stood suspiciously close to the wall.

"Well, young ladies," said Uncle Buck with a knowing glance at Leon. "I didn't know you were here."

"We were about to have a snack," added Leon casually while Buck flicked on the overhead light in the kitchen. He began taking bowls of leftovers from the refrigerator, turned on a low flame

34

under the coffee. He carried a dish of herring in sour cream sauce to the table and a basket of seeded rolls, a large salami and a jar of mustard, a white fish left over from breakfast, a bottle of seltzer. He placed a banana, without which no meal of his was ever complete, next to his plate. Charlotte brought milk and chocolate syrup to mix with the seltzer and make egg creams.

"We were just discussing your obvious talent for painting," Leon told her. Charlotte looked at Uncle Buck, who coughed disapprovingly.

"Is there something wrong with liking to paint?" she asked her uncle angrily.

Buck leaned back in his chair and swallowed a belch. He wiped his mouth with the napkin which, as always, had been tucked into his belt. He moved his banana from one side of his plate to the other. "Not at all," he said, looking over his rimless glasses at her. "I do wonder at times, I must admit, why you always paint portraits of—," he paused, "—your parents. I wonder if it doesn't verge on—," he leaned forward and looked at Lynda, a plea for support—"the morbid." He turned an affectionate and concerned gaze on Charlotte as if she were ill and he were waiting for a list of symptoms.

"It's called *practicing,* Uncle Buck. I have to paint what I feel," she snapped, pushing her plate away roughly. The memory of the wonderful color of the torn-off arm gave her confidence. She felt strong, fearless of what Otharose called "her way with words," and Aunt Rose called her big mouth.

"There's more to life than feeling," Buck responded gently, ignoring her anger. "There's history, science, and—."

"Pop," Lynda interrupted. "There's more to Charlotte's painting than feeling too. She has to make a lot of decisions. She has to plan compositions. She has to know about technique. She's not just Hannah George playing with paint. She studies, Pop."

Charlotte looked at her cousin, suprised. Lynda shrugged.

"I know. I know. And I admire your talent, Charlotte. I wouldn't want you to stop painting." Buck moved his banana back to the other side of his plate.

Leon swallowed a bite and looked sternly at his friend. "Artists too will be needed in the new world," he said. "Look at the wonderful new Soviet artists." Leon took another bite of salami on rye.

Charlotte hated the paintings she had seen from the Soviet Union, but she was grateful for Leon's support. She cut herself a huge slice of salami, spread mustard on it and nearly finished it in one bite. A bit of yellow mustard oozed out of her mouth onto her chin. Buck reached over with his shredding damp napkin to wipe it clean, repeating, "I know. I know, but, Charlotte, you're getting older. You're in high school now. You can paint, why not? But you're a smart girl. You could be useful in many ways. There are other things besides painting, that's all I'm saying. You draw at the table. You stay alone in the back yard and draw. Then for a change on Saturday night you paint. Nothing is good carried to extreme. Look at my sister, Mathilda. She only wanted to paint, like you. Now she can't do anything else. She needs to be supported like a child." His voice rose an octave. "In this country, if there's a social revolution some day soon—which it is my firm belief there will be—the new society will need the energy of people such as yourself and your cousins." He nodded respectfully at Lynda who fiddled with a crust of bread. "Your energy and commitment will help to sustain the victory."

Throughout this speech Charlotte kept her fists clenched and tapped her feet under the table. She felt her indignation grow as he proceeded. She felt it surging through her like a forest flame; crackling noises warned her of an impending explosion. He was telling her to be something other than herself. He was disapproving of what she most wanted to be. She didn't know if her paintings would serve the revolution. She didn't care. It wasn't just that she wanted to paint them; it was the only peace she knew. It was what she was best at. Didn't he see that? Didn't he think she was good?

She stood up and pounded the table with her fists. "I don't give a shit for the asshole of a revolution that will most likely never come," she shouted.

Buck looked as though he were considering the point philosophically. Then he looked hurt.

"Charlotte, sit down," Leon urged.

And Lynda echoed, "Jesus, calm down."

36

There were no two words more likely to induce fury in Charlotte. She continued, her voice rising in intensity: words, phrases, coming to her as if by magic. "Don't you believe at all in self expression? How come you always tell us about the glory of writers? How come you practically worship Otharose and her letters? Isn't that art? Isn't that self expression? She doesn't even show her letters to anyone. Is that socially useful? Seems to me it verges on the socially useless. Sure, maybe we'll read those letters some day and find out Otharose is a bona fide genius, a female Shakespeare. Then we'll publish them and we'll all be rich, or better still, they will serve the Revolution with a capital R. But meanwhile, you want her to keep writing them, don't you? Is there such a big difference between writing and painting?" She leaned over the back of the chair and looked at them all defiantly.

Leon smiled, impressed with her rhetoric. Charlotte felt proud for an instant and almost smiled back. Everyone drank a sip of seltzer, cut another slice of salami.

"You remind me of myself," Buck finally sighed. "When I was your age I was interested in prehistoric times—archeology really. I wanted only to pore through caves and mountains searching for bones and pottery. It was a passion with me." He took off his glasses and wiped them on the edge of his shirt which he pulled out of his pants. He blinked several times and fitted the glasses back on his nose, pulling the wire rims carefully over his ears, leaving the odd shirt tail hanging sloppily into his lap.

"But I had to learn, my girl." He leaned forward now, "I had to learn that my private desires were not all that mattered. Archeologists would not be needed. Historians would. And may I remind you that Otharose, as you call her, is a Negro? The Negro voice is essential to be heard in these times. If I can be of any help in encouraging that voice, it is my privilege to do so."

"Well fuck it," Charlotte answered. "My vision is just as important as Otharose's voice."

Lynda jumped up. "Don't talk to my father that way. He's under a lot of pressure. He's been through hell. He doesn't need you insulting him too."

She felt ashamed, trapped by the strength of her feeling, confused by the intensity of Buck's. "Well, the whole thing stinks."

She spoke softly, a kind of apology. "People should do what they want to do. What they love to do. You might have discovered something wonderful," she whispered, longing for his forgiveness. Perhaps he would correct Lynda, saying: I am Charlotte's father too; we are all the same here.

"George — my brother — your father," he nodded at Charlotte, "would have felt just as you do. He told me the same thing when I switched my major in college. He never found anything that pleased himself though. He was passionate about music, like Andre. Then it was playwriting. Then it was going off to war. Of course he was passionate about Mara. We used to say he was passionate about passion."

The phrase she had heard through the wall dissipated whatever was left of her anger. A wave of humiliation passed through her. Her head ached. Her eyelids stung.

"Is that supposed to be my fault somehow? That he went off to Spain and died?" The words came as much of a surprise to Charlotte as to anyone at the table. She didn't know why she'd said them. She was responding to something unsaid, something unsaid again and again for years and years. Somehow she always felt responsible. But what could she possibly have done to cause him to leave? To cause him to die? She was about to push the thought away, back where it came from in the older convolutions of her brain, when she noticed the effect of her remark. Buck looked up at her sharply and then quickly over at his friend. Leon shook his head, bit his lip and returned a harsh glance in Buck's direction. The atmosphere was so thick with silence even Charlotte hesitated to break it with a word.

It was obvious to her as soon as she was alone in bed what she might have done to cause George to die in Spain. The only thing she could have done because she was too young to have done anything else. She had been born. And that had caused George to go off to a war that was already nearly over, nearly lost. His wife followed soon after and they had both been killed. It seemed frighteningly obvious to Charlotte. She was not George's child. That had been the secret then, it must be — the reason she was the one who most needed Otharose's love; the reason her

38

mother had left to follow her husband to war. Then who is my father? she wondered as she lay in bed listening to Hannah George's slow, whispering breath. She heard Lynda's proprietary tone: "don't talk like that to my father." She stared at the painting, at George's blue eyes as if she could discover in them the answer to her suddenly uncertain paternity. Did she look like him? Her eyes were blue, like his. She looked at the eyes searching for suggestive similarity or definitive difference, forgetting she had painted them herself.

Lynda walked into the room, her bright green pajamas eerily incandescent in the dark, her thick hair wound up in a helmet of plastic pink rollers. She sat down on Charlotte's bed and took her cousin's hand. "It's all so confusing," she soothed, "for all of us."

"Why for you?" asked Charlotte, but only a small fraction of her attention was on Lynda's words.

"Why for me?—why for me?" She grabbed a pillow and, pulling back the case, began to fold the material back and forth between her fingers, making a snapping sound. Charlotte's attention remained partial, most of it still on herself.

"I live a secret life, Charlotte. Do you realize that? No one here really knows me."

"I didn't mean to hurt his feelings," Charlotte said, still holding tightly to Lynda's hand. Absently, Lynda moved her fingernail, carefully manicured and filed to a point, back and forth in Charlotte's palm. With her other hand she kept snapping the pillow.

"You think you're the only one who's confused about who you are, Charlotte?" The snaps increased. "You're the subject of everyone's attention. Is she an artist? Is she unhappy? Is she feeling too adopted? Andre loves you. Even Mama—."

"I know I'm not the only one," Charlotte answered, but she remained unmindful of what Lynda was saying about herself. There was more to discover this night, more to know. "But what made him so angry?" she asked, thinking, why would he be glad if I'm like George? Why would he mind if I'm like him when he was young?

"I don't know about Hannah and Jacob," Lynda continued,

39

making a fist of her cousin's hand and holding it in both her own. She looked into the dark room, out the window, then at the portrait. "They're so young—Hannah and Jacob, I mean. They seem to be apart from it in a way. Maybe lucky for them. But I—." She looked down at the tangle of hands, then pulled her own away. "No one here really knows me," she whispered.

Still, the declaration failed to penetrate Charlotte's attention. Her entire body felt driven along some track which had always been before her, never dared before. Now she was on it and she couldn't stop, not even for Lynda. It was her night, her thoughts, her life, and if she avoided the track, the direction of light now, it might not come again.

I don't see much of Mara's realism. She remembered Leon's voice through the wall. Then she must be like the Cohens.

And just as soon as she asked the question, she knew what had to be the answer. It wasn't George. It was Buck. That was why Rose had adopted her and Buck had not, why they never made her call him Father. Because it was the truth.

Slowly Charlotte got out of bed. She kissed Lynda's cheek and felt her cousin pull abruptly away. She walked over to her painting and picked up her pallet knife which she coated heavily with the paint she squeezed out of a large tube onto her recently cleaned and oiled pallet. Then she raised the knife into the air and brought it down softly on George's blond hair.

"Charlotte!" Lynda screamed. But by the time she reached the desk, Charlotte had covered most of George's pale, gentle face with wide strokes of thick black paint.

She had only asked one person, one time. In the late fall after the spring of her realizations, she made a lunch date with Aaron, whom she considered to be the most honest person in the circle of grownups she knew. Furthermore, Aaron was a neurologist with a suspicious (Leon said) interest in psychiatry and psychoanalysis. Leon insisted that all of philosophical psychology was reactionary and negated the absolute supremacy of economic forces. But Aaron remained fascinated with the ambiguities of human behavior, he said, and Charlotte remembered the phrase when she was thinking of someone to ask.

She met him on Fifth Avenue, near the park and across the street from Mount Sinai Hospital where he worked. Charlotte rarely came to the east side of Manhattan but, each time she did, she reprimanded herself for not coming more often, if only for a walk. The park was lush in summer, stark and peaceful in winter, and it immediately soothed whatever turmoil rushed through her active brain. She waited patiently for Aaron to appear as she leaned against the stone wall that bordered the large meadows, the fenced-in playgrounds, the horse path that ran under overlapping dogwood trees, the reservoir like a small country lake in a circle of elegant skyscrapers. Curved concrete paths wound around the grass and hills and, as Charlotte stared at them, her shoulder pressed against the cool stone, she recalled with pleasure the childhood Sundays spent at the zoo further downtown, the twirling rides on the merry-go-round, waiting eagerly for Uncle Buck's and Aunt Rose's faces to reappear at the entrance point. The

41

injustice of the unequal distribution of wealth notwithstanding, Charlotte thought, the great white buildings facing the park were a wonderful place to live. She imagined herself opening the long casement windows in the spring, walking out onto her tiny balcony, stretching her arms to the sky and saying, Ah, it's a glorious day!

Today the trees were bare, the last leaves crushed into a brown dust on the ground. It was cold and crisp, but Aaron wore only his white doctor's jacket over a thin shirt. Two tongue depressors, one ballpoint pen and a slender aluminum flashlight emerged neatly from his breast pocket. He waved to her as he hesitated a moment under the long blue canopy of the Klingenstein Pavilion.

Charlotte was wrapped in several layers of warm clothing — a black turtle-neck sweater and jeans, a knitted wool cardigan, a dark green loden coat with red plaid lining the hood. She was always cold, the first to take her winter jacket out of the plastic case in October, the last to part with it in March. She flipped the hood over her long brown braid and waved back. She felt a tantalizing agitation in anticipation of the luncheon she and Aaron had planned.

He took her to a small French restaurant on Madison Avenue. They both drank wine. There were white candles on the blue-checked tablecloths, and Charlotte felt very grown up. They were eating their dessert when Aaron finally said, "So, my dear Mademoiselle Cohen. I presume you didn't invite me to lunch just for the pleasure of my company though, if so, I should be greatly complimented."

Charlotte smiled down at her chocolate fudge cake, remembering his seductive formality in the bathroom that day. She wondered how to begin, since she wasn't good at beating about the bush, what others called tact and she insisted was gross dishonesty.

"I want you to tell me the truth, Aaron," she said, folding her hands in her lap. "Who is my father?"

Aaron wiped his mouth delicately with his white cloth napkin. "What makes you think there is some doubt about this question — as evidently you do?" he asked, as if he were speaking to an equal, taking care to control his obvious surprise.

She told him as much of the story as she could without

42

becoming confused. She related certain memories, alluded to the mysteries and described the scene at the kitchen table with Leon and Buck. When she was done they both remained silent.

"Would you care for some tea, dear?" Aaron asked, paternal now. Charlotte liked that even more than his debonair gallantry. She shook her head.

"Just an answer."

"My answer," he told her, leaning on his elbows, staring earnestly into her eyes, "would have to be that I honestly do not know. I never questioned that George Cohen was your father. I was never given any reason to question it."

She looked very disappointed. She had assumed it was a secret well-kept by most of the people who knew her. She had decided it was the reason so many of the adults seemed to look at her so meaningfully all the time, frequently treated her with special attention. She couldn't think of any other reason. Hannah with her curly hair and raisin-brown eyes was much prettier than she was; Lynda did better in school.

"But I can tell you this," Aaron's tone commanded her attention.

"Your mother was a dear friend of mine, a schoolmate and a colleague. I confess to you, my dear Charlotte, that I was in love with her myself."

Charlotte looked up at him, wondering if this was why he'd looked at her that way in the bathtub. The thought made her feel very irritated indeed.

"I was very jealous when she married your father, pardon me, George. But I took comfort in the fact that she was obviously as deeply in love with him as any woman could be. I imagined that was why she was even willing to leave her child to follow him to Spain. She gave up a brilliant career, a coveted position at the hospital, when there were almost no women on staff. I always assumed that you were a real love child, my dear. A product of the love between Dr. Miriam, that is Mara Friedman, and George Cohen, the artist, who had given her that name."

His use of their full names, especially his use of Mara's maiden name, made any further argument seem foolish. He mocked the validity of doubt with the language of myth.

But Charlotte continued to doubt, more so than ever before.

43

Now that she had two possible origins, two competing life stories rather than a simple mystery to ponder, she suddenly possessed a context for all the double truths which had chronically confused her. The small ones—such as Lynda calling her Oscar. The larger ones—the way she felt another Charlotte was in ascendance when she felt powerful or angry. She kept the intriguing question to herself and swore Aaron to secrecy. Anyway, there was no one to ask. Aunt Rose would call her foolish and refuse any serious opinion, since she believed that a disciplined silence in the face of any threat to daily equilibrium was the surest way to avert catastrophe. Buck was under too much pressure as it was. Charlotte had sworn, since her last fight with him, to exert some self-control, as he always implored her to do. Like Lynda, she was worried about his health. Moreover, she thought that if he could survive somehow, prove himself a hero, he would win his older son's respect, and Charlotte's beloved Andre would be relieved of the conviction of his father's hypocrisy. Besides, what could she expect Uncle Buck to say after all these years? Yes, Charlotte, you are my child? Then why had he not found the courage to claim her before? Some indefatigable loyalty to his brother, no doubt, or to a noble image of her mother. And, if he denied it, calling it nonsense or childish fantasy, she would be right back where she started—doubting, suspicious, ignorant still.

She certainly would not trust Mathilda even for a single minute. Aunt Mathilda was an artist, but she was insane. The last thing Charlotte wanted was her point of view. Leon was back in Chicago and, besides, she didn't know him well enough. Charlotte was just fifteen. She would wait one more year and then, reminding the one person in the world who would never break her promise, she would confront Otharose.

In the meantime, Charlotte packed away her oils, her canvases, even her sketch pads and pencils. She rarely went out into the garden and she kept her curtains drawn. All seven portraits of Mara and George stood in the back closet along with a suitcase filled with her other work. Charlotte painted her black desk a warm brown and covered it with Russian novels, several histories of the Negro people in the United States, and a few of the simpler works of Marxist philosophy including the pamphlet by Mao Tse Tung,

On Contradiction. She thought this would please Uncle Buck, but one day he came into her room while she studied the causes of the destruction of Rome for a history test, and he asked her why she never painted any more.

Jacob was playing cards on Lynda's bed. At ten he had become a card shark, an obsessive player of Gin Rummy, Hearts, Solitaire if necessary.

"Jacob, why can't you read a book sometimes?" Buck interrupted himself to ask his son.

"I don't like reading," Jacob answered in a pleasant tone, but his eyes, Charlotte thought, conveyed actual dislike. As if he were afraid to prolong the conversation, Buck looked away from him and over to Hannah George who was sitting in the old, lumpy armchair, her legs curled under her, drawing elaborate designs on a large pad with her new crayons.

"Charlotte isn't interested in drawing any more. She gave all her pads to me," she said, never taking her eyes from her work.

Buck looked at his niece with genuine alarm.

"God!" Charlotte exclaimed, raising her eyes to the ceiling as if begging for mercy. "I'm trying to learn something useful like you said. I'm thinking of majoring in history in college." She waited with pleasure for his smile.

"Charlotte—." He turned and walked to the door where he stood for a moment with his hands in his pockets looking down at the floor. "I know I expressed concern about your involvement with art. But you must follow your own star, my girl. Do you understand? Don't let anyone sway you from your path."

Charlotte folded down the page corner of *The Destruction of Rome* and tore off a neat triangle as she had once done to the corner of the drawing of her hands. She looked down at the black print which swam into wavy lines before her. She took off the black, cat-eye glasses she had recently started wearing and addressed her uncle with a big smile.

"I realize that," she said, a teacher explaining reality to an incurably romantic child. "Art is not my star. That's all. My path lies here right now." She pointed to her books. She put her glasses back on, walked over to her uncle and kissed him on the cheek. "Don't worry," she told him. "I'm becoming very realistic in my

45

old age. I'm not going to turn out like Mathilda. I may even consider medicine as a profession, like my mother."

Buck smiled sadly and shook his head. He kissed her before he left the room. He had an interview early the next morning, he had told everyone proudly at dinner. It was the closest he'd come to a real job possibility in a year. Charlotte heard him tell Rose and Andre, who were listening to music on the living room radio, that he was turning in early that night so he would be fresh in the morning.

Charlotte returned to her desk, glancing quickly at Hannah's design as she passed. "Pretty," she murmured condescendingly. It was very ordinary, she'd seen a hundred like it in her life. She found her place in the history book, pushed her glasses to the bridge of her nose and picked up her pencil. But the black print still swam before her eyes. He had called her "my girl."

Charlotte's interest in history had as much to do with her teacher, Mrs. Velkin, as with her desire to turn her life in a direction which would be more satisfactory to Uncle Buck. Mrs. Velkin, Aunt Rose might have said, was as skinny as a rail; as hardy as a little beech tree, Charlotte thought. She had short brown hair that was straight on top and ended in a tight roll of curls that reached all the way up to her forehead on one side and ended above her ear on the other side of her absolutely straight side part. She had small brown eyes which Charlotte described as "burning with a passionate intelligence." She began each class by referring to a stack of voluminous notes scattered over her desk, but by the time fifteen minutes had gone by, Mrs. Velkin was walking up and down the aisles, her glance darting out the window then back at the class, continually gesticulating as she gave her perfectly organized, always fascinating lectures on European history. Mrs. Velkin possessed a wealth of both conceptual and detailed information about Rome, the Middle Ages, the French Revolution and the discovery of America, which a momentary perusal of her notebooks would unlock, and she would talk for almost the full period. About five minutes before the bell she would stop, look intently at the class now that she had found her way back to her desk, and ask for questions or remarks. Charlotte was certain that Mrs. Velkin looked especially at her during these times, and she was never without some response which she hoped would please the extraordinary little woman who was the first person outside Charlotte's family to affect her intellectual life.

"Origins are always evident in history," Mrs. Velkin asserted over and over each time a new unit began. "There would have been no Renaissance without the Middle Ages; no Reformation without the Renaissance," she shouted, her finger pointed at them as if they were a religious congregation, her starched flower- print blouse dampening slightly under the arm. "Nothing happens without the thing that happened before."

Charlotte immediately realized that implicit in this most fundamental aspect of Mrs. Velkin's lessons in history was a lesson equally applicable to family life. She understood right away the idea of direct and indirect causality in Mrs. Velkin's lists of events that lead to revolutions and wars. The notion of opposing human needs manifesting themselves in alternating swings of the pendulum of religious philosophy — the need for an ordered catholic collectivity followed by the need for protest against authority awakened Charlotte to the meaning of the tension she always felt between her strong desire for Uncle Buck's approval and her yearning for personal adventure, her secret passion to think something no one had ever thought before. And when Mrs. Velkin introduced them, through the unit on the French Revolution, to the less obvious consequences of tyranny, the ways in which long years of oppression and slavery could turn a just man into a killer, when she suggested that freedom was in some ways the most frightening thing of all, so that throughout human history people who had nearly died for it turned it over almost immediately to a tyrant in a new guise — Charlotte was somehow reminded of the bitterness and increasing unhappiness of Andre.

He sat in the back of the history class on the other side of the room from Charlotte's front row seat. He had only one friend in the entire school, a remarkably ugly, very sweet boy named Myron Shatsky who played the flute. Myron, Andre and Brian, who played the trumpet, spent many evenings together on the fire escape, where Charlotte less and less frequently joined them, serenading the neighborhood until people began leaning out their windows yelling *Quiet down!* or Aunt Rose made them stop. But Brian, who was an athletic, socially confident boy, had another life as well among his friends at Our Lady of the Sacred Heart where he went to school. Myron and Andre had only each other.

48

As Charlotte's involvement with history and an extending circle of friends deepened, Andre seemed more and more to withdraw. When Charlotte offered her brilliant little questions at the end of history class each day, Andre looked at her resentfully. When she stayed up late pouring over her text on the French Revolution, he mocked her for what he considered a useless pastime.

The greatest source of his disapproval of Charlotte, however, was her involvement with Angel Lopez, a recent immigrant from Puerto Rico who was just learning English and studied auto mechanics in the commercial track of the school. Like Andre, he had curly black hair, and there seemed to be something smoldering in him, Charlotte decided, some hidden heart rarely revealed. She hoped that in spite of the language barrier she might be the one to unlock the secret core. Angel liked girls to look feminine, Charlotte realized, after studying the girls he stared at in class. She exchanged her black turtle-neck shirts for twin sweater sets in pink and yellow, her blue-jeans for plaid pleated skirts. She cut her hair to shoulder length and asked Lynda to show her how to roll it up in curlers so that in the morning it curved around her neck in a neat pageboy. She began wearing pink lipstick and mascara. She felt like a very wonderful, very ordinary girl.

After two movie dates and three parties during which they danced close to "Over the Mountain," Angel invited Charlotte to his house one evening when no one was home. She tried to make conversation with him as they drank cokes and watched T.V. on Angel's narrow bed beneath a large pink and white picture of the Virgin Mary ascending to heaven. Next to it loomed a large poster of Elvis Presley.

"Elvees Press-ly" he told her, pointing upward, because there was not yet much he could say in English.

Charlotte nodded up at the large, sultry face and, too loud, answered "Uh, huh!"

Previously, influenced by Andre's preference for folk music and his recent interest in Bach, Charlotte would not have tolerated a taste for Elvis Presley in any of her friends. But she was sure Angel was a sensitive, intelligent boy. He was poor, which made Charlotte think he was a socialist at the very least. He always wore corduroys and neat plaid shirts, never with the collar up, which

49

made her think he was respectful, not a delinquent or fast. At the crowded parties he had slowly circulated his hips against her with suspicious efficiency, but in the movies he only held her hand.

He nodded one more admiring time at Elvis, turned off the television and put a stack of 45s on his small portable record player. The familiar instrumental beginning to *Love Me Tender* filled the room and Angel turned off the light.

Charlotte felt her pants dampen, her mouth fill with saliva. She touched the Peter Pan collar of her light blue starched and ironed blouse. For a second the fifth portrait of Mara and George came into her mind, in which with soft pastel crayons she had drawn Mara's partially exposed breasts, experimenting with a new shading technique which she'd used to make them look full and round. The drawing ended right above Mara's nipples, but Charlotte had followed that one with a drawing of herself naked to the waist in which she had spent a great deal of time on the nipples. When she finished the drawing very much to her satisfaction, she had painted her real nipples bright red and then, in the dark, imagined an artist painting the real body of his model rather than an image. It had been the best fantasy she'd ever had. But that had been a year before, before she put her paintings away and gave her pads to Hannah George.

Charlotte tucked the perky curls of her frequently washed hair behind her ears and moistened her lips as Angel came back to the bed, took her chin in his hand and began to kiss her while deftly unbuttoning her blouse.

Not a cell in her warm sweaty body wanted to resist. Amazed at how little she cared for the lessons Aunt Rose had tried so recently to teach her, she helped Angel with her bra strap, stripped off her pink plaid skirt and within moments was bathed in a highly focused ecstacy that her fantasies had not come even close to providing. She sat on her knees as he caressed her breasts, brought both hands down to her waist, slowly pulled her pink nylon underpants down to her knees and ran his fingers rhythmically through her pubic hair.

Angel kissed her shoulders, her neck, her lips. This could not, she realized, be his first time. But she loved him all the more for his experience, and kissed him back, whispering "Angel" in his ear.

50

Suddenly, as he unbuttoned his fly and pulled down his corduroy pants, he smiled at Charlotte in a way that made her angry — it was arrogant, demanding — the sort of smile she would have loved to create on the mouth of her fantasy lover but which in reality she didn't like at all. Angel, assuming her silence to be acquiescence, pulled off his underpants and whispered, "You wanit, baybee, donyou."

Charlotte's cheeks went hot. Her hands went cold. She had no idea what she felt or wanted. He lay on top of her and began to urge his penis between her legs, but Charlotte turned on her side and whispered, "no." He pushed her head down to his torso and put his penis in her mouth where to Charlotte's astonishment he allowed it to remain, sliding it deeply into her throat and then pulling it back to the shallow shore of her gums again. She was scared. She felt utterly ridiculous. She thought she would throw up. When he began to come she turned her mouth away and felt the warm liquid oozing down her neck and over her breast. Angel moaned and grunted and finally whispered, "Charlotte, leetle slut, querida, my leetle whore."

Later he lay on the bed as if he were asleep, his slender penis curled softly against his thigh. Charlotte put on her bra, pulled on her underpants which were still around her ankles, dressed and combed her hair. Angel didn't say a word while he dressed. He kissed her cheek holding her face possessively and indicated he was ready to take her home. But Charlotte shook her head vigorously and swung her pointed finger back and forth, emphasizing her intention to go alone.

"*I'm going alone*," she shouted as if increased volume would cause him to understand. "*Solo*," she added proudly. She wondered for a moment how poor Angel managed in the academic classes in which he surely understood almost nothing. But she didn't contemplate Angel's position as a recent immigrant for long. All the way up Broadway to 106th Street she thought: I shouldn't have done that but my body wouldn't stop.

She thought how completely different it was from her private fantasies and how horrible Angel had sounded when he said, "you wanit donyou" as if he wanted her to want it and hated her for wanting it all at the same time.

51

She thought about the naked shoulders and breasts of Mara in the painting, and it was with complete certainty that Charlotte understood, in the moment when she entered the dimly lit wooden box of the elevator, that her painting and her obvious nymphomania came from the same place in herself; that just as she had forced herself to relinquish her obsession with art in order to learn to be useful, she would have to give up her interest in boys in order to be good.

She stopped curling her hair and went back to wearing jeans. She committed herself with greater energy than ever before to history, and she avoided Angel in the halls, returning a cold stare to his arrogant smile and the infuriating clicking sound he made with his tongue whenever she passed.

She returned to the fire escape on Saturday nights and was dismayed to hear that Andre's songs had become more somber and anguished than ever. Brian had abandoned them temporarily for parties and dates. Only Myron Shatsky's resonant flute and Andre's deepening voice singing about strangers and loneliness filled the night. Even the general joy in the family when Buck was hired by a private school had failed to lift Andre's spirits.

"He's surviving, like you said he wouldn't," Charlotte told Andre, hoping he would find in his father something to love.

"You call that survival?" scoffed Andre. "Don't you see how old he looks? He can't stand teaching in some dumb elementary school after the prestige of the university. He's ashamed, Charlotte. He likes talking big about the dignity of labor from the high horse of privilege."

"It seems like you don't want him to survive," Charlotte accused, and Andre turned from her in disgust.

His articulateness improved steadily, always in the service of insulting his father. Aunt Rose treated his angry outbursts as if they were symptoms of a disease, not something for which he could be held responsible. Whenever Andre exploded she patted his head, whispered, "relax, *ingeleh,* calm down" and she turned an angry eye on Uncle Buck. Buck never interfered. He accepted his son's accusations as if they were well-considered criticisms of his own highly faulted personality.

"I'm sorry to hear you say that, son," was all he ever said

when Andre's accusations began.

Charlotte had to admit that Buck didn't seem happy at all about his new job. In fact, he looked worse than he did right after the university fired him for being a dangerous subversive. But he discussed politics once more at dinner. He began to read again. Having accustomed himself to Charlotte's new passion for history, he engaged her in many conversations about Mrs. Velkin's theory of historical causality, arguing for a more strictly economic interpretation, denying man's *need* for freedom or authority or anything else as primary. "Needs are a function of economic forces," he insisted, peering at her over his glasses. Charlotte was delighted that discussion had replaced silence at dinner time. Still, they all worried about him. At times he ended an argument in the middle, muttering, "Oh, what's the use," and wandered away from the table. He steadfastly refused to talk about his job at all.

"You're ashamed of it, Pop, admit it," Andre sneered at his father's back once as he left the table.

"Come with me, Son," Buck said, and Andre followed him into his room. They remained there for over an hour, after which Andre emerged looking drawn and sad. He had not been hard on his father since. But for weeks, he was without energy for anything. The relief of his anger had left something empty inside him. He was obedient. He lost weight.

The whole situation made Charlotte feel anxious and depressed. So she encouraged her new best friend, Vivian Klein, who was always full of energy, to join them on their fire escape evenings. Despite Vivian's uncurled blond hair, which she wore pulled in back of her large ears and tied sloppily with a piece of old string, Charlotte thought Vivian was exceptionally beautiful. Furthermore she was smart. "Brilliant!" Andre assured her, shaking his head in awe when Vivian followed his songs with memorized recitations of the poems of John Donne, Dylan Thomas, e.e. cummings and a few of her own: "Always remember / that I can be broken / as easily as a Chinese lantern," was the ending of Charlotte's favorite of Vivian's poems.

She hoped that Andre would fall in love with their new comrade, and comrade she was in the most literal sense. Vivian's father was a wealthy lawyer but Vivian herself was an actual member of the YCL, the youth league of the Communist Party. She was always involved in direct political action of some kind. Most recently, she was working after school stamping and addressing envelopes, trying to raise money to help writers and actors fight the blacklist.

Andre listened to her tales of picket lines and meetings with renewed attention, asking respectful questions about ideological disputes in the party. Once he braided her long hair while Myron played a plaintive flute.

Vivian often slept over, sharing Charlotte's bed or sleeping on the floor, which she said was good training for inevitable future hardship when the revolution came. But one Saturday night in the spring that Charlotte was fifteen and a half, after an especially long concert on the fire escape and a little bit of red wine which Aunt Mathilda had surreptitiously shared with them after the others had gone to bed, Charlotte and Vivian had obtained special permission to use Otharose's room.

Tangled vines of dark green ivy and purple wandering jew crowded up the wall near the window. The curtainless glass was covered with hanging flowering plants so that the city outside was viewed through a lattice pattern of pink and green. A tall cactus and heavy rubber plants reached to the ceiling at the foot of the bed, and a garden of tiny home-grown avocado trees made a large circle next to the teak dresser in which Otharose kept the clothes she wore during the week. The walls were white. Only one picture hung in the room—a dark photograph of Otharose's children at five and seven years old, which was as old as they ever got to be. There was a desk whose smooth surface was empty except for a blank pad and three sharpened pencils. There was no rug, but the double bed was covered with a spread of the most pleasing green and purple pattern Charlotte had ever seen. On that night, Charlotte was surprised to notice a sheet of paper covered with writing lying on the desk chair but, out of respect for Otharose she turned it over immediately and laid it neatly on top of the empty pad.

Vivian gasped with delight when she saw the room. The numerous leaves and overlapping vines made intricate shadows on the wall from the light of one brass, red-shaded lamp which

54

stood on a tiny wooden table at the head of the bed.

"Ooooo, Charlotte, it's gorgeous," she whispered.

Charlotte smiled. The light made Vivian's dark blond hair shine golden where it curved over the back of her small head.

The girls undressed and slipped into thin cotton nightgowns, Vivian's yellow, Charlotte's white. They brushed each other's hair. Charlotte's was getting long again, and Vivian murmured, "Mmmmm, nice hair," as she loosened the braid. Then Charlotte cuddled under the dark blue comforter and watched as Vivian ambled around the room, stroking a leaf, praising a piece of furniture. "What's that?" she asked, pointing to the sheet of paper Charlotte had found on the chair. Her eyes twinkled mischievously.

"We can't touch it," Charlotte looked down at the pillow, sorry to deny Vivian anything.

"Oh come on," Vivian pleaded, jumping onto the mattress and shoving Charlotte's shoulder. "No one will know."

"I can't, Vivian," Charlotte said sharply, looking down at the pillow again. In all her rebellions, failures or shameful secrets, she had never lied to Otharose. She had even told her about the night with Angel, whose details she had kept an absolute secret from everyone else. She had been wild with curiosity about what he had made her do to his penis. She thought she hadn't swallowed any sperm, but maybe an especially good swimmer had made it into her mouth and reached her uterus by morning. Otharose had assured her that this was impossible. "But," she added, "don't ever do it again. If a man's gonna use you, let him use you right." She had kissed Charlotte with her wide lips painted purple for the subway ride uptown and called her a little woman which was infinitely better than being a bad girl. Charlotte could not repay such kindness with betrayal.

When she looked up from the pillow, Vivian was reading the page, her mouth slightly opened and her tongue resting on her bottom lip.

"Vivian!" Charlotte grabbed the sheet and put it underneath the pad, then slammed a New Testament Otharose kept on her night table on top of that.

"Oh I'm sorry, Charlotte." Vivian hugged her friend. "Forgive

55

me? You wouldn't believe what it said!''

Charlotte turned her back.

''It's a letter to someone, and it's all about sex. I only got to read a little but it said—'' Vivian looked straight ahead and spoke slowly as she did when she recited Dylan Thomas or John Donne. '''Ole Man, I've told you many things, of fire and labor, of the tribulations of delicate avocado plants and of confused white children. But now I'm going to tell you of my body. It is sorrowful in its loneliness. My breasts ache for the touch of a man.' Isn't it beautiful, Charlotte?''

''I see your memory came in handy,'' Charlotte said bitterly, her face still turned toward the wall.

Vivian shrugged. She turned out the light and crawled into bed. After a few moments of silence she reached for Charlotte's hand. As soon as she did, Charlotte began to sob. Raising herself onto her elbow, Vivian looked down at Charlotte's miserable face.

''You don't understand,'' Charlotte cried. ''She loves me best of all. I've never lied to her. And she promised to tell me a very important secret which if she ever, ever, ever finds out I read one of her letters she might never tell me at all.''

Vivian took it all in thoughtfully. ''Then don't tell her,'' she advised. ''Secrets are sometimes necessary in politics and love. Keep it to yourself, Charlotte, and bear your guilt heroically.''

Vivian seemed satisfied that everything was okay, and she relaxed onto her back, lifting her knees and crossing her legs so that the quilt fell down to her ankles. The passing headlights, streaks of light through the flowers and leaves, lit up the ends of Vivian's hair and the smooth white domes of her knees. She began to hum Andre's song about the women in the uplands. Soon she began to sing the words, the entire ballad, her voice becoming more controlled as she sang, but remaining soft so no one but Charlotte could hear.

Charlotte cried—from the song; from the new guilt she would have to bear; from the intensity of her admiration for Vivian; from the weight of alternative histories and the direct and indirect causes of Mara's abandonment; from the image of seven dusty portraits in the closet; from the idea of opposing human needs manifesting themselves in alternating swings of the

56

pendulum throughout human history; from the memory of the ecstasy she had felt at the experienced hand of a mean, beautiful Spanish boy who could hardly speak English; but mostly, she thought, from the idea of secrets—Lynda's belief that nobody really knew her, Vivian counseling lies as desirable, even right. A frightening sense of freedom burned her skin as Vivian's fingers traced a slow circle in Charlotte's palm. Without planning anything so incredibly outrageous or even really knowing what she was doing, except that once again she was succumbing to a power in herself which was beyond her control, in a kind of haze of light and traffic noise, her mind folded away from ordinary things in an enclosure of green and blue (perhaps a silk remnant used for the living room drapes), Charlotte turned toward Vivian and moved her hand slowly up the girl's pale thigh. Vivian looked at her with eyes more welcoming than Charlotte had ever before known. She brought her lips down on Vivian's full mouth and allowed her hand to play in the blond hair that grew between Vivian's thighs. As Vivian stroked Charlotte's shoulder and then her breast, Charlotte whispered, "Do I call you Angel and pretend you're a boy?"

"Call me Vivian," said Vivian.

They never spoke of the incident in Otharose's bed, and the silence which surrounded that evening in the shadows of numerous plants brought them even closer than a frank discussion might have done. The part of it which caused Charlotte to remain silent was Vivian's odd straightforwardness — as if she had been expecting it, even planning it, as if she were not astonished at all. Charlotte did not have the nerve to broach the issue with someone as unperturbed and unconventional as Vivian. She much preferred it to remain as it was — something powerful, exquisite, even holy between them, a foundation to their more ordinary attachment which, over months of sharing each others' lives and secrets, was becoming a strong and abiding love.

The Wednesday before the Saturday of Charlotte's Sweet Sixteen, they sat on the stone bench in the back yard where Charlotte had begun coming again, alone and with Vivian. Charlotte's birthday was in November. (She was a Scorpio, and people always told her this with a knowing *uh huh* as if the stars, if nothing less reliable, could be held responsible for her fiery nature.) The girls huddled in their wool coats and scarves, a large yellow pad between them, listing foods and sodas to be bought, records to be played, decorations to be hung from the walls and dresses to be worn.

Aunt Rose and Otharose were making Charlotte's dress out of a gold, part-silk material. She imagined it with a scoop neck, a tight bodice and waist, a skirt that flared wide over a starched yellow crinoline. She had described it to them as precisely as possible so they would know what she wanted, and she expected to be thoroughly pleased.

The lists were complete, including the guest list, which began with Angel Lopez. Vivian had insisted that Charlotte accept the challenge of this test. He would come to the party; she would ignore him politely and shine in her own golden light; she would be free. At four o'clock it was getting dark and the wind had risen. They had just decided to go inside when Andre, in his shirt sleeves, looking drawn and pale, and Lynda, who had begun to resemble her mother to a remarkable degree, came into the yard. As soon as she saw them, noting in an instant Andre's anxiety, Lynda's swift, efficient movements, Charlotte knew something had happened to Uncle Buck.

"Hi," Vivian called happily. She did love Andre, she told Charlotte who occasionally pushed her to a romantic interest in her cousin. But he was so sullen all the time. Vivian was tired of trying to lighten up the atmosphere around him. Her reluctance made Charlotte feel relieved.

"Something is wrong," Lynda warned solemnly, the three words everyone in the family used as a prelude to news of disaster. ("Give them an introduction," Aunt Rose always said, "if you come right out and say it a person could have a heart attack.") Charlotte stood up straight, awaiting further information.

"It's Pop," Lynda continued. "He's been taken to the hospital. He's alive, but he's had a heart attack. He collapsed at work." She was completely self-possessed, no one questioned that she was in charge.

"You go upstairs and help Otharose with dinner and the kids," she instructed Charlotte. "Andre and I are going to the hospital with Mama."

Charlotte was frightened to delay them even a moment but had to ask, "Is he—is he—is Uncle Buck gonna—."

"He's not gonna die," said Lynda.

"They *say*," Andre added.

"Aaron's with him," Lynda said. "He's got the best attention. Don't worry, Oscar," she whispered affectionately, using the old name from childhood, reminding Charlotte that although she belonged to the family she had been an outsider from the beginning.

"We'll let you know how he is," Lynda added possessively as the two of them walked swiftly to the gate which led to the street.

The real children, Charlotte thought bitterly and, confronted with this ultimate selfishness of which she was apparently capable, she tripped and fell, skinning her knee, as she and Vivian went upstairs to help Otharose.

It was very late in the evening when Rose, Lynda and Andre returned. Vivian had gone home that night, but everyone else was waiting up for them, including Aunt Mathilda and Myron. As they watched Aunt Rose hang her coat methodically in the front closet and Andre and Lynda sit down heavily on the couch, Jacob looked up from his cards, Hannah stopped sucking her thumb, Myron stood up from his window sill perch, and Charlotte and Mathilda ceased pacing. Otharose eased Hannah off her lap onto the floor and sat forward in her chair.

"Do not keep us in suspense. It's enough we were not allowed to attend him in his hour of need," Mathilda said irritably.

For once Charlotte agreed with her and nodded her head. Mathilda looked at her with gratitude so intense that Charlotte suddenly knew how lonely her aunt was. She patted Mathilda's shoulder. "Thank you Mara dear," Aunt Mathilda said without correcting herself, and Charlotte let it go at that.

"He'll be okay," Rose reported, sitting down in the torn black chair, looking at the worn-down heels of her shoes as she removed them from her feet and placed them neatly in a corner. "He needs rest. Aaron says several weeks at least. It's a warning, not a disaster — those were the doctor's words." She drew the tortoise-shell combs from her hair, pulling the loose strands from her face, tucking them in to the braided bun.

Everyone moved slightly, adjusting themselves to relief. Myron looked at Andre adoringly, as if he wanted to rush over and embrace him, but he only sat down again and looked out the window. Hannah began to cry softly, burying her face in Otharose's knee. Jacob walked over to his mother and sat on the arm of her chair, smoothing her coarse hair with his small hand. Charlotte squeezed into the small space between Andre's legs and the arm of the couch, and took his hand. Andre allowed his hand to be taken but he looked straight ahead when he said, "You should have seen him, Charlotte. He's old. He's weak with a million tubes in him. And that's not all," he added, looking over at Lynda, incapable of telling them the rest.

Rose too looked at her daughter, and in a voice much like her father's Lynda spoke, pacing her words, preparing her phrases as if giving a college lecture, looking at each of them individually as she turned her gaze around the room.

"There are times, it seems, when lies serve a purpose despite what we have been taught about the importance of truth. There are times when lies protect not only ourselves but the feelings and expectations of those we love."

If Buck had been dead, Charlotte would have believed in the transmigration of souls at that moment. Almost immediately she remembered the last time she had heard this philosophy of the considerate lie, in Otharose's bed with Vivian.

"You are his heir," Mathilda echoed Charlotte's first thought.

"Lord, girl, tell us what you have to say," ordered Otharose in an odd strident tone.

"Pop was brought to the hospital by two of his co-workers," Lynda said after an obedient but majestic nod to Otharose. "It is therefore clear — now — where he has been working in the past months. It seems he has not been teaching in a private school after all, as we had been led to believe." She faltered.

"Lynda!" Charlotte exploded, unable to bear the tension any more. "Please!"

But Lynda couldn't continue. It was Andre who finally told them, tensely, in a monotone, staring at the floor as he talked.

"He's been working as a cashier in a coffee shop in midtown. At lunch hour it gets very crowded — people piling in from work, irritable to get back when their hour is up. Often they're rude, demanding. Even insulting." His voice became steadier as he spoke. He looked up at his family with hurt, uncompromising eyes. "Mario, the cook in the place, has become Pop's friend. Professor Cohen, he calls him. He's the only one who knew Pop's real work. Pop was never rude back, Mario told us. Always a man of dignity, Mario said. Polite even to the rudest customer. Today was especially crowded. A young man pushed ahead of the line

61

and banged his check and a five dollar bill on the counter. He shouted at Pop so loud the whole place could hear him yelling, 'gimme some change old man.' '' Andre's voice cracked, but he collected himself. ''Pop refused, suggesting that he wait his turn. Mario imitated Pop perfectly saying 'I suggest to you, young man, that you await your proper turn.' The guy raised his fist to hit Pop and he actually pushed him slightly. That was when Pop fainted. Or had a heart attack rather. He fell off the stool which sits on a big platform behind the counter. He fell to the platform and then to the floor. He has a black eye and a cut on his head on top of everything else. Mario nicknamed him the Royal Flush, since he's a poker player. He says Pop looked like a king sitting up on that throne.''

Andre's face was twisted into an excruciating smile as he uttered a noise somewhere between a laugh and a cry. He wrung his hands together like an old man in mourning. Charlotte separated the knotted fingers and took one hand in each of her own.

''What?!'' Jacob's voice broke the incredulous silence. ''Daddy works in a coffee shop?! A history professor in a coffee shop?! Oh my God.'' He shook his head back and forth, as if he could not imagine how he would cope with this newest humiliation brought on by his incomprehensible father.

''That is correct, Jacob,'' Rose answered in a steady voice, warning her son with her eyes that he'd better manage the correct response. ''Your father lied to us to save his dignity. He thought we'd be ashamed. We owe him our support now. All of us. Your brother Andre was the only one who knew.''

Everyone looked at Andre. Otharose murmured, ''Lord have mercy,'' and she crossed herself, which she rarely did in the presence of the family. ''You knew, Baby?'' she asked Andre in a voice filled with concern. Mathilda, Charlotte noticed, was the only person in the room who openly cried.

''He told me a few months ago and swore me to secrecy,'' Andre explained. Myron stood up again, crossed the room at a quick pace to where Andre sat, and stood still right in front of his friend.

''Myron,'' Hannah said sternly, lifting her curly head off

Otharose's knee. "I can't see Andre."

"Ssshhh, Hannahla," Rose said. Then she added, "Myron dear." And he sat down on the floor right where he stood.

"I've been to the shop a couple times," Andre continued. "That's how I know Mario. Pop did his job well. At first I was a little embarrassed, but he didn't seem to be. At least not when I was there. He spoke to every God-damn customer as if they were lords and ladies and he was a well-trained manservant with a lineage reaching back to kings."

Later, when Otharose had put some leftovers from dinner on the table, Aunt Rose told Charlotte, "Your Sweet Sixteen will go on as planned. Your Uncle Buck insists. He asks that you visit him in the hospital before the party so he can see you all dressed up." She looked at Otharose who immediately went to the closet and pulled out the sewing machine along with the silky gold, half-finished dress.

In bed that night Charlotte was aware of dozens of sounds. She heard the slow wind in the back yard as if it were a hurricane on an ocean beach. Hannah's breathing sounded like the snoring of a breathless old man. Lynda called out in her sleep once, an indecipherable sound, and Charlotte thought it was a death cry. She turned over in her narrow bed so many times and with such ferocity that the sheets became a tangled rope inhibiting the movement of her legs. In the midst of all the discomfort she heard the sound of voices coming into her head from the past — Buck's voice through the wall, Angel's calling her whore, Vivian's shameless sigh in the dark, screaming voices from way in the past which Charlotte could never identify but had always heard. A truck backfired on the street in front of the house and, even though it was two rooms away, Charlotte was certain it wa a gun shot. She rushed into the living room and looked out the window but the block was empty, the night still. She went to the bathroom and found some cotton which she tore off into small pieces and shoved into her ears. When she went back to bed, having straightened her sheet and crawled back under it, she tried to call up a sex fantasy since it was unquestionably absolutely necessary, but she could not excite her body no matter how fully she elaborated the

63

scene. It was the first time in her life that Charlotte lay awake for a full night, a powerless victim of her own racing thoughts. When the room lightened from the sunrise, a platinum fog behind the thin, white-cotton curtains, she heaved a sigh of relief and, for the hour which was left before everyone in the house awakened and began moving around, she slept.

She danced. In the mellow light of the blue bulbs Vivian had put in all the lamps, Charlotte's cheeks turned a dusty rose from exertion and excitement. Her long brown hair had been curled at the ends, a cluster of tiny white artificial flowers carefully twisted around her pony tail by Lynda. She danced all the fast ones, with several boys in her class, with Andre, even with Myron, best of all with Brian who was handsome enough to make Angel look twice. She refused to dance slow and refused to dance with Angel at all. She moved her hips in perfect rhythm to the music while Brian's eyes traveled from her face to her gold silk hem and back up again. She let him fling her onto his hips while she raised her legs absolutely straight into the air. Long strands of artificially curled brown hair came loose and hung over her forehead like jungle vines. Her dress did not swirl as high as she would have liked over her crisp yellow crinoline; the cut had been a disappointment. The top bloused when she'd dreamed it would hug her breasts like a seventeenth-century peasant dress. The skirt was an A line instead of the full circle she had so carefully described. She said nothing about it to Aunt Rose or Otharose who had stayed up late several nights in a row finishing it. But the two women looked at each other, crestfallen, when they saw Charlotte's lips turn down. She told them how beautiful it was, but it was one of those transparent lies told in families that no one mistakes for the truth.

Nevertheless, Charlotte swirled and turned and took pleasure in the two inches of thick layered net of her crinoline exposed above her knees. She lost any modesty which she had always been enjoined by her elders to demonstrate—"in public at least," Aunt Rose would say with a piercing look. She danced with the part of herself that had stripped off her clothes in Angel's bed. It was that or not dance at all. Once, as Brian folded her arms around

64

her waist so that she stood with her back to him and felt his chest against her shoulders, she caught Angel's eye. His look shot through her, planted itself inside her like a national flag placed on imperialized land: this is mine, said the look and the half-smile that went with it. For an instant Charlotte yearned to be possessed by him, to run to Angel and in front of everyone throw herself at his feet. She tightened her grip on Brian's hands and, when he tried to untwist her body from his own in a twirling motion, she held fast, feeling the comforting pressure of her forearm against her breasts which sweated profusely behind her new, white lace bra and her golden dress.

Uncle Buck admired it greatly. "A golden angel," he had sighed when she entered his room and saw with horror the tube in his nose, the intravenous needle stuck in his thin arm which was spotted with black and blue marks from injections, the white bandage over his right temple, his tousled white hair which looked thin and yellowish now instead of silvery blue. Isaac Cohen, the man whose brother, invoking the masculine power of wild forest animals, had named him Buck, stared at his niece and tears came to his bloodshot eyes which seemed oddly naked without the rimless glasses he took off only to sleep. He reached over to his night table to put them on and murmured, "It's like Mara walked into this room, no Rose?"

"She resembles her," Rose answered and sniffed.

Charlotte bent over to kiss Uncle Buck on his damp forehead and brushed his thin, white hair back from his eyes. "Thank you for letting me have my party," she whispered.

"Dance till the sun comes up, and you'll be queen of it all," he said hoarsely and extended a pale hand to indicate the world.

Under the stark, fluorescent bulbs of the immaculate hallway, Charlotte's dress looked brassy and Aunt Rose looked almost as pale as her husband.

"Why do you get mad whenever my mother is mentioned, Aunt Rose?" Charlotte was spinning theories. "Didn't you like her?"

"Not now," Rose said.

"Why not now?" Charlotte insisted as they waited for the

65

elevator. Aunt Rose opened her black leather purse and dug around inside pulling out a package of mints. She popped one into her mouth and gave one to Charlotte. "Your breath," she said.

"Will you please answer me, Aunt Rose?" Charlotte sucked furiously on the mint.

"Sshhh!" Aunt Rose hissed, ominous as a snake. "It's a long story. I did like your mother, of course. What a question. I loved her. Her death was a great loss to me. Perhaps the greatest I've ever known. How can you ask? Didn't I take her child as my own?" She turned her face from Charlotte and pushed angrily for the elevator again.

"Well, you get angry every time Uncle Buck or Aunt Mathilda mentions her name."

The elevator was crowded with visitors leaving the hospital, several nurses, an orderly pushing an old man in a wheelchair.

When they were in the taxi riding across town under the shadowy trees of the east-west transverse through the park, Rose spoke again, looking out the window as she did.

"Your Aunt Mathilda is a fool, as you no doubt have guessed, Charlotte. You're always watching everyone, and I doubt you can have missed that obvious fact. She makes everything romantic, from politics to her brothers' natures, and she always has. She can't take care of herself. If not for Buck, she'd be in the poorhouse. She understands nothing of the twists and turns of your history. Just like she understands nothing of the history of the world, which I sometimes wonder if any of us do. As for Buck, well," she paused as she handed the money to the driver and got out of the cab. Cold air soothed Charlotte's cheeks as they walked to the building.

"Well what?" Charlotte implored.

"Nothing," Aunt Rose snapped. "Don't push me any more. We'll talk about it another time. I promise. You should enjoy your party."

"It's always another time." Charlotte was nearly in tears as, alone this time, they rose to the fourth floor in the elevator. "Everyone's always going to tell me another time. I don't know anything about my parents All everyone ever does is weep and practically pray when I mention their names. I don't know how

I came to live here, or why my mother really left, or why you adopted me, or why everyone always looks at me as if I'm about to ascend to heaven or descend to hell. And everyone will tell me *some day*. Otharose, and now you."

"What has Otharose told you?" Aunt Rose asked sharply. "Don't listen to her, Charlotte," she warned with sudden affection. "Rose loves you. She always has. She's a fine woman, and she might have been a great talent, no doubt, under different circumstances, if there was any justice in the world, which there is not and sometimes I wonder if there ever will be. But she's a broken human being. An angry woman. With all her wisdom, and I'm not denying it, she's—she's not well, Charlotte." Rose held Charlotte's cheek in her open palm and looked into her tearful eyes.

It jolted Charlotte to hear this description of Otharose. But Aunt Rose's hand on her cheek softened her entire being, and she asked, "Aunt Rose? Do you love me?"

Rose pulled Charlotte to her abruptly, but the embrace was shortened by the elevator door opening, and they stepped into the hall. She removed Charlotte's coat as she might a young child's, straightened the folds in the golden dress. She brought a small comb out of her bag and combed the curly pony tail, holding the strands tightly as she combed so it wouldn't hurt. She held Charlotte's chin in her hand and whispered, "Why don't you use my pink lipstick, dear, since it's such a special occasion?"

Charlotte stuffed the last of the paper plates and cups into a large garbage bag. The intoxicating high from the spiked punch had turned to fatigue. Her feet burned from fast dancing in tight, black, patent-leather pumps with skinny two-inch heels. The shoes lay tossed on their sides in the middle of the living room. Popped balloons covered the rug, an unbroken yellow one bouncing airily about in the breeze from an open window. A remaining strand of pink crepe paper hung from the ceiling. Everyone had gone to sleep, which was perfectly fine with Charlotte who was lost in her thoughts as she cleared the garbage and put dishes in the sink. Or more precisely, she was lost in a single thought. Everything that had happened during the evening swirled into a background chorus line in her head, as the other dancers had swirled into the background when she danced with Brian. Uncle Buck's alarming appearance, her talk with Aunt Rose, her disappointment in the dress, her failure to establish her freedom from Angel's possessive smile. She thought only of the following morning when she would be sixteen years and one day old, when she had a special appointment with Otharose.

Otharose lived in a building at the foot of hills which formed a large park. As she walked down the long, stone stairway that threaded through the brush to St. Nicholas Avenue, Charlotte realized how odd it was that she had never before been to visit Otharose's other home. Her anxiety lessened when Otharose opened the door, flooding a corner of the tiny, dark hallway with light. "Hey, Sugar," she said, and turned into the living room where so many photographs of her children hung that only small portions of wall were visible. On top of an old radio were three color photographs, each in a filigreed silver frame. They were of the children again, and one of Otharose's husband, all dead, their faces surrounded by the elaborately folded satin of the coffin beds. Every piece of furniture in the room was beige, as were the heavy drapes that covered one window from ceiling to floor.

"Come on in the back," Rose said over her shoulder as Charlotte followed, meek and intimidated. The back was a space larger by half than the living room in which the light was so dim it took a moment for Charlotte's eyes to adjust. An ancient-looking woman sat in a large, old-fashioned bed propped against a wall of at least five pillows which reached around her shoulders like a royal couch. The bed linens were white with a tiny border of hand-embroidered silky white flowers. The curtains that covered the window right behind the bed were of an opaque, white cotton that completely shut out the daylight. The old woman's hair was stark white too, undisturbed by a single strand of black or gray. The thick hair formed a large, shining circle around the old woman's head, was clipped into a wide silver barrette at the nape of her neck and woven into a thick braid that fell over her emaciated shoulder onto her tiny, flat breast. Even the chest of drawers was painted white and covered with a long, draping piece of intricate white lace. The only relief from all the whiteness was the dark wood of the tall bed posts and carved head board and the coffee brown of the old woman's face and hands.

"This is my grandmama," Otharose told Charlotte as they stood at the foot of the bed. "She's one hundred and one years old. Say hello, Charlotte. She can't hear you but say it anyway. She'll know."

"Hello, Ma'am," Charlotte whispered and found herself performing a small curtsy.

The child says hello, Grandmama, Otharose shouted, and the old woman nodded her head and smiled.

"Grandmama was born into slavery," Otharose continued. "She remembers Sherman marching through Georgia. Come on in the kitchen, Sugar. We'll get Grandmama some biscuits and feed her while we talk. Don't think I don't know what you came for." She chuckled as they left the room. It was an unfamiliar sound coming from an Otharose Charlotte didn't know, just as she had never known of the existence of the ancient, beautiful grandmother. She felt an unexpected discomfort with Otharose in these surroundings, in Otharose's other home.

The kitchen was colorful—yellow walls, red pots on the stove over a low flame emitting strange and tantalizing aromas from foods Otharose had never cooked for them. Seven or eight philodendron plants crowded on a low shelf, their long vines twisting almost to the floor. Charlotte relaxed a bit in the familiarity of the plants which she always associated with Otharose.

Otharose wore no makeup that day. Her lips blended into the brown of her skin. Her hair was braided but small wiry wisps stood straight out from her head.

"Come on now, Sugar," she said, carrying a plate of warm biscuits, "take that tray of tea and we'll talk."

They sat in two straight back chairs at the side of the bed while Otharose slowly put small crumbs of warm bread into her grandmother's toothless mouth. Charlotte heard thunder outside and the beginning of a hard rain.

"Storm," said Otharose serenely. Her grandmother raised a long, bony hand and turned toward the heavily draped window. Her eye caught Charlotte's and she said in a high-pitched voice, "Pretty little white girl, Rosie." Otharose said, "Ain't she?"

After several minutes Charlotte found the courage to speak to this new and unfamiliar Otharose. She felt like calling her Rose. Or even Mrs. Moore.

"I came because I'm sixteen," she said. "And you promised me a story," she stated firmly. "Remember?"

"Mmmmmm, hmmmmmm," Otharose crooned.

Charlotte remained silent. Otharose spoke slowly as she continued picking up crumbs with her fingers and holding them to the old woman's mouth.

"When I was a child, I was very very poor. I lived with my mama and my grandmama here in a tiny shack in the back country of Georgia. There was a dirt floor, almost no food, and I had three brothers. I can't rightly recall his face but I remember my daddy, or a man I was told to call Daddy. He left when I was three years old. Once I was talking to Mama, shortly before she died, and I asked about Daddy. She told me, 'That wasn't your daddy, baby. You and Rodney and Brother got another daddy. That man you call Daddy was only Alphonso's daddy.' And she would never tell me who my daddy was. Many times as I asked her she would just mutter or laugh or tell me to hush. Even this old woman here wouldn't say if she knew, which I can't be sure she did."

Otharose wiped her grandmother's mouth with a napkin. Then she held a thin china cup to her lips so she could sip some tea. The grandmother's skin glistened in dark amber highliights against the white cup.

"Couldn't you convince your mother to talk it over with you?" Charlotte asked. She felt immediate sympathy for Otharose whose history had been, surprisingly, so like her own.

"Shoot, honey," Otharose laughed. "We didn't talk things out the way y'all do. If I'd said, 'Let's talk it out, Mama,' she'da looked at me like I was pure crazy." Otharose, still laughing heartily at the image, ended with an mmmm, mmmmm, mmmmm that was so familiar to Charlotte she regained the courage of her mission.

"What about me, Otharose?" She sat up straight. "It's time to tell me the secret."

Otharose put down the dish and turned toward Charlotte. She laughed again, a long, high, strange sound which ended with a lilting, "Oh Lord," that sounded like part of a song. "Some secrets are better kept," she warned.

"Not this one," said Charlotte, her voice steady and low.

"Well—you're just like me, baby. That's the secret. It's why I've always loved you best. Why you always needed a little extra." She let go of Charlotte's hands and, opening her arms wide, broke into a faraway smile. "I worked for your Uncle Buck and Aunt Rose before you were born, you know. Started out helping in the house, but your uncle, who is a fine, fine man, saw I needed to write my letters, so he gave me a room and insisted I take time to do it." She paused and repeated, "They don't come any finer than your Uncle Buck. His brother, George, was a handsome man, extremely attractive. Thick blond hair with white already in it. A strong body. Women loved him, girl. You listening?"

Charlotte was listening so intently saliva was collecting in her mouth.

"Dr. Miriam, he called her Mara—the sea—Lord, he was romantic—she loved him too, like all of them. But he loved her back. But, here's the secret and Charlotte, you must never tell, promise now."

"I promise," Charlotte shouted and sucked in her breath.

"She was introduced to Buck and George by Aaron, you know, who I'm sure was in love with her himself. And in the beginning, no one could tell which brother she was going to choose. See, George was a much more romantic figure, like I said. But your Uncle Buck—was, well, a man you could lean on. Everyone felt that way. And he's no ugly duckling either, just a quieter sort. Not so flashy. Of course, he was already married to Rose at the time. Rose was no match for your mother in looks. But she has her own strength, your Aunt Rose, a power I call it. No man would ever leave her for another woman—might go off with someone, you know—but not leave her, no matter how much he might be in love. And baby, Buck loved your mother too.

72

Rose—well, she's a woman who knows her own power. She wasn't a bit scared. Took Dr. Miriam under her wing, they became real good friends. Rose would sew her pretty things to wear. And Dr. Miriam would bring lots of presents for Lynda when she was born. Rose had Andre and your mama had you about the same time. And then—well, you know the rest. They up and left you. Everything was secret in those days. Lots of talking behind locked doors. Lots of crying and shouting. Kind of crying and shouting you only hear in politics and love. Something about both was in the secret. Your Uncle Buck and George were both active in politics then. Rose too. Dr. Miriam was worried about her job, but she believed in the politics too. Anyway, after all the shouting and crying, George went to Spain to fight in the war and she followed. You came to live with us."

"Which one was my father?" Charlotte demanded. The shouting she had always heard reached a crescendo in her head.

"Don't know, Sugar," Otharose said, looking up at the ceiling. "Don't even know if it was one of them. I know there was something about who was your father though. But it could have been Aaron. George left very angry, saying it was as good a place as any to die. And she followed. It could have been George who was really your daddy. Just like he's supposed to be. I just heard enough to know all the uproar had something to do with you and who your daddy really was. And something to do with politics too. Couldn't go by looks either," Otharose added suddenly, intrigued anew by the old mystery, "since you are the image of your mama, except she was prettier. And those bluish eyes of yours could've come from George or Buck."

Charlotte was stunned. After all this, she didn't know any more than she'd known before. She'd figured out the secret for herself. Otharose couldn't solve the mystery that remained any more than anyone else. She felt a disappointment so keen it threatened to immobilize her entire body, cause her brain to shut down her arteries and veins, her blood as deathly still as pond water in dry summer heat. Only the edge of rage that threatened to storm the stillness reminded her that she was alive.

What was all this white, and pictures of people in coffins, Charlotte wondered angrily. Where was this strange world of

73

Otharose's other home? Did any of them know this dark, affectionate woman whose being radiated comfort and power and whose room radiated exquisite peace—or so she had always thought?

"You're different today," Charlotte heard herself say. And then she couldn't stop. "You don't seem like I know you. I always thought you knew everything, Otharose. I always thought you weren't—confusing. I thought you were totally strong. But today you seem weak, Otharose." Charlotte was crying softly. "And I'm not sure what's your story and what's my story and whether I believe anything you say, if you want the truth. I always thought you were the smart one," she repeated, weeping now.

"That's because you don't really know me," Otharose answered in a matter-of-fact tone. "I'm no different from you, Charlotte. I'm no weaker and no stronger. I'm as crazy as you are. I had a mama somewhere and a papa. I lived in dirt poverty. I brought two babies into the world and watched them die in a terrible fire 'cause some old white landlord wouldn't give us a new stove. I loved a man who was so broken by those deaths he shot himself. I live in a white world—white as this room, white as the whiskers of God, white as bones, and I'm not saying anything against white. I loved a white man once and I love you, but white can be empty and cold as arctic ice, Charlotte, and I am a colored soul lost in that ice. And I'm a woman too," she cupped her thin breasts in her hands. "Why shouldn't I be as weak or as mad or as crazy as anyone. Is this a world to make people sane?"

Charlotte's need for her father's name seemed suddenly irrelevant compared to the hardships of Otharose's life. All she wanted now was to mend things, to somehow apologize for her outburst, for past betrayals, to assure Otharose that she understood things she hadn't realized before.

"Otharose," she said in a voice so strong and unhesitating that Otharose seemed to step out of her anger. The old grandmother pointed to Charlotte, nodded, and in a kind, firm voice she said,

"Speak, child."

"Otharose," Charlotte repeated, scared and determined to confess. "I know lies are necessary sometimes. But I don't want to lie to you."

74

Otharose's expression anticipated possible disaster.

"I once read one page of your letters," Charlotte said.

Otharose broke into a smile which instantly became a passionate laugh. Her grandmother had not been able to hear Charlotte's confession, but when she saw Rose laughing she began to laugh too. She chuckled and called on the Lord for mercy. Tears came to her eyes, and her tiny shoulders shook so hard her braid bounced as she rolled back and forth on the pillows.

Charlotte laughed at them laughing, repeating several times, "What's so funny? Tell me." And at last Otharose gained enough control to say, "That ain't nothin, girl." She pulled the long-legged Charlotte onto her lap. "I thought Lord knows what this strange little girl's gonna say. You can read my letters any time you like, Sugar. I don't care. I'd like for you to read them."

"But I thought they were a secret." Charlotte was amazed and greatly relieved to be on Otharose's lap. She pulled the wiry wisps of hair straight back from Otharose's forehead and tucked them neatly into the overlapping braids. She wiped her fingers, oily from the hair grease, on her jeans.

"I never said they were a secret," Otharose said, "but no one ever asked to see them. No one seemed interested. So I didn't never show them to nobody."

Charlotte loved the way Otharose used double or even triple negatives to intensify the importance of something not done or not said. It was so clear, and clarity of language was becoming one of Charlotte's newest passions. Just as an orderly arrangement of her toys had lead to her pleasure in an orderly pallet which in turn had led to her infatuation with Mrs. Velkin's orderly concept of history, lately she lay awake nights figuring out absolutely clear ways of saying things. *Didn't never show them to nobody,* was all in one category—negative. Charlotte still didn't know nothing about no daddy, she thought, and burst out laughing herself. The muscles in her legs and shoulders felt suddenly loose. For a moment she heard, as if it were sound, an altogether new, penetrating quiet in her head. She was starving and tired; she wanted to be alone.

She left Otharose's apartment having performed a full curtsy to the grandmama, and having managed to avoid looking at the photographs of the dead family on the way to the door. It was still raining. Nevertheless, Charlotte walked the twenty-five blocks from Otharose's apartment in Harlem to her own. As soon as she was in her room she cleared her history texts off the desk, took her oil paints out of the closet and began the eighth portrait of Mara and George.

"It will constitute a profound crisis of belief," Buck warned them. "There will be chaos. We're already under attack from the outside. Now the party will be in shambles." He looked at Aaron, eyes filled with sorrow and disbelief, perhaps even shame, Charlotte thought, amazed. "It appears we have made terrible mistakes, my friend."

"It may be a lie," Mathilda offered. "That Stalin could do such things? I don't believe it." She poured herself a second glass of wine from the decanter in the center of the table and spilled some on the voluminous sleeve of her bright blue caftan.

"Don't be absurd," Rose told her. "It's Krushchev who speaks. At a Soviet Congress. Not Nixon in the Congress of the United States."

"It's the bitter truth," Buck assured his sister, dipping a napkin in water and handing it to her to wipe out the stain of wine. "A Soviet congress," he repeated. "And they tell us what the red-baiters have been saying for years is the truth. All those dead."

They all crowded in the kitchen, some seated at the table, some standing around it. Lynda, who attended Queens College, had cut her last classes when she heard the news. Andre and Charlotte, in their last year of high school, had taken the day off. Even Hannah and Jacob were considered old enough to understand. Myron, who by now practically lived in the Cohen apartment, stood shuffling uncomfortably next to Brian, who, with white shirt sleeves rolled up above his strong forearms, had grown handsomer than ever in Charlotte's opinion. Vivian was the only one of the children whose life was directly threatened, and the grownups included her in the inner circle of those who were seated around the spread of bagels and cream cheese, noodle pudding and thick golden sponge cake baked by Aunt Rose as soon as the news came in. Otharose was there, listening quietly as usual as if she were planning her letter for the evening. Leon was visiting again, writing another article for a Chicago weekly. It was worse in a way than June of 1953 when the Rosenbergs were killed, an afternoon which they would never forget. The family had sat in a circle around the small black radio, weeping openly. Later they had joined the throng of demonstrators at Union Square. But that was simple defeat—the lines between innocence and guilt were never unclear to them.

"As far as I'm concerned," said Rose after a long period of mumbling and repeated expressions of general consternation during which everyone poured wine and filled their plates with food, "it's over. Everything is in question now. We better look that right in the eye. Our survival depends on it." She leaned forward on her elbows and implored her husband, "If the great Joseph Stalin is no better than Hitler . . ."

"That's going too far, Rose," Buck interrupted angrily. "There may be reasons, factors of which we are unaware."

Aaron smiled cynically, a smile full of pain. But Leon said, "There are no factors, Buck. Rose is right. A group of men followed a policy of murder and mayhem in a government thousands of miles away. And our own history, our personal *lives*—" he caught his breath, gulped a sip of wine, "are in devastation. For me there is no question. I resign from the party today."

With that announcement they all began to talk at once, splitting off into angry exchanges with the person nearest them, shouting and accusing each other of naïveté or betrayal. The young people, except for Lynda, withdrew to the living room. They all looked at Vivian.

"I agree with Leon," she said. "It makes quitting the only sensible thing to do. But," she glanced at Charlotte, "if I'm not a communist, I'm—I don't know what. Nothing makes sense. There's nothing to believe in. And then what am I?"

"You're Vivian," said Andre, whose infatuation had not

diminished in the two years he'd known her. "You're exactly what you were yesterday, except you found out something you didn't know before."

"Hah!" She shook her loose, blond hair over her shoulders. "You're a great one to say that, Andre."

They all thought of Andre finding out about Buck's secret job more than a year before, and how different he'd been ever since. Robbed of the anger that had kept him in touch with something strong in himself, he had submitted increasingly to melancholy. His skin turned pale. He cut his hair very short the moment it began to grow over his ears. He even neglected his guitar.

"It's different, Vivian," he murmured.

"No, it's absolutely the same. You believe in something absolutely. It keeps you going. Then you find out you were fooled. It doesn't matter what the thing was—politics or love—even if *part* of what you believed remains true, it's all ruined. It's a trauma. A shock to your system. Don't minimize it. I feel like my guts have been shoveled out. I feel humiliated. I feel exposed. I feel like I want to die," she threatened with blazing eyes. Brian said, "Vivian, listen." He took a deep breath, as if planning his words. "About a year ago, I stopped believing in God." He looked at Charlotte and blushed. Everyone followed his glance to Charlotte, then looked back at Brian. "I don't know," he continued. "Something just happened, and I knew it was all a kind of lie—Jesus being his son, Mary being a virgin, all of it. At first, well, I wanted to kill myself. And I couldn't figure it out, you know? How would I, well, sort of, live? Until I realized that I was still the same. I mean I—well—still believed in the same things. I know it sounds stupid. But I thought most of the things I believed in were still right, even without Him. The people who thought up the ideas were right about a lot of them, and the ideas are still good. I know how angry and empty you feel. But you'll find something again."

Vivian had told Charlotte innumerable times that she thought Brian was beautiful but simple minded. Now she looked out the window as if she were embarrassed by what she agreed was his stupidity. All she said in response to his speech was, "This isn't about God," to which Andre and Brian exchanged a sad shrug.

79

"Brian's right," Jacob surprised them all by saying in a collected tone. He brushed his long brown hair out of his eyes and stared at Vivian. But when she began to argue her point of view, lecturing Jacob on dialectical materialism, he kept his eyes on his feet. When she was done talking, he bent down to tie his sneakers. Then he walked out of the room.

In the kitchen they could hear the volatile discussion continuing. Leon shouted, "You're naïve at best, my friend, perhaps blind or even mad. I'm sorry to say so, but it's a naïveté so great it borders on the criminal."

"Relax, man." Aaron tried to calm him down. "We're friends, remember?"

"I'm no friend of a collaborator," Leon said as if he were addressing a mass meeting. "And his stubborn innocence," he pointed to Buck, "amounts to collaboration."

"This is too much," Mathilda screamed. She stood up and pounded the table with her fists.

"You are a collaborator if you don't reconcile yourself to the obvious and take appropriate action. Quit, Isaac, quit today."

"You told me to join. Now you want me to instantly quit? Leon, sometimes I think you're a religious man."

"Don't be philosophical, Isaac. What do you mean, religious? I'm a pragmatic man."

Buck looked pale. He tried to stand up to answer the accusations, but as soon as he did so he faltered, clutched Otharose's shoulder, and sat down again. Buck had been weak since his heart attack, unable to return to work. A soft crew neck sweater with a blue or white sports shirt underneath had replaced his suit and vest. An empty plastic cigarette holder or an empty pipe through which he perpetually sucked air and saliva had replaced the small line of butts lining the edge of his desk. He stretched the neck of his shirt collar a bit, as if he needed air.

"Calm yourself," Otharose said. She dipped a napkin in a water glass and gently wiped Buck's forehead. She remained standing behind him with a hand on each of his shoulders. Watching her from behind, standing like that with her hands on Uncle Buck's shoulders, Charlotte noticed the strength and youthfulness of Otharose's body. Wide shoulders, small waist, broad bony hips, long legs. Her hair was pulled straight back that day, parted severely in the middle and stretched behind her ears where two thin braids met and joined at the nape of her neck, outlining her head like a crown. Her face was completely unwrinkled, though she was over fifty years old. He dark purple lipstick complemented her lavender dress. In the moment of realizing for the first time that Otharose was a beautiful woman, Charlotte noticed also the confident and gentle way she placed her hands on Buck's shoulders.

"Leon," Aunt Rose said sternly, eyes unwavering on her old friend's face. "If you continue, I shall have to ask you to leave my house."

"Oh my God," Charlotte moaned from the living room. But Hannah George responded sharply, "Don't say 'Oh my God,' Charlotte. If Leon says things like that he has to leave. Mama's right." For one moment Hannah herself flashed before Charlotte's eyes—not the littlest girl wearing clothes Lynda and Charlotte had worn before, teasing her only form of aggression, but a strong, clearheaded almost woman. Like her mother. The image disappeared suddenly as Myron, usually all but mute except when he was alone with Andre, shouted, "Correct!" All the adults looked into the living room.

Lynda, for whom Leon had always been a favorite (he had encouraged her talent for writing, taught her the elements of a well-constructed article) put her hand on her mother's arm and said, "Mama," as if to beg her for silence and offer support at the same time. She turned to Leon. With open fingers she combed her dark hair back from her forehead where long ringlets, like Andre's and Hannah's, fell. Leon's expression, when he looked at Lynda, was full of anguish, of passionate longing, Charlotte thought, and she remembered the way Aaron had looked at her in the bath.

"Leon," Lynda said, "we're all upset. Don't ruin a friendship for politics." She looked pleadingly at her father who nodded his support.

Leon answered, "It's not politics, Sweetheart, as if that meant something out there. This is a time when politics rests here." He pounded his chest with his fist, turned red and looked at Buck.

Buck winced as if in pain. But it was Rose who spoke.

81

"So you can act like a friend who disagrees, Leon, not like a party official bringing charges, or you can leave this house."

"Mama!" Lynda objected.

"I?" Leon asked, genuinely astonished. "Like a party official? I am the one who disclaims the party!"

"You are the one who is offering condemnations," Rose intoned with a resigned, deadly calm.

"Rose," he pleaded. "You yourself said what we have to do. Will you let him equivocate and philosophize again? Just as he always does? As he did with Mara and George?"

Rose's mouth thinned into a tight line. She sucked her cheeks into her jaws and her eyes flashed.

Charlotte walked into the dining area and stood behind Buck, near Otharose, and stared at Leon. Buck stood up suddenly and, sounding angrier than the children had ever heard him before, said "Leon! The children! What do you think you are doing? You don't know what you're talking about so the better part of valor is, I would say, to remain silent." Buck pointed a professorial finger at his friend.

Aaron jumped up from the table and went over Buck, putting both hands on his shoulders. "All right. Calm down. Enough," he said. He forced Buck away from the table and led him into the bedroom. They heard the door slam shut. Everyone, especially Charlotte, looked at Leon, who was nearly in tears. Clumsily, he pulled on his plaid lumber jacket and stretched his dark blue knit cap over his bald head.

Lynda stood up and started to follow her father, but turned back suddenly to Leon. "We'll work it out," she assured him, and then to Rose—"won't we, Mama?"

But Rose looked down at her glass which she clutched in her fist like a rock about to be thrown and remained utterly still while Leon walked over to her, placed his hand on her shoulder for a moment, looked around at everyone, resting his eyes for the longest moment on Lynda, and left the house. As soon as he was gone, Lynda turned to her mother.

"I thought in this house we reasoned and talked things out," she said. "How could you do it?" Her voice was abnormally controlled. There was no mitigating childish rebellion in her eyes.

82

"I can do it because he's a tyrannical man, Lynda," Rose said softly. "And tyrants cannot be reasoned with. You will try. You will fail. And you will learn one of life's bitter lessons. I've known Leon a long time. He comes to conclusions with the speed of light." She waved at the overhead lamp. "And anyone who disagrees with him is dispensable, because the one thing he can't stand is uncertainty and doubt. He didn't think Mara and George should go to Spain—" Rose looked at Charlotte quickly, as if this simple phrase could wipe out the impact of Leon's provocative accusation. "So no one who maintained an open mind on the subject could be listened to, was even suspect—of what, I never figured out. A failure to perceive the truth according to Leon, I suppose. With people like that you cut the cord fast and clean." Rose sliced the air with her hand. She had gotten carried away with her own passion, forgetting Lynda's indignation. Charlotte was impressed. She glanced over her shoulder at Hannah, who sat in her mother's habitual chair staring at them. The new aura Charlotte had perceived was still there. Hannah. She faded into the background because she was not a chronic rebel like the rest of them, but she was like Rose, perceiving necessity, accepting the price.

Lynda continued in the same bitter, calm voice, as if Rose had not spoken. "He was *my* friend. He liked me best of all, Mama. He thought I was special." She turned her back on the family and walked down the hall to her room. Before she entered, slowly drawing the door closed behind her, she stopped and, looking with cold, dry eyes at her mother, said, "You know. The way you feel about Andre."

Several days afterward, Charlotte once more put away her paints, but this time not in anger or self-denial. It was only an interim during which she needed her energy for something else. In fact, she left out one large drawing pad and her charcoals because somehow, though she had no idea how, she intended to turn everything she planned to learn in the next few weeks into sketches in preparation for a mural—the most ambitious work she had ever conceived. The eight portraits of Mara and George leaned against the far wall in a line. In the past year, Charlotte had turned to portraits of herself which were, in reality, double and triple portraits—two or three faces attached to each other like Siamese twins, each registering an emotion different from the other. This time, thought Charlotte, as she oiled her pallet and placed the tubes of paint into the little compartments of her cherry-wood paint box, she would paint history.

On her desk she piled several books she had found on Uncle Buck's shelf: *What Is Communism?* by Earl Browder, *History of the Communist Party in the United States* by William Z. Foster, the first volume of *Capital* which she had never dared attempt before, and a volume by Edmund Wilson which Aaron had given her for her sixteenth birthday. It included an essay called "The Partnership of Marx and Engels," which he had suggested she read. Charlotte had never read any of the book, nor any of the others on her desk. But for the next two months she applied herself to their pages with the intense dedication of which crises frequently made her capable. "Politics and love," Otharose had said. Vivian had said it too. And now Leon had suggested a connection. There was something in her history waiting to be discovered if she could penetrate that connection, and when Charlotte was on the trail of her history her energy knew no bounds.

T hroughout the spring and early summer Charlotte studied the complicated history of American Communism and attained an elementary understanding of its philosophical roots. On the wall above her desk were dozens of sketches; everyone in the family, individually and in various groups, stared down at her in shades of brown and gray. There was a watercolor sketch of Otharose's grandmother, only a thin line of black ink separating white from white. Some of the family members sat for Charlotte, and she had drawn their portraits with an eye to actual likeness as well as to her own emotions and memory. She had not yet convinced either Vivian or Andre to sit, however, and tonight it was her intention to do so. In addition to the portraits, there were sketches of cities—broken down tenements on 106th Street between Broadway and Amsterdam Avenue Charlotte had drawn, hoping to replicate the feel of industrial poverty she had read about in *Das Kapital*. There were sketches of Stalin, Hitler, Joseph McCarthy; of Marx's daughter Eleanore who had ruined her life with devotion to a cruel and selfish man; of Emma Goldman whose autobiography Charlotte had read several times, marveling at the interweaving of her struggle against personal tyranny as a woman and the social tyrannies of the ruling class.

"She had to fight twice for her freedom—once from capitalism and once from men," Charlotte told Vivian in an frenzy of indignation. But Vivian was uninterested in Charlotte's newest passion. Ever since she quit the YCL, she had been languishing. She wandered away from political discussions after dinner. She

85

would be leaving for college in Massachusetts in September, but she made no attempt to find a summer job. She took a large allowance from her father, which she had sworn she would never do, and spent her days wandering around the city with Andre, who infuriated Buck with his aimless inactivity. In the evenings too she sat out on the fire escape with Andre and Myron singing and staring into the hot night.

Charlotte worked all day in a mid-town office as a file clerk. For seven hours she moved from her desk where she organized correspondence by date to a tall file cabinet in which she organized them by company. She took her lunch hour at Chock Full O'Nuts later and later each day in an attempt to shorten the interminable afternoon and thereby create the illusion of shortening the day. At five, she joined the packed throngs on the uptown local, her feet swelling in her tight white or black patent leather pumps, her cotton dresses sticking to her broad, sweaty back. As soon as she got home she changed to shorts and a tee-shirt and went to work on her mural plans.

High on the wall, above the overlapping collage of sketches, was a long sheet of paper covered with dates, some referring to crucial events of recent political history, others to crucial events in Charlotte's life — 1939: Hitler-Stalin pact, Charlotte's birth, Andre's birth, Mara and George go to Spain; 1941: Hitler attacks Soviet Union; 1944: Browder attacked for rightest deviationism; 1949: Smith Act Trials; 1953: Isaac Cohen fired from the university; 1955: meeting with Otharose; 1956: Twentieth Congress of the Soviet Union, invasion of Hungary. And many more in between. In small letters toward the very bottom of the page, Charlotte had written, "June, 1956: Brian Sullivan."

She'd had sex with Brian one Sunday morning a year before when everyone else had gone to the beach. It was her first time, but Brian had a whole year and two different girls of experience behind him. He brought the hesitant, thoughtful gentleness with which she was so familiar in his conversation to his lovemaking, giving her a sense of safety which enabled her to express her considerable passion without restraint. When he lay on top of her, his penis pressed against her thigh, not yet daring to put it inside, kissing her lips and forehead and eyes, Charlotte became so wild with excitement that Brian asked her if anything was wrong. All resistance to going all the way was overcome by the sweetness of that question. She laughed and murmured, "uh, uh," between heavy breaths, then watched mesmerized as he sat up on the edge of her bed and rolled a slippery transparent rubber onto his penis with dexterous fingers. He whispered her name as he rolled himself back on top of her and gingerly spread her knees wide apart so he could get inside. Once there, it was Brian who seemed to lose control, and it was her turn to be concerned. She had lost all sexual arousal in her fascination with the process she had heard about and dreamt about and imagined for years. She felt his large torso heave up and down against her soaking wet belly and breasts. While he writhed against her, she held his shoulders and pressed her palms against his back, a grateful and amazed witness to her possession at last of this crucial piece of knowledge about one of life's primary mysteries. During his orgasm he said, "Jesus, Mary and Joseph," in a husky voice edged with delight which made Charlotte laugh out loud.

Brian told her he loved her, that he always had, but Charlotte didn't respond. She knew she didn't love Brian. Or, she knew she didn't love Brian any differently from the way she loved Andre — there was no feeling that came near to what she had read about in books. She loved Brian simply, with her whole self intact. That's why she had chosen him for her first experience. It felt nothing like it had with Angel, she realized with immense relief. Charlotte suspected that the closest she had come to love in her almost eighteen years was the feeling she retained for Vivian.

She luxuriated in the slight breeze that came in from the back yard at dusk as she scanned the dates posted above her sketches and aimlessly drew a possible composition for the mural. So far she had no idea how to proceed, how to express in paint the complicated ideas that came and went in disorganized images. But she was only working as a file clerk until the end of the first week in August. Then she would have a full four weeks before her classes began at Queens College to complete the painting she'd been planning for months. She pinned her braids to the top of her head so she could feel a coolness at the back of her neck and went out to the fire escape to see if Andre or Vivian would sit for her. She wanted to complete the preliminary portraits that night. She was in the right mood. All the many ideas she had encountered in the past weeks kept her at a paramount pitch of aliveness. Long-forgotten memories exploded in her mind with lightning clarity. She saw Uncle Buck's face before it had aged, the color of the kitchen walls ten years before. She heard the first tentative sounds of Andre's guitar when he first learned to play. She even saw, or felt, or somehow knew again the amber light she had vaguely remembered in her home with Mara and George, and she smelled the aroma of furniture polish. It all seemed to float right behind her eyes, as did the more recent information she had gathered in her attempt to discover the link between politics and love which was still so difficult to apprehend.

It had something to do with the passion for justice which had been thwarted again and again throughout history and the equally constant frustration of that other passion—an end to loneliness through love. She felt the immense waste of human life that lay like a fuel-burning incinerator at the center of the wealth of nations. She had understood this connection through rereading the wonderful essay recommended to her by Aaron. She felt with no less a sense of fury the tragedy of the life of Karl Marx's wife, Jenny, who had watched three of her children die and finally been broken herself, in part because of the sacrifices the family made to the work of the father. Charlotte was not unaware, even at seventeen, of the irony of Jenny's tragedy when set against her husband's analysis of the sacrifices of the working class—their failure to assume responsibility for their inherent power.

As she slowly ambled through the kitchen where Aunt Rose sat sewing hems and seams on everyone's clothing for the fall, Charlotte felt she had come a small step closer to perceiving the shape of the madness which she knew lay at the heart of her family's life, just as there was (she had been completely convinced by what she understood of the first volume of *Capital*) a suicidal madness at the center of society itself.

The night was hot. It had not gone below ninety-five degrees in more than a week. Andre wore only a pair of white shorts. Brian, too, was bare chested over his cut-off dungarees, and

Charlotte blushed a shade darker than her suntan when she smiled at him. Myron's long-sleeved shirt stuck to his rounded back in great circles of sweat. Vivian sat at the far corner of the fire escape, her back to the railing, next to Hannah George who had begun joining them on evenings when she didn't go out. Only Jacob and Lynda kept themselves apart.

Charlotte leaned out and smiled at Andre. "Want to sit for me now? Please?"

"Soon." He moved his head up and down to the beat of the music, trying not to break his concentration. Vivian climbed over to the window sill where Charlotte joined her, her tanned legs pulled up to her chest, knees meeting Vivian's mid-sill.

"This—this family—is the only thing that can ever really matter, Charlotte. You're so lucky to have it." Vivian whispered as Andre hummed a melody along with Myron's flute. Charlotte looked down at her knees. She felt very differently but she didn't want to argue with Vivian.

"Oh, I know you don't agree, Miss Revolution, 1956," she persisted, " but you'll find out, just like I did. It's bullshit. The idea that we can make the world better. You'd better keep painting those portraits, Charlotte. I'm telling you. And find yourself a husband and have babies like I plan to."

Charlotte didn't answer. She was feeling peaceful and contented from the force of the energy that had carried her from day to day since the beginning of the summer. No fog clouded her thoughts; there was no noise in her ears; she felt in charge of things and appreciative of the family. Uncle Buck was in his room reading the newspaper. Jacob sat next to his mother at the kitchen table reading a magazine. Aunt Rose had set up a system of three fans through the main part of the house, and a soothing breeze moved from room to room.

"Will you let me draw you now?" Charlotte asked Vivian, giving up on Andre for the moment. She put her hands on Vivian's knees and felt a surge of pleasure move through her arms.

"Do I just sit here like a bump on a log?" Vivian asked through clenched teeth, her head held at a stiff, artificial angle. Charlotte giggled and put the pillows behind Vivian's back, picked

89

up her feet and put them on the bed.

"Now relax," she said, "just sit reasonably still. And talk to me."

"About what?"

"About something important. I want to draw the deepest you. Tell me about politics. Why don't you care any more? Just because of one disappointment?"

Charlotte had begun drawing as she talked. A line drawing of Vivian's features took slow shape on the page.

Vivian sighed. "Naturally you would go right to the most upsetting subject—except of course for one—" She smiled mischievously.

"Don't talk about *it,* Vivian," Charlotte pleaded, "or I can't draw."

"Politics then," said Vivian, "okay." For the next hour she described her history in the YCL beginning when she was thirteen—how furious her father had been, how her mother, the daughter of a socialist, had defended her, the ecstasy of the picket lines and demonstrations—and all of it revolving around the belief that revolution was not only necessary and right, but possible. It had happened in Russia, and it could happen here. This aspect of it was crucial to Vivian—she longed for something which could be achieved.

"I could never believe in anything like that again." She shifted position crossing her legs at the ankles.

Charlotte had outlined the shape of Vivian's face by then and modeled the chin and cheek bones in dark gray. She was particularly satisfied with a new technique for doing hair. Vivian's was pulled back from her forehead and the part down the middle looked perfectly real.

"All I can tell you—" Vivian continued, "I mean if you asked me what I thought was the deepest things in me now—is that I'm different. Totally changed, in a way I never thought possible. Everything inside feels different. I'm scared I'll never be the old Vivian again. And at the same time I'm scared of ever being her again. I don't know if it's growth or fear I'm feeling, but I'm just so different, Charlotte. That's why I can even talk about that night. It's like a different me did it. Before the revolution." She laughed. She was close to tears.

Charlotte felt her cheeks go hot again; she kept her eyes on her drawing. She knew Vivian needed her to say something, that she needed her to understand, to sympathize. But she was afraid of losing her concentration. Vivian waited. She stared at Charlotte until she had regained control. Then she said in an altogether different tone of voice—harsh and loud—"I've had sex with two other girls, too. And also, Charlotte, I've had sex with Andre."

Charlotte's hand stopped on the page. Then she continued the line of Vivian's neck and shoulders as before. "That's not very surprising," she lied.

"Well, you can't really call it sex." Vivian smoothed out the wrinkles in the spread. "Andre—well, *can't,* Charlotte. I mean, he can get hard, but then nothing happens, no matter what I did or he did. He just gets harder and harder until it looks like he might burst. He's in actual pain, he says. It happened twice. Then we decided to stop trying and just be friends. But Charlotte—" Vivian moved out of position.

"Sit back," Charlotte ordered, "I'm nearly finished." She felt a stiffness in her shoulders and neck. She was in danger of losing the power she had felt in the beginning of the evening, in danger of closing down. "And be quiet," she added shortly. "I'm doing your mouth."

Vivian shrugged, looked down at the floor. "Just one thing—I mean two things. One, don't ever tell Andre I told you. And two, Charlotte, Andre is scared he's queer, well, homosexual I should say. He told me while he was crying once, right after—you know."

Charlotte heard this and knew she had somehow known it before. No one in the family would ever suggest the possibility that one of them was homosexual. No one would use the formal word. Even Uncle Buck, usually so proper in his language, said "fag" or "pansy" derisively when they saw men like that on the street. Once she had heard Leon say it was a bourgeois perversion. Aaron had said no, it was a sickness which maybe couldn't be cured. What if Andre was? What name could he give himself? What name would she put to her experience with Vivian in Otharose's bed? "What's a queer, Vivian?" she whispered, laying her pencil on the floor. "Andre hates himself. I've always known that much."

Vivian got up and stretched her arms to the ceiling, then bent down to touch her toes. Her hair fell over her face and caught the light from the desk lamp which danced in stripes across the darker blond. When she stood up her eyes were filled with tears. Charlotte put her arms around Vivian. She rocked her and smoothed her hair, wiping the sweat from her forehead. She wanted to kiss her but she could not, wanted to speak but was silent. The ideas that had haunted her all through July came to her in shouting voices now, intrusive, unwelcomed. She was afraid she would never figure it all out, that she would never be able to paint the mural that, to her surprise, she had begun to care about more than anything else.

"Oh, it's just as well," Vivian said in answer to Charlotte's silence.

"What?"

"That I'm going to Massachusetts next month." Vivian managed an artificially light-hearted smile.

They went back out to the fire escape but found that the singing had stopped. The kitchen was empty and the house dark, except for one small lamp in the corner of the living room. Hannah was asleep on the living room couch and Brian had gone home. Myron and Andre stopped talking so abruptly when the girls came out that they knew they were intruding. Andre looked into the street and Myron said haltingly, "I guess I should go home," but he gave no sign of leaving.

Charlotte and Vivian went back to the bedroom and lay down in the dark. Soon they heard Lynda's key in the door. She came into the room, undressed quietly and got into bed. In a few more moments they heard Myron's shuffling walk, and the door closed again. Charlotte lay awake for an hour hoping that Andre would come in and offer to sit for her that night, but he didn't come. It was several days later, on a Saturday morning, that Charlotte finally had the opportunity to complete her last preliminary portrait.

An all-night rain had broken the heat wave. Charlotte and Andre went out to the back yard for the sitting. He leaned against the ivy-covered concrete wall which separated them from the adjacent yard. They were rarely alone together lately, but the strong connection between them was undiminished, and as soon as Charlotte sat down on a small triangle of grass opposite Andre, her sketch pad propped against her knees, they smiled.

"So how the hell are ya?" Andre asked. He turned his head to the right. "This is my best side."

"Just look at me straight, creepo," Charlotte teased. She had already begun shading in Andre's broad forehead. She sketched swift, flat areas—his temples, his bony jaw, the long side of his nose; below a pointed chin she drew a slender neck. "Take off your shirt," she said so firmly that Andre instantly obeyed. She suddenly knew that Andre's whole body would appear somewhere in the mural, the indented cavity of his chest clearly visible. It looked deeper today than ever before, which meant he had lost weight. She was disturbed by how little she had noticed him in recent months, and neither had he paid very much attention to her. The old sense of perfect comfort between them dissipated somewhat.

She picked up a newly sharpened pencil and began to draw his features, looking closely at him, as if she didn't know him well at all. He looked confused for a moment, then angry.

"Make sure you get this in," he said holding back his hair and pointing to a small ugly scar on his temple. "It's my best imperfection." A slightly contemptuous sneer distorted what had been the sensual line of his upper lip.

"I'm not drawing you to be critical." Charlotte held her pencil still for a moment.

"It's not your drawing," he answered stiffening. "It's your manner. You seem so damn—*interested*—so self-involved."

"Well Jesus, Mary and Joseph," she shot back, trying to be light. But Andre would not bend. "Well, how am I supposed to be when I'm drawing?" she asked seriously. "Besides, I can still listen to you. It's been ages since we talked. What's happening with you? What do you do all day walking all over the city with Myron and Vivian? What do you see?"

"Oh, I get it. Charlotte Cohen, the Serious Young Woman, the Responsible Wage Earner, the Dedicated Artist—no time waster, she. Isaac Cohen's niece, head to toe. You sure have changed."

She understood the truth of what he said and why he was so angry at her. She almost lost her concentration but she clenched her teeth and tried to recall the sense of layered ideas which had opened walls around her several days before. She finished his face, unavoidably replicating the sneer that still hardened his mouth. She shaded the curve of his shoulders, drew in a light suggestion of the outline of his chest, hips, legs, the unlaced torn sneakers on his large feet. Then she looked straight at his chest and with a softened pencil she began to model the rib cage, the chest bone, the indented curve which looked so deep today.

"I feel like a fucking fly being pinned," Andre complained.

In order to keep her concentration, Charlotte began to list all the reasons for his anger with one part of her brain so that the rest of it would be free to draw him. *For being different than he thought she was, for drawing a mural of the family, for being completely engrossed in her drawing of him instead of himself, because he loved her best.* She knew him well enough to know these were the reasons although she didn't understand why any of them except the first would make him so angry. She knew that the longer she persisted in her concentration, the angrier he would become. But she couldn't stop. She didn't answer him, or try to comfort him, or in any way try to assuage his anger. She didn't apologize. She just assumed he would keep his promise and sit there until she was done.

She was finished with his chest and moved down to his feet, becoming very focused on the detailed rendering of his sneakers (the loose laces, the torn hanging tongue, the frayed bulge of canvas just over his pinky toe) when he lit up a cigarette, took a long drag and said, "You and Vivian have sex together?"

She stopped drawing. She longed to have their closeness back again, to help him out of the rage which seemed to enclose him like rusted armor through which no other feeling could penetrate.

Andre flicked the end of his cigarette across the pavement and picked up his tee-shirt. "You finished?" he said, indicating her pad.

"Andre, why are you so mad at me?"

He stood up and arched his back, which was lined with long, red crevices from leaning against the stone. He looked down at her and said, "Let me see," pointing to the drawing again. She held it out to him. The face was harsh, the mouth set in an angry sneer, heavy lids covered most of the dark eyes. Andre kept his hair so short now his flamboyant curls looked more like tiny waves, but Charlotte had drawn them in uninhibited strokes so that they fell over his forehead the way they had years before. Stark, shadowy geometric planes indicated tremendous tension at the sides of his forehead. But the shoulders and neck were delicate, and the sunken chest and torn sneakers gave a sense of vulnerability to the figure that startled Andre out of his bitterness.

"Jesus, Charlotte," he whispered, "You are good. God, I am so fucking angry."

Charlotte touched his thigh from where she sat on the small patch of grass. He knelt down and laid his head in her lap on top of the sketch pad. Charlotte removed the pad and placed his head more comfortably on her thighs. He stretched out, turned over, and closed his eyes while she brushed his hair with her fingers. After a long period of silence Charlotte said. "I love you, Andre. Best of all. I always have. But you can't just spend your life sitting on the fire escape with Myron Shatsky. And I don't have sex with Vivian. It only happened once. It was weird and I doubt if it will happen again."

"Weird?" Andre said, a trace of anger creeping back into his voice. "Upsetting, maybe. Shocking. Shameful? Yeah—I would definitely say that. But not weird. It's like being with yourself. With someone even closer than a brother—or a sister in your case."

He was quiet while Charlotte took in what he had told her. She resumed the rhythmic stroking of his hair. Andre kept his eyes closed when he said, "And I had sex with Vivian too, Charlotte. I just thought you'd want to know. Just like I know about you and Brian. It's nothing like they tell us—everything in pairs. Nice and neat. It's really the birds and bees—everybody's fucking everybody. And only Jesus H. Christ himself knows what the old folks did. Dr. Miriam, as Otharose calls her, seems to have shtupped everyone in the family. Or so I heard Mathilda saying once behind a closed door I wasn't supposed to be standing near. But Aunt Mathilda was probably just jealous she didn't get a turn.

95

Poor old Mama's the only one who's been faithful and true, I'd wager, and that's probably because she hates a mess."

He laughed scornfully at his own cynicism. It was a misanthropic perspective on the world that had given them moments of grotesque comic relief in the past, and Charlotte couldn't help a short laugh at the odd mixture of Andre's deadly realism and his obvious agony in the face of what he saw.

"You know what I wish?" he said. "I wish Otharose would decide to get back at the white landlord who was responsible for the fire that killed her kids, get back through us. I wish she would set fire to our house and destroy everything. Except you of course, Charlotte. You and — let's see — Hannah George. You two would survive." His tone made their survival sound like a sin.

He jumped up and put on his tee-shirt. He offered a hand to Charlotte who rose, brushed the dirt off the seat of her pants, and put her arm through his. As they walked up the stairs to the apartment, Andre put his arm around her shoulders, pulled her close to him and said, "And it was very very good with Vivian." He leaned over and licked the inside of Charlotte's ear. She pulled away shouting, "Andre!!" slapping him with pretended good humor on his arm.

He laughed at her. "Andre!" she repeated harshly, "for God's sake."

He raced up the stairs ahead of her, laughing loudly. "Andre," she said very softly, after he'd gone.

In the end, Charlotte decided to use the long roll of paper filled with significant dates as the first layer of the final painting. She stretched it taut inside a wooden frame and rewrote every word and number in black water-repellent ink. Over this historical record, she used watercolors, in various levels of transparency, to paint the portraits of the family, the city scenes, the faces of significant people from history. The ninth portrait of Mara and George was of their corpses lying in a common grave in the Spanish earth. An unidentifiable couple made love at the center; all that could be seen were the man's back and ass and the woman's wide open legs. Two young girls, naked and on their knees, fondled each other's breasts, but this image was faded into

96

the background; only the observant would notice. Everyone in the family was drawn with admirable accuracy and was immediately recognizable, although Aunt Rose thought she looked too fat, Brian said with a blush that he wasn't that muscular, and Uncle Buck said he looked pretty damn old. But Charlotte thought they all looked wonderful. Even Aunt Mathilda looked poignant rather than foolish in her huge orange and blue striped dress. Aaron was dressed in his white hospital jacket and stood next to Charlotte's old math teacher, Miss Sipinelli — Charlotte's private joke with herself. Otharose looked straight out from the paper, her head surrounded by green vines and flames. The old grandmother sat on her bed looking out at them all with bright, piercing eyes. What held all the images together, giving some sense of unity to the potentially fragmented mural, were the words and dates. They threaded in and out of the faces of Stalin, Vivian (between Mrs. Velkin and Brian Sullivan), Uncle Buck, Aaron, Emma Goldman (who stood behind Lynda), Jacob (playing cards with Leon), and all the rest, like a background of loose, black tweed. From 1939 to 1957; from the Popular Front through Taft-Hartley and the Smith Act to the party debate on Lenin's concept of the centralized elite (which seemed to be written on the forehead of an anguished looking Vivian); from the Hitler-Stalin pact to the firing of Isaac Cohen (these words ended abruptly at the shoulder of Andre); from the crib with *Oscar* written on the side to a self-portrait in which Charlotte had experimented with Cubism, painting her face from three different angles at once; from the beginning of Charlotte's life to the present, the major events of the world and the family framed a background to the portraits. In the top right corner, surrounded by a circle of blank white paper, Myron Shatsky stood on the fire escape playing his flute.

Everyone was amazed at the detail. Aunt Rose wept. Otharose smiled proudly. Aaron said he had never seen symbolism used so obviously and so brilliantly by one so young. Uncle Buck toasted her with expensive French champagne. On the crest of her joy in their encouragement and respect, and even, she supposed, their love, the colossal mystery of her paternity seemed to shrink to an ordinary question. Through tears of relief she kissed Uncle Buck and decided, suddenly and simply, to ask him as soon as

97

she could find the opportunity to talk to him alone.

The next morning she had to leave the house at seven in order to register for her fall classes. Lynda, a junior, had mastered the complicated procedure. She calmed Charlotte's panic when desirable classes filled up unexpectedly, requiring last minute changes in programming. Together they read and reread the enormous catalog, finding substitutes, trying to choose courses for subject, teacher and time all at once. At twelve, when Charlotte had registered for only half her credits, the entire system closed down for lunch. She and Lynda sat on a grassy hill eating sandwiches and drinking cokes.

"Is this where you live your secret life?" Charlotte asked, smiling into her tuna fish sandwich.

"Jesus H. Christ, Charlotte. Your memory. What was it? Three years ago I said that to you? You never asked me. You hardly paid attention to me that night. But there it is, in your memory, just like one of those inked-in dates on your mural. You really do have a strange mind."

"So answer the question." Charlotte leaned back on her arms and turned her face to the sun. "Is this it? The world you don't share with any of us? Is the real Lynda Cohen this competent college girl? What were all those secrets you held back then?"

Lynda balled up the wax paper and tin foil which had contained her corned beef on rye and sucked the remains of her coke loudly through the straw. "You're the one with all the secrets, Charlotte. You and Pop, and Mama too I guess. I'm an open book, Kiddo. Just what you see is what you get. I was lying to you, just trying to make myself important. I had some idea that I'd scare you into thinking I was doing something bad. Then you'd tell Mama. Then she'd have to come begging to me—to try and find out. No, Oscar. I don't have any secret identity. No romantic lies surrounding my birth—much the worse for me. I'm just who you think I am. I go to school, where I do very well and am highly respected by my teachers. I come home when I'm expected. I have no secrets." She chewed on a piece of ice. "Well," she said slowly, "maybe just one."

"Tell," Charlotte demanded, leaning forward on her knees.

"It's a real one, Charlotte. Promise you won't tell until I'm ready."

"I promise," Charlotte agreed.

"I've applied to work on an English language newspaper in Paris. One of my professors recommended me. It's a special apprenticeship program. You learn how to be a reporter. You help cover real events, and you study French at the same time. They give you a stipend for rent and everything, even a small salary. It wouldn't cost Mama and Pop anything. I'm supposed to hear by next month."

Charlotte stared, amazed at the bravery of this decision. She could not imagine leaving home and had been secretly relieved when told she would have to attend a city school, like Lynda and Andre, where she could work in the afternoon and tuition was free. "You'd go that far away?" she asked.

Lynda stood up and brushed grass off her skirt. She flung the remains of her lunch into the trash can and pulled Charlotte's arm. "Come on," she said. "All the classes will be closed if you don't hurry. Yes, Charlotte. There is nothing I would like better than going far away from home. Pop's the only one I'd really miss. He's the only one who makes me think maybe I should stay."

"But everyone loves you."

"Maybe. But they don't need me. So I can go. And remember," she added, "don't tell anyone. Not Andre. Not anyone. Do you promise?"

Charlotte nodded her head. Lynda had to leave her while she completed registration, saying she would meet Charlotte at home. While she managed to find five courses which were open, and required, and interesting, then matched classes with room numbers posted on an enormous sheet at the end of the room, Charlotte thought about the secrets and lies which had framed her childhood, stories eternally hinted and never told. Lynda's lies were harsher, more ruthless perhaps. They did not arise from a need for myth or clarity, as did her own. Nor were they pathetic, like Andre's, made from shame. Lynda simply kept her business to herself. The boundaries implied by this fact caused Charlotte to feel a certain awe and somehow afraid.

She returned home exhausted and hot, felt the small relief

99

of the slightly cooler air in the lobby, and walked up the four flights of stairs as the elevator was broken for the third time that summer. She found several policemen standing in front of the door to her apartment. And as she had always known whenever tragedy struck Uncle Buck, she knew then, before she opened the door, just from looking directly into the Hispanic policeman's sympathetic eyes, that Uncle Buck was dead.

Everyone in the kitchen stared at her for a moment while she stood absolutely still. She rushed past them following a trail of nurses and police until she reached his room. Slowly, she walked to his side and knelt beside him as if there were still time for something, one last word. He was covered by a thin sheet, never having woken up from his last night's sleep. His face was white and gaunt, his eyes closed. She put her arm across his chest and with her other hand she smoothed his soft white hair. She kissed his forehead, his cheeks, his lips and wet his dry skin with sweat and tears.

Aaron came in and lifted her up to a standing position. She leaned against him and allowed him to take her back into the kitchen where he began making funeral plans with an efficient and precocious Brian, and more immediate plans with one of the policemen.

Aunt Rose stared at them all, as if she could see her future right up to its very end, while Aunt Mathilda wailed her completely uninhibited grief.

Otharose sat silently between Andre and Jacob holding both their hands. Their eyes were dry, but for very different reasons, Charlotte knew. And which was worse for the son of a dead father—a worshipful adoration always doomed to disappointment, or a disinterest so cold it verged on contempt?

She walked past Hannah and Lynda to the living room window and climbed out to the fire escape. She put her head on her knees and wept, calling for her uncle to return, begging him not to die, knowing that something far beyond his person would never return again. In the midst of her grief the thought came to her that she would paint him the way he had looked just now in his bed, and she felt so guilty for thinking it that she called out to Buck for guidance. *Too emotional,* she heard him say in his tone

100

of affectionate, critical concern. Only then, when she looked up from her knees to consider what he had given her, did she notice that Myron Shatsky had been sitting there all along.

His long face was covered with red mounds of chronic acne. His eyes, however, Charlotte noticed for the first time, conveyed attention and sympathy. She realized with some shame that she had never tried to get to know Myron because Andre loved him so much. As if he had witnessed her realization and her apology just as he had witnessed her private grief, Myron smiled gratefully and picked up his flute.

Book Two

Moonwalk

The green and blue curtains were frayed at the edges. The leaves of the dining room table were kept folded down to allow for more space in the room. "And what's the point of keeping it open?" Rose asked Charlotte, "when there are never more than three for dinner?" The old couch that had served as a bed for Aunt Mathilda, now dead three years, or Myron Shatsky—the occasional third for dinner—had been given to the Goodwill long ago.

Charlotte hated the emptiness of the room which had once been so crowded and busy. It was always clean, since it was easy for Aunt Rose to maintain order with only herself and Andre to worry about. The lights were kept dim.

"But Alex and I come," Charlotte insisted. "And Jacob comes too, with Marilyn and the baby."

"So once in a while I open the table," said Aunt Rose, rising from the old black chair with a grunt and walking over to an end table to straighten a lace doily that ruffled out from under two polished candlesticks. "Is this what you're coming to talk about Charlotte? My table?"

Charlotte leaned against the lumpy back of the corduroy couch, placed her arms across her expanding belly. Aunt Rose knew what she had come to talk about. She wanted family history, Charlotte had told her over the phone, though Rose insisted she couldn't remember a thing. Now, after a few moments of silence, Aunt Rose began to talk. She told Charlotte about the first time they all met Miriam Friedman. "She played the guitar for us." Rose looked at the wall and spoke as if Charlotte were not in the room.

105

"She didn't have such a good voice. Nothing professional. But it was a sweet voice. And there was something about the way she played. It was nice. George thought so." Rose looked back at Charlotte. "That I can tell you. George fell in love with her from that evening on." Suddenly she looked harshly at her niece.

"You can't live in the past, Charlotte," she said. "The past is past. You have a life now. You're young. It's enough already with your mother. All you ever did was ask questions. What was she like, how did she feel, why did she go. Why, Charlotte? What are you hoping to find out? There was nothing. You know everything there is to know."

"First of all," Charlotte began, and heard anger in her voice, old anger she thought she was done with. She changed her tone. "First of all, I don't know everything there is to know. I never have. I hardly know anything, and that's the point. I'm about to be a mother, Aunt Rose. I need to know more than ever before. Don't you see? I never had a mother. I have to imagine her before I can be one myself."

Rose looked at Charlotte, amazed. "Never had a mother?" she said. "What's a mother, Charlotte?"

Charlotte failed to notice the pain in her aunt's face. "That's right," she answered. "I've got to force myself to remember her. Even if I have to make her up."

"There's a big difference between remembering and making something up, no?"

"No," answered Charlotte. "Not really." She sat back and pulled wisps of hair off her forehead as Rose had done with her comb. She reached around for her long braid and wound it into a bun, retrieved a barrette from her pocket and pinned the braid to her head. The two women stared at each other, wide, stubborn mouths set in identical grimaces, each fingering curly wisps of hair escaping from thick, tightly woven buns.

"And Alex," Rose pushed. "What does Alex think of all this?"

"It's not a question of what Alex thinks," Charlotte snapped. "I'm the one who wants to know."

Charlotte had met Alexander Cayne in her first year of graduate school where she had gone to accumulate the education credits which would qualify her for tenure as a history teacher. Bowing slightly, staring into her watery spaghetti and meatballs, he asked if he could sit at her table and she agreed. Before he began to eat he unfolded his paper napkin and stuck the corner into his belt. She talked non-stop for an hour. Most young men would have fled. But Alex, a graduate student in psychology, was entranced. "You are the most open person I've ever met in my life," he said. She received the compliment with pleasure, feeling that he saw her just the way she wished to be seen.

Early that spring, on an unusually warm day, Alex drove Charlotte out to Jones Beach so she could be near the ocean, the place in the world she most loved to be. Sitting in the damp sand he bent his long, tanned legs at the knees and leaned over to watch the water. The tide was high and the surf was rough. Very few swimmers were in, and he kept a steady eye on Charlotte as she surfaced and dove under the waves, swimming too far out, he thought. Still, in the midst of his anxiety, he would tell her later, he enjoyed watching her swim. He walked to the edge of the water and began to call her name.

Charlotte looked back at Alex. She hadn't realized she had gone so far out, and she turned around. When she was a few feet from the shore where the waves were breaking, she allowed herself to be thrown onto the beach by the force of the water. She bumped her head on Alex's ankles when she was thrown. He kneeled down to help her, thinking she was hurt, but Charlotte was laughing. When he began to laugh too, she saw how deeply he was in love with her.

She lay next to him wrapped in a large towel on the nearly empty beach. She admired his body, which was angular and flat in a way she considered appealingly Christian (he reminded her of Brian). She considered him to have an unusually perceptive mind, although Jacob and Andre told her he was not so special when she described him as "brilliant."

"He's smart," Jacob said. "He's not brilliant, for God's sake."

"He's got that waspy intelligence. You can buy it at Yale," Andre added. They were both growing to like Alex, though, especially Andre who could assume an abstract interest in his own chronic depression and had begun to pick Alex's brain on the

107

subject as if they were two clinicians discussing a case.

Charlotte dismissed their doubts as jealousy. She loved Alex's familiarity with elegant food. He prepared delicate meals bounded by nutritional concern, far from the syrupy sweet rolls and oven-softened brisket to which she was accustomed. She loved his comfort with the woods where he had spent his childhood summers, all the things he knew about flowers which he had learned from his mother, an expert gardener. Alex spoke of gardenias, forsythia, crocus—magical names to Charlotte, who would have called them only flowers in the past. He took her on a weekend in the woods and pointed out a beaver dam, the morning mist hanging like silver silk over the slate gray pond. She loved the fact that he could swim, and ski, and skate several miles without even breathing hard. He taught her to ski, and to her amazement she was good at it. She soared down the elementary slope but she couldn't stop at the bottom and flew like a plane crashing into his arms. The Jewish-Communist ghetto of Charlotte's childhood had been like a hothouse of thick, overlapping plants compared to this cool field scattered with tiny wild flowers you had to be very near to name. She loved everything about Alex that was different from everything she had known before. But she fell in love with the fact that before he ate, he tucked his napkin in his belt.

Charlotte turned toward Alex on the blanket and opened her towel, inviting him in. Their wedding was small, in a rabbi's study (reformed) since Alex's parents (Lutheran) were dead. Charlotte wore a purple satin dress with a broad-brimmed purple straw hat. Alex wore a dark suit and a yarmulka to accommodate Aunt Rose's cousins. Without Uncle Buck around, she said, she didn't feel like fighting with them all.

For the next year and a half Alex and Charlotte lived in a perpetual mood of adventure. Shackles had been cast off. (He hadn't known such joy since he was a boy, he said, marveling at her energy. She had never known such peace, she responded, sleeping through every blissful night for the first time in her life.) They were in an intense but protective dress rehearsal for adulthood, slowly becoming one with the parts they played. They imagined themselves speaking lines no one had spoken before,

108

with no audience to mark their failures or note a torn seam in their disguise.

At the end of a year and a half, Charlotte went off the pill, frightened by the medical predictions of blood clots and cancer. She was fitted for a diaphragm, which she used carelessly. When her pregnancy test registered positive, they drank champagne at a dozen parties. They savored each word of the announcement they made to family and friends.

That was when the past came back like an avalanche of volcanic ash, a mud river cascading down the slopes of their mountain peak. Charlotte quit her job teaching history, which she had performed with dedication (recalling Mrs. Velkin) since she graduated from college. Encouraged by Alex, she decided to spend the months of her pregnancy painting. The trouble was that by the third month she found she had no energy for anything apart from her body and the baby growing inside it. Only thoughts of Mara could engage her interest, and she hadn't thought of Mara in years, not obsessively the way she had once done. Alex pursued her every evening as she paced around the rooms, jotting down memories in an old journal.

"What the hell are you doing?" he demanded, at his wit's end. "You're withdrawing from me. From everything. You're changing, Charlotte, into something I don't know."

She tried to explain the old mysteries, but Alex insisted it was destructive to live in the past. Charlotte wanted to be the woman he had fallen in love with, full of energy and drive. But she languished, was distracted. She watched the first wall rise between them.

One night, unable to sleep, she began to pace the dark living room. Every so often she leaned out the window so that she could see the shadows of Central Park. She remembered leaning out the window as a child and the memory made her uncomfortable. She pulled herself inside again. "Catch your death of cold," she muttered to herself.

Her flannel nightgown felt warm against her skin. She fixed herself a cup of tea and held it in both hands, an amulet against bad fortune. She walked around in the the dark some more, then sat down in the old maple rocking chair. She was no longer worried about what to paint. She thought she was thinking about the small being inside, whose fluttering movements she had just begun to feel. But when she got up from the rocking chair she knew she wanted to see Aunt Rose, to hear as many stories of the past as Rose could remember: to turn those stories into a painting of some sort. Charlotte walked back to her bed and fell immediately into a deep sleep.

Now, after their first meeting, Charlotte returned home and opened a newly purchased notebook. She began writing the story she had wondered about all her life, filling in various details missing from the history as it had been told by Rose. In the weeks that followed that initial meeting, Charlotte did almost nothing but work and rework the scene when they all met Miriam, adding details, eliminating a clumsy phrase, drawing pictures in the margins which often extended right over the words. Alex told her she was going crazy. He had just entered analytic school and was beginning his private practice.

"Is that your diagnosis, Dr. Cayne?" she sniped.

"I'm not a clinician at the moment." He returned her fire and turned his back.

Charlotte had always loved the way he translated her feelings into words that gave new meaning to her behavior. She loved to sit up late and listen to him describe his patients or Andre, waiting for his interpretations which would turn something she had thought obvious into a thing of a very different sort. She saw, again and again, that his analytic distance was a way of managing the love he felt for the broken people who found their way into his tiny consulting room, as it was clear to her that he had developed a strong love for Andre who, in his increasingly sour depression, reminded Alex of his mother. She loved the process of his insights as much as the content: he worked with layers of translation as she did in her portraits. But now she refused to talk to him about the story of Mara. She could only handle one layer at a time.

"You used to be so open," he complained, and she knew he was remembering his childhood—the slammed door of his mother's room.

110

At night, when they might have talked, she walked to her desk as if in a trance, often still standing while she began scribbling and sketching.

"I thought you were going to paint," Alex said to her. Charlotte refused to hear the need beneath the irritation.

"Mmmmm," she said, not turning to look at him. "I am."

It was only occasionally that she had a chance to walk through a museum or gallery. Usually she was working or too exhausted from working to do anything but sleep. But every so often, and always because she felt some inner emergency, a state of tension for which there was no other response, Miriam visited museums. In museums she could feel a unique kind of calm inside she could find nowhere else in the world except sitting right at the edge of the ocean.

Miriam's mother, Constance, had been raised by wealthy parents in a small New Hampshire town. She had sacrificed wealth and position to marry a young Jew from New York, Mark Friedman, a passionate man, according to Constance, who had died in an accident a month before his daughter was born. The young mother, too proud to turn to her family for help, got a job as a secretary and named her child Miriam, hoping to invoke courage and fortitude. She raised her in a two-room apartment on the Lower East Side of Manhattan where she lived comfortably among the Jews who reminded her of her dead husband. She was determined and cheerful, a woman without an ounce of self-pity. "You have to play the hand you're dealt as best you can," she told Miriam in a flat, emotionless voice.

Constance rose in the business from secretary to Assistant Administrator in the course of fifteen years. She could be counted on to be home when she said she would, lugging a large bag of groceries filled with the ingredients of nourishing meals and treats. She almost never raised her voice. And each evening, from the time Miriam could remember, she would retire after dinner to her bedroom (Miriam slept on the living room couch) where she would read and write poetry until she fell asleep. She died almost immediately after Miriam was accepted into medical school, having met her daughter's friend Aaron and assuming

111

they would marry. She had been a good mother, Miriam thought.
She could not recall many harsh words. Certainly, she had never
been hit. Yet she would never, except in the most dire emergency,
have dared to enter that room after dinner or, for that matter,
questioned why her mother assumed ownership of it year after
year, even when Miriam was an adolescent and craved privacy
as a colicky baby craves rhythmical movement without which
it becomes hysterical and wild. Constance had been unassailable
in her devotion to her daughter. They had led a peaceful, isolated
life whose material requirements were attended to, a life of
routine and predictability that looked to anyone who knew them
like evidence of love. But Constance was impenetrable at her
center, and it was in relation to that center that Miriam's lone-
liness developed. Her loneliness was chronic and therefore some-
times unnoticed, but it erupted occasionally, engulfing her in
a panic so vast and fluid that Miriam thought she would go in-
sane or die.

Charlotte tapped the desk with the tip of her pen and stared
at the page before her. It was too extreme, she thought. It was
how *she* felt, and she was attributing it to her mother. It was that
very confusion that pleased her though, in a way she could not
describe. She was trying to stick to the facts, but at times the facts
were not enough. She turned on her desk lamp. She only had
several more hours until Alex came home. She picked up her pen
and wrote.

That special panic had come upon her only four or five
times in her life. She felt as if she were literally the only person
on the planet: no one else could see her; no one was like her;
she could not scream loud enough for anyone to hear. The first
time it happened to her she had been walking near a museum
and, terrified, she had rushed inside. She had wandered through
the enormous galleries staring at the paintings and sculpture,
and the next time she realized where she was an hour had passed
and she was calm. From then on she rushed to museums
whenever the attacks came on. She had met Aaron in a museum.
Miriam had no family she was close to. She had never known

her father's family, and Constance's relatives had long since disinherited her and her half-Jewish child. Aaron was her first and only close friend. He helped her with her studies, being a resident when she was a first year medical student. He took her with him to political meetings where the collective intensity of feeling, the disciplined studying, and the belief in the possibility of a better world allowed Miriam to believe she had escaped the loneliness of her childhood. He introduced her to George, Isaac and Rose Cohen.

The night she met them was her first night off in ten. She was very tired and after a small glass of wine served with dinner, she felt a daring lack of inhibition. Otherwise, she would never have agreed to play George's old guitar and sing for them. She played badly, but she had a pleasant alto voice and since they were all high from the wine, everyone joined in. During her second song, Miriam looked up from the guitar strings at her audience. Aaron sat on the floor, his forehead resting on his knees. Isaac sat on a couch with his arm around his new wife, Rose, tapping the rhythm of the song on her shoulder. Miriam felt drawn to Isaac that evening. She felt him to be strong, reliable, capable of loyalty which, once assumed, could never be broken. She felt drawn to Rose as well—or the world she created in the apartment crowded with furniture, books, food: to the cinnamon rolls and the small embroidered lace napkins placed carefully on the backs of chairs and the way Rose straightened each one as she passed through a room. Isaac's and Rose's apartment drew her into its warmth. The fact that Aaron had brought her here made her feel closer to him than ever before. But it was George she fell in love with.

When she put the guitar aside and folded her hands in her lap, he leaned forward, looking at her with a gaze so presumptuous she shifted uncomfortably on her chair. It was as if he were looking through her clothes, her skin. He proposed a toast, and Rose passed around carved crystal glasses filled with amber brandy. Miriam spread her hands in her lap and played nervously with the folds of her black dress, pulling the material over her knees, fingering the pleats.

"To our new friend," said George. "A new member of our

113

*family. To her lovely voice, and to the power of her presence. To
a woman who should not be looking down at her knees" (he
smiled) "but into the faces of her subjects."*

*Miriam was a shy person, unconfident, and yet when George
said that, she felt as if he were describing a hidden self.*

*"To Miriam," he continued and raised his small, sparkling
glass. "But why should anyone have named you 'bitter sea'? You
should be Mara. The sea. May I call you Mara?" She lifted her
eyes to meet his, nodding. "To Mara then," he finished. "May
you always remain in our lives."*

*Then he turned to his brother and, with grand explanations
about elk in the forest and leaders of men, he changed Isaac's
name to Buck.*

*They all drank. Miriam's cheeks burned. She felt a melting
of walls inside, light spread through her. She thought of her
mother's room, of the few times she had been embraced by Constance, of the large photograph of the young, dark-haired man
who was her father. George's hair was blond, but he had the same
penetrating eyes. In Isaac's and Rose's house, a week later in
George's bed, she felt herself to be her father's daughter —
passionate, opening and unfolding in a warm climate, needing
desperately to be loved.*

*"Such drama," Rose smiled after they finished their drinks
and replaced the glasses on the wooden tray. "Always with
George," she told Miriam, "we have drama. If he's hungry, it's
the best meal ever prepared on earth. If he's happy, the revolution is at hand."*

*George laughed, caught his sister-in-law in a bear hug,
nearly toppling her tray. He took the tray and gave it to his
brother so he could complete his embrace. He swung her in a
circle off the floor. When he put her down she looked at Miriam
and, serious eyes contradicting a playful smile, she finished,
"And when he's sad, Dear, the world and everything in it can
go to hell because it's not worth it for anyone to live another
minute."*

*"He's an artist," Miriam answered softly, looking at George.
"His moods are his tools. I remember my mother saying that.
She was a poet. Of course her mood was usually depression,"*

she smiled at Aaron. But she felt strongly that she was finished with all that, with the part of herself that had been Constance's obedient daughter, as if Constance were really dead once and for all. She felt, and she knew it must be madness (out of the corner of her eye she saw Aaron looking at her sadly) as if she would never be lonely again.

Charlotte put down her pen and sat back in her chair. On the wall above her desk was a large portrait of her mother. It was a series of portraits really, in the style Charlotte had used right before she went to college and still found useful for expressing the overlapping images she saw whenever she planned a painting of someone she knew well — a collection of faces, some facing front, some profile, some hidden in the boundaries of a larger face. In every painting Charlotte was obsessed with revealing everything she knew. Every secret seemed a deception, every withholding a lie.

The portrait was full of broken lines. The shaded areas were unclear and tended to overlap what ought to have been a light plane. Paintings had never soothed Charlotte as they had her mother. (But then, Charlotte remembered, that was one of the details she had made up.) They excited her to a frenzy. Now, gazing at the inadequate drawing, then at the increasing pile of papers on which she was constructing her mother's history, Charlotte felt agitated. She gathered the papers together, feeling anxious to get back to the old apartment and talk more with Aunt Rose, to elicit more information than she'd been able to acquire thus far. She was trying to figure out how to ask what still seemed to her to be a crucial question — the nature of Mara's relationship with Uncle Buck.

Charlotte looked out the fire escape window and, for a moment, she thought she saw Andre and herself sitting there. The

116

past was more and more alive in her as the days went by. She felt threatened by it, though she couldn't admit it to Alex, too engulfed to struggle against its pull. She thought of the following fall when Hannah would be moving back to New York. They would have a big Thanksgiving feast like the old days. Jacob and his family would be there. And she and Alex would come with their baby. They would even go to the nursing home in Washington Heights where Otharose lived and bring her home for the feast.

"We'll all be here then," she told Rose.

"Not all." Aunt Rose sniffed angrily. "Not Lynda."

Lynda had won the scholarship to apprentice on a French newspaper and left home soon after her father's death. Never completing her American degree, she had settled in Paris where, in the last few years, she had begun to achieve a solid reputation as a journalist. She sent them her articles, written from wherever in the world she was traveling—most recently, Vietnam. But she had not come home. Not in almost ten years.

"Can we talk about the more distant past?" Charlotte asked softly. Aunt Rose nodded, shifted position, removed a comb and replaced curls.

"Why not?" Rose asked. "But what's to tell, Charlotte. I can't remember anything."

"Last time you told me about the time you met," Charlotte urged. "What happened between the night my mother played the guitar for you and the time she finally married George?"

"What happened? Nothing. They fell in love right away. He always had that effect on women. He sat and stared until everyone was embarrassed. A year later, they were married. By that time Miriam had become Mara and Isaac had become Buck, thanks to the decree of King George. We all went to City Hall. So." She straightened her back and clasped her hands in her lap.

Charlotte remained silent. She looked pleadingly at her aunt and rested her open palm on her belly which was round and large though she was only in the beginning of her fifth month. They heard a shuffling from the other room—Otharose's old room which now belonged to Andre. He was reading through the huge stacks of newspapers he collected, Charlotte presumed. She forced her thoughts from the disturbing image of her cousin.

117

"You didn't like my father?" Charlotte suddenly asked.

"Didn't like? Of course I liked him. You couldn't help liking him. We saw them every day." Rose spoke firmly, as if to emphasize her affection for George. "Except when Miriam was on duty, most nights they would come here. Later they would go to George's dumpy little apartment on Barrow Street. But, for relaxation, for a good meal and good conversation, she came here. Often with Aaron too. We would eat. We would talk. She would help me with Lynda. She would hold her and feed her the bottle."

Rose pulled a comb out, although no wisps had escaped, and combed the top of her hair. She replaced the comb and stole a quick glance in the ornately framed mirror which hung on the wall next to her chair. "Believe me, Charlotte," she said. "It wasn't just George she fell in love with."

"And then?" Charlotte felt a small flutter in her belly—a thigh perhaps, or a tiny foot.

"And then? And then nothing. Look, Charlotte. It wasn't a simple time. George—your father—he was—a passionate man. He swept her off her feet. He was handsome. He could talk beautifully. Could he talk, Charlotte! About literature. About politics. She was a lonely girl, your mother. Successful, yes. A doctor. But—you can understand, Charlotte. She was a baby. A crazy mother from what I heard who hardly spoke to her. Took care of her but hardly spoke to her. She was lonely and didn't even know she was lonely. She told me that once. Those were her actual words. You can't blame her, Charlotte."

"Blame her for what, Aunt Rose?" Charlotte sat forward abruptly. She felt a sharp pain in her groin.

"Who said anything about blame?" Rose straightened her white nylon blouse, smoothing non-existent wrinkles from her skirt. "Blame is not the issue, Charlotte. You said you wanted to understand more about your mother though it's a waste of time in my opinion. What's past is past. But so, okay, so I'm telling you. She was smart. She was beautiful. But mostly she was lonely. She loved to be here." Rose indicated the dim kitchen where a narrow shaft of light danced on the dark wood of the highly waxed floor. "She loved Lynda, Isaac—the family. She was happy with us. But she was crazy about your father. I mean crazy,

118

Charlotte. Even Aaron was worried about her. She neglected her work. He talked to me about it. You know what it is to be crazy about a man? I mean crazy?"

Charlotte thought about her strong desire for Alex to make love to her, about his growing reluctance to do so the more the distance between them grew. Alex's knowledge of psychology had once caused her to feel safe and important. Now that same knowledge frightened her, a weapon he could use against her if she let down her guard. But no more than when she was a girl could Charlotte talk easily to Aunt Rose. She opened her mouth to speak, but no sound came.

"You don't know," said Aunt Rose, smiling ruefully. "Your Alex. By him, everything's inside." She pointed to her head. "There's no world by him. So no one can be a victim of anything. I feel everything that happens to me is my fault, by Alex. He can't be easy to live with. But he's not like George, Charlotte. He's —" she paused, " — a predictable man. More like your Uncle Buck."

She got up and walked into the kitchen where she nearly bumped into Andre, who was leaning on the counter, his soiled tee-shirt stretched around a skinny neck, his hair cut so close to his head you could not find a curl.

"Talk, talk, talk," he said. "Here we are, cozy, cozy, cozy in the past. That little guy's gonna save us or bury us." He pointed to Charlotte's belly.

Charlotte walked over and kissed him, ran her palm across his head and teased, "You'll be bald soon, Andre. And *he* is gonna be a *she.*"

Aunt Rose turned on the light, covered the narrow table with a white cloth, and began to take food from the small old-fashioned refrigerator that fit snugly into a rectangular space in the wall. The three of them sat down to eat. Not much was said. Every so often they looked at each other and smiled. Rose asked if Charlotte had been to the doctor, and she said she had. They spoke briefly about the escalating war in Vietnam. "And my Lynda there," Rose said, cutting salami, placing slices on Andre's plate. "Taking her life in her hands. I don't know if I can take another death." Charlotte and Andre met each other's anxious eyes and returned their

119

attention to bananas and sour cream. Charlotte, knowing she would pay with heartburn later, cut herself a large piece of salami, spread it thickly with a layer of mustard, and ate it on the torn-off heel of the seeded rye.

That night she dreamed she gave birth to a deformed child who was actually Andre. She awoke screaming and Alex caught her in his arms. He held her and stroked her hair while she cried. When she finally calmed down he said, "Baby, it's the Mara story. It's going too far. Maybe you should stop. What are you trying to do? Rush to give birth to your mother before you give birth to your child?"

"Let's make love, Alex," whispered Charlotte, who did not wish to be analyzed.

But Alex refused, saying he was tired and, within several minutes, he was asleep.

Miriam had been involved with George Cohen for about six months when Aaron noticed a change in her. He decided to express his concern on an afternoon when she was leaving the hospital early to meet George for dinner at an Italian restaurant. More than anything in the world, lately, she loved being alone with George. She would even cut short her time with her teen-aged patients on the acute psychiatric ward to meet him when it was convenient for him. This shocked Miriam because working with the young girls who had a real chance of recovery had been the greatest joy she knew.

Ever since she had decided, on Aaron's advice, to try a residency in psychiatry, changing over to the hospital where he was on staff, Miriam had found a place in the world where she felt completely at home. It seemed like her place, that part of the medical profession in which she could be most useful, where everything she had learned from lecture and text combined with intuition and instinct so that her senior colleagues not only noticed her competence but spoke of unusual talent.

But that afternoon, Miriam had rushed through her sessions. As she left, she saw her last patient sink into a languid posture that she knew was the signal of a new depression. She ought to have remained for fifteen minutes at the least. But she left, telling herself she could make up for it the following day.

She was trying to push doubts from her mind, ringing for the elevator when Aaron approached her.

"Can I walk with you?" he asked, as if he expected to be refused.

"Sure," Miriam answered. "But I'm in a bit of a rush. Can we just walk over to the bus?" She pushed her straight dark hair behind her ears. The ends were cut evenly, as were the bangs across her forehead.

("You always look like you just had your hair done," Rose had told her accusingly.

"It's my mother's training in the maintenance of appearances," she had replied, pulling at her bangs guiltily, as if she could jerk them out of shape, make them jagged with her fingers.)

Aaron and Miriam walked out into the cool evening. The sun was going down.

"You look tired, Miriam," he said, and immediately corrected himself. "Not tired. Drained. I don't mean you look bad," he added hastily. "I'm trying to say something to you, Miriam. Help me." He zipped up his blue jacket and plunged his hands into the pockets of his white pants. "You seem preoccupied in a new way. You seem tense. You have rings under your eyes." He sounded paternal, clinical.

"Aaron," she said gently. "I'm trying to get used to being Mara, not Miriam."

"Mara's a very pretty name." He looked down at the sidewalk, quickening his pace. "And its meaning's simpler. But it's not your name." He pulled her arm through his, keeping his fist clenched in his pocket.

"I like it though," she insisted. "It takes me away from everything I hate about my past. My life was bitter, Aaron, though I never saw it before. I don't know by what miracle I didn't end up like one of the girls on the ward.

"I am tired," she admitted as the bus appeared on the corner. "But I've never been happier, Aaron. That's the truth." She leaned over to kiss his cheek, but Aaron turned his face suddenly and kissed her mouth instead. She pulled back, then quickly hugged

121

him so that her chin pressed into his shoulder. He was stiff in her embrace. He mumbled, "Sorry," and she kissed him on the cheek before she boarded the bus.

As she approached the restaurant she tried to prepare herself for whatever mood George might be in. She had learned in the last few months the necessity of anticipating his moods this way because if she expected only the happiness she desired, and he was depressed or self-critical, she would be unable to restrain herself from making the situation worse by allowing him to see, and feel guilty for, her own disappointment. She walked slowly down the street and felt suddenly tired, which she attributed to how hard she had been working. Four days on the ward, and this was her first evening off. She should be home, asleep.

But Mara had given up her apartment the previous month and moved in with George. There was little space to relax in the clutter of his two small rooms. She needed order, cleanliness, another holdover from her life with Constance for which she was repeatedly apologetic. "I can't find anything!" George had insisted when she began organizing his possessions, dusting the old furniture, clearing a corner for her neatly stacked medical journals, when she had placed her sweaters, each one enclosed in a zippered plastic case, in the small oak chest of drawers that was the only piece of furniture she had moved from her apartment to his.

George sat at a corner table in front of a large poster of Venice. The blue of the Venetian sky framed his dark blond hair, which waved in long curls over his forehead and ears. He wore a navy blue shirt opened at the neck, its soft collar pressed without starch, a pencil sticking out of the breast pocket. A half-finished glass of beer was on the table. He was reading some pages of notes, but when she entered he looked up and removed his large glasses from his face. He smiled tentatively at her as she sat down.

Mara opened three buttons at the neck of her dark green cashmere sweater, feeling suddenly warm. She ordered a cool drink. She took out a cigarette from her Philip Morris pack and smoked.

"Are you writing?" she smiled at him, indicating his notes. He folded them and thrust them into his pocket.

"Just some notes," he said.

They were silent. Mara waited for a sign from him to indicate his mood, how she could best make him comfortable, how she should be.

When George ordered their food from the waiter he sounded gruff. Mara put her hand on his. "What's wrong?" she said. He freed his hand, finished his beer, and put his glasses back on.

"Is it the play?" she persisted. "Is it going badly?"

"I'm no playwright, Mara," he answered. "I know it and you know it. So why don't you just level with me?"

"I don't feel that way at all." Although there were moments when she did feel that way, she spent the next several minutes encouraging him, reminding him that all artists suffered from self-doubt, asserting with a conviction she did not feel that he would be successful some day if he just stuck to it, that within a year he would finish this play. He appeared to listen as she spoke. She stopped when the waiter brought food and wine, but as soon as he left Mara continued. While she spoke, George ate listlessly, as if lulled into boredom. Mara ate almost nothing.

"There is something special about you, George," she finished, as he wiped some butter angrily across a thick piece of bread and tore off a bite. "It's just a matter of getting that special part of you onto paper." And feeling she had reached him, helped him, she stopped and drank half her glass of wine, chewed a small piece of veal.

"When you played the guitar that night, I thought you were what was special about me, baby," he said, taking off his glasses again and rubbing his eyes with his thumb and forefinger. Mara ached from the pain on his face.

"I thought you were going to come along and save me. I thought you were an angel, Mara. A real angel."

She felt a tinge of shame for her obvious failure. The image of her last patient came into her mind and she realized — yes, the desire to save everyone. And hated herself even more. She pushed her hair roughly behind her ears, jerking off her gold earring in the process. It rolled across the table into George's lap.

123

He picked it up and held it out to her, retaining it in the tight grip of his finger and thumb. "I don't mean to accuse you, baby," he said. "It's your nature to tantalize with that promise. Just like my brother who would, if he could, save every goddam soul in the entire world. I, well, I myself am merely mortal." He smiled at the immensity of the failure this view of himself implied. He reached over and replaced the earring on her ear. He freed her hair from behind her ears and leaned across the table to kiss her softly on the mouth, his lips slightly opened so that she could feel the tip of his tongue.

At that moment the waiter came over to see if they wanted coffee and Mara, blushing, declined. "You don't have to be a god to want to help people. You help people all the time," Mara said. "That's why I fell in love with you."

George looked forlorn. "People are dying in Spain." He stared at his glass as he raised it to his lips. "It's the prelude to worldwide fascism over there. I believe that. I ought to be there with the brigades. Besides," he added, as if reminding himself, "my play's not going well." He tapped his fingers on the side of the white china cup, considering. "Let's go to Buck's for coffee, baby. Okay?"

She had hoped to go home after dinner, to make love. But she agreed, pleased by his elevated mood.

Rose had coffee ready as usual for anyone who happened to stop in, and there were sweet rolls stacked on a large plate. George grabbed one and popped it into his mouth whole as he entered the room.

"What kind of manners!" Rose pushed him and slapped his hand.

Buck smiled at them all. He pulled Mara toward him, nestling her in the comforting arc of his arm, and ushered her to the most comfortable chair, lifted her feet to the ottoman.

"Take off your shoes, Miriam," he said to her. "You're just off work, I bet. Rest. She works hard," he said to George. "She should be home, asleep."

"Her name is Mara," George said, looking at her at last with the expression she had been waiting for all evening. When he said Mara his eyes shone, his mouth spoke the word adoringly.

124

He looked like he wanted to make love.

"Mara," Buck muttered. He pushed his rimless glasses up the bridge of his long, narrow nose. "I don't mind Buck. I've gotten used to it. I might even say I like it. But for some reason, I don't like Mara, George. She's Miriam." He held out his hands, then returned them to his sides and looked at the liquor cabinet. "I have scotch. You want a drink?"

"Mara's a beautiful name," George told his brother. "Yeah. I'll take a small one."

"What do you think?" Buck turned to her. She had almost fallen asleep. It wasn't just the fatigue. There was something about Buck's maternal attention that disarmed her, induced an hypnotic relaxation that cleared her mind of everything but the desire to rest.

"About my name?" she asked. She had been thinking about the way George kissed her in the restaurant, the way he had looked at her just now. Mara was shocked at her own need for George's love. She had never needed love. She had lived all her life without it except in its most pedestrian forms. Now she felt ready to give up anything for it, for the right kind of moment with George Cohen. "I like Mara," she said to Buck. "It's beautiful."

"It's Mara then," Buck agreed. "We'll drink to its permanence. Rose — it's Mara," he said to his wife, who was walking into the room.

"Big surprise," said Rose, falling into the black chair and pulling long brown curls from her forehead with her tortoise-shell comb.

There was a moment of silence while they all sipped their drinks. Then George said, "It's Mara Cohen." He drained his scotch and raised the empty glass to all of them in a belated toast.

Mara sat up, fully awake. Her chest felt hard, as if she had sustained a blow. Her cheeks felt hot. She smiled.

"Well, congratulations!" Buck shouted and came over to kiss her on the cheek. But as he pulled away he looked at her skeptically, as if, with his back to his brother, he could warn her of something. "Congratulations," he repeated more softly, stroking her cheek.

"So," Rose said when Buck moved away. "My darling Mara." Mara walked over to Rose's chair and kissed her friend. Rose flushed, embarrassed and pleased. Then Mara turned to George. She knelt down on the rug and looked up into his face. His eyes were sad, free of his previous anger. His jaw was loose, his lips soft and slightly opened as if he were about to plead for something, and she stood up and sat on the arm of the couch, put her arm around his shoulders, and pulled his head into her lap. She leaned over him and kissed his hair.

When they got home George made love to her as passionately as he had ever done. He moved his hands slowly all over her body, looking at her as if she were a priestess he alone had the power to please. He leaned over her, holding himself far above her as he entered her. He balanced himself on his forearms so that he was like an arch spreading across her sky and slowly moved in and out of her. He smiled as she sank deeper and deeper into a river which seemed to lift her body from the bed and hold it suspended on a wave as he moved out of her, into the edge of her and then at last deep inside of her where he stopped moving altogether, but remained perfectly still, holding his weight off of her with his arms, watching her as she moved. She began to moan in hoarse, pleading cries, and he moved his face very near hers, ran his tongue slowly across her lips, ears, neck and, when at last she had nothing left to keep from him, when she was calling to him in low tones which must have come from her dreams, when she begged him and dug her long manicured nails into the flesh of his shoulders, he screamed, laughing, "Ouch! Bitch!" and fucked her hard, losing control, until they both screamed and rolled across the bed while they came.

Later, when they lay beside each other in the hazy gray of a city night, he began to talk about going to Spain.

126

Charlotte lay quietly in bed. She didn't have to be a therapist to understand why she had written that sex scene in the afternoon. She had lost any inhibition that might have come from imagining her parents in bed in the building of her own desire. After she completed the scene, she had begun to imagine sex with Alex who — she didn't care if it were crazy — was probably also George. She thought of how exciting sex could be with Alex, how she used to look forward to it all day and then, the next morning, call him at work, even if he was in the middle of a session, and whisper, "Wasn't that good?"

The pain in her back that had begun the week before eased only when she was lying down. She relished the feeling of freedom from the nagging pain. In that moment of comfort, she began to think in images, something she had not done in months.

Her mother's story was being pieced together from Rose's skimpy descriptions, her own memories, the look of faces in old photographs and, she had to admit, from her own imagination. She was adding assumptions, desires, even experiences of her own. Charlotte saw her story floating in front of her as a patchwork design, a part of Mara's face modeled in detail, another part drawn with incomplete suggestions, a third part missing altogether. Then she knew that she was painting after all, and that thought relieved her because she had not understood any more than Alex what she had been doing all these weeks.

Thoughts of composition, perspective, color sucked away all remnants of anxiety. It wasn't just some chaos of power inside

127

her as she and Alex had feared. She picked up a pad and pencil and began to sketch, giving material reality to the feeling of calm. Of course. She had been away too long to face a canvas immediately. She was writing her way into the part of her that could paint, moving blindly at times, at times purposefully, edging around blocked doorways, under low hanging beams, stepping across holes in the floor, moving toward the Charlotte she had left behind.

Charlotte turned off her bedside lamp, but left the room dimly lit by Alex's light. It was his late night. He had sessions until ten, but he would be home soon and she didn't want to fall asleep before he arrived.

She thought about her years as a history teacher in a Bronx high school, of the years before at Queens College where, after Buck's death, she devoted herself to the study of history as if her fervency could bring him back to life. Andre had criticized her for her choice. "You're a coward, Charlotte," he told her. "You could be a great artist. You'll be an ordinary history teacher." But Vivian, at nineteen already married to a young architect named David, supported Charlotte. "You can't change the world," she informed Andre, just as if she hadn't been informing him of the opposite for years. "As a painter she'll be insecure all her life. As a history teacher she'll be safe." "Oh, safe," Andre sneered.

Charlotte turned her energies further and further from Andre and counted on Vivian who lived in Massachusetts, but who was happy to spend hours on weekly long distance telephone calls. That spring, however, Vivian became pregnant and began to have little attention for anything else. Charlotte had blamed her at the time. "You're just like all the others," she had accused Vivian. "You think all the world's disappeared inside your belly."

Turning onto her side, she pulled her nightgown up to her waist and massaged her belly. Charlotte missed Vivian. How could she have kept out of touch for so long? Vivian didn't even know Charlotte was pregnant, but she would call tomorrow, Charlotte decided as she heard Alex's key in the door. She tried to retrieve, once more, the image of the painting that would come out of all her words, but it was gone. She got out of bed too quickly, causing a stabbing pain in her lower back as she walked down the hall to meet Alex in the kitchen. How could you be expected to think about anything else, she wondered, defending Vivian, when every breath you took was characterized by what was going on inside your body which, however powerful it might seem to mythological history, seemed well out of control to you.

Alex was piling food on the table, setting himself a plate, sipping wine as he organized his feast. "Hi," he said when she touched his shoulder. He looked down at her belly and said "Hi," again. He turned from her abruptly, communicating a discomfort by now familiar to Charlotte.

She glanced at her large breasts and loathed herself. She thought perhaps she smelled. Futilely, she tried to fluff up her unwashed hair. Even after working twelve hours, Alex's blue and white striped shirt had remained miraculously unwrinkled and hugged his chest in neatly pressed folds. He had loosened his tie, but it hung down his button line, a pleasant stripe of wine red against the pale blue. His dark blond hair and small, straight nose would have made him look youthful except that he had lines around his mouth and eyes that made him appear older than his thirty-two years. His mouth was full and sensual, an anachronism to his New England Protestant roots that Charlotte loved better than any other part of him. When, as often happened, Alex drank too much (though he never got drunk, he insisted, only tipsy) his lips would soften even more, remaining open and damp after he'd finished his many declarations of love for her.

She felt desire rise as she watched him pour a large glass of wine, gesturing to her to see if she wanted some, frowning at her when she refused. She was afraid that later, in bed, she would be taken over by this desire and make matters worse by pressuring him.

She imagined him leaving her after the baby was born. What would she do? Who would bring home the meat, she wondered in a panic. She pictured tigers with dead rats in their mouths, gifts for their hungry cubs. She felt like an animal, her belly dragging her down to the jungle floor, growling for food and attention, a freakish animal who, despite being pregnant, was still, repulsively, in heat.

Having finished setting the table for himself, five bowls of

129

leftovers lined up in a semicircle around his white plate, Alex smiled at Charlotte. Then, as if he were about to engage in an act of sinful gluttony, he sat down in the blond, straight-backed chair. He picked up his napkin, tucked it into his belt, and ate with complete attention for several minutes. When he paused to drink more wine he looked at the living room, which was in shambles. Bedroom pillows lay across the floor where Charlotte had used them to support her back. Discarded sheets of paper filled with rejected portions of Mara's story covered the rug and couch. A coffee cup, a glass filled with separating orange juice, a plate crusty with tuna-fish, and a small crystal goblet half filled with red wine covered various end tables. Charlotte's desk, the one she had used as an adolescent, now refinished to its natural oak, was so laden with papers its surface could not be seen. If Alex were to touch the furniture, instead of just looking at it, he would find his fingers black with dust, Charlotte thought guiltily as she followed his gaze around the room.

"Charlotte," he began, pushing his plate a fraction of an inch away from him and refilling it with another piece of cold chicken, a helping of broccoli salad.

"Don't start lecturing me," she said, louder than she had meant to. "I have things to do besides clean up all day. Besides, my mind's cluttered right now, so the room's cluttered too."

"Nobody's asking you to clean up all day," he said in the tone of voice she hated most, his therapist's tone. He added with a tolerant smile, "You don't have to get defensive."

"I'm not defensive," she shouted. "And don't talk to me like I'm one of your fucking patients, Alex." She hated the fact that they were fighting. It eliminated all hope that he would want to make love.

Alex began clearing his food away. He stacked everything in the sink, wiped the table with a sponge and washed the dishes in silence. When he was done he said, "I wasn't trying to be critical, Charlotte. I just can't stand all the mess. It makes me nervous. It reminds me of my mother's house when she had her breakdown. All she ever did was scream, smoke, drink and sleep. I'm sorry if I overreacted." He pulled a red checked dishtowel from the rod over the sink and began to dry the few dishes in the

130

drain. With his back to her, he added, "And look at Andre, Charlotte. His room is always a mess. It's a sure sign of breakdown."

Charlotte remembered a wonderful day on a lakeside beach with Alex. She had been depressed for months, and during that time she had done one secret drawing which she had not shown to anyone. He had initiated a discussion about her sadness, telling her that he believed he knew what was wrong. Then he had described her love for painting, the strength it gave her, her fear of it. He pulled together all sorts of seemingly unconnected details — memories she had shared with him, parts of her paintings he had admired, the links between her desire to paint and her fragmented family history. He ended by saying, "You're an artist, Charlotte, and so you have to paint no matter what else happens in your life." She remembered the powerful gratitude with which she'd received that naming, a relief from the unspeakable shame she felt whenever she used the word artist in relation to herself. She cried in his arms, and when they returned home she had shown him the drawing, which he had studied and praised and, most important, completely understood, describing it to her better than she could have done herself.

She told him now, "I just realized that what I'm really doing by writing all this stuff about Mara is planning a painting. I'm writing out everything I know about it all so I can clear my head for a mural." She felt a surge of strength pass through her which made her feel the wind in the back yard as it brushed her neck the day she drew Andre's portrait when she was seventeen. "I'm sure of it," she added emphatically. "I feel stronger than I've felt in months. The mess is part of it, Alex. I have to live in that chaos for a while." She indicated the disordered living room, thought of her father's chaotic apartment as she had described it that afternoon. "I know Andre's in trouble, Alex. Don't threaten me with Andre."

She felt afraid, longed for his walls to come down, waited for his confidence, his love. But he looked at her with an expression of doubt.

"Why are you looking at me like that?" she demanded. "And what are you drying those few damn dishes for? There are three damn dishes. Can't they sit in the drain for one night for God's sake? And Alex, for a therapist, you have a suspicious capacity to confuse your wife with your mother. I'm not her. I don't drink. Much. And I'm not having a breakdown." She pulled her braid over her shoulder and began to twirl the edges in a newly acquired habit Alex described as compulsive. She looked down at her old seersucker robe tied around her bulging body with a long piece of wool. It was a comfortable robe and she suddenly felt ashamed. What was a breakdown anyway? How did you know you were in one?

"I'm sorry, Alex," she said as she flung her braid off her shoulder. Her eyes filled suddenly and easily with tears. He put his arm around her back, pulling her head against him.

"I need you, Alex. I'm scared."

"I'm scared too. Why aren't you painting like you said you would? Painting always makes you feel strong. This story you're writing—it's like a bad obsession. That's why the mess bothers me. Disorder is a characteristic of obsession."

"Well, I suppose I am obsessed. I suppose I have been off and on all my life."

"Where's it all coming from, Charlotte? This story."

"Where do you think it's coming from?" She was suddenly stern. "It's coming from me. From my head. It's my story, Alex. I'm doing it. I don't know exactly why, but I'm doing it. It's mine."

"But you know so little about her," he whispered.

"I know what I've heard all my life from all of them. I've known two men who were in love with her. I'm imagining the rest."

Facing Alex's doubt, his obvious inability to understand her, Charlotte suddenly felt strong, as if she were being pushed to a bottom line where she had to stand or bend. She wasn't going crazy as a result of writing Mara's story. She would go crazy if she didn't write it. And before she gave birth she would paint it. She felt free of all doubt. She would return to her story in the morning. She would call Vivian in the morning. She wanted to make love.

She pressed her head against Alex's belly, rubbed her lips across his crotch. She stood up and took his face in her hands, kissed him on the mouth. He pulled away from her sighing, "I'm exhausted," faking a yawn.

When he went into the bedroom, she attempted to straighten up the living room, trying to compromise. She gathered up discarded pages intending to throw them out, but when she held them over the garbage can, she couldn't go through with it. She picked up the crust and flung it into the kitchen can, and made her way down the hall. The light was out and Alex was pretending he was asleep.

Charlotte lay down in the dark and heard trucks rumbling down the avenue as if they were driving down the center of her room. A group of boys hung out on the corner, shouting at each other and playing a radio. She stormed over to the windows and slammed each one down, drawing the heavy drapes although it was a moderately warm night. The noises filled her head nevertheless, until she felt as if the boys, the trucks, the radio were inside of her, as if there were no quiet place, no privacy, no silence anywhere on earth except right near the ocean which would always be far out of reach. For a long time it had seemed to Charlotte that with Buck's death she was free of her past and her obsession with it. She heard the high-pitched, lilting melody of Myron's flute as she had heard it the day of Buck's death—as a coda to eighteen years of separating herself from the portraits of Mara and George. And now suddenly it was all here again—the old questions screaming in her brain, the restlessness, the sense that in trying to write or paint their story she was chasing a part of herself she was always in danger of losing—the past as present as it had ever been.

She breathed heavily, loudly, and couldn't suppress a long belch which eased her chronic heartburn. She felt a small hill protrude on her belly moving into a lump against Alex's thigh. He withdrew his body from hers a fraction of an inch.

"What is it?" she whispered, her face turned away from him. "Why can't you stand it, Alex? This is our baby, Alex. Yours and mine. I want you Alex." She pushed her fist into her mouth.

"I don't know, I feel like it's coming between us, Charlotte. Like it's yours. It is your body, after all. I don't feel connected to it at all. It's all too incredible to me. Oh, it's probably nothing. I just have to get used to it." He reached around and hugged her wide waist. "You seem so far away from me," he mumbled into her back. "That damn story. This."

133

Charlotte felt huge. She felt a building strength that threatened to break the muscles of his arms, crack the bed in two; she felt a rumbling inside which she feared might drown the baby—high tide waves rolling over tiny silvery fish. Charlotte felt larger than Alex, larger than the room, the apartment, the building. Her mouth opened and she felt a rushing relief as the ocean poured out. She feared her size, her huge high tide self—as Alex must, tall waves destroying everything in their path, white foam spraying and racing along its crest, foam that became white sheets of paper covered with her writing, spilling over the land, leaving nothing but layers of mud, dark and velvety and filled with strange, primitive life forms, salamanders and anemones and starfish which looked lovely when they were dead and hard, but when alive, were repulsive with their pink slimy underside covered with hundreds of tiny, protruding needles of pulsating flesh.

Then the sound of the rhythmic wave drowned out the boys on the corner, the radio. The trucks rumbled down the avenue, over her belly, her eyes, her throat. She moaned a long, low sound that sounded like a cry but was in truth a shout of relief as the ocean poured out of her gigantic lungs. Alex moved his hands over her breasts when he heard the sound. He undid the buttons of her gown and played with her large, dark nipples.

"Are you crying, Charlotte?" he asked urgently, and sensing what he wanted, what she wanted too, she lied, "Yes. I am."

"Don't cry," he crooned to her, a love song in the dark, a lullaby. "Don't cry, baby." He stroked her arms, her thighs, and parting her legs he entered her from behind, his face pressed to her broad shoulders, moving in and out of her gently, quieting the noises, calming the ocean, for a quick ecstatic moment parting the thick curtain through which she groped each day to find her former, ordinary life.

He removed his hands from her breasts as soon as he came, resting one on her thigh, the other reaching around her head to feel her eyes, which were damp, and her nose, which was running. He apologized again but Charlotte felt only relief. She felt small, ordinary, lying there in the curve of Alex's chest. She did not think of the story of Mara and George.

"I feel good," she told him. "Quiet. There are no sentences

134

about Mara running down my eyelids."

"Good," he murmured. "Maybe the story really is getting out of hand, Honey. It's not good for you. There's something crazy about it. Don't you think?"

But Charlotte listened to his words only as vehicles for the lulling sound of his voice. She curled around her belly. The trucks rumbled like distant drums, comforting, down the street.

In spite of awakening at six to the sound of a garbage truck on
the corner, Charlotte felt quiet inside. As soon as Alex left the
house, she reached to his side of the bed and checked a number
in an old telephone book.

"Hello? Who is this?" Vivian had always answered the phone
as if she were waiting for bad news, a death call. Charlotte heard
a child crying, the tinkling music of a morning television program.

"It's me, Vivian. Your long lost . . . " Charlotte giggled.

"Charlotte? Is that you? Oh my God."

She told Vivian she was pregnant, and within seconds was
pouring out the story of her narrative of Mara's life, her visits to
Aunt Rose, alluding to her troubles with Alex. She talked to Vivian
the way a pregnant woman eats in the afternoon—filling up a
hole.

"Remember? I told you. Listen. I'm coming into New York
tomorrow to see my parents. My father's sick. It's incredible you
called today. I haven't been to New York in two years. Can I see
you, Charlotte?"

"Can you!" Charlotte sat up in bed and, pulling the quilt over
her head, slouched into the tent she had created. The darkened
space underneath was tinted blue from the silvery purple of the
material. Her mouth was pressed close to the receiver. "When do
you get in?" Leafy vines arching around Otharose's windows
encircled her, dragged her into that past which was lately so alive
in her. "I'm going to Aunt Rose's tomorrow. You want to come?"

They arranged to meet at Grand Central Station at eight-thirty and have some time alone together before they went to the old apartment.

As soon as they hung up, Charlotte dialed Aunt Rose to tell her Vivian was coming. Rose was delighted and thought Andre would be too. Right before she said good-bye Charlotte asked, trying to be casual, "Oh, Aunt Rose, by the way, did my mother ever talk to you about wanting a baby? Did she mean to get pregnant?"

"You're coming to continue your questions. And with Vivian who will encourage you, heaven help me. Yes, Charlotte. She wanted to get pregnant very much. But she had a job convincing George. He was talking already about going to Spain. But I told you how much she loved Lynda. She wanted you very much. Is that what you want to hear? It's true. And Charlotte, when she went away, she meant to come back. She left you with me because she knew I loved you as much as she loved Lynda, although to talk to you and your cousin no one ever loved either of you, certainly not your mothers. So good-bye. I'll see you tomorrow. I'll make lunch. Don't eat." Rose hung up.

Charlotte remained in bed for some minutes looking at the ceiling, the telephone receiver propped on her stomach as if some message were expected from within.

For the rest of the morning Charlotte attacked the disorder of the living room, getting rid of dirty dishes, lifting pages of writing and sketches to dust underneath. She and Alex had dinner at a neighborhood restaurant, both of them chatting and lively during the meal. Sex had always worked this way for them, pushing them beneath the conflicts of ordinary life to a safe place they did not need to name. But Charlotte lost control while she was chattering about Vivian. She told him everything she could recall about their friendship, even confessing to him the experience in Otharose's bed. Alex's eyebrows arched suspiciously—a clinical suspiciousness, Charlotte noted with distaste.

"Oh it didn't mean anything, Alex. Lots of girls did it. It was just that I loved her so much. The body doesn't make cultural distinctions about who it wants to touch, you know."

Alex looked into his lap. "There's a certain narcissism to it, you must admit, Charlotte."

She softened, seeing clearly for a moment what she had done;

137

she reached across the table for his hand. "I love you," she whispered, pausing as the waiter removed dishes from between them. "And I always will love you. No one else could put up with me."

"I agree," said Alex, a mixture of irritation and acceptance in his voice that made her feel remarkably free. She ordered chocolate fudge cake with whipped cream on top and offered Alex bites from her spoon until they consumed every last crumb.

On the bus going downtown the following morning, she took out the notebook that contained the story of Mara and George. It was difficult to write on the moving bus. But Charlotte was resolute, holding the pencil nearer and nearer the tip for greater control.

Mara and George were married by a civil court judge at City Hall. Aaron, Isaac and Rose were the only witnesses in attendance. Lynda whimpered and fussed throughout the ceremony and, finally, Rose had to leave to nurse the baby in the ladies' room.

One Saturday afternoon when Buck and George had gone to a meeting, Mara was sitting quietly in the Cohen living room, when Rose came in with Lynda on her hip and her blouse damp with milk. Her hair was loose, falling in soft kinky waves over her shoulders and she pushed it behind her as she sat down to nurse. The baby reached up and grabbed a piece of her mother's hair, clutched it in her small fist and pulled hard so that Rose had to ease the hair out of the hand where it became tangled and braided into the tiny fingers. Her white nylon blouse was opened completely so that one large breast was fully exposed, except for the nipple, which was suctioned into Lynda's mouth.

Mara walked over to the black chair in which Rose always sat — talking, reading, now nursing the baby. She knelt by her friend's knee and stroked Lynda's fine sparse hair. The fontanel had not yet closed and, touching it with her thumb, Mara uttered a tiny cry of awe at the velvet pulsating softness. Rose reached a free hand over to touch Mara's cheek. "Do you want one?" she asked.

Mara felt a sensation of speed within, as if a sleek vehicle

138

were racing down some part of her rarely visited but always
there, not experienced directly but infusing every experience of
her life with an unavoidable character. She felt as fragile as the
orange Chinese lantern that she pulled from a vase and crushed
between her forefinger and her thumb. When she looked up at
Rose, she was crying.

"I'm sorry, dear." Rose was only five years older but she felt
as if Mara were a child. "I should have kept my mouth shut?"

"No," Mara stroked the baby's head again, tilting her own
head so that it nearly touched Rose's arm. She kept her eyes on
Lynda. "I do. I want one terribly. But George doesn't. Or says
he doesn't, especially if he decides to go to Spain."

Rose eased her breast out of Lynda's mouth and lifted the
baby to her shoulder where she patted the tiny back until Lynda
finally burped. Small drops of milk fell onto her waist, into her
lap. Mara got up and brought some tissue. Rose wiped her breast
efficiently, transferred Lynda to the other side, tucked the drained
breast into her heavy cotton bra and exposed the other one, gently
teasing the infant's mouth with the large, brown nipple until
Lynda sucked and the connection was forged.

Charlotte pressed her forehead against the cool bus window
and cried. She could picture it so clearly. Vaguely, she could
remember Aunt Rose nursing Hannah George. Phrases and
photographs from a dozen books about infancy swirled through
her mind. She didn't know how she would survive the emotional
intensity of being a mother. She wanted it. She feared it. Perhaps,
she thought, looking down at her notebook again, she was putting too much intensity into Mara and Rose. Perhaps life was easier,
more comprehensible to them than it had ever been for her.
Perhaps she was only writing about herself. But then she thought,
I know Aunt Rose. I know how she would be. And that provided
a moment of confidence just long enough to begin writing again.

"You seem so relaxed with it," Mara said, watching Lynda's
face, tracing her finger across the shadow of an infant eyebrow.

"I watched my mother and my sister with babies all the time
in the old country, then here," Rose said. "But I'm not always

139

relaxed. *Sometimes when Buck is home, it's very tense. Everyone these days looks down on nursing. We're supposed to be modern, use bottles, always afraid of spoiling babies. We're supposed to let them cry. I can't stand to hear her cry so there's no use thinking about supposed. All the party people think I'm crazy. It's part of why George says he doesn't want one, believe me. It's supposed to be a diversion for a true revolutionary."* Rose sniffed indignantly. *"Good thing for them their mothers were willing to have a little diversion."*

"I know," Mara said. *"He told me that part. He's worried about my work. He says I'll have to stop working, or I might even want to. He says that would be a loss to humanity. I want one so much, Rose."*

"So have one," Rose said with her customary abruptness whenever she said anything outrageous.

"You mean, don't tell him? Don't use anything and pretend I am? You mean pretend it's an accident? Oh, Rose. I couldn't."

Rose nodded her head, respectful of Mara's feeling but clearly in complete disagreement.

"Is that what you mean, Rose? Do you really think it would be right?"

"Right, wrong," Rose intoned. *"It's all I hear around here. You might have noticed, Mara, I'm not a very good Communist, in the strict sense. I listen to their rights and wrongs. I understand them. I admire their passions. Buck's. George's, too. I feel differently, which I don't say. I just go about my business. What I need, I need. What I know is right, I know, even if I can't explain it to them. If you want a baby so much,"* she looked down at Lynda who had fallen into a luxurious doze beneath her mother's large breast, the wet, elongated nipple hanging like a last, uneaten grape at the curl of her bottom lip, *"then have one, Mara. That's my opinion."*

She handed the sleeping Lynda to Mara and replaced her breast inside her bra.

"It's hard with George to know how to act," Mara confessed, rocking Lynda. *"You're lucky, Rose. Buck is so —,"* she groped for words, *"kind,"* she finally said. *"George is —,"* she stopped.

Rose buttoned her blouse and tucked it back into the waist

140

of her black skirt. "George is selfish," she declared. Then, walking over to the mirror on the far wall and turning on the table lamp which flooded the shadowy room with a sudden yellow light, she began to braid her hair.

She hadn't been in Grand Central Station in years. The enormous domed ceiling, its blue silhouettes of constellations punctuated by pieces of shining crystal stars, arched over the large stone columns, the gold carvings, the enormous photograph on the east wall of a snow scene in New Hampshire that would radiate familiarity for Alex, but struck Charlotte as remote and unappealing. She felt better looking up at the dome, finding the stars in Orion's belt, the claws of her Scorpio, the water crab.

Huge, tight packs of commuters rushed out of the doorway from the dark track into the brightly lit station. Men in business suits carrying attaché cases extracted cigarettes from pocketed packs and put them into their mouths with one hand, still managing a smooth discourse with other men who looked just like them. Women in equally tailored suits walked past her and Charlotte admired their coordinated outfits of tweed suits, navy shoes, strings of pearls. Suddenly, she heard music, and winding toward her was a long line of bald men in long, orange robes. They played a haunting melody on tambourines and sang about Hare Krishna. Through the line of commuters they moved, a stripe through the dark and blue and gray. Two Black men with enormous circles of glistening hair walked by. The world was changing. Charlotte placed her hands flat against the baby, wanting it to feel her excitement.

An older woman (going to visit her daughter who has just had a baby, Charlotte decided), stood for a moment in the entrance, assessing direction. Pearly white hair stiffly haloed her small head. "Do you know where a taxi stand is?" she asked Charlotte. "Of course," Charlotte answered, embarrassed to be caught staring at the woman, and she pointed to a large staircase in the middle of the room. "Just go up those stairs—"

The woman reached into her square black bag and retrieved a hard candy wrapped in cellophane paper. "Thank you. *Dear,*" she said, placing the candy delicately on her tongue. "Would you

141

like one?" But Charlotte declined. Right behind the woman's left shoulder she saw Vivian who, at the same moment, spotted her.

They screamed each other's names. They raced into each others' arms with such force that Charlotte nearly fell backward. She pulled away from the embrace and cradled her belly in her arms.

"Oh God. I'm sorry," Vivian yelled. "Come here. I'll be more careful, I promise. Oh Charlotte," she pressed her cheek to her own, ran her palm across Charlotte's still-damp, freshly washed hair until she reached the braid which she fingered all the way down to the tip, pulling it over Charlotte's shoulder and moving back a bit to look into her face. "You're still beautiful, Charlotte. Especially when you smile."

Charlotte blushed. "Oh, come on," she protested. "My mouth is too wide for my face."

"And your hair's gotten so long," Vivian said.

Vivian's hair was cut short now, the platinum highlights sparkling across what looked like a fitted blond cap. It was cut straight across the back and tucked behind Vivian's ears. A moon-curve of bangs fringed her wide forehead. She looked the same otherwise, however. Charlotte noticed her trim figure, her sun-burnt cheeks.

"Oh you look wonderful, Vivian," she said. "I'll never look like that again."

Vivian laughed and put her hand through Charlotte's arm. They decided to walk several miles uptown. It was a warm day in the spring and a comforting breeze drifted off the Hudson River as they entered Riverside Park, catching up on the facts of each others' lives. Charlotte told Vivian what Alex was doing, when her due date was, that Jacob lived on the East Side in a fancy apartment — his wife's money. Jacob was a successful graduate student in Sociology, devoted, Charlotte added sarcastically, to analyzing social organization as a complicated series of learned responses to a variety of stimuli. "He won't even march in the demonstrations against the war in Vietnam," Charlotte told Vivian, her voice rising an octave in outrage. "He says ideology means nothing any more; he sees everything that happens in the world as an opportunity to analyze the structure of the situation.

He's like a man describing the mechanical construction of a car as it speeds over a cliff with a whole family inside.''

Vivian looked down at the sidewalk and sighed. "He was always the one most uncomfortable with politics," she said. "I'm not sure he's so wrong, Charlotte."

Charlotte ignored this remark and continued, "Andre's not good, Vivian. I ought to warn you. He's a sacrifice to something. He doesn't work. He hardly goes out. He writes in a journal or something, reads interminable newspapers. The only person he ever sees is Myron—besides the family of course. Or what's left of it. And even sweet old Myron comes around less."

"Do you still see Otharose?" Vivian smiled at the old name.

"She's sick. And older than her years. She lives in a nursing home in Washington Heights. I visit her from time to time. Not half as often as I should."

"What ever happened to all those letters?" Vivian asked. "There must have been hundreds of pages."

"She keeps them in a box under her bed. I don't think she writes much any more."

"Not much good news," Vivian smiled as they sat down on a bench to rest.

Charlotte shrugged. "Well, it's not all bad. Hannah's coming back to New York next fall from her rather extended college education. She's been so involved with politics. Jacob's wife Marilyn is having another baby. I want a girl so much, Vivian. I am literally dying for a girl. How are your kids?" Charlotte finally asked.

Vivian had three between the ages of two and seven years old. "Oh, they're wonderful, my darling," she shouted in a stage voice conveying artificial passion. "It's their mother who's dying on the vine." She let her head fall lifeless to her shoulder. "But you'll see them this summer, Charlotte. You must come up and stay with us in the country. The baby's easy so far. The middle one's kind of distant, hard to reach. The older one's too sensitive, and he can be a tyrant. Like his father." Vivian looked resigned.

"What's David like as a husband?" Charlotte asked.

"If I were still used to such profanity," said Vivian, pulling Charlotte from the bench and beginning to walk again, "I'd say he's an asshole. But I don't speak that way any more." Then she

143

amended, "Oh Charlotte. It's only that marriage is so hard after you have kids. It changes completely. David's a good man. He works hard. Builds beautiful homes for people to live in. It's only that we had a fight this morning before I left. It's just that we have nothing to say to each other."

"Are you going to leave him?" Charlotte was concerned, and a bit amazed.

"Leave? No, Charlotte. I'm not leaving. I'm having another baby. I found out this week."

"Vivian! How can you take it? Four babies in seven years!" Charlotte pulled Vivian's head down onto her shoulder as they walked, and kissed the smooth blond hair. "That's wonderful," she whispered doubtfully.

"I like it," Vivian said turning a somber face to Charlotte. Tiny creases appeared between Vivian's mouth and nose, at the edges of her eyes. Charlotte kissed her on the corner of her mouth.

Andre met them at the door. He stood there staring and fingering the collar of a neatly pressed shirt he had clearly put on for the occasion. He moved his hand from the shirt to the tiny bristles of his hair as if he were trying to stretch it back into long sensuous curls.

"Andre," Vivian whispered, and hugged him.

Charlotte edged past them and found Aunt Rose attending to last-minute details of an elaborate lunch. The lights were bright in the kitchen as well as in the living room beyond. The table was cluttered with many delectable dishes which Vivian stared at while she extricated herself from Andre's embrace, moaning with delight.

"Oh, Rose," she sighed. "I haven't had New York bagels in ages. Or lox. Or Greek olives!" She popped one into her mouth. "Or chopped liver!" she screamed. "Oh my God! Chopped liver!" She turned from the feast and, sucking on an olive pit, she kissed Rose.

"So sit down right away," Rose said, untying her apron and bringing coffee to the table. "We can eat."

Later, fortified, they moved to the living room where, Charlotte noticed, the dark rug had been vacuumed, the blue and green drapes pressed. All for Vivian, or the lost time in their lives she represented.

144

Vivian and Andre were engaged in conversation so exclusive that Rose retreated to the kitchen where she began cleaning up. Charlotte followed and, lost in thought, crashed into the kitchen counter. She doubled over with pain and anxiety from the blow. She felt the baby jolt and turn.

"Rmmmm, Crash!" Andre roared from the living room. Charlotte turned to smile at the old humor not shared for many years.

"Be careful, for goodness sakes," Aunt Rose shouted. She ushered Charlotte to a dining room chair. "Sit," she ordered.

"God," Charlotte muttered, self-critical. "Jesus H. Christ."

She knew she was about to say something she shouldn't, something which would upset her aunt, even hurt her deeply. Maybe that was why she'd used Lynda's famous epithet — old words of the errant daughter wandering as far as possible from home.

"Aunt Rose," she began when she caught her breath. "You've helped me a lot with my story." With her eyes she placated, she paused. "I'm almost ready to paint — " adding legitimacy, objective value to her obsession. "Well, there's one more question I have to ask. A hard question." Charlotte looked down at the floor. She felt like a little girl again.

"So?" Aunt Rose asked gently. "What is it?"

"It's about Uncle Buck. About Uncle Buck and my mother."

Rose moved dishes from the counter to the sink. She turned on the hot water. Charlotte watched her aunt's face for a sign of upset, a sign that she had gone too far. Rose sucked in her cheeks slightly. "How can I be doing this?" Charlotte wondered. "How can I do this to her?"

But how would she ever know anything if she didn't know this? She realized that, in a certain sense, it was unimportant. But in another way it was the key to everything. Once she had thought the only question was which one was her father. Now that she was pregnant, although it had taken her months to put it into words, she knew that it was Mara she was trying to understand. Charlotte remembered her shame, sitting on the fire escape the day Uncle Buck died, thinking about painting his face which still hovered weirdly between the soft look of sleep and the stony look

145

of death. She remembered how she had annoyed Andre with her concentration on his portrait. But the portrait had been good. The mural had been a great success. It hung in the girls' old bedroom now. Almost no one ever looked at it. Still, it existed, a small space in the world, on a wall in an unused room, where all of it was integrated, all the chaos worked into a whole. The fact that it existed, anywhere at all, that she had caused it to exist, carried her through disappointment and failure, even real loss. Charlotte could not have said why, but she knew she thought about that mural hanging on the wall of her old bedroom whenever she felt she might fall apart — just like Andre — and thinking about it made her able to go on doing what she had to do, instead of staying in her darkened room the way she wanted to do, like him.

Charlotte walked to the sink, keeping her voice low so that Andre and Vivian wouldn't hear. "Aunt Rose —," she began. "Uncle Buck and my mother. Did they — Aunt Rose?" She grabbed a dish towel and a plate and began frantically drying. "It's just that — that all my life people have suggested, intimated, that there was some doubt about who my father was. It was a long time ago. Maybe it can't hurt you any more —."

"Are you going to dry my dish until it breaks?" Rose took the dish from Charlotte, wiped it gently and put it away.

"Is there any chance Uncle Buck was — really my — well, my actual father?" Charlotte held the dish cloth absolutely still. She leaned her back against the counter. Why had she done it? No one else in her right mind would have done it. An hour ago it had seemed the only honest thing to do. Now it seemed cruel.

"Don't be ridiculous," Rose snapped. "What nonsense are you talking." She looked past her niece, past Andre and Vivian where they sat, heads bent together at the far corner of the living room, past the curtains and out the window. An early afternoon rain splashed against the pane, darkening the house. Vivian reached over and turned on a table lamp. Rose stared at Vivian for a minute. Then she looked back at Charlotte, her expression changed. "And if I told you it wasn't true, it never happened? Would you be satisfied then?" She looked at Charlotte tenderly. "The truth is," she said, her voice hoarse, "I don't know. I always thought they were friends. Buck loved Mara very much, but like a

146

younger sister, I always thought. It could be, Charlotte. George thought so. That's why he took off for Spain soon after Mara gave birth to you. Your uncle, my husband, Buck, Isaac—he was very badly hurt. Mara stayed angry at George a long time. She kept wanting to talk to me about it. But I never found out exactly what she wanted to say, whether she was angry at him for a false accusation or for something else. If it was true, I didn't want to know. Because what I wanted, Charlotte, was my family. Not only Lynda and Andre who I was pregnant with then. But more children. With a father. A family. And if it was true, then I would never have that. I don't expect you to understand this, not now. And if it wasn't true, it was just another example of how George could be."

Charlotte wondered if she would ever know. Could you exhume bodies from the earth and examine bone structure, find a gigantically oversized gene? She needed something definite, but she did not dare speak. She reached out to touch Rose's shoulder, but her aunt turned back to the sink and continued talking.

"Your generation didn't discover sex it may come as a surprise to you to know. Lots of people did lots of things. You want to know something, Charlotte? I myself deceived my husband once. Isaac was away for a week. I was mad at him or I was affected by all the sex talk always going on. I don't remember. But I slept with Leon that week. Only once. You look shocked. Is it so shocking? I was sorry afterward, but while it was happening—."

Rose nodded, refusing to deny the old moment of pleasure.

"And yet you turned him out," Charlotte whispered, "even though he was so important to Lynda."

"You think it was Lynda who was important to him?" Rose snapped, pulling curls from her face and tucking them behind her ears. "Oh, I guess he liked her honestly enough. But she was a child. He was using her. Of course, I would never say such a thing to Lynda."

Charlotte mumbled, "I'm sorry, Aunt Rose."

"You're sorry. But you said it. You brought it all back. And I don't blame you in a way. It's your life. I can see you'd want to know. Would have to know. I wish I could tell you for sure now that you ask. And maybe it's better to have it all out, just like Alex always says."

Charlotte felt doubtful. She wished she could replay the last ten minutes. Instead she insisted, the power inside, familiar and foreign, urging her on. "So you never knew?"

Rose turned on the tap again, but didn't speak any louder. Charlotte moved closer to hear. "What can you know? I only think. And what I think is it was more of George's craziness. So he practically drove himself crazy over it. And her too. She gave birth premature, after eight months of a miserable pregnancy. George accusing her every other day. Buck afraid to go near her — as a brother, I mean, as a friend. And me —," Rose shut off the water, placed her palms flat on the edge of the sink, looked down into the gleaming porcelain, "and me, I was nice to her, Charlotte. Nice. But never close. Rose Moore was the only one who talked to her like before. And all because of George. If you ask me, there's a good chance he was just mad at everyone because his dreams were one thing, his laziness another. Then, you were born, and you were a strong baby, thank God, Charlotte. Right from the start, in spite of being premature. As Andre was weak, you were strong. I know what strong babies are. My girls were strong. Jacob, too, I guess wasn't weak. Only Andre. Anyway, after a month or two, he left. He also cared sincerely about the war." Rose looked critically at Charlotte. "We all did. There were a few things more important than love at the time. Mara left very soon to find him, and to prove to him, maybe, that she cared too. Both of them died a month after that. A hospital was bombed. I never talked about it much with Isaac and he never mentioned it to me. Out of respect or guilt, which one, I never knew that either. When we heard the news of their deaths, he asked me to legally adopt you, and I said of course. Maybe he didn't think he needed to because he was already your father. But Isaac came from the old school, Charlotte. He would have thought he was your father then even if he was really your uncle. Family. Kin. He was trying to provide for you in case something happened to him. Do I know the truth now? I don't. I only assume. I loved Miriam, but it was never the same. It was always between us. She wanted to talk, either to confess or to deny. But I wanted to forget it. Either way damage was done. And if she confessed, what could I say after Leon? That she was bad? But she was bad, to me. But — I blame myself Charlotte. I

148

was scared. I was a coward. You and your Alex are right about things in the open. Look at my Andre, Charlotte. God knows what crazy ideas are stuffed inside his beautiful head. Like the piles of garbage in his room."

For the first time in her life Charlotte craved her aunt's reserve. Anything better than this confusion, this endless ambiguity.

Rose snatched the towel from Charlotte and dried her hands, ran the damp linen over the edge of the sink, polishing. "Your mother was not a bad person," she said again. "A lonely person. More than anything else, a lonely person. I abandoned her, Charlotte. Through you I try to make amends. Not always completely successful, I know."

"Who wasn't a bad person?" Andre demanded, walking into the room, a mischievous grin on his face. Vivian followed, radiating energy, her cheeks pink as if they'd been chafed by the wind.

"You look happier than I've seen you in years," Rose told her son, ignoring his question. She had resumed her habitual stance, a bemused, slightly distant witness to the crazy passions in other people's lives. Charlotte felt herself relax.

"I feel good," Andre said. "It's having her back," he looked at Vivian adoringly. "You know what I'm gonna do, Mama?" He turned suddenly and punched the counter hard. "I'm gonna make a big bonfire in my room. Throw away all the garbage. All the papers and clippings and everything. I'm gonna clean it out. Start fresh. I'm gonna get a job. Myron says there's an opening for a clerk in the music school where he teaches. I'll be a clerk to start. If Pop could be a cashier, I can be a clerk, right?"

"Who ever said anything was wrong with a clerk? It's an honest job," Rose muttered, her chin almost touching her chest, hiding her hope.

"That's wonderful, Andre." Charlotte put one arm around him, one arm around Vivian. "And we should do something active together," she told them. "Something political. You've been hanging around your room too long, Andre. And I've been obsessed with this story of Mara, living in the past." She glanced guiltily at Aunt Rose. "Let's go to that demonstration against the war on Saturday. I'll get Alex to come too." She was pacing the kitchen as she spoke, her own energy sudden and effusive like her cousin's. She pushed the story of Mara and George to the back of her mind, which Alex would like, she thought happily, and she resisted the thought that Andre's transformation seemed brittle, too sudden, too strong.

"I don't know about a political meeting," Vivian hesitated.

"Oh, come on. It's important," Charlotte insisted.

"We're all starting fresh," Andre pleaded, taking Vivian's hand. She looked at him, to Charlotte's amazement, with sexual desire in her eyes.

"Oh, okay," she said, not breaking her stare. "Now, let's clean out your room."

"And no bonfires. The incinerator's good enough if you want to get rid of all that stuff," Rose called to them as they walked down the hall. Her voice, Charlotte noticed, had returned to its old strident tone. Maybe she hadn't been badly hurt after all.

She was as angry as anyone in the street. She felt a sense of power in her voice as it blended with the voices of thousands of others. She had never considered America *her* country, not in the sense that she belonged to it. She had grown up in a marginal corner, identified by its alienation from traditional American values. "Profit," she could remember Uncle Buck saying, "is the root of all exploitation." And Leon: "We must fight, children, to topple the American empire for the good of the world." The only thing about official America she'd ever heard praised was the constitution itself, the individual liberties it assured, the declaration of a people's inherent right to freedom to govern themselves. Now, Ho Chi Minh was declaring such freedom for his people. It was easy for Charlotte to see herself as a supporter of Ho Chi Minh.

Hundreds of people marched down Fifth Avenue screaming, banners piercing the air before them like rifles, shooting words into the heart. Songs of peace—"All we are saying is give peace a chance,"—mingled with vengeful shouts—"Hey, hey, LBJ, how many kids you kill today?" Charlotte placed her palm on the baby. Its legs, she thought. The body count of the week before, during the height of the Tet Offensive, painted in large, black letters onto a white sheet, waved before her in the breeze.

150

Andre and Alex walked in front in a rare moment of congenial, simple agreement. Raised by upper-class Protestant New Englanders to be proud of his country, Alex's disappointment was genuine, his indignation clean. Andre was marching on the swift, light steps of private hope. No doubt, energy of many origins joined in his adrenalized blood stream that day.

Charlotte castigated herself for allowing personal emotion to pollute what ought to be a purer commitment to historical justice. She would have given anything to put her private concerns behind her and enter wholeheartedly into the real meaning of the march. She looked at Vivian who now walked silently, sullenly, no chant or song threading her into the fabric of the crowd. Charlotte was so engrossed in her thoughts that she hardly noticed the fifty blocks she walked that day. She wanted to force her attention into the world. She cared very much about the war. She was as angry as anyone, but she sang the anguished cry for peace with more than Southeast Asia in mind.

Her thoughts were a whirlpool pulling her attention down to the foundations of her private history. She condemned herself for self-indulgence. She attended faithfully, after that day, every meeting and demonstration against the war she could find.

"You asked her? You actually came right out and asked her?" Alex sounded outraged, but he liked the fact that she had done it. He turned to look at her and had to swerve around another car. Fortunately, the passing lane was empty and they had only to withstand the shock of a horn blowing loudly as they sped by.

"Yes, well I had to. Or I would never know. Would you please keep your eyes on the road, Alex?" She laughed. "Even now I don't know. Seems I'll never know since all the ones who do know, the two who do know, that is, are dead." All her life she had been trying to penetrate that wall, as if she were listening through the bottom of a glass for secrets. Beginnings were so tangible, sensuous. But endings were abrupt, the colors of the world changed forever and nothing you could do. "But I suspect, Alex. Especially after that incredible part about her and Leon. I think she was trying to tell me something. Don't you? I think she was trying to say Uncle Buck was very likely my father. Don't you think so, Alex?"

He turned off the turnpike onto the narrower road of Route 116. Signs to Turner Falls, Massachusetts, where David and Vivian lived, began to appear. "I think," he said when he completed his turn, "that you want that to be the truth. Which doesn't mean it isn't. I think you're right when you say you don't know. But, Jesus, I can't believe you asked. I love that about you, Charlotte." He unlaced his fingers from hers and placed his hand on her thigh, playing with the thin cotton of her pink and white flowered maternity dress. He pulled the dress up her thigh and touched her bare

152

skin. She opened her legs a bit and said, "mmmm."

"Hey," he laughed, returning his hand to the wheel. "We better wait or we'll crash for sure." Charlotte moved over to him, her body too large to be encased in the seat belt. She leaned on his shoulder, looked up to kiss his cheek, sunburned pinkish gold from playing tennis every afternoon with Jacob. In one more month they would start their childbirth classes. Then he would really feel a part of it, she knew. Anyway, things had been better for the last few months, ever since the lunch at Aunt Rose's.

She had put her story about Mara in the drawer as soon as she got home. She had not told Alex about that day until now because she was so pleased by his approval when he saw the desk cleared and the living room clean. Charlotte didn't attempt to paint either, or even to draw. She told Alex she needed a break from it all. She began to spend her afternoons reading and her evenings, while Alex was still in the office, attending political meetings in the neighborhood. She was writing short articles for a small radical newspaper. She had written several reports on meetings between the local Black Panther Party and some white radical activists, their continuing attempts to form a coalition. She had written an essay on the suggestive beginnings of the Women's Liberation groups, one of which she attended every Monday night. Alex encouraged her. He approved of what he called her re-entry into the real world.

In the mornings — since during the summer Alex began work later — they stayed in bed together reading the papers, drinking coffee, lately making love. They laughed as they watched her body move around whenever the baby shifted position. They both hoped for a girl and called the belly *Mira* — after Mara, but also Spanish for *see*. Charlotte said she was exchanging the mystery of *sea* for the clarity of *see*. Alex laughed, saying she was the one who was mystical. Charlotte's breasts were enlarged, her nipples constantly damp with the clear liquid that precedes the coming of milk. Nevertheless, Alex seemed less anxious about it, closer to her than he'd been since she first got pregnant. Often he kissed her body, each gigantic part of it, and she would sit on top of him rocking back and forth on his tight thighs, her breasts held gently in his large, open palms.

Andre continued to improve, working part time in the music school, spending evenings with Vivian during her weekly visits to New York to see her father who was still not well. Vivian's pregnancy didn't show yet. She just looked as if she were putting on weight, and she had made Charlotte promise not to tell anyone the truth. Andre thought she looked great a little bit plump. "You look full of life," he told her repeatedly whenever Vivian complained that she was getting fat. "You look like a gorgeous Reubens painting—a naked nymph leaping through the woods," he said once, expansive, chuckling, daring to run his hand down her sunburned arm.

"Vivian," Charlotte said to her in the ladies' room of the restaurant that night, "what in hell are you doing with Andre?" Vivian smiled wickedly, but she said, "Oh Charlotte. Nothing. Just enjoying his company. I'm pregnant, for goodness sakes."

Andre's hair had begun to grow in. Black curls grazed his collar and fringed his thick eyebrows. His room was clean. He had not exactly thrown everything down the incinerator chute. But he had stacked all the papers into a huge cardboard box which was kept in the corner of the room, covered with a blue cloth and used for a stand for his guitar, which he had begun playing again. Andre's papers reminded Charlotte of Otharose's letters, then of her story of Mara and George. And it was that thought, that her unfinished story might never be taken out again if she left it there much longer that caused Charlotte to risk all her new-found contentment and bring out the pages again. She had done it yesterday morning, as soon as Alex left the house. She had cleared her desk of political pamphlets, galleys for her recent article on a small but significant women's meeting she had attended, and begun reading the story again. She read it through without stopping, entranced, riveted. As soon as she finished, she added several pages, bringing it up to the time when Mara followed George to Spain but leaving out the scene in which Mara gave birth. She cried as Mara prepared to leave. She described Aunt Rose holding Andre, Uncle Buck holding her, Lynda toddling at the side of her mother, all five of them standing at the dock watching the boat pull away. Mara stood on the deck waving madly until she couldn't be seen any more.

Aunt Rose had given Charlotte one letter from Mara written

154

from Spain, which Rose had kept for twenty-five years. Everything else, Rose told her, she had thrown away—letters, George's unfinished novel and attempts at plays. "What would I keep them for?" Rose asked. The past was past. Mara's note read: *I have found him. I will work in a hospital here for a few months, until his immediate assignment is complete. He is sorry. He seems to understand. In a few months either we will both be home or I'll be home alone. Some day I will have to explain to my darling Charlotte why I had to leave her, how I long for her now. And some day, my dear dear Rose, I will explain to you. My best to Buck and the children, to Mathilda and, of course, to Rose Moore. Mostly my love to you, my friend. Miriam.*

Charlotte kept the letter in a small carved box bought for the purpose. It was lined in blue velvet. She had called her "my darling Charlotte." She had longed for her touch. She had meant to come back. She had signed the note, "Miriam."

When the figure of Mara moved into the fog and out of view, Charlotte started to cry, wetting the last page of her manuscript, having to type it all over again. As she thought of it now, sitting in the car near Alex who had begun to sing, she burst into tears again.

The road was nearly empty of cars now that they had turned onto an even smaller country highway. They were only five or six miles away and soon she would have to pull out the directions, telling him where to turn, looking for mailboxes. Alex smiled at her, accustomed to her tears.

"It's not my pregnancy," she said.

"What is it, then?" he urged, gentle, no analytic distance in his voice.

She told him. She spoke slowly, afraid of losing the closeness. She confessed she had written another scene. Alex sighed deeply and his jaw muscles tightened.

Charlotte pulled a wad of papers from her canvas bag. "I'll read it to you," she offered. "It's not really a scene. Just notes. Or snatches of something. Sketches. Will you listen Alex? I'm sorry. I couldn't help it. I think it's good for me to finish it."

Alex didn't say anything, but he nodded, giving her permission to go on. Charlotte read the unconnected descriptions out loud.

155

Mara and George had a good winter. They moved to a larger apartment which excited them both. George had abandoned his play, but he'd begun a book which he said was the best thing he'd ever done. Mara worked long hours at the hospital, meeting George late in the evening for dinner. Frequently, George cooked meals and served them elegantly on linen tableclothes with crystal glasses, by candlelight. They made love to the music of slow jazz and fell asleep in each others' arms. When she didn't work late, Mara accompanied him to meetings. On weekends there was always a demonstration or discussion. Energized by his new book, George was articulate, magnetic, full of conviction. On demonstrations, he marched in the front, holding up large signs and leading everyone in choruses of "Hold The Fort, For We Are Coming." Whenever she had time, Mara decorated the apartment: hung curtains, bought furniture, arranged books. She left the second bedroom empty, for storage, she said, waiting until George had finished his first draft to mention a baby. They were exhausted and busy. They seemed to have so much.

But as he reached the halfway point in his book, George began to show signs of depression again. He became uninterested in sex. He remained angry for weeks on end.

Mara began to have trouble concentrating at work again. One afternoon she left early and went to Rose's and Buck's where she was expected for dinner that night. Rose might still be in the park, but Mara and George had their own keys. She was surprised to find Buck there, baby-sitting for Lynda while Rose went to the doctor. Buck seemed delighted to see her. He fixed her a cold drink. He put a new Mozart record on the Victrola. They sat together in the shadowy living room, sipping whiskey, talking about the hospital and the university where Buck had just landed a wonderful job. "A tenure-track position. Imagine, me," he said smiling, "a revolutionary with security too."

When the record finished he got up to turn it over. He smiled at her as music filled the room again and returned to the couch.

"Mara dear," he said, putting his arm around her shoulder. "You look tired. Are you all right?"

"Oh yes, I guess so," she answered, trying to make light of her *obvious tension. "It's just George. Things were so good for a while. But he's depressed again. He's angry at me. I know it. He says he's not, but I can tell. He acts, at times, Buck, as if he almost hates me." She thought of the night before when she tried to touch him, to make love. He had grabbed her hand and snatched it away from his leg. She had been alarmed at the way he looked at her, an expression of loathing on his face. "You look like you hate me," she whispered.*

"I hate myself," he said. "Why can't you understand that?" And he had turned his back to her.

Mara leaned into Buck's arm. She let her head rest on his shoulder. She wept.

"George has always been difficult, ever since he was a boy. He was temperamental. It's not your fault," he soothed. He reached over and dried her tears. He lifted her face so he could look into her eyes. He leaned toward her.

Charlotte paused, Alex shook his head. "Jesus, Charlotte," he said.

"There's more," she told him. And she continued.

He leaned toward her and suddenly he was kissing her on the mouth, running his hand down her breasts, onto her belly, pulling her skirt above her thighs. Mara melted beneath his fingers, longing to feel this energy, longing to believe her loneliness was gone after all. She returned his surprisingly ardent embrace, reaching up to hold his smooth, shaven cheeks in her hands. She opened her mouth as his hand reached her upper thighs and moved underneath her silk underpants. She lay back, feeling the weight of him gladly, as an immense relief. She thought of nothing when he entered her except how relieved she felt, to have someone there, someone so deeply there again, someone with her at the closest place. It was Lynda's cry, waking from her nap, that jolted Mara into reality again, into a guilt and horror so penetrating she felt as if it had shoveled out everything inside of her, everything decent, leaving nothing but corruption behind, corruption and horror and filth. She shouted, a cry of shock, as if she had been attacked. Buck whispered, "My God,

157

*Miriam, I'm sorry. My God. Forgive me,'' as if he had attacked.
He left the room to attend to his child.*

"Then I decided that was wrong," Charlotte said. She was
still sniffling from tears. "I decided it was impossible. I wrote it
all over again." Alex remained silent, his jaw still tight. "Go on,"
he said, turning toward her. He jerked the car over to the side
of the road and stopped.

*Mara leaned into Buck's arm. She let her head rest on his
shoulder. She wept. He reached over and dried her tears. But the
hypnotic, relaxing fatigue she so often felt under his maternal
attention enveloped her. Tension flowed out of her body. She was
asleep. He remained on the couch with her, fearful of waking
her, allowing her to sleep in the curve of his arm. They were still
sitting that way in the dark when George, using his own key,
came into the apartment.*

*"What the hell," he shouted, and woke Mara with a jolt.
"What the hell are you doing?" he shouted, grabbing her wrist,
pulling her up from the couch. She was confused. She had just
emerged from the deepest sleep she'd had in weeks.*

*"What is wrong with you?" Buck shouted at his brother. "Are
you crazy? Are you mad? What are you suggesting? What are
you thinking? Let go of her!"*

*"George stepped back. He looked ashamed. Then he looked
doubtful and furious. Then he looked ashamed again. "I'm
sorry," he said, sounding genuine. "I'm very very sorry," he said
again, this time sounding snide.*

*As the three of them stood there in a small circle staring at
each other, they heard Lynda beginning to cry. At the same
moment they heard Rose's key in the door. She burst into the hall
and started towrd her daughter's room. "Three of you here and
the baby's crying?" she accused. "And what are you doing standing in the dark?" But her tone contradicted her apparent
annoyance. She had just been told she was pregnant again.*

"So which one is it?" Alex said. This time Charlotte would
have welcomed analytical distance.

158

"Why are you so mad at me? I've put it away for months. I wanted to finish it. It's not making me upset. I'm not going crazy. I just want to see where it goes. Though as you can see, I'll never know." She was angry and confused. He liked it when she pursued Rose for details of the past, but he got mad when she wrote it down. She didn't understand. She shoved the remainder of the story back into her bag.

Alex pulled her into his arms. "I'm not really angry, Charlotte," he whispered into her ear, as he peeled long, damp strands of hair off his lips and tongue. "I just don't understand what you're doing any more than I did before. Why do you describe it like that? It's practically pornographic for one thing."

"I just have to," she answered. "I have to know what happened."

"But that's crazy, Charlotte. You don't know anything. You're making it up."

"I have to feel it, then, even if only as it might have been. Then I have something to move forward from."

"But doesn't it matter if it's false? If it might have happened completely differently?" The same question Rose had asked. And she answered the same.

"No. I know it might have. But I have a possibility here. It's more than I had before."

"I'm worried, I guess," he continued. "Things have been so good with us since you stopped. And it's only two more months till the baby's here. I just want us to live our life. I don't want you obsessed with something in the past. It's as if you *like* the uncertainty. You're seducing yourself into two equally plausible histories. I presume, if you want my opinion, that your father was George, just as he's supposed to be. That second scene sounded very realistic to me, from what I've heard of him. You can't make Buck into your father just because George was obviously a bastard." He kissed her again.

Is that what it was then? That Buck was responsible, protective, good? But she liked George too. Rose had said he cared about Spain. Whatever private redemption he sought, he had volunteered and had lost his life. And also, she liked the way he made love. This thought, however, disturbed Charlotte so much she pulled

159

away from Alex. What did she know about the way George made love? Especially if he were her father, for God's sake. She had made it up. The second scene seemed more realistic to her, too. But was that because the first seemed repellent, even frightening in a way, or because it didn't happen? The questions energized her. She liked the precariousness she felt when sliding between the possibilities.

Then suddenly something else was clear to her. Alex hated her writing because it was a mystery to him, another closed door like her pregnancy in those early months, an awesome fact no biological description could fully explain. Alex solved mysteries by naming them—family histories brought into line by one determined consciousness (his patient's) supported by a confident guide (himself). By the time the patient had finished therapy and begun to suspect the neatness, question the finality of the explanation, Alex would be uninvolved, that patient's story complete, like an elegantly structured novel, in his file. She had loved his capacity to believe in his theories. And he loved her openness, that he could see, or believed he could see, all there was to see in her. Charlotte did not disbelieve in Alex's vision. It was fiction, she thought, as good as any other, as good and as real as her story of Mara and George. But beneath the fiction, which was not untrue, were all those other layers, echoing, contradicting, pushing up through apparently solid ground like faults in the earth, hinting at other stories, equally true, equally false. If Charlotte responded to this confusion with a certain vertigo, she was willing, happy, to wander around the edge looking down. The dizziness attracted her. She had spent most of her life so far trying to unmask secrets at the same time as she needed to keep them in place. But Alex had to believe in the reality of final stories, written once and for all. What arrogance. Or confidence. He was a man you could lean on, like Uncle Buck.

She was surprised by this last thought, seemingly unconnected to what had gone before. Yet, it was the truth of her feeling. She understood that somehow Alex was wrong in the way he saw the world. Yet the fact that he believed so deeply brought her close to believing it too.

"You have to believe one thing or the other once and for all," Alex whispered. "And I do think it's likely that your father is George."

160

'It's not only that.' She heard her voice on the verge of break-ing. "It's my mother, Alex. I want to know about my mother." She leaned toward him again, pressed her forehead against his chest. He held her tight. He rocked her. A sense of safety filled her. It had nothing to do with fiction or fact but emerged from older layers, before any stories began. Enclosed in that safe grip she did not care to question the truth or the lies. The discomforting and seductive mysteries paled before his wonderful conviction.

"I want my mother," she sobbed.

By the time they spotted Vivian's mailbox, Charlotte had collected herself. Alex kept her hand in his as he turned the car onto the long dirt driveway. "Dry your eyes." He patted her thigh. She relaxed. Things were good with them again.

They rode up a narrow, winding road, bumping over rocks and into small ditches in the sand. Thick layers of leaves arched over them, shading the road, creating dark, filagreed patterns on Charlotte's dress and Alex's legs. Suddenly they emerged from the trees and were in a circle of bright sunlight in a newly sanded driveway. To their left was a wide field reaching toward a blue-green mountain. To the right, the woods. Charlotte noticed more shades of green than she'd seen in years. A dark red doorway opened and Vivian flew out, screaming "Hi'" followed by two small, almost naked children, their skin bronzed by the sun. Another child, his long straight hair an incredible white gold, stood shyly in the open doorway, sucking his thumb. Behind him Char-lotte noticed David, surveying the arrival scene, looking drawn.

Vivian's father had begun to improve and she hadn't been to the city in weeks. Andre had made Charlotte promise to get Vivian to New York that month. But when Charlotte saw Vivian she doubted she'd have any success. Vivian no longer looked fat. She was clearly pregnant now.

Charlotte watched Alex's long arms pull through the lake water, his body moving swiftly from the shore to the white raft, and she was entranced.

"He's beautiful," Vivian said. She passed Charlotte a peeled orange.

161

"Maybe our daughter will be like him," Charlotte smiled. "Disciplined and certain of her place in the world." She pulled off a piece of juicy crescent and popped it into her mouth.

"Or maybe she'll be like you," Vivian teased. "Or maybe she'll be a he. What are you going to name it if it's a boy?"

Charlotte hadn't considered boys' names. She expected a daughter. She began building a small hill in the warm sand, lifted handfuls which she rained slowly over her tanned calves. Every so often she looked up to watch Alex dive. Suddenly David ran past them at a breakneck pace and dove off the ground into shallow water. In several minutes he was out at the raft, hoisting up his thick muscular body in one movement. Vivian winced.

"He's a strong swimmer," Charlotte noted. But she didn't like David's looks. He held his body stiffly, his shoulders pushed slightly forward, his chin down, as if he were prepared for a fight. Vivian stood up.

"Mmmm. He's a good athlete," she said as she looked down the beach and began calling for Andrew and Matthew who were fishing for salamanders at the edge of the lake. Nora, who was only two and a half, waddled over to Charlotte's hill and began sticking her fingers in the center, making holes.

"Cake," she said.

"Shall we make a cake?" Charlotte jumped up and grabbed Nora's hand. They ran down to the edge of the water to build mud cakes just as David and Alex came butterflying into shore. David grabbed his daughter's ankles, whirring through the shallow water like a motor boat, reached up for her arms. and lifted her onto his belly as he floated out to the ropes. Nora began to scream, "stop, stop." She was crying loudly by the time her father stood up and shifted her onto his hip. She arched her back away from him, gasped for air and called for her mother while Alex and Charlotte exchanged a disapproving glance. Vivian, trailing the two boys, ran down the beach, marched angrily into the water and grabbed Nora from her father.

"For Christ's sake, Vivian. Would you please not interfere?" David clenched his fists but didn't move.

'I don't think this game is fun for her," Vivian said coldly and turned her back. David plunged under the ropes and swam back out to the raft.

"Mom, don't you think you were just a little bit mean?" Andrew, Vivian's oldest, accused. "Daddy was just playing," he chided in a voice remarkably like Vivian's. Andrew was small for seven, and slender.

Already a proficient reader, he walked back to the blanket and dug his book out of Vivian's large straw bag. He fished out his eyeglasses, fitted them over the non-existent bridge of his tiny pug nose, curled away from his mother and the sun, and began to read. Vivian, who had shown only irritation at her husband's disapproval, was obviously daunted, even shamed, by this criticism from her son. She looked guiltily at Alex and Charlotte, shrugged her shoulders as if in apology and then, forgiving herself, muttered, "Well, you'll find out soon enough."

In the shade of the willow trees he had planted on the northeast side of the house he had built, David's mood improved. He described for them every stage of the building, a project which had already taken him over a year. Soon he insisted they relinquish their shady corner and go inside with him so he could give them a detailed tour of the house, which was still unfinished.

The kitchen had been completed only that week. David opened cabinets to demonstrate the neatness of the door fit. "Mexican tile. Really authentic," he said, running his hand over the gleaming counter. "Vivian designed it," he added proudly. "She really likes the house a lot." Huge thick beams stretched across the high ceiling. "Not a nail in the entire external structure." David tapped the rough wood, approving. "It'll last forever. I mean it. Andrew and the other kids'll be playing with their grandchildren here."

Then he ushered them upstairs so he could show them the old claw-footed bathtub salvaged from a junk yard and built into a dark rosewood frame that blended soothingly with the dusky pink of the bathroom walls. Indeed, Charlotte thought, it was the most beautiful house she had ever seen. As he guided them from room to room, even though she felt somewhat bored and wished to be allowed to return to her seat underneath the willow tree,

163

Charlotte felt a moment of attraction to David. She was touched by his longing to build something that would last. It was an affectionate attraction that contradicted her strong discomfort with the man. She could imagine a blunt sort of pleasure in sleeping with him. She was impressed with David's forethought, his control.

Alex appeared genuinely interested in the tour, so Charlotte was able to excuse herself and return to the back yard where Vivian was waiting for her with a vodka tonic and a plate of crackers and cheese. They were obviously unhappy, Charlotte thought. She wanted to give Vivian the chance to confess her troubles but she didn't know how to begin. Vivian looked over at her sons rolling down the dirt hill at the far corner of the yard, her face set in a smooth, untroubled smile.

"It's all so beautiful," Charlotte said, "the mountain, the land." She eased her bulky body into a low chaise lounge. "It must be amazing to own such a wonderful house."

"David owns it," said Vivian without rancor or regret. "I live here. I raise my children here. And I'm comfortable here." She took a sip of her drink. "It is beautiful. It really is."

When she paused, Charlotte plunged. "Do you want to talk about David at all? I mean, I have trouble with Alex too, even though things are good right now. I told you about the Mara story and how upset it makes him."

Charlotte shared her troubles with a friend as a host might offer a carefully prepared appetizer to a full course meal. It was an invitation to a claim on her attention, the chance to confess. But Vivian shook her head.

"I don't want to talk about it. I've made my peace with my choices for now. I may be only twenty-nine, but I've been married for twelve years. I wanted all this. And it's not as bad as it seems today."

"It does seem bad."

"I have fun with David. I love doing the things he teaches us to do—you know, all the outside things. He's not as serious as all the men we grew up around. He's simpler. He's just mad today, and jealous like he always is of my friends. Especially you, Charlotte. He's heard about you for years. I think he really likes Alex though. Don't you think they're getting along well?"

The two men walked across the yard toward David's large garden. Charlotte could have watched Alex contentedly for the next hour as he wandered up and down between the rows of vegetables, pulling ripe tomatoes off a vine, twisting an enormous zuchinni off its stem, stuffing fresh basil leaves into the large pockets of his khaki shorts.

He had gardened all through his childhood with his mother on her farm in Vermont, and continued to do so until she died when he was twenty-three. They would sit on the porch until it got dark, drinking martinis, sucking on olive pits, talking about the size of tomatoes that season, the expectations for corn. They would play tennis in the afternoon, both of them lanky and strong. But since her husband left, abandoning his first family for a new one, efficiently run by a younger, simpler wife, Alex's mother usually drank three or four martinis until her voice became loud, her laugh hoarse, and her inevitable confessions upsetting to her son. It was better when he could catch her before the third martini. Then they would leave their drinks and cook a gourmet dinner together, eating it slowly on the dark porch by candlelight. There would always be a fresh salad from the garden.

"I am going to make you a dynamite salad." Alex grinned at the women as he walked by, arms laden with beans and red-edged lettuce, ripe tomatoes and four kinds of spice. "It'll be enough for all four of you—for Mira, the Belly and—what's yours gonna be, Vivian?"

"Oh, on your fourth it doesn't matter," Vivian said. "Maybe Carolyn or—well, actually, I was thinking of Isaac."

Charlotte felt encouraged by this reference to their shared history. When Alex had gone to join David in the kitchen, she said, "Why won't you talk to me, Vivian? Revealing yourself makes you strong." She reached for Vivian's foot with her own and stroked the arch with her toes.

"Because it doesn't make me strong," Vivian said. "And I'm not so sure it always makes you strong either, Charlotte."

"Well, strong or weak," Charlotte answered, "I just can't keep anything in."

She wondered about it all, feeling guilty but immobile as Vivian fed the children, bathed them, read to them, put them to

165

bed. Power. The moment of sexual attraction to David which she tried to forget as quickly as she could. Revelation. Her desire to know everything possible about Mara and George, and her desire to have Alex know everything she knew. Anything left out, inadvertently or on purpose, made her feel as if she were trapped in a net of lies. Control, or her lack of it. She thought of how she had asked Aunt Rose about Mara and Buck, knowing she shouldn't, unable to stop the words coming out of her mouth. She thought of all the chaotic rooms she had known—Andre's, George's (the one she'd made up), her own. She began to imagine a painting of a messy room, a room filled with dirty dishes, pencils rolling off surfaces onto the floor, caught in mid-air by Charlotte's eye and brush. As she arranged the mess in her mind, she placed someone in the middle of the room—a man—no, herself, holding one neat stack of papers in her hands, like a child constructing a sturdy block tower in the corner of a disordered room. Alex was an orderly person, like Aunt Rose. Mess upset them. The careful drying of a dish, the preparation of a balanced meal, the ordering of memories—naming one thing, forgetting another—in these small behaviors and efforts of consciousness, they found solace. She wanted to be like them. Charlotte pulled a straying curl from her forehead and tucked it behind her ear. Well, she was a little bit like Aunt Rose. She could see it more and more as she got older. She had a no-nonsense streak in her too. Did some tragedy strike? Get everyone together and pass out drinks. Does a war threaten? Is the world about to fall apart? Get the dinner on the table and we'll talk. Charlotte felt a lump of heel, or buttock, or side, turning over inside her. She smiled, satisfied with herself. There was some order in history. Nothing happened without the thing which happened before. It was all a matter of perspective, of generations, of seeing the generation of things until they fell into place. That was why complete honesty seemed so important to her. If there were too many blind spots, how could you get a sense of the whole picture without distortion? She knew what Aunt Rose would say, and Vivian too—"Lies can protect people too." She remembered Lynda saying it when they found out about Uncle Buck's job as a cashier. But Charlotte didn't want to be protected. She wanted to know. Or both amounted to the same thing for her.

Lies told for too many years affected you as if they were the truth. What a waste that was. And secrets made her think of ships moving away from her, clouded by fog until they disappeared. Charlotte saw the ship as a painting, dozens of yellow lights shining from the broad white hull, rigging like winding spider webs across the sky, rope ladders entwined with the legs of climbing sailors, protective railings reaching around a deck, and all of it suddenly obliterated, wasted, removed by a thick wash of dirty paint.

How did all this connect to the sense of mystery and relativity she had come upon in the car? How did the tantalizing confusion of conflicting stories fit with her uncompromising need to knw *the* truth? She wondered if the painting she had just seen, the ship moving into fog, was what would come in the end of all her writing. No mural. Just the boat moving away. Settling for a fragment, a small piece of the whole, that Charlotte realized suddenly might tell everything there was to tell. "God," she said aloud and she tapped the aluminum arm of the deck chair as if it were a drum.

When Alex called her into dinner she was jolted into ordinary time. She jumped up. For a moment she was scared. He was standing in the open doorway between two huge picture windows, holding a bottle of wine and a glass. "Come on, dreamer," he called. "You gotta eat too."

Charlotte climbed the stairs to the house, suddenly starving. The sun was almost down. She pulled a cotton shirt of Alex's over her dry swim suit, combed and rebraided her hair. The table looked inviting—a red cloth, white plates, tall white candles in silver candlesticks, a black wrought-iron pot in the middle steaming with fish smells. A long, crusty bread overlapped the edges of a tray. At the corner of the table, filling a dark wooden bowl, was Alex's garden salad. David sat watching as Vivian completed the setting, six empty beer cans lined up in front of his plate.

"So tell me about giving birth," Charlotte demanded of Vivian when they had finished eating and praising the main course. Vivian was clearing the table, serving homemade blueberry pie. She looked at Charlotte as if in warning. "It's hell if you want the truth."

David shook his head. "For Christsakes, Vivian. It's not that bad."

"Not bad for you."

"Was Nora so bad? She was easy. It took you two hours. You were laughing when she was born." His voice conveyed the same restrained tension Charlotte had noticed that afternoon.

"Nora was number three. You remember Matthew? Eight

hours of misery. And with Andrew? Thirty. I thought I would die."
Vivian spooned out a large helping of pie from the serving dish
and ate it. "I'm gonna suffer for this later," she smiled. Dark purple juice ran over her lips. She caught it with a napkin and giggled.

"Oh Vivian," Charlotte begged. "It can't be that bad. Is it?"

David looked at Alex—a comrade, a sympathizer. "What is
it with them. It's a fantastic thing. They give birth to a baby, a
brand new life, and it's a complaint. My mother always said it was
the most beautiful thing that ever happened to her."

"That's what mothers are supposed to say," said Vivian, and
she proceeded to eat more pie.

"You were very young," Alex explained. "Scared. Naturally.
Charlotte knows very deeply that she wants this baby. She's not
ambivalent. She's more sure of herself as a woman. Well, you were
so young when you had your first. Charlotte is strong, and in the
childbirth classes these days they teach you how to control your
pain."

"Ha!" Vivian guffawed as she stood up. "Charlotte thinks
revealing everything is power. You think everything can be controlled, Alex. And David just believes in bossing everyone around."

"Shut up, Vivian," David shouted. Then, "Sorry," he said,
and moved the empty beer cans into a circular pattern.

Charlotte poured herself more wine. Strengthened, as always,
by Alex's praise, she kept her eyes from Vivian who was leaning
against the sink with her arms crossed over her waist.

"Okay, okay" Vivian relented, breaking the uncomfortable
silence. "I guess I'm just an unreconstructed lapsed Communist,
a believer in impotence and chaos. But I'm sure what you're all
saying is true." A derisive expression passed over her face, quickly.
"It probably won't be so bad for you." She stared at Charlotte,
maternal. "Like I said, there are some things it doesn't do any
good to reveal." The look of derision softened into sadness. "I'm
sure it'll be fine." She turned her back to them and ran steaming
hot water into the sink.

Charlotte remembered how several months ago she had realized the truth of everything Vivian once said about being pregnant. She watched small clouds of steam rise off the water and
thought of fog.

But that night in bed, after making love (she was passionate, recalling Alex's strong body in the water; he was tender, in awe of what he had decided was the extraordinary psychological strength of his wife) Charlotte felt a contentment so near ecstasy she refused to diminish it with thoughts about Vivian. Alex was right about her strength. She had made herself strong by writing the story of Mara and George. She had cleansed something, buried something. Just as she hoped Andre was burying something, thanks to his attachment to Vivian. He was so much better. Almost as if he were reborn. And she would give birth to a wonderful new person, unburdened by old ghosts. *Mira.* Or maybe, as Alex had recently suggested, *Ruth,* which she had discovered meant *compassionate* and *merciful.* Like him. Before she gave birth herself, Charlotte planned to write the scene of Mara giving birth, to see if she could do it, and because then she would be finished. She would have gone as far as she could go, all the way to the foggy morning on the dock when Mara left for Spain.

Loud voices from upstairs interrupted her. David spoke in a voice so loud Charlotte could hear some of his words through the ceiling. She heard him call Vivian a cold bitch. Then the words were muffled again.But she could tell it was David's voice and she wondered if Vivian was talking low, trying to calm him down, or saying nothing at all. "I don't give a fucking damn who hears," she heard through the ceiling. Then quiet again. She was very worried about Vivian. Would she end up leaving this man, with four children between them? How could she? Did she even have any money of her own? She certainly couldn't figure it out, if Vivian wouldn't discuss it. She turned onto her back and lifted her legs to the ceiling, doing a pre-birth exercise she'd read about in a natural childbirth book. Her thoughts returned to their previous track.

How had Mara found George? Why had she resumed using her original name? But somehow Charlotte knew that whatever had happened in Spain, even the ultimate solution to the mystery of her own paternity, (if that solution should ever be known) would have to wait for another time in her life. She just couldn't imagine it now. She needed to know more.

She was aware of noises again. Different noises this time, the creaking of the ceiling, the sound of deep sighs and moans. Surprised, she realized they were making love. There was so much about Vivian that Charlotte didn't understand. There always had been. She turned her naked body toward Alex and reached around to his chest, placing her hand over his heart, resting her head between his shoulder blades. She watched moonlight shine behind thin gauze curtains, then disappear.

In the morning, they all went for an early swim after a light breakfast. They took a picnic basket and the Sunday papers to the lake, and they baked in the sun. Vivian and David were getting along much better. He kept his arm around her as she sat on the blanket talking to Charlotte and, every so often, he'd kiss her on the mouth, interrupting her, or place his hand on her breast as she talked, demonstrating ownership. Vivian stiffened, but she smiled.

Then, standing waist deep in water, they threw the children back and forth to each other. Nora's head went under and she came up frightened, but she didn't cry. Andrew was happier than Charlotte had seen him all weekend, especially when he was allowed to swim alongside his father out to the raft. Matthew, the middle child, would tolerate being thrown only once, insisting he didn't like it though he was a better swimmer than his older brother. "Come on, let me throw you again, Matt," David insisted. But Matthew refused, his posture, much like his father's, stiff as a hard little nail. "Matthew!" David reached for him. But the boy turned and ran off singing and laughing down the beach where he began stalking frogs.

When they returned to the house in the late afternoon, Alex and Charlotte showered and packed. David was fixing a large plate of cold cuts and cheese. Coffee was brewing on the stove. He seemed to have decided that he was glad of their visit. Or maybe his sudden hospitality was only relief at seeing them go.

"I'm sorry I've been kind of depressed all weekend," he said.

"Oh, we all get angry and fight sometimes." Charlotte's dislike was now too strong to do anything but avoid a confrontation. She didn't want to upset Vivian. But David demanded that she see it his way.

171

"No. We don't fight a lot. We really don't. Things are very good with us. The house. The kids. Everything's good. It was just a bad weekend. I've been tired from work. This house takes up too much time, and I'm working on two others." He forked several pieces of turkey onto Charlotte's plate until she put her hand up to stop him. As Vivian came into the room with Nora on her hip, the phone rang.

She picked it up with her free hand. "Hi!" she said, sounding pleased. "I thought you were out of town." Then her mouth opened and she squinted at the receiver as if it had ceased working, begun emitting static instead of words. "I thought he was okay. Are you serious? Oh my God. Yes. Tonight." She hung up and stood still, clinging to Nora with both arms. Nora rested her head on her mother's shoulder and sucked her thumb. "My father's dead." Vivian sucked on a piece of Nora's hair. "He died today. I have to go to the city with you," she said to Charlotte. "David?" She walked over and placed Nora in his lap.

"Don't worry," he told her. "Don't worry about anything here. I'll take care of everything. I'll call you tonight. I'll bring the kids in tomorrow or Tuesday."

He put down his daughter and embraced his wife. She leaned stiffly against him, her arms at her sides. Charlotte felt stunned. Here it was again—an ending before you were ready. This death, happening now, would have an effect on Vivian's marriage. It would have an effect on Andre. A wave of anxiety passed through her. What questions would never be asked, she thought, what completion forever curtailed? Charlotte felt Vivian's father's life close down. It was over. It had to leave a hole whose dimensions they could not yet fathom. Every ending did, even the end of a painting, even the end of a book you were reading. She remembered the feeling she'd had the night before of the life inside her being new, unburdened, and she looked with sorrow at the faces of Vivian's sons who were now coming into the room.

When the children realized their mother was leaving, the two younger ones began to cry. David told Andrew to take them upstairs, which he dutifully did, telling Nora he would read to her, dragging Matt by the hand, affectionate but firm, a small version of his mother.

172

"He acts so old for his age," Charlotte told Vivian, holding both her hands. (Was she suggesting that somehow Andrew could take the place of her father?)

"He's great," David agreed.

"Too old for his age," Vivian complained, trying to collect her things, counting her money. Mostly she was walking around in circles. She stopped and ran her hands through her hair. She uttered one cry and stopped it with her fist.

In the driveway David tried to embrace Vivian but she pulled away from him. Then he kissed Charlotte, his hands grazing her breasts as he pulled her toward him. But perhaps it had been an accident, she thought as she returned his kiss.

In the car Vivian cried. She recalled the many instances of her father's disapproval of her until her marriage. "He thought David was the best thing that ever happened to me," she said.

Charlotte sat in the back seat with Vivian. Alex remained silent at the wheel, anonymous and efficient, a professional driver taking the women where they wanted to go.

"In the middle of all this, I'm worried about Andre, Charlotte," Vivian said. "He doesn't realize I'm pregnant. I was going to write to him, but now he'll see without warning. I'm sure he'll come to the funeral."

"Well, why worry about that?" Charlotte noticed Alex's shoulders shift, his neck stiffen. He had not approved of Vivian's flirtation with Andre.

"Just take my word for it, it's a problem," Vivian said "Can you tell him before he sees me, Charlotte? I can't handle it. Can you?"

Charlotte said of course she would help in any way she could.

"I'm sorry you have to hear this, Alex," Vivian spoke to the back of Alex's head. "Just pretend you don't, if you don't want to." She lowered her voice as if that would make it easier for him not to hear. "But Charlotte, I do love Andre. I love him in a way I will never love David. I want you to know that. I wanted to help him. He looked so awful when I saw him. All those days we spent together were the best days for me in a long time."

She moved closer to Charlotte and looked down at her knees. Then she looked up at Alex again and lowered her voice even more. "But it was just like the last time."

Alex made a graceful turn off the small highway and entered the turnpike. As he turned his face to check the cars behind him he looked fully concentrated on the road, as if their words were inaudible to him.

"It was just like the last time," Vivian repeated in a whisper. "He couldn't. Andre, I mean. But this time it didn't matter so much. It was wonderful anyway. You know what I mean, Charlotte?" She pressed Charlotte's hand and then, as if a simple distortion could ensure Alex's ignorance, as if he had not heard because she was whispering, she raised her voice to a normal speaking level and added, "I mean, you know, Charlotte. It was wonderful. How close we were. The way we talked."

Charlotte was furious at Vivian, but when she began to cry she took her in her arms. She said, "I know, Vivian, it's so hard," remembering Uncle Buck. And maybe it wasn't all Vivian's fault, she thought. She felt weary of all the men, especially the dead ones who so blatantly and indelibly left their marks. But she felt grateful for Alex too, so kind compared to David, or to George. Then she felt angry at Vivian again in Alex's behalf. She reached her bare foot along the side of the seat until she touched Alex's leg. He took her foot in his hand and continued to hold it as he drove, while Charlotte, in the back seat, stroked Vivian's hair.

A week after returning to New York Charlotte went to visit Otharose in the nursing home. She hadn't been in months but Otharose greeted her as if she'd been there the day before. Sitting up in a turquoise plastic arm chair, Otharose reminded Charlotte of the old grandmother in the white room. Two thick, dark braids crowned her head and met at the root of her skull. She wore a slightly frayed, white quilted robe. Dark shadows underlined sharp cheekbones and softened a slender neck. Dark purple lipstick made her face look strangely youthful in the frame of gray hair.

Charlotte told her all the news. Otharose insisted that she take good care of herself, rest in the heat, or she would faint from the weight of the baby. "You look more and more like your mother," she said, stroking Charlotte's cheek with her long fingers.

Charlotte walked to the window and looked down fifteen floors to the street below. "Aunt Rose told me all about what happened before my mother went to Spain," she said. "She told me you were the only one who was really good to her."

Otharose looked around effortfully to see Charlotte's face. "Come sit down, Girl," she said sternly. "I'm too old and too sick to be twisting every which way to see you."

Charlotte sat on the bed. Her eyes filled with tears.

"Well, what are you crying about, Sugar?" Otharose said.

"It's just the past. Here I am about to have a baby and I can't think about anything except the past. I'm afraid it's bad for the baby. I know it's bad for me."

"The past don't rest like we want it to. Of course I was good

175

to your mother. I understood how she felt. I didn't know what she did or didn't do, but I understood. Cause I loved him too, Charlotte. We all did."

"You mean — ?" Charlotte looked up, astonished and furious that she was about to be forced to sustain another revelation. "Otharose!" she warned.

"Oh girl, I don't mean what you're thinking. I never slept with your Uncle Buck. Lord, no. But does that really matter? It's who we love that makes our lives what they are, not who we sleep with. You're old enough to understand that. You ain't no baby any more."

"Sometimes I wish I were," she announced, petulant. "And sometimes I feel the way you used to, like I want to give into Ole Man Death who tries to get me every day."

Otharose laughed. "Why does he try to get you, Sugar? You got a husband. You're gonna have a baby. You have no cause for despair. Shoot, girl. You even have a gift. You're an artist." Otharose waved her hand in air, as she said the word, as if the stars were the limit to Charlotte's hopes.

"Well, my mother had hopes too. She was a doctor. Everyone says she was beautiful. And look what happened to her."

"Your mother didn't have what you have. She didn't come from a big family who loved her. She even gave birth alone. No one even knew she was in the hospital until you were born."

Charlotte's attention was captured, as always, by a new detail about Mara. Something intervened between herself and her sadness. "Do you remember anything else?" she looked hard at Otharose.

"I remember I gave her chrysanthemums. Yellow chrysanthemums. Lord, there were a lot of flowers."

It seemed unreasonable, even ridiculous, but each new detail filled her with energy, with hope. Yellow chrysanthemums. Perhaps the story wasn't done. She had been thinking she had only one part to go — her own birth. And with this new detail, that part fell into place. (An image came to her: a young woman alone in a bed surrounded by flowers, the room so large the woman looked tiny, insignificant.) There was suddenly the possibility of going on.

176

"Do you have any idea what happened in Spain?" Charlotte asked. Rose stood up with the help of a cane and limped over to a metal cupboard. She unlocked the door and took out a box of butter cookies. Slowly, she tore the outer paper, lifted the top and removed four cookies. She handed two to Charlotte and put the other two into the pocket of her robe. Then she closed the cupboard, walked back to her chair and leaning heavily on the cane, she sat down.

"Open the window, Sugar," she said. "It gets so hot in here."

Charlotte obeyed and returned to the edge of the bed.

"No," Otharose said. "I don't know, Baby. You know who knew, I think? Your Aunt Mathilda."

"Aunt Mathilda?" Charlotte was shocked. She had hardly thought of Aunt Mathilda in the years since she died. She had certainly never considered her as a possible source of relevant information on any subject whatever. "Aunt Mathilda?" she repeated.

"Well, why do you look so surprised? She was their sister, after all. And she was a little like you, Charlotte. Oh I know she was crazy, or everyone said she was crazy. Maybe they made her crazy by saying it so often, you ever think of that? But she was an artist too, Charlotte. Whatever happened to all those paintings?"

"Who knows," Charlotte said. "They were all of herself anyway. Probably in the closet somewhere."

"Why should that matter, that they were all of herself? She was still an artist." Otharose raised her arm again, indicating the sky. "She wanted to know things. Anyway, if I remember right she was the only one who kept writing to them in Spain, and some letters came for her."

"Well what ever happened to them?" An entirely new perspective opened up, something resting on tangible evidence — letters.

"Don't know," Otharose said.

An attendant came in with a tray of dinner. Otharose picked at her meat and vegetable, ate two cubes of raspberry jello. She pushed the tray away with a snort. "Terrible food. Don't pay to eat it," she sniffed.

Charlotte moved the tray from the chair and helped Otharose over to the bed. Once propped up against the pillows, Otharose reached into her pocket and pulled out the cookies. She nibbled the edge of one, cupping her hand beneath it to catch the crumbs.

"What it comes down to," she chuckled, "is saving a cookie for after dinner, eating it slowly so you can kind of draw out the pleasure and putting another one away for before you go to sleep." She patted the remaining cookie and returned it to her pocket.

"Come on, Otharose. There must be more than that," Charlotte objected. "Don't you ever write letters any more?"

"Me?" Otharose laughed. "Lord, no. What would I have to write letters for?"

"You know," Charlotte smiled as she rose to go. She looked in the mirror and carefully applied her new iridescent lipstick. She took out a comb and straightened her hair. Otharose watched Charlotte prepare to leave as Charlotte had once watched her. "Write to Old Man Death so he can't get you," Charlotte finished as she turned around.

"Lord help me," Otharose responded as she dusted the remaining cookie crumbs off the spread. "I'm not fighting Ole Man Death any more, baby. I'm just waiting around for him to come on by."

S*he worked until the first pains came. When she knew it was time, she found Aaron and asked him to call George when it was done. Then she walked to the maternity ward, left a message for her obstetrician who was attending another birth, and checked herself in. The labor room was small. She was glad to be alone. As soon as the serious contractions came they would put her to sleep and then there would be only darkness, lost time. It would seem like a minute later when she awoke, and she would have a child. It seemed perfectly right to Miriam that she be alone. She thought about Constance, recalled every detail of her face as she had looked when Miriam was a child. Fair skin. Small creases around her eyes and near her cheekbones when she smiled. A wide mouth, too wide for her face. Fine reddish blond hair tied into a bun most of the time but, in the evenings, hanging loose over angular shoulders, long, shining tresses which occasionally she allowed her daughter to comb. "I wish I had hair like yours, Mama," Miriam heard her child's voice say. "Long. And blond." And Constance would object: "Oh, but my darling, your hair is beautiful. Like the polished metal armor of a knight. Remember the poem I once wrote for you? 'She has the hair of knights / black as polished metal armor.' Remember? Your hair is just like your father's. Oh, I have always wished for black hair."*

Miriam's pains intensified. Long and blond, long and blond, she hummed, forcing herself to sit up. She fell back again just as the nurse entered the room.

"Time for a shot, Dr. Cohen?" she asked. Cheerful tone, respectful words, carefully chosen.

Miriam smiled and shrugged, an acceptance of impotence, a resignation to mourning, but the nurse interpreted it as an agreement and prepared the injection. What was she mourning? Mara watched the nurse move the intravenous attachment to the side of the bed. She felt the smooth, cool cotton wet the inner curve of her arm. She had not been lonely in so long, not completely lonely, like this. She had been naked in the arms of George Cohen—naked body, naked heart. Mara smiled when the needle pierced her skin. Naked and not lonely. Knight and mourning. She felt the cotton bed sheet and thought it was blond silk.

The first thing she saw when she woke up were flowers. Dozens of them. She thought she had landed in a garden. For a moment she thought she was dead. Then she saw George.

He was crying. He took her hand. "You have a daughter," he said.

Mara looked away from him and noticed a small square card settled among a dozen roses: "All our love, Rose and Buck, Lynda and Andre." And under an enormous bouquet of violets: "To the sweetest girl in the world. Love, Aaron." A pale blue card almost hidden in yellow chrysanthemums said simply: "Rose Moore." On the other side of the bed was a large crystal vase filled with at least twenty white gladiolas.

"You name her," Mara whispered. "Give your daughter a name."

George, weeping profusely now, said "Okay, baby. If that's what you want."

"You're the namer, George," Mara said as she drifted back into an irresistible sleep. "You named me, no matter what. You named us all."

"I'll call her Charlotte then," George reached over and stroked his wife's hair. "Charlotte," he said again.

She felt unbounded as she drifted back into fog. She felt him drift back with her. "Charlotte," she whispered, and longed for the touch of her new girl.

Charlotte covered the white canvas with white paint. While it was still damp she began an outline in pale green. She didn't

180

know what would emerge from her brush—the ship, a disordered room or a series of portraits in her old fragmented style. She squinted at her canvas, trying to separate her hand from conscious control. The hand, holding a thin sable brush covered with green paint, drew. At last she achieved that moment she'd been reaching for, free of intention. She felt her eyes nearly close. She swayed and regained her balance. She saw long shapes emerge on the canvas, delicately outlined shapes, petals on long stems. When she knew she was painting flowers she allowed her mind to focus, only slightly, as if she could keep part of her brain in the other state. She rubbed the brush in green again, outlining as many flowers as she could until they covered most of the canvas. No vase or bowl, just long stems emerging from the lower border of the canvas, the upper petals disappearing off the top. She swallowed, licked her lips, found her square bristle brush and covered it with white. She prayed the phone wouldn't ring. She hoped it wasn't time for Alex to come home. She felt sweat run down her bare chest. She held her belly with one hand, rubbing small circles where the pain had begun as she had learned to do the previous week in her childbirth class, and with her other hand she dipped her brush, layering white on white, the only thing separating the white of the flowers from the white of the canvas, a thin green line. She used green for the stems too, breaking the line every so often, letting the background white show through. She wanted no rigid borders. She wanted to negate the boundaries of the painting with her paint. She shaded the petals a darker green, and in three places, with pink. For a moment Charlotte's ordinary consciousness returned. She studied the painting. It needed something dark—slight and peripheral—but something dark. She mixed a pinkish brown. She knew she had lost time, but she didn't know how much. She smiled, feeling the unique energy, the power. She went back easily to the other place and added brown to a shadow, to the underside of a low petal resting against the stem, a thin line of it to give the stem dimension. Then, with a white brush in one hand and a green in the other, she painted with both hands, carefully, yet in a kind of frenzy. She had to finish this work today. She was afraid she might forget something. It was not the kind of thing she could do over time.

181

She opened her eyes fully when she realized the room had gotten dark. Avoiding the painting, she went into the bedroom and put on a cotton sundress, a new one she had bought so she could be both comfortable and attractive when Alex came home at night. It was loose enough to hang in soft folds over her body. Charlotte was in her ninth month.

She turned on the lights in the living room, looked at what she had done, and smiled. It was a still life, she realized. After all her words, only this. *Still life.* She smirked at her pun. The white was clearly shaped by the green line and brown shadows. It was a canvas full of gladiolas, the flowers without a card. The ones that must have been from George.

The following evening men were landing on the moon. Aunt Rose and Andre had come over so they could all watch together. The television had been moved into the bedroom, the coolest room in the house, and Charlotte lay spread out on the double bed wearing a thin nightgown, her thighs, stomach and breasts covered with damp towels to ward off the heat. It was the hottest week of the summer and, between the weather and her sweltering, swollen body, Charlotte was nearly faint with exhaustion. They had turned off all the lights to cool down the room as much as possible, and the four of them sat around the pearly light of the television screen, Alex at the foot of the bed, Aunt Rose in the maple rocker, and Andre on the floor, leaning against several pillows propped up against the wall.

On television, white snow veiled a barely visible space capsule while Walter Cronkite described his own excitement, alternating with a narration of the capsule's slow movement toward the moon. Steel rods unfolded from the bottom of the craft and, like the legs of a praying mantis moving slowly toward the ground, remained eerily suspended in dark space as the capsule descended.

Aunt Rose rocked. "On earth people starve to death," she said.

"Ma, can we forget the starving masses for one evening? This is human achievement!" Andre sounded sarcastic. He looked thin. Charlotte was worried about him.

She had told him about Vivian's pregnancy the day after they returned from Massachusetts. Andre had not gone to the funeral.

He had refused to answer Vivian's calls.

"Andre," Charlotte had pleaded. "This doesn't change her feeling for you. She has three, soon four children. She needs security. You know how she was. She wasn't just disappointed when the Party fell apart. She was very young. And I think she felt like her father got the last word. Like her whole life had turned upside down. She really loves you, Andre. She told me."

"She's running away," said Andre. He paced the room, his chin jutting out belligerently, his fists clenched.

"So she's running away," Charlotte had responded. "People run away, Andre. People don't always live up to themselves. Remember Uncle Buck? How you always thought he was so weak?"

"But I was wrong about him, Charlotte." Suddenly he smiled, delighted at his own defeat. "I've been wrong about everything ever since I can remember. Wrong about Pop. Wrong about politics. Wrong about Vivian."

She felt cornered. Everything she said would be twisted to his ends. She felt invisible, as if he would grab an isolated word of hers and inject it into his private dialogue with himself. She reached out to touch his hand. He jerked it away from her.

"And wrong about me. No, Charlotte, she doesn't care about me. Why should she? I'm nothing. I'm a clerk. I was a clerk."

"You quit?" Charlotte looked at him warily.

"Of course," he answered proudly, as if he were describing an act of courage. "I know why she went off and got pregnant. When she saw me again she thought we had a chance together. Then she realized she was wrong. That I couldn't make it—hey, Charlotte, know what I mean?" He punched her shoulder and burst into a long self-loathing laugh.

She had tried to explain to him that he had it all wrong, that Vivian had been pregnant when she first came to New York to see her father.

"You're saying she lied to me?" Andre laughed again. "Come on, Charlotte. You can't make everything okay with a few lies. You of all people should know that."

For weeks, according to Aunt Rose, he had remained in his room all day. He came out at night to eat something, she supposed. "Like a mole-rat," she shivered. "Foraging."

183

They had begged him to watch the moon landing. They had both needled and nagged so much he had finally agreed.

"Here I am, " he said to Alex when he entered the apartment, "thanks to the Harpies."

The capsule descended as slowly as snow. The television snow remained static. "It's coming down! It's coming down!" Walter Cronkite gasped. "My God. It's really coming down!"

Charlotte raised herself with effort onto her elbows so she could see. She moaned from the heat and threw her head back. "Alex," she begged, "I think I'm going to faint." The temperature had been close to 100 for three days. Even at night it dropped only five or six degrees.

Alex seemed not to hear, but Aunt Rose jumped up and pointed her finger at Charlotte. "Just hold on. Don't faint. I'm getting more wet cloths." She disappeared but returned in a moment. Gently, she removed the dry towels from Charlotte's torso and replaced them with damp, cool ones. Charlotte moaned her appreciation. The fires that seemed to be racing over her skin diminished, as if embers were being watered down.

"Alex," Charlotte pushed his back with her toes. "Aunt Rose had to get up. Didn't you even see?"

"Let him watch, *Meideleh,*" Aunt Rose chided. "Men are landing on the moon. If Uncle Buck were here he'd never believe such a story."

"I'm sorry, Charlotte," Alex said, his eyes glued to the set. "But you should watch this. It's a great victory."

Andre laughed. Alex looked at him, annoyed.

"Sshh, sshhh. No arguing," Rose said and returned to the rocker.

Square metal beings with small windows for eyes emerged from a door at the bottom of the space craft. They bounced onto the moonrock and jumped high in the air. A mechanical-sounding grunt came from one of them as he leaped a circle in the greenish light.

"He says it's fun!" shouted Walter. "Well, this is just truly amazing. A major step in man's mastery over nature. A truly grand historical moment."

184

"I don't like it at all," Charlotte complained. "Really, on the moon. God only knows what they'll do now that they're up there. It'll be so different looking up at the moon at night. It feels almost sacrilegious. And what about the ocean?" She felt carried away. "Maybe the waves will be different with men walking all over the moon. And what about my period?" She shoved Alex playfully. "What if they screw up my period? No kidding, Alex. I don't like it at all."

Alex moved away from her nudging toes. "Jesus, Charlotte," he said. "Will you stop relating it all to yourself? And why do you say *they*? It's *us*. *We're* on the moon."

"We are?" she said. "Then why am I so hot?" She lay back and cried, "Oh God."

"What?" Rose jumped up. "A pain?"

"No, Aunt Rose, it's okay. It's just one of the Braxten-Hicks contractions. Not a real one."

"*Braxten-Hicks,*" Rose muttered. "I don't understand that any more than men on the moon."

They were quiet for a while. The moon film had been eclipsed on the twenty-two inch television screen by the distinguished faces of the newscasters. Walter Cronkite and Eric Sevareid informed the American public in awed tones that a miracle had indeed taken place that night. They showed clips of the rocket lifting off days before. An enormous cloud of fire and smoke obliterated everything for a moment so that it was unclear whether the liftoff had been a success or a disaster.

"Fire," Andre said into the silence. "It's more miraculous than the moon. It's everything in one. It turns the dark old ugly moon into light."

"What are you saying? Don't be crazy, Andre," Aunt Rose's eyes met Charlotte's for a second. She looked scared.

"Oh nothing, Mama," Andre said as he rose to his feet and walked out of the room. "I was just thinking about Otharose."

"He's bad," Rose told Alex as soon as he was gone. "What do you think, Alex? Is he bad?"

"He seems to be in trouble again," Alex agreed. "I'll go talk to him. It's over now anyway."

The station replayed the landing, and this time Charlotte

185

watched it with interest. The men moved as if filmed in slow motion. Every time their feet left the ground (but if the ground was the moon what did the word ground mean any more?), it seemed as if they might never return, just keep drifting upward in that weird slow swim-walk in the air. Charlotte couldn't have felt more distant from them. Her world had funneled into her uterus. Even when she'd painted the gladiolas, she had felt as if her eyes were lodged in the uterine wall, x-ray vision eyes looking through flesh at canvas, serenely watching her hand's difficult search for the precise line. Tonight, with men walking in space, bouncing off the moon like the tiny red balls she and Lynda used to use for playing jacks, all she could think about was her own body — not the way her body had once been, not even the baby's body which lumbered rather than floated insider her own, but her body as it was this minute — huge, hot, a weight to contend with every moment of her waking and sleeping life. This was all that existed any more — arid minutes, desert-slow, like the minutes on the moon between the time the astronauts' feet left the ground and returned to it. In several days, they were told, the men would return to earth. After blinding, deafening, shocking moments of re-entry, they would crash into the ocean. It was the most dangerous part of the journey. Now they turned in air (but there was no air). They laughed, or so Cronkite reported, with the lightness of the absence of time. But Charlotte's time warp was heavy. She lived inside a large weight of time, and all she could think of with real interest was the moment, which she presumed must come in a week or two when, in a miraculous historical event, she would be freed. And it was appropriate, she thought — as the moon landing faded to Cronkite again who said, ''Now this,'' making way for a Coke commercial — it was perfectly appropriate that time measurement had become so distorted. In the last nine months she had relived most of her life. All those years in Uncle Buck's and Aunt Rose's apartment stretched behind her perfectly visible, like a beach with no obstruction whose miles are foreshortened to inches when you look back to see the distance you have walked. She knew the details of those twenty years would form the story by which she would understand the meaning of all her coming reality. She felt like a baby, lying in the moist sheets, her legs spread apart, her hair damp with sweat. She pushed the warm towels onto the floor. Her threadbare cotton gown stuck to her breasts and belly. She sat down on the floor near Rose's chair and leaned against her aunt's knees. Rose rocked, and Charlotte's head moved slowly back and forth with the rocking movement.

"You'll be all right." Rose kept her palm on Charlotte's forehead, pressing it against her knee as she rocked. "You've had some bad luck, but you were born with more strength than some people acquire in a lifetime. Look at my Andre. He's no survivor. Who did this to him? Me? The times? I don't understand. But I understand you, Charlotte. We're not blood, but I understand. Soon you'll have a baby. In the fall, we'll have Hannahla back. And, with a little luck, Lynda will reappear before I die. You'll watch them come back and go away again. Like me. And while you wait and watch," Rose stopped the rocking of the chair, "you'll paint."

Charlotte was still. She neither blinked nor swallowed. Her head slipped between Rose's knees and she felt the pressure of thighs against her temples, Then, as if she were being born, her head was lifted into her aunt's hands.

She changed into a bathrobe while Aunt Rose stripped the bed of damp sheets. When they came into the living room, Alex was pacing the floor and draining a glass of white wine. Andre was sitting on the couch, bent over the coffee table, lighting match after match, blowing each one out with tiny gusts of breath so the flame flickered back and forth, back and forth, before it finally disappeared. Each discarded match was added to a pattern he was forming on the coffee table.

It started with crawling on the floor, naked, her breasts and belly grazing the parquet as she moved down the hallway to the bathroom. Like a large animal, she thought, and felt comforted.

Two hours later she was lying on a bed in the labor room breathing in and out with Alex as together they tried to control her pain. As they breathed, he chanting directions at her as he had been instructed to do, she became more and more furious.

"Shut up," she told him after an hour. "Just hold my hand.

Rub my back. Get me ice. I'm not breathing and I'm not blowing. I just want to lie here and scream."

"You've got to try, Charlotte," he urged. "You've got to control the pain."

"Shut up," she said, and she wished Vivian were there.

Dr. Galen came in and sat down on the bed. He began to tell her about his recent trip to the Soviet Union. Once, in a moment of recklessness, Charlotte had allowed herself a sexual fantasy about Dr. Galen, who was in his middle forties, dark haired and handsome. *Dr. Galen lifted the sheet to her thighs and spread her legs with a commanding hand.* She had enjoyed her childhood imagery, turning her examination into sex. Now she told him to shut up too.

"Charlotte!" Alex said, looking embarrassed.

Dr. Galen laughed. He patted Charlotte's thigh. "Oh, it's all right," he assured the husband. "I've heard it all before. Take it easy, Charlotte."

But Charlotte took it hard. It was over fourteen hours later when they wheeled her into the delivery room. She was nearly unconscious with exhaustion and pain. Alex, his graceful frame draped in a large, green hospital smock, his blond hair covered with a cap of the same green, ran behind her as they wheeled her down the halls. As she floated in front of him, he reached over to touch her shoulder, and muttered something she couldn't make out, but she was glad to hear his voice. "Talk," she ordered when he stopped speaking. "What?" he asked, coming up beside her, leaning over to kiss her sweaty forehead as she rolled around a corner. "Talk!" she screamed. She needed his voice, precious vehicle for some kind of peace she had never understood, never known except in his arms, she never figured out why, but there it was, a silence inside her from the sound of his voice. *Talk, talk, talk, talk,* she pleaded, gasping between each shouted word. Alex talked. When she entered the blinding white light of the delivery room and while they lay her on her back, strapped her arms down, lifted her legs into the air, he kept on talking. She had no idea what he was saying, but when she felt herself moved, spread, draped, entered, she heard his voice behind her and although she knew she was dying she felt that to the harmony of his voice that would be all right too.

188

Darkness replaced the white light then, a darkness so narrow she had to keep her body utterly stiff in order not to be bruised by the black walls. She slipped downward, eyes closed, mouth opened, feeling the silky slipping as the dearest comfort she had ever known. She saw Mara's face as she moved down and she called Aunt Rose. Then she whispered, "Mira," and "Ruth," while low in the black hole a steel shelf inside her began to push itself down, out of her, the bottom half of her body tearing away from the top like the discarded part of a spacecraft that has served its purpose and is blown away. She whispered, "Ruth," once more, or so Alex told her later, and as she was blinded by light, deafened by sound, shocked into re-entry, the blackness was gone, the white light turned on again. "It's a boy," Dr. Galen said proudly and she opened startled eyes to see the tiny wrinkled body of her son. There was only a split passing second of loss as she thought the words for the first time, *my son,* and Mira or Ruth drifted back into the blackness she'd left behind.

They placed him on her chest and she raised her hand slow as a low-tide wave rolling onto his tiny head. She tried to breathe evenly to comfort him. She felt the wet satin of his body against hers and at the same time she felt as if she were he, finding firm ground after what must have been as much his trial as her own. Then she remembered something that had happened when she was pushing the head out, in that moment of pain that was greater than any she had imagined. Flat on her back, her legs spread wide apart in the air, she had longed for a foundation, a floor, a ground at the bottom of the tunnel. She would have given her life for it gladly, a place to sit squarely and push. A place where her strength seemed measurable, finite, known. It was a feeling she'd had only when she painted. But when the head came out and the pain dramatically diminished so that she emerged from the darkness and felt the tiny torso between her thighs, she saw that solidity didn't exist at all. On the contrary, everything was mobile, changing, fluid. That was what had always frightened her. She loved the idea that nothing happened without the thing that happened before because it seemed to negate that awful fluidity. But in that moment of making something out of nothing—stories, babies, paintings of the world bounded by the deception of frames—it seemed not to be awful at all. It seemed merely descriptive. She would never possess the whole of anything, once and for all. The realization itself was incomplete, but danced like a white spotlight around the edge of a circle of clarity so compelling the darkened stage around it seemed, for the moment, not to matter at all.

That was what Charlotte saw in the instant, the age of agony that turned the well-lit hospital room into a dark tunnel and back again. But when Alex leaned over them, crying and laughing, running his hand over the back of their child, kissing Charlotte all over her sopping wet face, blocking out the world with his shape, she forgot it again, and she would not retrieve that small piece of knowledge, crucial as it was to her, for fifteen years to come.

They all sat around the table which had been enlarged by the addition of extra leaves, covered with a white linen tablecloth, and laden with dishes of traditional Thanksgiving foods. Rose had taken out her best china and her real silver. Charlotte smelled the mixed aromas of sweet potato pie, almond stuffing, roast turkey and then turned abruptly to the stove where she smelled smoke.

"Ach!" Aunt Rose snorted. She had burned a tray of muffins.

Otharose wore a navy blue gabardine suit, slightly lavender with wear, buttoned up to the throat. The thin edge of a red silk scarf was visible under the collar.

As soon as she arrived, she had walked slowly into her old room followed by Charlotte. Andre was sitting on the bed. The room was a mess again.

"Boy, what are you doing?" Otharose had demanded, leaning on her cane, chastising him as if he were a child. "Look at this mess." She had lifted Andre by his arm to a standing position. He bent down and kissed her head. "Let's clean up before dinner. How're my ghosts supposed to roam free?" Her eyes twinkled.

Andre laughed at her, but he began to straighten up a bit. When they were alone for a minute Otharose whispered to Charlotte, "That boy's in trouble. Does your aunt know?"

At the table Otharose kept a keen eye on Andre, noticing his movements, looking up each time he spoke, and Charlotte kept a keen eye on Otharose.

Next to Rose Moore sat Jacob's daughter Jennifer encased

191

by the tray of her highchair and a large plastic bib covering her white organdy dress. Marilyn, Jennifer's mother, a small, thin woman with dark hair curled into a trim page boy, kept smoothing the bib, holding a cup to the child's lips, and smiling at Jacob, who sat at the head of the table, in Buck's old chair.

"Andre refused it," Rose snapped when Charlotte worried about the older brother's due. "Sometimes I get so impatient with him. So let Jacob sit there. He's got a family. He's doing well. So let him sit at the head."

Aunt Rose, Charlotte and Andre sat on the other side of Jacob, and next to Andre sat Hannah George. She had returned to the city in September after a few months of hitching across the country. (*Hitching?* Rose had shouted. *A girl alone hitches? Is my daughter out of her mind? Are all my children out of their minds?*) But Hannah had come home safe, moved into a sprawling apartment with three other women, and begun working for a committee to end the war in Vietnam. She earned just enough to pay her share of the rental and often had to eat at her mother's or Charlotte's house.

She had been very excited when Charlotte showed her the Mara and George notebooks. "I love the mixture of truth and what you made up," she said. "Do you think it's true about Mara and my father? God, Charlotte. We never really knew any of them." She tried to convince Charlotte, who was still overweight and out of shape from her pregnancy, to exercise with her and eat health foods. So far, Charlotte had refused, but every time she looked at Hannah's strong, slim body she was tempted to give in. Her black curls were shaped into a long, disheveled Afro. She wore large, red-framed eyeglasses. She dressed casually, in the costume of newly liberated women, but her tee shirt was a beautiful shade of aquamarine, her corduroys were pressed, and her high boots were tied with blue laces that almost perfectly matched the shade of her shirt.

"Don't you dress for Thanksgiving?" Rose had said when Hannah came in. "And don't you brush your hair, Hannahla? What's wrong with you?"

"I'm dressed, Mama," Hannah answered, looking down at her pressed pants, obviously hurt.

"Aunt Rose!" Charlotte came to her cousin's defense. "Hannah looks beautiful. Her hair is perfectly in style."

"Relax, Mama," Andre said, putting his arm around Rose. "This is a special occasion. Almost like Passover. Hannah looks fine."

Charlotte had never seen him so paternal. His calm tone disturbed her. "What are you feeling so good about, Andre?" she questioned him, suspicious.

"Can't I feel good?" he laughed. "I feel good, that's all." He took a seat next to his younger brother.

In the middle of the main course the bell rang and everyone assumed it was Myron who was coming late from a concert. But it was a telegram from Lynda. *Mama, everyone,* it said. *I wish I could be there. I miss you all. Kiss the little ones for me, especially Ivan, our newest arrival. Maybe I'll be home for Christmas. Love. Lynda.*

The telegram came from Stockholm where Lynda was covering the trial of the American government for crimes against humanity in Vietnam.

"A telegram we get." Rose pocketed the yellow paper and helped herself to more meat. "Here, Hannah," she pushed. "You don't eat meat. So eat more vegetables." She spooned string beans onto Hannah's plate.

"Lynda's living her own life, Mama. That's what you always told us to do," Jacob reminded her from his magisterial seat.

"We lose our children one way or another." Otharose reached across the table and patted Aunt Rose's hand. Rose looked resigned to mourning, the way Charlotte remembered her looking the day Buck died. "They leave. They die. Or they change into something we can't recognize. Here, Sugar." She handed Jennifer a corn muffin covered thickly with butter. The child reached for it eagerly. Marilyn smiled, looked at Jacob and shrugged.

"No, Marilyn," Jacob objected. "No, I'm sorry, Rose. No bread before dinner. That's what we always tell her. We'll just confuse her by giving it now." Marilyn returned the muffin to the platter and pushed some green beans across the plate toward Jennifer, who began to scream and kick her feet.

"So give her a little bread this time?" There was deference

193

in Aunt Rose's tone, which Charlotte didn't like at all.

"Come on, Jacob," Charlotte tried to be harsh. "It's Thanksgiving, for Christsakes."

Sensing the pathway to bread and butter through their disagreements, Jennifer began to scream louder, "I want bread!"

Jacob shot Charlotte an irritated glance. He rose from his seat and pulled his daughter out of her highchair. He put her in the girls' old room, shut the door, and walked back to his seat. Piercing cries began from behind the locked door. "She'll stop in a minute," he told them calmly and sat down to finish his meal.

"You're a tyrant, Jacob," said Hannah. She pushed her glasses up the bridge of her nose. "Marilyn, don't let him tyrannize you. Why'd you give in to him?" The way she said *tyrant* reminded Charlotte of the day, years before, when Rose had dismissed Leon.

"Hannah, would you please mind your own business? I raise my children my own way. You don't have to agree." Jacob didn't sound angry, only certain.

"She can express an opinion, Jacob, no? In this house we always expressed opinions." Rose had clearly expected Buck's spirit to emanate from his chair. "Your father always encouraged the expressing of opinions, no matter what," she continued, in case he hadn't gotten the point.

Jacob was not even thirty, though he seemed much older than that. His hair was well cut and he wore a neatly trimmed beard which, along with the formal blue shirt and tie, added years to his appearance. He wore rimless glasses, exactly like Buck's.

"Need I say I am not my father?" he answered, the first trace of annoyance in his voice.

"May he rest in peace, Jacob," said Otharose. "Remember the day he died? How upset you were? I've never seen a child so upset. Not Charlotte. Not Andre. Not even Lynda. You were the most upset of all. I knew because your hand was clammy with sweat. Old folks say sweaty hands indicate a deep upset." Otharose wiped her long, pale palms with a linen napkin. "I can still feel the sweat in my hands from holding yours."

From between Otharose and the empty chair at the foot of the table which was reserved for Myron, Alex sighed audibly. He shaded his forehead with his hand. They all knew what his sigh meant—here were the dead, without whom no Cohen reunion was ever complete. Here were the ghosts, the past. Charlotte felt no pity for her husband's discomfort. She had warned him. Ghosts aren't that easy to dismiss.

On the way uptown to pick up Otharose for the Thanksgiving dinner, Charlotte had tried once again to imagine the deaths of Mara and George. She wanted a final scene, to leave it all behind. When she nursed Ivan at two or three in the morning, the city silent, only a few windows across the avenue shining with yellow light, Charlotte felt calm. Her body softened in the dark, muscles loose, one palm cradled around Ivan's small buttucks, her fingers tracing lightly the puffy undersides of tiny pink toes. Alex wanted her to be done with it, and she pretended to him that she was.

But she could never imagine their deaths. Aunt Rose couldn't help her with this part. Charlotte had nothing to go on. The story was on the shelf, unfinished. The "Gladiolas" hung over the kitchen table, unsatisfying to Charlotte, partial.

The slightly sour smell of the river had blown into the car. But if she turned her face the other way, toward the park, she could smell the dry leaves of late autumn. She thought about burning leaves in the country. The thought was so strong she smelled the sweet musty aroma of the smoke. (It was the first of three times that Charlotte smelled smoke that night.)

She closed the car window all the way as Ivan began to whimper. She unbuttoned her coat and blouse and unhooked the flap of her nursing bra. Ivan was a strong sucker, she was told by the more experienced mothers she'd met in the park when the weather was still warm and the benches were lined with women nursing infants, feeding toddlers plastic bottles of juice, handing them crackers and raisins. Ivan was three months old. He'd be up to juice soon.

"This is gonna be quite a reunion," Alex sounded wary.

"Everyone except Lynda. Too bad Vivian and her family couldn't come. But everyone else—all the living anyway. And the usual ghosts."

"There's a new generation, Charlotte. There are Jacob's kids. Now Ivan. Maybe the Cohens could let the ghosts rest for once."

195

Ever since the summer and her story's last installment, Alex had argued for transcendence, for final burial. "You can't live in the past, Charlotte. If you're this obsessed, there's something unresolved," he warned. "Maybe you should go into therapy."

Charlotte thought she would, as soon as Ivan was a year old. Now, she lived too much without words to contemplate describing her life every week. She felt rushed into feelings she couldn't name. She had never loved anyone as intensely as she loved Ivan. Yet there were moments when she hated him as well. Once, when she had been trying to paint all afternoon and had been interrupted ten or fifteen times by his cries, she began to scream at him until he was screaming too. He stiffened and turned red, gathering his wet, crumpled sheet into desperate fists, his feet jabbing the air in rhythm to his convulsive cries. Charlotte fell into a rounded ball of rage on the floor near him. She pounded her head, pulled her hair in gestures she remembered from movies about the mentally ill. She could not calm him. She could not bear to hear him cry. She could not help him at all and this was one mystery she could not handle. For a moment she thought she might slap him. But when she stood up she saw green shit running down his leg and her heart raced with relief. That was it then! That was the reason. His stomach had been upset. The storm of confusion settled, impotence ebbed. She wept as she bathed him, changed him, listening to his cries placidly now, because she knew that as soon as he was clean she could nurse him into a peaceful slumber. They fell asleep on her bed curled into each other, his lips caressing her breast as she stroked his fine brown hair.

Charlotte knew perfectly well her rages at Ivan were connected with Mara and George. She saw Mara's face whenever she screamed. But she couldn't talk of it to anyone, not to Alex who might think her a bad mother, certainly not to a strange therapist. She painted a series of dark, carefully planned abstractions of windows. She tried to picture the deaths of Mara and George.

Charlotte had looked forward to the reunion, but as usual she was worried about Andre. He had refused to emerge from his room once again for weeks, and tonight, if he didn't come out for dinner, Charlotte intended to insist. She wouldn't allow him to indulge himself any more. She expressed her intention to Alex as they turned off the West Side Drive onto the dark winding streets of Washington Heights.

"Andre needs to be in a hospital," Alex told her. "He's severely depressed, Charlotte. I think he needs medication."

"Are you kidding, Alex?" she exploded. "We've got to get him to a therapist, I know. But not a hospital where they'll burn out his brain." She had begun researching therapists who followed the ideas of R. D. Laing. She had found one in Philadelphia and had his name and number with her. She would give Andre the number tonight.

"I don't agree," Alex insisted. "He's beyond therapy right now. But far be it from me to argue with a Cohen."

"Oh Alex, you know you love my family. And you're part of us. Everyone respects you."

"Aunt Rose is always asking my advice, then she never listens."

"Aunt Rose never listens to anyone, Alex."

"Well, she'd better listen to me on this. And give me a little credit for knowing my business, Charlotte. Andre's in big trouble. He's a baby who never left home. At the age of almost thirty, he still feels guilty about hating his father. And you know what, Charlotte? I really think Andre is homosexual. That's what's eating away at him."

She was flooded with all the past conversations, Vivian's remarks, Andre's own sneering references to his love for Myron, Uncle Buck calling such men fags, pansies and queers. Yet she had never taken it seriously, nor imagined the anguish he must be in. "Maybe he's really sick" she murmured, afraid Alex might be right after all.

"I agree with the analysts who say it isn't a sickness," Alex continued, trying to comfort her now. "But Andre has to face it."

"Andre will never face it," she said, feeling a wash of anxiety as she realized this was the truth. "He can't face it, if you mean look at it squarely, accept it, take it like a man? He'll look at it sideways, run away, then sneak back for another peek. He'll never find a peaceful solution. He's at war, Alex. Some wars never end. Like mine with my parents. We have an uneasy truce, but they'll be back. I know it."

"You're working yourself up, Charlotte, keeping things going too long. History isn't everything. Look, I'm a therapist, take my word for it. There are people who finds ways to transcend the past. I'm one of them, Charlotte. I know I can never make over my rotten childhood, but I'm not obsessed with it either. It's over. I go on from there." He turned into the circular driveway of the nursing home. Alex lived as he swam, Charlotte had thought, as she handed him the sleeping Ivan and buttoned her blouse. Efficiently. Always trying to keep one eye open so he was assured of his direction. Figure things out and move on. That was the secret of health.

"But Andre doesn't have your strength. He starts out behind," she had told him. "Ghosts aren't that easy to dismiss." Then she had walked to the desk in the lobby to ring Otharose's room.

"Well, I agree with Alex," Jacob said as he rose from the table. "Let the dead rest." He went into the bedroom, and they all realized that Jennifer had stopped crying. Jacob returned with her in his arms, wiped her eyes with a damp paper towel, and handed her to her mother. Marilyn gathered her into her lap and began to feed her string beans which Jennifer ate swiftly. Then she said, "Now I have bread?"

Jacob nodded and Marilyn buttered a large piece.

"God!" Hannah exclaimed, and lit a cigarette.

"God what?" Jacob asked as if he were genuinely inquisitive. "God, she's learning obedience? God, she's learning healthy eating habits? God, she's learning manners? Exactly what god are you appealing to, Hannah?"

"The god of independence," she retorted. "The rebel god. The god of anti-fascism."

"Oh, for the love of Pete. Now I'm a fascist. Why are we always so measured in this family?" Jacob cut a neat slice of turkey from the large drumstick on his plate.

Alex leaned his forearms on the table in a way that made Charlotte know he was about to speak. She feared what he was about to say.

"Well, I thought you handled that very well, Jake," Alex said. "You weren't harsh. You were clear."

"The voice of mental health," Charlotte grumbled. "And who the hell is Jake?"

They were about to start arguing when Ivan woke up and began to cry from his carriage in the hall. In a few seconds, his crying woke the other baby, Jacob's younger daughter, Annie. Marilyn and Charlotte rose from the table and, fingers on blouse buttons, headed toward their respective carriages. They carried the babies into the bedroom off the kitchen where some changing apparatus had been arranged. As soon as they began nursing, all noise from the bedroom ceased.

"Peace," Andre said. He put his arm around his sister, reached over to pat his brother's hand.

"Is that a prayer, a description, or a command?" Hannah nuzzled his neck and scratchy cheek.

"All three," he said, pulling Hannah and Jacob toward each other.

"What's with you, Andre?" Jacob asked. "You're not known as the peacemaker of the family." But Jacob seemed relieved. He smiled at Hannah. She got up to hug him, messed his hair so roughly that she knocked off his glasses.

"I feel peaceful tonight," said Andre. "I feel very happy having you all here."

Listening to the conversation from the nearby bedroom, Charlotte looked up at Andre's remark and through the frame of the open door she met the alarmed eyes of Otharose.

Just as they were all sitting down in the living room, Aunt Rose, Hannah and Marilyn finishing the cleaning up, the bell rang.

"Myron. At last." Andre jumped up and went to the door.

Myron was still not handsome, but he looked much better than he had as an adolescent. Old scars and crevices from acne gave a rugged cast to his face. His dark hair was long and combed back from his forehead in shining waves. He wore a dark suit and a white shirt opened at the collar. He lay his flute on the table and began hugging them one by one. When he embraced Charlotte he whispered, "You're beautiful as ever." She introduced him to Alex, indicated Ivan with pride.

"Oh, it's good to be having a party in this house again,"

199

Myron said. He sat down next to Andre and patted his friend's thigh. Myron's jazz band had played that evening at a local club. "I think there were more musicians than audience," he smiled, "and everyone was eating turkey while we played, but it was good. The music was great. Our clarinetist is superb."

Rose brought him a heaping plate of food which he accepted gratefully, listening all the while to the facts of all their lives for which Myron seemed as hungry as he was for the turkey and sweet potato pie. He insisted on hearing Otharose's news.

"At my age, there's not much news," she said with no resentment. "I eat, I sleep, every so often I watch T.V."

Before the evening was over, maybe when they took her back uptown, Charlotte was determined to ask Otharose about the old letters. Maybe there was someting in them she could use to finish her story. With all of them sitting there again, Charlotte was thinking about a mural. The "Gladiolas" were clearly not sufficient. Impulsively, she got up and walked into her old room.

There it was, hanging on the far wall, curling at the edges — all their faces, ten years before, all the history that had contained their lives. Charlotte removed the tacks and rolled the canvas into a tight tube. She taped the edge and carried it out to the kitchen. "I'm taking this. Okay?" she announced to Aunt Rose. "It's my mural. I need to use it."

"It's yours," Rose replied. "Take it if you want it. You're doing another one, Charlotte? When will you have time, with the baby?"

"I'll find some time," Charlotte answered. "Thanks, Aunt Rose."

A chilly breeze drifted into the living room. Charlotte walked over to close the window and remained for a moment looking out at the fire escape. She heard the sound of Andre's guitar and thought it was the past again. But he had picked up his instrument, and Myron was taking out his flute.

"Oh, wonderful! Yes, play," Hannah shouted. "Oh, Alex, Marilyn. Wait until you hear them."

"Maybe you should play out there. The neighbors probably missed us all these years." Charlotte nodded at the fire escape.

"No," Andre said, too earnest to match her joke. "Not the fire escape. Not tonight."

They began with some of the old union songs and ballads from the Spanish Civil War. Then they moved to civil rights and peace songs, which Andre and Charlotte sang in harmony while he played soft chords and Myron played the melody on the flute. They played the old song about Ireland, and Andre sang alone. When he reached the line about the language that the strangers did not know and looked at her, Charlotte's eyes filled with tears.

"What ever happened to Brian?" she asked when they finished.

They all teased her and she blushed. Alex looked confused and Hannah jabbed him playfully in the arm. "Old loves," she announced grandly.

"He lives in Berkeley," Myron said. "He's married and has a baby. He's a doctor, Charlotte."

She smiled, curled into her chair. "Play that song one more time," she said.

After a while Andre put down his guitar. "Now for some real music. Okay, Myron? Come on." He walked to the archway that separated the living room from the kitchen and leaned against the wall.

Myron stood near the window in front of the fire escape. They all turned toward him while he played a haunting Beethoven sonata. Charlotte's emotions swayed easily between melancholy and joy.

Everyone applauded so enthusiastically that he agreed to play again. "Oh, Myron. You are truly wonderful," Hannah gasped. "Isn't he wonderful, Mama?"

"Myron was always a special person. "Aunt Rose stated an objective fact. "He's a real friend. A week doesn't pass that he doesn't come for dinner. And it's not always so nice, like tonight, I can tell you. Aren't I right, Myron? Sometimes it's pretty grim."

She glanced at Andre to make certain he wasn't offended. But he wasn't there. In the moment that they all looked over and discovered Andre's absence, Charlotte, for the third time that evening, smelled smoke.

"God!" Jacob leaped out of his chair. "Smoke!"

Andre's door was locked. A dark mist seeped under the crack, filling the hallway. Jacob moved back down the hall and ran at the door. It burst open and they were choked by huge gusts of smoke. The curtains, the bed, the papers were in flames.

The fire department had come soon enough to save the rest of the apartment. Only Otharose's old room was destroyed. But an acrid smell permeated the air, hung from the walls, emanated from the rugs.

Alex and Myron had followed Jacob into the room and dragged Andre out. Jacob thought to slam the door behind them to contain the flames. The three men carried him out to the street while Rose rushed behind them, leaning on Hannah George, moaning, "My God, My God, *mein ingeleh,* my little boy."

Alex had screamed, "Get Ivan! Get the babies!" But Marilyn was already clutching one child in each arm, Charlotte holding onto Ivan as tightly as she'd ever held anything in her life. With her elbows she shoved Otharose ahead of her, nudging her along with whispers. "Come on, Otharose. Walk fast, Otharose. We've got to get to the street." When they finally made it to the lobby, Otharose stopped still. She leaned on her cane and said to Charlotte, "No hurry, Sugar. I know the smell of Ole Man Death. He's been here all night."

Charlotte raced past Otharose to the street where fire engines already gathered. Two firemen climbed up and entered the apartment through the fire escape. Andre was placed on a stretcher as soon as the ambulance arrived. His left arm and the left side of his face were black with burns. By the time he arrived at the hospital, Andre was dead.

Charlotte painted them all against a dark brown with purple shadows, only the faces in detail. Their bodies were merely streaks of white paint, as if they were all dressed in shrouds. She painted them as they appeared to her at his funeral when she said her few words. She didn't care if no one ever liked or even saw the painting. If she didn't paint, she felt she might die too, just go to sleep and slip away to Andre. Alex remarked that he never saw her so driven. She was hardly able to hear Ivan's cries. She worked in a frenzy, trying to reach a quiet place, witness to a history she could neither understand nor leave behind.

Lynda, who had arrived the day of the funeral, left a week later to return to Stockholm. She seemed like a world traveler, somehow rushed, radiating a distance that none of them could penetrate. She supported her mother's arm throughout the ceremony, but when Charlotte and Alex took her to the airport, she boarded the plane long before departure time. She seemed like a stranger. None of them felt, later, that she had really been home.

Jacob was strong, attending to arrangements, ordering flowers, supervising the cleaning out of Otharose's old room.

Hannah moved in with her mother for a month, someone to be there in the middle of the night.

Aunt Rose was broken. Her portrait was at the center of the mural, large and gaunt. Charlotte tried to capture the expression of resignation in paint. "My son was no survivor," Rose repeated many times during the initial days of shock. "My son," she would cry and retreat, sobbing, to the burnt-out room.

They had rummaged through the ashes looking for remnants of Andre — an explanation, a farewell, even an accusation. Vivian finally discovered a note, singed at the edges, in the back of a drawer. They would never know if he had forgotten to take it out or had mixed feelings about them finding it. It said: *It's not Pop who was too weak. It was always me. I know you will get me to a hospital no matter what, Mama. But I plan to be Dead on Arrival. And that's how my life has always felt to me. It's not your fault. I'm tired of hurting you.* Then there were explicit directions for his funeral.

Charlotte was the only speaker. She had clutched the dark wood podium, trying not to fall, telling them how much she had loved him. "With him, I never felt I was a stranger," she said. "With Andre, I never felt adopted." She told them about the Irish ballad and the line Andre loved.

Then she looked over at Myron who stood up from his second row corner seat and played the song on his flute.

The coffin rested on a metal platform on wheels. When the pallbearers rose to push it down the aisle of the long austere room, Aunt Rose stood up and waved them away.

"I brought him into the world," she said. "I'll take him out."

And taking her place at the head of the coffin, leaning into the metal bar for leverage, wiry curls scattered untended all over her forehead and cheeks, she pushed her son out of the room.

Book Three

Charlotte's Place

By any conventional standards Charlotte Cohen was not a good wife. She did not assume Alex's personal needs were her own: she neither bought his clothes nor remembered his appointments. It was difficult for her, especially when she was in the middle of a painting, to demonstrate the calm spirit or convey the lucid directions which are generally associated with high standards of domestic efficiency. From the very first day of his life she was passionate about her child, but it took her several years of hard work to learn how to be a good mother.

Charlotte was accustomed to testing limits in order to probe her feelings to the greatest possible depth and thereby find something new and interesting to paint. Her tendency, therefore, was to become amused, then angry, when Ivan overstepped limits out of curiosity or mischief. There was chaos in the house before Charlotte acknowledged the reasonableness of Alex's pleas.

"We can't live like this," he told her, shoving an armful of brightly colored plastic toys to the side of the room. "You tell him to take out one toy at a time and then you let him bring everything he owns into the living room. You tell him he has to be in bed by seven and you pick him up as soon as he makes a peep. There has to be some consistency, Charlotte."

But it was not the argument of consistency that swayed her. No more than when she was a child could Charlotte tolerate disorder. She was at her wit's end with her failure to manage the natural chaos of a toddler. Gratefully, she allowed Alex to take over certain issues of Ivan's developing discipline. He bought boxes of various sizes in bright colors and stacked them in Ivan's room. Over time, and daily, every evening when he returned from work, Alex ordered his son's belongings with the same care he gave to garden rows of vegetables and spice. He achieved no miracles; Ivan remained as messy as most children. It was the father's patience and dedication that accounted for the order of the nursery.

He was equally determined about rules and regulations. At eight o'clock Ivan was put to bed and the door to his room closed. No amount of screaming could alter the father's resolve. Even when Ivan crawled out of bed and banged on the door Alex would only shout from the living room an encouraging, "We're right here, Ivan, but you can't come out." For several weeks the tearful pleading lasted for fifteen minutes. Then after a period of silence, Charlotte and Alex would tiptoe to the room where small fingers could be seen reaching out under the crack in the door. "The Count of Monte Cristo is asleep," Alex would announce. He'd ease the door open and lift his son gently into bed.

Charlotte marveled at the impenetrability of Alex's resolve. He was, she knew, a rock against which his patients' imaginative neuroses battered themselves until they were spent. He would never budge. Mistaking her own needs for her child's, she submitted to Alex's methods. Only much later in Ivan's life would she use this incident as a cause for one of her many maternal regrets. Then, she covered her head with pillows or went out for a walk. The sound of Ivan's screams was a lever pushing open doors in her brain behind which other screams were released until Charlotte's head felt like a long, dark tunnel through which grating, unplaceable noise echoed. She thought she would go mad.

"Just shut him out," Alex advised. "He'll be fine. You're too receptive, Charlotte. You can't give everything equal access in your mind."

It was not the content of the advice, which she could never heed, but the echo of Uncle Buck's voice which calmed Charlotte. She stuffed her ears with cotton and felt contented in her choice of a husband.

Charlotte Cohen never changed her name and that fact, along with her domestic failures, caused some of Alex's friends to pity him. "Charlotte *Cayne?*" she would scoff when people asked her why she did not comply with the usual symbol of the marital bond. "Who the hell is Charlotte *Cayne?*" To their son they bequeathed a name symbolic of each important piece of his heritage: he was Ivan (after Buck) Martin (after Mara) Cayne (after Alex), and the parents were content with this arrangement.

"This is Charlotte Cohen, my wife," and later, at the height of feminist consciousness of naming, "my partner," Alex would say proudly whenever he introduced her to anyone. "The painter," he would add, as if she were known. Charlotte would blush and look down at her toes. But she depended on Alex's pride. As much as he disapproved of her need to re-create in words the story of her parents, as intensely (fearfully, Charlotte thought) as he objected to any sign in her of obsession with her family, he understood completely and instinctively the demands of translating her experience into the images of her art. Like most analysts, Alex was infatuated with the idea of creativity. He saw her, Charlotte sometimes suspected, as his private laboratory for the book he wanted to write some day on the making of art. More even than herself, he guarded the privacy of her studio, a small, bright room in the back of the apartment, and he trained Ivan not to enter that sanctum without the permission of his mother.

Charlotte thought the whole situation was nothing short of miraculous. Her artist friends were awed by Alex's encouragement and support of her work. "A regular Leonard Woolf," they remarked. She was aware of her domestic faults, that she fell short of the highest standards of wifely virtue, but she was an ardent lover to Alex, and a good friend. She learned to keep her obsessions about her family history to herself. (Perhaps he was sick of such stories after listening in his office all day long.) She enjoyed, however, the life stories of his patients, admiring the way he gingerly separated strength from neurosis as if he were loosening the multiple twists and turns of Ivan's always knotted shoelaces.

Charlotte liked Alex's slender torso and long, slightly gangly arms as much as ever. Nestling in them at night she felt a serenity more complete than she had ever known and in her head a silence which existed despite the noise of the street, the rustling of unfinished paintings, the whining of ghosts. And if she felt an undeniable distance even at the height of their passion, she attributed it to the boundaries they allowed each other and the growing importance of her always private internal world. Contrary to the opinions of her friends who considered her deprived of the thrilling fevers of true erotic passion, Charlotte believed that edge of distance from her intelligent and devoted husband to be a necessary and valuable condition of both her art and abiding love.

Charlotte remembered the first time she knew that the characters she was accustomed to casting in her erotic fantasies were masks for herself. The realization had come on a night when her painting had opened her. (She remembered the opening in the image of an ice wall which suddenly returned to water and dripped away.) Charlotte imagined the opening, saw the wall melt, and knew it had been some time since she had felt that way. Perhaps since Andre died.

For the first few years after his death, she did not go to the grave. As Ivan moved through his early years, she thought less about death than ever before. When he entered kindergarten and they no longer had to pay for an all-day nursery, she quit her teaching job and began to work as a substitute, using two days of every week to paint. During the first year, she painted a series called "Horizons." Each painting consisted of long, broken, angular shapes of muted color. Pinks, pale greens and browns reached from one end of the canvas to the other. The "Horizons" resulted in her first participation in a group show of women artists at a Soho gallery for which she received one rave review in a daily newspaper and one respectful mention in an art magazine. Alex was extremely proud, then dismayed when, soon after the opening, Charlotte sank into a depression which, after three months, had become a chronic gloom. She felt undone by her moderate success. She couldn't paint. Substitute teaching emphasized her sense of a fragmentary existence. There was no coherence or order to the history she taught. One day she'd be called upon to teach the American Revolution, the next week it was Ancient Rome. She had approached in her art the edge of the world. She'd been encouraged, applauded, was scared and withdrew to a familiar place.

She dreamed, once again, of Andre. She was chasing him. She was losing him. She heard him sing. His death seemed to proclaim a failure in her so gigantic there was no reprieve, a verdict of guilty for which there was no appeal. Then the verdict turned into a plea; she pleaded for guilt which had become redemption. She stared for hours on end.

For the first time since his death, Charlotte began to visit Andre's grave. She sat near the tombstone and talked to him, sang to him, cried. She placed her hands on the earth and longed for the obliteration of boundaries.

Alex approached her one Saturday as she dressed and prepared to go to the cemetery.

"You work all week, Charlotte. Sundays you have classes to plan. Ivan misses you. I miss you."

"Alex." There was a look of impatience in her eyes, as if she had already left. "I'll be back by three, four at the latest. I have to change the flowers. I need to go, Alex." She turned to adjust her scarf.

She was going with Myron. She had begged him to come and play the flute.

"God," Alex sounded out of control the way only Charlotte's private obsessions could make him. "It's morbid. He's dead. You hardly pay any attention to us. You haven't painted in months."

Charlotte said nothing. She knew she was almost done. But she had to finish something. She needed to go one more time.

She stood by the grave, dry eyed, as Myron played the old music. Every time she had come in the past year, Charlotte had chronicled her guilt. *Maybe if I had shared your secrets more, like when Uncle Buck got the cashier's job. Maybe if I had paid more attention to your loving Vivian. Maybe if I had tried to convince her to leave David. Maybe if I hadn't had Ivan just when I did.* "Were you really lovers when we were kids?" she asked Myron.

He shifted his long body uneasily. He stroked his throat with a large hand, adjusted his collar, buttoned the top button of his shirt. "Once," he said, and scuffed some dirt with his toe. "Just once. I was very confused about sex. I loved Andre more than anything else in the world. My parents were so old—immigrants, but not like Aunt Rose was an immigrant. Real immigrants. They

211

spoke only Yiddish to me, did you know that Charlotte? Your family was like some exotic, wonderful planet I had come upon in outer space. The politics! The way they talked to children! The love! I adored all of them. But I really loved Andre. Just as I've always loved you." He said it straightforwardly, an emotion to which he'd long ago become accustomed and had no trouble revealing. "I was not the most attractive adolescent, as you may remember."

Charlotte looked up at the tall, bony man. His long nose and dark eyes conveyed sternness, contrasting a mouth that seemed always about to smile. His forehead was a series of broad angular planes. The acne scars on his cheeds were fading as he aged.

"Girls wouldn't have much to do with me. I did have strong feelings for Andre. Andre — well, I never figured it out. I think he was probably in love with Vivian all his life. But I was the only one he could confess to and he had lots to confess. One night he began crying after he told me about how much he hated his father. Of course he didn't hate Buck. He just felt he could never live up to his expectations. He started telling me about how much he loved his father. I think he was in love with Buck in a way. But there I was, filled with my own passion for him and his family and we sort of fell into each other's arms. Next thing we knew we were kissing and after that we were touching each other and, well, and all the rest. I was such an oddball already, Charlotte. Somehow I wasn't that surprised. I was homosexual for the next five years or so. And now, occasionally." He shrugged. "But Andre was deeply ashamed. I always felt partly responsible for his death."

Charlotte told him about all the confessions she had made on this spot. She told him about the "Horizons" and the guilt she did not confess to Alex for fear of upsetting him. "But what would your confession be?" she asked. "Maybe if I hadn't loved you so much? You were always there. You always stood by him, right up to the end, like Aunt Rose said. You have nothing to be ashamed of, Myron."

Abruptly, he pulled her into his arms. He began to cry and they sank to their knees, rocking, each of them calling Andre. Then they began to laugh. "He'd think we were nuts," Charlotte said.

They sat cross-legged on either side of the grave. She took some long-stemmed roses and a wilted bunch of daisies from her canvas bag and placed them in a criss-cross pattern over the earth.

"Are you happy, Charlotte?" Myron asked.

"Yes," she answered quickly. "Alex has made me happier than I've ever been in my life. And having Ivan has made me feel I belong here, not off climbing the Pyrenees somewhere. I just wish I could find the energy to paint more. But with Ivan, and the job—"

Myron stared at her. A possessiveness in his eyes stirred her until she felt the opening inside, the wall melting. Charlotte stood up and brushed off her skirt.

"My life has a lot of death in it. It's made me scared of the world. Alex makes me safe. The world strikes him as ordinary, controllable." She paused, searching for words. "He never seems to stand back in awe, he's never struck impotent, or dumb, by it all." She gestured toward the sky, the ground.

Myron stood up. "I think we've completed our ritual," he said with the habitual half-smile of a patient man.

Charlotte kept her promise to Alex and did not return to Andre's grave. She complied with his request to go to a therapist and began seeing one named Clara. But Charlotte was so taken with the woman and so engaged by the process of self- exploration that Alex did not have to convince her to stay. She didn't exactly feel happier after working for several months with Clara, only determined to retrieve control of her life. Hannah helped her learn to run and diet until Charlotte could do an easy two miles and was thin for the first time since Ivan's birth.

She applied herself to organizing her house. She transformed Ivan's nursery into a little boy's room, buying and painting furniture, throwing out tiny blocks and small wooden animals and replacing them with puzzles, books and a set of electric trains. She bought him dolls and a carriage which infuriated Aunt Rose. "Are you trying to make him into a *fegaleh?*" she said. Charlotte painted walls, tore through closets, wiped shelves clean, boxed old clothes to give away. Finally, she piled a mountain of photographs on the dining room table and worked for days until they had all been ordered chronologically into three thick albums. The night she finished the last album, she and Alex made love. When he touched her she felt burned, as if her skin were turning an instant blazing red, an infant's first exposure to the sun.

"I've always loved you, Alex," she told him that night, "and I always will."

He had never asked her to explain her pain. He had tended her from a distance, assuming responsibility for the house and much of Ivan's care. There were times when she hated Alex for his infuriating tending, his unbreakable, patient reserve. He had left her underground, kept alive in a prison of maddening remoteness, impenetrable to her Count-of-Monte-Cristo cries. But now it seemed as if he had been watering a dying plant, refusing to give up on the browning leaves, unperturbed by its scrawny ugliness. "Welcome home," he said that night, and the following evening he had come home laden with two canvasses and a new set of paints.

With those paints Charlotte began a new series that she liked much better than the "Horizons." She painted self-portraits—some nude, some dressed, some of her face. To these ten she added the painting of her family after Andre's death and "Gladiolas," accompanied by a written description of their meaning: "These are the flowers I imagine my father to have given my mother at my birth," she wrote. "The painting represents my attempt to reconcile their differences in myself."

The gallery that had shown "Horizons" was happy to welcome her back, having received such good notices the first time. But the critics hated her second show, called her self-indulgent and reductively autobiographical as they were calling many women artists that year. Charlotte felt far stronger in the face of this condemnation than she had two years before in the face of her limited success. She told Clara she felt solid, as if they had pushed her to a place where she had to stand or bend. (She remembered feeling that way the first time Alex had failed to understand her, and during her old arguments with Uncle Buck.)

"You are beginning to claim your own powers. You are burying your dead," said Clara prematurely. Still, it felt like a graduation to Charlotte. The two women embraced for the first time

214

at the end of that session and when, a month later, Charlotte became depressed again (as she now knew she would after the completion of every series) Clara didn't accuse her of masochism, as Alex might. "Well," she shrugged, as if to the inevitable mystery of life, "it's like this, back and forth. Let's start again."

Soon afterwards, Myron spoke to a friend and helped Charlotte get a job at an art college so that she could both work part-time and experience a consistency of presentation. It was the teaching that kept Charlotte from succumbing again to that wretchedness between vanity and blighted hope. Teaching was a reasonable enterprise — you provided students with encouragement and technical direction and they forced you to transcend your moods in *their* self-portraits. They admired you out of all proportion and were grateful for the smallest amount of attention. Good teaching was not a matter of taste, or politics, or fashion. You were praised for a job well done.

At the college, for the first time, Charlotte had become friends with many other artists, including a woman named Sybila Abele who became her most trusted critic. She had come to the United States from Latvia when she was a girl, been raised on a farm in Michigan, and moved to New York at twenty determined to make her way as an artist. After a short, failed marriage which left her with a daughter to support, Sybila had gone to school to become a librarian. She sculpted at night — long, lean clay women and tall abstract forms made of tree branches. Sturdy yet slender pieces of wood reached almost to the ceiling of her studio and were tied together with carefully placed twine. Even the knots of the twine, Sybila showed Charlotte, were tied with attention to comparative size, so that they became smaller as they moved toward the top of the stick.

"Are they boats?" Charlotte moved her hands through the various shaped spaces created by string and wood.

"Who knows," Sybila answered distractedly. "Yes. I guess they could be boats. I'm interested in the contrast between the definiteness of the wood and the open space outlined in string."

"Riggings," Charlotte insisted.

"You have a strange mind for a painter." Sybila sounded

215

delighted by this ambiguity. "You attach symbolic meaning to everything, the way a writer would do."

"My father's side of the family." Charlotte moved through a narrow opening between two tall branches painted a dull red. "They loved words."

"We'll call them 'Boats,' " Sybila decided. "And you can make up my titles from now on."

"If you give me lessons in technique." Charlotte picked up a wire tool and traced the perfectly modeled shoulder of one of the sculptures. "See that line? That plane it outlines? I'd like to get that sense of flatness into an oil."

For the next month, while Sybila prepared pieces for a show, Charlotte worked with clay and achieved a sense, in her fingers, of flatness bordered by the sharpest possible edge. "I can get it onto canvas now," she declared one morning. Sybila set up an easel, and the two women worked together silently until late afternoon. When she completed the experiment, Charlotte stood back from a canvas depicting four flat planes crisscrossed by barely visible black lines.

Sybila stared at the canvas for a long time. "You've got the sense of flatness down. But Charlotte—this isn't you."

"It isn't me, you're right." Charlotte felt inexplicably grateful for the small recognition. "It's more you, Sybila. Your discipline. Your knowledge of color and line. But this is only an experiment. Not a real work. It will be me, eventually, now that I've got it in my fingers. You know?"

Charlotte felt strong on the day she went downtown to the opening of Sybila's show. She had run four miles that morning, the farthest she had ever gone. It was late June and she, Ivan and Alex would be going on vacation the following month, to a small house they'd rented upstate which nestled into mountains and looked onto a calm, deep pond where she could swim each morning while Ivan—and Vivian's children if she came to visit— fished for salamanders and frogs. She would invite Sybila too, she decided as she neared the small gallery, and perhaps this would be her chance for a real break. Leonard Genetti, a successful sculptor and critic who had once been a teacher of Sybila's, would be there. Charlotte wondered briefly what he would look like. She had admired his work.

There was a moment in which she might have seen it all from beginning to end, but it wasn't possible at the time. It was a joyous moment in which everything seemed woven together in a fabric of warm wool, rich color, simple line. She could not have seen it would be a tight-fitting fabric, useful for swaddling clothes, or a shroud.

During the months of her involvement with Leonard Genetti, Charlotte became interested in clothes. Why not? she reasoned, recalling the way her childish love for Angel Lopez had changed her style of dress. Weren't clothes another aspect of the aesthetic world? Like her apartment whose colors and spatial arrangements could occupy her for hours when she was having trouble with her work? Charlotte could not imagine why she hadn't become interested in costume until now. She cleared dungarees and cotton tee shirts out of her drawers and replaced them with the soft, clinging skirts and high-buttoned loose blouses that were in fashion that year. During the worst of it she almost, but did not, cut her hair.

Leonard Genetti was forty-five when Charlotte met him, ten years older than herself. He was a man of strong build, who chewed almost continually on an unlit pipe. His hair was a neatly trimmed but uncombed mass of gray and brown curls. A thick, wiry moustache fell over long, narrow lips.

He loved to cook Italian meals, drink scotch and good wine. He could be charming and sophisticated to the point of fraudulence, Charlotte thought much later, as she watched him banter about art world gossip with a famous painter she knew he loathed. His interest in politics was peripheral, his opinions passionate and unexamined. He believed the Catholic church to be the most evil force in history and this conviction, as far as Charlotte could see, was based solely on his hatred for the priests who had corrupted his early sexual awakening with images of hell and a legacy of guilt it took him twenty years to overcome. (His wife left him, he said, because he had not yet learned how to love and screw the same woman. His son, now twenty, had no such problems, he laughed.)

He was one of a dozen men in 1969 to answer a call for an army of volunteer freedom fighters to go to North Vietnam, as their forebears had gone to Spain, and he was ready to go. But the cadre of internationalist warriors had never gotten off the ground. He ended up going to Hanoi with a group of artists and writers for peace. There, he produced a series of sketches that were collected in a book that was commercially successful and highly acclaimed.

Leonard's mother, even at seventy, catered to her husband, a painter who had made a great deal of money from a three-volume set of popular books on American art.

"He was an uninspired painter," Leonard said of his father, "but an inspired manipulator of the art world. His son," Leonard would explain, mock bowing as he pulled the pipe out of his mouth, "did not have the usual struggles gaining a reputation."

Still, the son was not satisfied with his own progress to date. "I'm respected as a sculptor, but feared as a critic," he told Charlotte once as they walked arm in arm through the riverside promenades of Battery Park. "I want to be feared as an artist. To create awe. I want to be that good."

Charlotte was entranced by his arrogance, calling it genius at the time. She pulled him around to face her and pressed her lips to his throat.

At Sybila's opening, Charlotte was introduced to him as "a very fine artist whose work danced between the real and the surreal." He was introduced to her as "the brilliant sculptor and (with a wink from the introducer who was an admirer of Charlotte's work) a powerful critic." Charlotte swallowed hard. Her feet felt

219

nailed to the floor, her tongue to the roof of her mouth. But she was released into relative social normalcy by the brilliant sculptor/powerful critic's opening remark: "Your friend Sybila is a magnificent artist. Her work has a power which is entirely female. Men can only stand in awe."

Charlotte's heart lightened in her chest. She laughed out loud, lost all her shyness, grabbed his hands, shouted, "Oh, Mr. Genetti. I'm so glad you think so!" She imagined the reviews the following day.

It was at that moment that Leonard Genetti looked at Charlotte Cohen in a way which might have revealed the whole story for her, from beginning to end.

"I saw your 'Horizons' and admired them," he said in a soft voice that seemed at once to mock and defer to her loud tones. She bowed her head, breaking his stare.

"But I admired your family portraits even more," he added. When she lifted her eyes his had not moved, were waiting for her.

"I got a few reviews. They were awful." She heard bitter pride in her voice.

"I wanted to write about them, but—well, you know, there wasn't room in the column that week. Then I wanted to write to you, but—." He flushed slightly. "I felt shy. I especially liked the one of yourself from the rear. The weird realism of the braid. It looked almost like a forest. I loved the way it contrasted with the impressionistic lines of the body."

The painting was a nude seen from behind. Charlotte stepped back from ordinary, private feelings about her body, as she had long ago learned to do when it came to her art, and responded to Genetti's interest in her style. They spoke about art for some time, Charlotte growing less intimidated as her interest was engaged by the ideas. She referred once to her alternating involvement in history and art, her as yet unrealized desire to find a way to join the two passions in her work. But Leonard considered history an enemy which had to be outwitted or transcended by the artistic soul. This difference would eventually serve as an example to Charlotte of an unbridgeable gap between them, a sign that their alliance could never have lasted through time. But it was only one thread in a fabric that took years for Charlotte to

220

describe accurately. She was always mistaking a part for the whole.

At the time there was a moment of uncomfortable silence. "Of course no one will like such paintings," Charlotte said to end the discomfort, adding a self-deprecating laugh. "No one likes realism today, and certainly no one likes history mixed into art."

"I would like to see your recent work," said Leonard Genetti, "and perhaps, if you were interested, you might see mine."

He looked at her again as he had before, a gaze which, she would know months later, revealed the whole of the man and his danger for her. It was a possessive gaze, naked in its desire, compelling in its need, arrogant in its expectation.

Suddenly he turned to the crowd gathered in the small gallery and raised his glass flamboyantly. "To Sybila Abele," he shouted. "A fine artist. To a magnificant show!"

Sybila's pale cheeks turned a deep pink. She hugged herself when the crowd broke into applause. Leonard Genetti threw back his head and drained his glass of scotch just as Charlotte once imagined George Cohen to have done.

The next week she visited his studio on Green Street where, under an enormous skylight, surrounded by his large wire sculptures, Charlotte, for the first time in ten years, made love to someone other than Alex Cayne. Leonard undressed her himself, as if she were a sculpture in mid-creation being unwrapped. He lead her to a full-length mirror and placed her in the position of her painting, the nude seen from behind. For a long time he played with her hair, making his way, he said, through the forest she had created. He had fallen in love with her, he told her, as soon as he saw the painting of her jungle hair. He unbraided it, spread it across her back. He knelt behind her and traced her buttocks as if he were sculpting them himself, retracing the lines she had drawn. When he stood up again and met her eyes in the mirror, she nearly fell against him in a swoon. He brought his hands around to her breasts and remarked with a smile that she was obviously as ready as he was. He pressed himself against her; she felt him hard and eager, and turned. He knelt again and spread her legs. He drank from her, licked her until she shouted. He led her to his bed and laid her down. He removed his clothes. He entered her slowly and remained for as long as she needed until

221

there was liquid between every pore of their bodies, and they danced their boundaries away with no concern for the dangers such melting invited into already formed lives, filled with favorite colors, decisive lines, familiar shapes hardened by time.

If it had ended with simple rejection Charlotte might not have been so changed. As Vivian said, it was preferable to know the potential depths of one's passions than to die in ignorance. Charlotte would get over it, Vivian assured her, just as she had once herself. Sybila understood better how close Charlotte had come to being destroyed, not because Leonard eventually left her, but because, in the end, he condemned her art.

She could never say whether it was the man himself or the power he represented that released her most primitive desires. There was something about him that undeniably reminded her of her image of George. She was amazed to discover, in the months of their involvement, how much she craved recognition, the feeling of being known. It started with their life stories. They poured out to each other as many details as they could remember, learning all the major characters of each others' lives. Leonard seemed enraptured by her memories and began referring to her famiy, the dead and the living, as if he knew them well. Once he sat for her as she drew his portrait, obediently immobile for several hours, and when she was done he was full of praise. "You were such a wonderful model," she said. "It was to repair the wounds inflicted by Andre in the back yard," he said with the expression of a man offering jewels.

She told him more, everything she could remember. She got out the old portraits of her parents and brought them to his studio to be admired as "early brilliance." She read him sections of the story of Mara and George. Unlike Alex, Leonard saw her obsessions as the ground of her art, an act of creation that had carried her from the confusions of childhood to the threshold of maturity, he said. He showed her sketches for his latest sculptures. "Now you must break out of realism," he advised. "Allow your imagination to travel unburdened by the literal."

"I'm not sure I feel burdened by the literal," Charlotte said tentatively. How different from Sybila, she thought, who noticed the same quality but described it in a way that made her feel strong.

"You can do it," he insisted, as if she had questioned her own capacity rather than his remarks. "You have more talent in your little finger than I can ever hope to have in my life."

He seemed to enjoy the conviction of inferiority, that she was an ideal for whom he continually had to prove himself, in work and in bed.

"You've made me understand sex," he would tell her, caressing her body with modeling strokes. She felt he wanted to understand her completely—every image in her paintings, every crevice of her flesh. And the more they conspired in her idealization, the more she felt known.

Until she met him, her painting had seemed a private thing, any small commendation a gratuitous surprise. But when Leonard Genetti praised her she heard the applause of the world. In the tone of his voice, his approving smile, she flew to giddy heights of fantasy in which she joined the Cezannes, the Michelangelos, the whole panoply of aesthetic immortality. Perhaps she imagined his fame would carry her to her own. She never forgot the exact manner of speech in which he complimented her work. But she didn't make a great effort to understand it at the time. She settled for saying she was in love.

For the first and only time in her life, Charlotte was oblivious to noise. From a person who could be awakened by a voice on the street ten stories below, who could not paint if Ivan called his father from the other room, she became a person who didn't hear much of what went on around her. For once Charlotte didn't mind the disharmonious sounds of human life. She took to leaning out the window again, but this time her window faced the street and she relished the voices below, the cars rushing down the avenue, even the police sirens and fire engines speeding by.

At the pond that summer, separated from Leonard for a month, Charlotte cried a lot. Alex asked her repeatedly what was wrong, used to her depressions but not her tears. She said she didn't know, that maybe it had to do with a painting she was trying to finish. They spent quiet evenings together after Ivan was asleep, reading side by side, or her listening to his stories about his childhood and his work.

223

"Until I met you I didn't know what it meant to love someone I could trust." he confessed one night. He talked about his mother's temper, rages he could neither penetrate nor understand. "You were the first person I could really depend on. I realized that time when you were reorganizing the house how much it means to me—that you prove your resilience each time I think you're about to fall apart."

He said it to her now, she knew, because he feared she was falling apart again, with all the crying.

"I'm not falling apart," she told him and pulled his head down into her lap. He pressed his face to her belly while she stroked his hair.

"Don't ever leave me," he whispered.

She told him she would not, not knowing, for the first time since she met him, if it were the truth.

When she awoke the next morning Ivan and Alex were already coming in from fishing, hauling a net full of sunnies.

"Mommy!" Ivan shouted. "I caught breakfast!"

Watching the two of them clean, bread and fry the fish, Charlotte burst into tears again.

But she wasn't crying from weakness, not then, in the beginning. She felt the force of something within her stretching, growing, something whose birth she could not control any more than she had Ivan's. The only time she could remember feeling this way in the past was during the height of her concentration, painting the first "Horizon," the "Gladiolas," the seventh portrait of Mara and George.

When Vivian and Sybila came up for a weekend, they found Charlotte distracted and depressed.

"Where the hell are you, Charlotte!" Vivian shook her arm as they lounged on a small beach fronting the pond. "Ivan's been shrieking for you for ten minutes!"

"Oh, I'm sorry." Charlotte sat up. "It's the sun. What is it, Ivan?" She waded into the water to inspect and admire his netted frog.

She returned to the blanket where Sybila and Vivian, shining in baby oil, lay with their faces to the sun. She pushed in between them and told them about Leonard. Vivian, the validated cynic,

224

smiled. Sybila murmured something which sounded like, Oh my God.

"Are you shocked?" Charlotte asked in surprise.

"No, of course not. Worried. He's had affairs with lots of women artists, Charlotte."

Charlotte heard, and tried to ignore, an unusual flatness in Sybila's voice, recalling the flatness of the painted planes she'd accomplished in the studio that day. "I feel so guilty about Alex." She covered her eyes with her arm and pushed the impression away.

"Don't let him find out," Vivian advised. "Remember what I told you long ago about secrets? Secrets aren't always bad. They protect."

"How can you say that to me?"

"And I'd include Mara's secret in that," Vivian insisted. "Have you told Sybila the whole story?"

Sybila turned onto her stomach and looked ahead, toward the trees. "I've heard it. What I think is that secrets are inevitable. Not good or bad. Just inevitable — unless you want to go around causing everyone, including yourself, a lot of pain."

"And supposing Mara did sleep with Buck?" Vivian rubbed baby oil into her tanned skin. "Supposing she went around blabbing it to everyone. What good would it have done? Certainly no good for Rose, as you understood yourself when you were writing that story. Definitely no good for Buck. And you? Well, who knows, Charlotte? Unburdened of that painful mystery maybe you never would have begun to paint. Your painting always comes from a need to make sense of things. Right — Oscar?"

Charlotte was startled at the sound of the old name. She realized how much she had been missing Lynda.

"You're a mess," Vivian said.

"How long can I go on like this? Should I tell Alex? Should I leave him?"

Vivian lowered her voice as if there were someone around to overhear. "As you know perfectly well, I've had several affairs. The only man I ever thought of actually leaving for, though, was Andre." Vivian flushed and chewed her lip. "And think how crazy that would have been. God! I had some romantic idea about saving him — Andre and Vivian going out to sing the world to its senses. I never told David about any of them, not about Andre and not about the others. I know you'll say I'm not as attached to David as you are to Alex, and that's certainly true. In fact, there's no other man, but I'm trying to get up the guts to leave him all the time."

"Vivian! I didn't know things were that bad."

"It takes guts to leave," Sybila said, the disturbing flat tone gone now. "But after you do it, it won't take guts at all. Living alone after a bad marriage is complete relief. I used to slap myself every morning to make sure it was true."

"Somehow I think it might take me years," said Vivian. "I used to tell myself I loved him. Now I know that isn't true. Sometimes I'm not even sure I like him. But I want this family thing so much. The point is, Charlotte, you're totally confused. If you say anything now you'll tell more than you should. Above all, you will make yourself miserable which, I assure you, is no virtue and no favor to anyone. It's obvious that you're not about to end it with Leonard and you'd be crazy to leave Alex. Wait, Charlotte. It'll hurt, but bear the weight of your secret for a while." She echoed her words from long ago.

"Wait, Charlotte," Sybila agreed. "Don't do anything for at least three months."

"Why three months?" Charlotte leaped upon this small certainty, hoping for an unambiguous prediction from her experienced, clearheaded friend.

"Because," said Sybila harshly, "three months is about how long the good part lasts."

Back in the city Charlotte was so thoroughly obsessed she couldn't paint, but she was gaining a perspective on herself which, she felt sure, would fill her studio with new and exciting work when the right time came. She would paint out of a new sensibility, she imagined, a new life having nothing to do with Spain, Uncle Buck and Andre, the ghosts of Mara and George. Here, she felt, was the part of her that had closed down with the disappearance and death of her parents. Charlotte allowed herself a fantasy about leaving Alex, even Ivan, and beginning a brand new life ʷᵗʰ Leonard as they traveled all over the world. She toyed with ⸱ ⁿf Charlotte Genetti as a name. She was being reborn.

She could not back away from such promise despite older obligations. (Well, she thought, she would not leave Ivan. Of course not.) She might discover strengths in herself of which she had only dreamed. Already she could distinguish what was important to her from what was not important with a single-mindedness she mistook for clarity. What was important was Leonard. What was important was art. What mattered was expressing honestly and fully all that was within her. When she was sitting by Ivan's bed one night, assuring herself she would never leave him, she remembered the moment right before his birth when she had understood the connection between ordinary life and partiality—that wholeness could be apprehended only occasionally, short of death. The memory made her uncomfortable. She returned to bed and pushed close to Alex's back as he slept. As soon as he left for work in the morning, Charlotte called Leonard at his studio, as she always did, and arranged for their next date.

"I was waiting by the phone for hours," he said. "Come down right away."

She loved his demands on her. He required her presence, he said, for his life to have any meaning at all. He liked them to paint together, in his studio, which they often did, but Charlotte only pretended to paint. She splashed color on the canvas and told Leonard she was experimenting. In fact, she could concentrate on nothing but him.

By the end of November, with the family obligations of the holidays and the mid-term obligations of school squarely upon her, Charlotte was nearly immobilized in an emotional crisis of major proportions. Leonard Genetti's love had waned.

"I certainly do love you," he insisted to her one afternoon as he paced his studio, "and it enrages me when you suggest I do not."

She sat on a beige velvet couch checking her watch. In a half hour she had to be uptown to pick up Ivan. Their passion, as well as their battles, were always bounded by the clock, as if they were engaged in some deadly serious game of charades.

"Well, I can't go on like this," Charlotte said. "I am not a good liar. Whatever anyone else may think, I cannot live a lie. I can't paint when I'm living a lie. I haven't painted in months,

227

Leonard. I want to leave Alex. I want to tell him. I want us to be together honestly. If you love me, you should want it too."

Leonard paced and thrust his pipe into his mouth. He threw it onto his desk across the room and fell on the couch next to Charlotte. he put his head into his hands and cried.

During the first weeks of their love affair, Leonard had cried often—when she left him to return home, after they made love, once in the middle of a drawing he was doing of her in which her hair was braided into a crown on top of her head. Charlotte thought the drawing looked remarkably like Aunt Rose. She had laughed. "That looks like my aunt, not like me." "You're majestic with your hair like that," Leonard had responded. "Completely unpossessable."

Confronted with this myth of herself (in fact she had been ut-terly possessed) Charlotte had remained silent under his gaze which conveyed an attention so compelling her own life outside the mo-ment paled. Guilt, maternal love, friendship, even sorrow and mour-ning did not so much disappear as diminish into fractional pro-portions of her consciousness. Perhaps, Charlotte had thought, astonished at the changes in herself, this was the way such emo-tions ought to feel. Perhaps from this extraordinary vantage point, the high-water perch of her new obsession, she had finally learned how it felt to be unobsessed—as if there were an imaginary spot between the old obsession and the new in which she was free. She had tried to bring Uncle Buck and Andre to mind, but they seemed gone. Not forgotten, but gone. She felt their absence as she had not allowed herself to feel it before, and she felt her spine relax. She thought of Mara and George and saw two young people die in an explosion. She watched their bodies blown apart, two senseless deaths, and she held her ground in time. She was no baby clutching a dark wood crib, but a grown woman who had survived. The aroma of furniture polish faded into Leonard's tobacco smell.

Now, as she insisted once again that they end the secrecy of their affair, Leonard's expression was one of inward focus, a man who could not be disturbed.

"You haven't painted in months," he said, staring at the highly polished floor. "I'm ruining your life. I'm set in my ways, ʻlotte. I don't want to live with anyone. I do love you, but ʻing too. I've made a life for myself which feels right

228

to me." He put his hand on her knee. "I couldn't do what you're doing—not paint for months." It was an accusation, a denial of her seriousness. "And," he finished, standing up and facing her, "I can't work with daily confrontations like this one."

She felt ashamed. She knew she had begun pushing him for rendezvous more often than he wished. Sometimes she called him when she thought Alex was asleep, risking cruelty to one man, waking another. She watched herself from afar, wondering if she would ever recover from what she had begun to see as an illness.

"You're driving yourself crazy, Charlotte," Sybila warned, the odd flatness in her voice again. "He's not worth it. He's had lovers before, and he'll have more when you're gone."

"It's going too far," Vivian told her. "You're worth a hundred Leonard Genettis."

"What's the matter with you?" Aunt Rose asked her one Friday evening when the family was gathered at Charlotte's for dinner. "You don't concentrate. You have bags under your eyes. You look like you're crying all the time. You look like your mother, and I don't mean it complimentary. You look like she looked when George went to Spain."

It was one of many moments when Charlotte felt she might lose her mind if she didn't discover a new perspective. (It felt like the times she had gotten stuck on a painting, unable to go forward, afraid of blotting out the failed attempt, working toward a deadline with no hope of success, each new line adding to her sense of incompetence, fraudulence, mediocrity. She had saved herself, each time, with a new perspective—a front-faced portrait changed to a profile, a distant landscape seen instead up close. During the first "Horizon" she had stretched the pale colors across the top of the painting and had gotten lost trying to envision the land below. Finally she had washed over the land with thick white paint and brought the horizon line down to the center of the canvas. That was her focus. There was no land, only the horizon line, narrow stripes of textured color suggesting a partial glimpse of earth and sky.)

In search of new perspective, Charlotte confessed to Aunt Rose. "Did you ever feel this way with Uncle Buck, or Leon?" She watched her aunt scour the sink.

229

'Whether I ever felt that way doesn't matter. You feel that way. Just like I told you once before. You remember? Your mother did. Maybe you, I hope, won't kill yourself over this Lenny Genetsky.''

Charlotte laughed so loud she almost disturbed the others. "Leonard Genetti, Aunt Rose. He's not Jewish. He's Italian." She felt a sudden distance from it all, as if she were sucked away on a wind. She was far away, at the wind's end, and saw the possibility of laughter. A hurricane, a cyclone of laughter.

"So it's Leonard Genetti. He's Italian. Makes no difference to my point." Aunt Rose slipped plates efficiently into cupboard shelves. "You feel this way. You're in love."

Charlotte leaned against Rose's back, hugged her shoulders and would have dropped to her knees clutching Aunt Rose around the thighs had not the older woman disengaged herself and turned around, her mouth set in a grim frown.

"I'm not finished. Listen to me. So you're in love. And it's not going to work out. That's obvious. You're going to be very unhappy for a while. You can be unhappy and survive, Charlotte. You won't be the first one. You don't think I long for Buck? At night you don't think I long for him? You think it's easy for an old lady like me to find a replacement? No one wants an old woman. You can live with pain, Charlotte. I promise you. You won't die."

They had all said it, but when Rose said it something shifted inside. Not permanently—there were several more months of desperation, chronic ambivalence, weeping, begging, and occasional moments of ecstasy in which she pretended everything would turn out all right—Leonard would want her—Alex would understand, and she would paint again.

But the shift was undeniable. The next time she and Leonard fought about the issue, she felt the shift assert itself and before it could pass—a moment of minor earthquake which is over before damage is done—Charlotte stopped time. She eased herself down into the narrow gap in the earth and possessed her pain.

" we part," she said.

"ssumed just the expression she feared—

"I'll always think of you as I first saw you in that painting," he said quickly. Tears flowed down his cheeks.

For an instant Charlotte saw it all as she might five years hence. Leonard Genetti in love with an image. Charlotte Cohen using one obsession to defeat another. She saw the fragility of his wire sculptures, his isolated world. At the moment, however, she felt nothing but rage at him for his self-deception which she mistook for a purposeful deception of her. Well, she thought as she was about to go out the door, I won't let him get away with it. Why should I? she asked herself instead of preserving whatever dignity she retained.

Charlotte turned on him and made a very long speech. She accused him of being a liar, a coward, a hypocrite. She accused him of being a fraud. She cried and pleaded with him. Then she raged again.

"Don't ruin it like this," he said, an edge of contempt in his voice. She was like all the others, demanding, shrill, unable to understand.

"Don't *you* understand?" she resumed in a controlled tone. "You've changed everything. You're everything to me. I have nothing left." She thought of Alex and Ivan and was mystified by her own words.

"You have your art," he said. But they both believed that if she really had it, he wouldn't have to remind her.

She went out the door like a woman escaping—broken, empty-handed, and relieved.

For the first two months, under the illusion that she was managing without him, Charlotte painted day and night. She used so much energy, drained so much anxiety away in the studio that in the evening she was able to pay attention to her family. Alex began to relax. Ivan stopped waking in the middle of the night. At the end of that period, she had produced four canvases, two depicting erotic passion and two of large-scale battle scenes, a man leading one army, a woman another. All the figures were done in flat pink planes, only an outline of black suggesting human shapes, and Charlotte thought the abstraction of form saved th paintings from being too didactic. (She had practiced the techni

231

with "Guernica" in mind.) Sybila thought they were wonderful and offered to include them in a group show she was curating at a small gallery. Charlotte agreed, then felt instantly terrified. Leonard would possibly review that show. Obviously, she had been painting for him all along.

On the morning after the opening, Alex went out early to get the paper. When he returned his face was drawn. "He hated the show," Alex told her. "But he singled out your paintings for special criticism." His eyes conveyed pain and concern, his mouth cynical rage. It was suddenly clear that he had known for some time. She grabbed the paper while he turned his back to her and walked to the window.

She could never remember the entire review. For the rest of her life she would be like a soldier who wishes he might have seen the gun that tore off his arm. She threw the paper away immediately and forbad anyone she knew to discuss it with her. She spent days in bed with a high fever. She had caught the phrase, "A certain desperation which trivializes her passion," and the phrase, "A lack of discipline which drains subtlety from her form."

For years she wondered why he had done it. Did he think he was helping her, sending a public warning to what he thought was a wrong road for her to take? Was it simple revenge? Adoration turned to scorn? Or did he never feel the attachment as she did so that he was free to treat her like a stranger as soon as she walked out the door? Whether or not it was true, the last explanation gave Charlotte the most comfort. She could not understand how, if he had loved her, he could have betrayed her so completely. And as much as ever, Charlotte was uncomfortable with mysteries out of her control.

When she was well enough to be cogent, she told Alex much of the story and asked him not to leave. He assured her he had no intention of leaving, but when she insisted on knowing how the whole thing had affected him, he said, "I don't think I'll ever ~ble to trust you completely again."

~id that was a good thing. No one should trust anyone were a fool. Sybila came every day and nplimenting her work, assuring her that othing to do with art. It was Ivan, however, who finally got his mother out of bed. For days he came in to cuddle her, read to her, draw her pictures as he lay across the rumpled sheets. One night he offered to sing her to sleep before he went to bed himself, but in the middle of his lullaby he began to cry. Charlotte rocked him in her arms, kissing his hair, whispering, "What's wrong, Baby, tell Mommy."

"I feel like I don't have a mommy," Ivan said.

Charlotte rose early the next morning, made Ivan's breakfast and went to her studio to begin a new series like a soldier determined to live without his arm.

But it wasn't her arm which was crippled after her affair with Leonard Genetti. It was her cervix. She didn't menstruate for six months. After several Pap smears and four different gynecologists, she finally found a woman she liked. Dr. Lepard diagnosed a "precancerous condition" the treatment of which was cryosurgery, a new technique in which the offending cells were frozen off with liquid nitrogen.

"Pre-cancerous?" Charlotte inquired over the phone. "How pre?"

"Oh, it's nothing," Dr. Lepard assured her. "It's one of those catch-all medical phrases we use. Many things are pre-cancerous. Some people might say that living in New York City is a pre-cancerous condition."

But Dr. Lepard was not trained to do cryosurgery, and Charlotte was recommended to Dr. Richard Bryton, a well-known expert in the field.

He froze the tip of Charlotte's cervix, that very door through which her beloved Ivan had entered the world. Afterwards, she had a "colposcopy:" the doctor examined her through a large microscope which looked like a dental X-ray machine to see if the treatment had been effective. Charlotte passed her tests with flying colors.

She painted it — a white glacial mountain shimmering purity from stark white to pale blue surrounded by a sunburst of flying colors. She had been joking with herself, but it looked like a landscape to most viewers. "When did you see such a thing? Have you been traveling?" Aunt Rose inquired. Sybila thought the colors

233

were daring and urged Charlotte to do more paintings in that vein. "Your work has always been exciting," Sybila told her. "But this represents new territory, a building on those 'Horizons' but more powerful."

Charlotte took her friend's advice and painted more apparent landscapes, partly abstracted, that in fact depicted her vision of the insides of her body. There were mountains, rivers and deserts. There was a dark red and brown cave filled with once lush, now dying greenery—her uterus after Ivan was born. There was a small mud mountain, rich with shells and polished stones, but with an underground stream of polluted water carrying dead fish—a pre-cancerous condition. But Charlotte's condition was cured to everyone's satisfaction.

"Problem resolved," Dr. Lepard told her happily.

"But no sex for another month," Dr. Bryton warned. Alex shrugged gallantly. "Are you circumcised?" the doctor inquired next. "Because wives of uncircumcised men have a greater statistical chance of contracting uterine cancer."

Alex nodded, and Charlotte sighed. The whole business with Leonard must have contributed to her condition. (One gynecologist had described her cervix as raw, as if it had been gashed. Perhaps romantic love was a pre-cancerous condition.) But also, Leonard was not circumcised. Avoiding Alex's eyes, she looked at Dr. Bryton who continued to avoid her and converse with Alex. She couldn't get his attention. He was praising Alex for his circumcised state.

"After a month of abstinence," Dr. Bryton continued, "it will be necessary to wear a prophylactic for some time."

"Do I have to cover my fingers?" Charlotte asked pleasantly and finally got his attention, but the doctor didn't smile. Alex blushed, and Charlotte felt near tears.

"Meanwhile," Dr. Bryton concluded, shuffling some papers around his desk and standing to indicate the meeting was over, "You will have to wear a sanitary pad for five or six weeks." He looked at her at last. "Your cervix is dripping. The offending cells are simply dripping off."

Charlotte got through the sexless months with ease. Since the whole business with Leonard had ended, despite the quiet and

234

the alleviation of guilt, despite the new paintings and a renewed tenderness toward Alex, she had not felt one moment of sexual desire. Charlotte's insides were frozen stiff.

The last painting from that period showed a cave of ice with a long central stalagtite dripping slow, sticky, colorless vaginal tears.

In the years after the end of her affair with Leonard, Charlotte grew strong again. Beneath his domestic criticisms, she felt Alex's continued attraction to her personality. They tended each others' wounds as if their friendship existed apart from their marriage.

For the first time in her life, out of love for Alex, Charlotte learned the difference between generosity and hypocrisy — she finally comprehended the meaning of a kind lie. As much as possible, she maintained a calm exterior, trying to give him confidence in a wholeness and strength she did not really feel. Charlotte became the listener in her family, stopped confiding much herself. With her compulsion to tell all suddenly gone, she looked at the world from a comfortable distance. But no matter how intense her concentration on a painting, she rarely lost time. Following Sybila's example, she labored over the development of her technique. She learned to manage the competing demands of domestic, maternal and artistic life and began to make lists. Her lists calmed her, focusing her eye on the task at hand.

She hadn't had a show for years, since the travesty of Leonard's review, and had claimed she would never have one again. But in the spring of her forty-fourth year, she decided to take a leave from teaching to concentrate on painting for a show scheduled for the following May. Sybila had convinced her it was time to venture into the world again, she and Alex praising Charlotte for her courage and her advances in technique. But what they saw as fortitude was in reality a lack of expectation. When Charlotte entered her studio, she donned hope the way some women over forty use makeup and fashion—a premeditated, unsentimental effort to present a smooth picture to the world with no illusion about the reality underneath the aesthetic mask. She had lost hope, for exactly what she couldn't say. A belief in her capacity to affect events most important to her, perhaps, the price for having allowed her hopes to get so out of hand.

Just as she was wondering where she might vacation for the summer, to think in peace about plans for new work, Jacob bought a house by the ocean. He had gambled on the stock market and won. "A stockbroker," his mother said, amazed and disappointed. "A rich man."

"A generous man," Charlotte reminded her aunt. Jacob had invited them all to use the house as they wished. "We'll make room," he said. "An ocean house is just the thing for everyone."

"And the ocean is where I want to be," Charlotte agreed. Alex didn't mind the ocean, or Jacob for that matter. It was the rest of the family that sometimes still got on his nerves. But he complied with Charlotte's passion for the sea.

She remained in the beach house for the entire two months. All the others came and went on weekends and alternate weeks, the children back and forth from camp, the adults from work. For the last three weeks of August, however, they all came together, crowding into the small rooms, sharing the cooking of enormous meals at the end of the day, sharing, to Alex's dismay, one bathroom.

"I have to plan my shits," he complained, as always both attracted and repulsed by the intensity of his in-laws.

Charlotte told herself it was to accommodate Alex when she began organizing everyone into rooms, moving beds around, even keeping lists of who was sleeping where so that when some left and others arrived she knew instantly which rooms were available, whose turn it was to sleep on the floor.

"What are you, the Commissar of Sleeping Arrangements?" Hannah asked. Charlotte liked the title, dubbed Hannah Commissar of Athletic Activities, Hannah's new lover Paul, Commissar of Tides (he had to keep track of the highs and lows), Rose, Commissar of Cakes, and Alex, Commissar of the Emotional Region. When Vivian called to announce she'd be coming up the following week with one or more of her children (she had finally separated from David) Charlotte was ready with a detailed map of rooms occupied and unoccupied and easily fit Vivian in.

"When do I get off the mattress in the hallway, Your Majesty?" Ivan complained.

"Ivan!" Charlotte was offended. "I'm not a majesty. I'm a commissar!" She consulted her lists. "Not 'til next week."

"No, Ma," Ivan muttered as he left the room. "We're talking serious monarchy here."

Charlotte was so glad to be with everyone, so pleased in her capacity of Orderer, she hardly thought about the paintings she had failed to begin.

But then she began waking several times a night from recurring dreams. One morning before dawn she was awakened by the nuclear holocaust dream. All around her were stretchers of wounded—people missing limbs, with bandaged heads, faces cut by glass or burned. She was sweeping an ever-increasing tide of blood from the floor of a huge armory. It was a hopeless task. She sat up in bed with a shout—I can't! Alex turned over and pulled her back down, saying, "Are you okay?" She said, "I'm sorry. Go back to sleep." She lay there thinking about Spain, that there was nowhere to go any longer, no concrete place to make a last stand, no amount of bodies which could block the bombs.

If the war comes, she thought when Alex had fallen back to sleep, his deep breathing a background to the ceaseless buzz of insects against the window screen, think of how lucky we will consider Andre and Uncle Buck then—to have missed it. Then she thought perhaps they were with her, witnesses, as she was, to the mingling of the family's history and the earth's.

As she did each time she had the holocaust dream, she went to lie down near Ivan. She held his large sleeping body in her arms, protecting him from nuclear destruction. "I love you, Mom," he muttered in his sleep. "I really do." She had gone in to hear him say it. He was so frequently angry at her during the day. Then she put on her swim suit, took a thermos of coffee, and walked the mile to the ocean.

It was the first time in eleven days she had risked being alone. As she climbed over the dunes, she wondered why she had thought it a risk. She felt fine out here on the solitary beach. She would not only walk. She would swim.

But as soon as she saw the water she knew she would not be equal to the surf. She walked along the shore, glad high tide was early today. By the time Ivan came down to the beach, the waves would be more manageable. He had been five when he felt able to dare the most violent water, and now that he was fifteen, Charlotte felt no less the anxiety that he would disappear in the white foam. In a single moment, he could cease to exist. At times, Charlotte felt as though Ivan had been born yesterday. Then it was as if she had known him all her life.

But the tide would be low when they all came down to the beach. Ivan would swing his fists in the air, railing against the phases of the moon. "The waves will come back tomorrow, don't worry," Aunt Rose would say. Then Jennifer or Annie, Jacob's daughters, would race him in. Charlotte felt sorry for her son's disappointment. But she was glad the tide would be lower by noon.

She walked in a little deeper, unable to imagine herself diving into a dangerous surf as she had done the day she watched Alex fall in love with her. She pulled off her old straw hat, flipped up the hood of her sweatshirt. She must have walked over a mile. Scattered translucent clouds were already beginning to fade. The remnant of a quarter moon etched a placid curve in the sky. She pulled back from an especially large wave and sat down on the sand. She dug her feet in, up to her ankles, and looked down the beach in both directions. It was empty, the sand unmarked by running feet, slumbering bodies. An elaborately designed sand castle from yesterday was only a mound of low hills at the edge of the tide. She nudged it with her toe. It would be erased soon.

Her period was three weeks late. She reached between her legs feeling for wetness, for blood, but it was dry. Her breasts were swollen and her thighs ached. Perhaps that was why she had dreamt of blood. Or it could have been the news program they'd watched the evening before, first mangled bodies in Iran, then in El Salvador. "We're on vacation, for God's sakes," Alex had told her afterwards. "Try not to think about it. We have a right to enjoy ourselves."

239

She must be pre-menstrual, she thought, drowning in feeling, sniffing back tears. What a curse, to be pre-menstrual half the month with no relief of blood. "I'm pre-menstrual almost constantly since I passed forty," Vivian had once complained. Charlotte should consider herself lucky.

She tried to consider herself lucky, as Alex wished. She didn't blame him for his impatience with her new bout of sadness. She found it tiring herself. "It's not sadness," he had told her. "It's fear. You're scared of painting full-time again. Scared of having that show. Are you going to make us miserable about it all summer?"

She felt gratitude toward Alex, for sticking by her, and toward Ivan, for existing, but her attachments to them, her domestic tranquility, did not fulfill her need for power, her longing to believe she could break through some crucial wall. In the past years, she had organized abortion rights meetings, marched against nuclear destruction, chaired a women's studies committee at the college which created a series of courses on women artists in history — all the efforts were grand, the results limited and small.

What remained of her feeling for Leonard, she wondered, rising, walking into the water again. She'd known for some time that he had been Sybila's lover too. The two women had talked about it for years, analyzing attraction, describing every aspect of erotic passion, hoping that description would peel back layers of mystification to the simple heart. Still, she couldn't dismiss Leonard Genetti as a coward and an old-fashioned rake as friends encouraged her to do. There had been an opening. Something important had changed. She had been able to imagine the actual deaths of Mara and George. At last, those two seemed gone forever to her. Perhaps, she thought, that small piece of undeniable growth was, in part, a cause of her hopelessness as well.

Her painting had always been a vehicle toward them. Now she doubted the value of her work. She doubted her judgement, even her desire. "You're just scared of facing this year," Alex repeated, his voice tremulous with fears of his own.

She began to make her way down the beach toward the section where shortly they would make daily camp — towels and

240

blankets and rubber thongs, the umbrella, a basket of paddles, balls, Scrabble and frisbees, three liquid coolers for iced tea and lemonade, two knapsacks filled with sandwiches, cookies, apples, pretzels, leftover dinner from the night before, a large watermelon. The teenagers ate so much. They never stopped, it seemed, sitting down after each swim to another meal. It took almost an hour to get lunch ready every day. Ivan and Annie ate with the careless gluttony of the naturally thin. Jennifer ate guiltily, taking tiny bites and looking over her shoulder. She insisted on unwrapping only half a sandwich at a time. Five minutes later she would take out the remaining half. Then she took one cookie and put the box away, only to take it out again and shove a second one in her mouth. And so on. She sat in a graceless position, her knees tucked under her chin, nibbling. Annie, arrogant, and Ivan, oblivious, stretched their nearly naked bodies in the sand while they slurped watermelon down to the rind. Their bathing suits were merely stripes of color covering what Aunt Rose futilely called their private parts. They sauntered down to the nude beach every afternoon, callously begging Jennifer to join them. "It's all such hypocrisy," Jennifer said. "Making believe it's all so natural while everyone's staring at each other thinking about sex." But the real reason was her weight, of course.

"Go on, Jen, don't be so uptight," Jacob told his older daughter.

"Leave her alone," said Charlotte. "I agree with Jenny, it's all hypocrisy. We're fine right here." (Though she wanted to try it herself, and now she couldn't since she had taken Jennifer's part.) "You'll grow out of it," Charlotte told her. "You're not fat, just a little rounder than the fashion. You have a hungry soul." Jennifer was a musician, and reminded Charlotte, and Jacob as well, she feared, of Andre.

Every detail of the Thanksgiving dinner almost fifteen years before, the night Andre died, was clear to Charlotte. She remembered Jenny begging for bread and butter and Jacob's argument in favor of consistency and future health. But Marilyn had remained fat after giving birth to their third child, Michael, and Jennifer ate the way her mother did, in great excessive spurts. Both daughters were feminists and accused their mother of inactivity and submission, but whenever Jennifer played her clarinet, Charlotte noticed, Marilyn looked enraptured, the only time her attention was inaccessible to her husband.

Perhaps you had no conscious power over your children's development, Charlotte thought as her thermos came into view. Ivan had been responsive to her attempts to interest him in art when he was younger. He borrowed her paints and was grateful for any lessons she had time to give. Now he refused to accompany her to museums. He told her Picasso's paintings were simple minded, no better than he could do himself. "It's pure reputation, Mom," he informed her. "You're programmed to like him, so you do." He reminded her of Jacob when he talked like that, about "programming." But then, in the middle of the night, after she'd been sweeping blood off the armory floor, he whispered, "I love you, Mom. I really do."

She poured the last of the coffee into the thermos top and lay down on the sand. It would soon be nine o'clock and the first of them (Annie and Jacob, Hannah and Alex and Paul) would arrive at the beach, her solitude ended for the day. Their company had been a relief, but now that she was alone she found pleasure in her roaming thoughts and resisted the thought of distraction again. At noon Jennifer (the caretaker) and Ivan (the late sleeper) would appear shepherding Aunt Rose in her flowered-cotton bathing suit that came down to her knees. Charlotte picked up a straw and drew a picture of waves in the sand.

A large fishing boat was suddenly visible on the horizon. Its dark hull stretched on the high angular waves reminded her of Sybila's old sculptures. Two white sails formed glistening triangles against the sky. Old Man Death, she thought for no apparent reason. "Morbid," she muttered, disgusted with herself. She shaded her eyes with her palm to see if she could make out any life on board. But the boat was too far off, though it seemed to be heading inland.

She lay back and closed her eyes, unable to rid herself of the double image of the dark boat as a coffin. Even now, years after the story, more than forty years after the actual departure, Charlotte could not think about boats without seeing Mara disappear. Her experience with Leonard had forced her to an understanding

242

of Mara's choice. (She thought she would return, after all. Charlotte remembered the old note, signed "Miriam.") But nothing, since then, could have made her leave Ivan. Not the Spanish Civil War, nor Alex, nor the invitation she'd received a year before to teach in an art school in Chicago for a semester. No demand of intimacy or history could induce her to leave her child for more than a week or two at a time. In the last year, he had begun to need her less. She could go now to answer some call, follow some star of her own—maybe for as long as a month or two. She felt unanchored, afloat.

She lifted herself onto her elbows and looked out to sea again. The fishing boat moved in a slow horizontal line, parallel to the shore. In the last few years, Charlotte had relied as much on her teaching as on Alex and Ivan to provide a foundation beneath the chaos and omnipotence of art. Her increasing ability to unify subject and technique enabled her to tolerate the sobering limitations of teaching and motherhood. (She could not protect Ivan from nuclear war, she thought sadly.) Now, she was to have a year off, a whole year without the tender boundaries of classes to plan, students to advise, meetings to attend.

Charlotte sat up. The sky was completely clear now, the morning sun intense. She took off her sweatshirt and applied tanning oil to her arms and thighs. She crowned her head with her long, graying brown braid. She walked to the water and stared at the fishing boat for a while. It was still too far out to distinguish any life on board, but the tide was beginning to lower and Charlotte dove into the chilly water. She swam parallel and close to the shore. When she floated in on the crest of a gentle wave, Alex, Hannah and Paul were waving to her at the water's edge. Annie and Jacob were tanning their already golden bodies in the sun. A large extended family of Chinese people—about fifteen adults and six children—were setting up blankets, umbrellas and food coolers a little way down the beach. Two of them stood up and pointed to the boat, which now seemed to be anchored about a mile out to sea.

243

There had been an easy intimacy between Charlotte and Paul from the first. He was a writer whose first book was described by one reviewer as having been "written like music." "I liked that," Paul confessed to them all when Hannah proudly quoted the reviewer's words, "since I'm a closet musician too." He played them a tape of a jazz piece he'd written for clarinet and piano. By the following day, Jennifer had memorized the clarinet part, and Paul sang the piano's melody while she played. Charlotte liked him as much for his attention to Jennifer as for his interest in her work. She had done one pastel portrait of him, accenting the dark brown shades of his skin with silver. Hannah joked, "You think he's a god or something, to be painted in silver?" Then she dragged Paul away, complaining that all they ever thought about was art while the world went to hell.

"You think you have to drag the sun up or it won't rise?" Paul teased Charlotte, now, as she walked out of the water, shivering.

"Well, the sun's here, isn't it? It was tired today, wanted to let it rain. But I got it out despite great resistance."

Running past them to get a towel Charlotte heard Alex say to Hannah, "Omnipotence. They joke, Hannah. But they really believe it. Get involved with an artist at your own risk."

Jacob complained, "Charlotte! Get out of my sun. You're spoiling my tan." Like his father, he was authoritative and formal. ("Authoritarian," Hannah accused, lately supported by Jennifer and Ivan.)

244

"You're vain." Charlotte picked up a handful of sand and poured it onto Jacob's tight belly. He shouted and threw some back at her, laughing as she jumped away. When Marilyn and Jennifer arrived, Jacob would be irritable. Invariably, one of them did something to earn his disapproval. Then Aunt Rose would tell him not to be so hard on her granddaughter, who was like the son she still mourned. Then Jacob would tell his mother not to interfere.

Charlotte loosened her braid so her hair would dry. She could write the day down before it began. The only mysteries were old ones, she thought, looking hopefully from the fishing boat to the Chinese family.

When she approached the water, Alex was only a small, light shape on the waves, breast stroking out to sea. Hannah and Paul were kissing. His large, dark brown hands moved down her tanned back, stopped at her waist resting on her hipbones. Later, when the beach was crowded, sunbathers would look at them embracing. Then they would pretend not to be looking. Finally, they would look over at the family, at Aunt Rose, for a sign of disapproval. Aunt Rose would remain stone faced, or she would smile pleasantly as if she were wondering what they might want. Once she had said to a particularly unabashed starer, "Hello, Sir. Do you need something?" He had blushed and turned away.

They moved apart as Charlotte approached. "Jesus H. Christ," she said. "Don't you two ever stop smooching?" They giggled. "It's downright disgusting," Charlotte mocked, admitting with her eyes how jealous she was of their passion. She remembered Leonard stopping once in the middle of the street to kiss her. Cars honked as the light turned green. Several people applauded.

"Alex!" she called as he bobbed up and down just past the breaking waves. "Come on. Take a walk with me."

They walked past families eating and playing paddle ball until the crowd thinned out to isolated groups of sunbathers, some lying nude under the heating sun. Then there was no one except a young man in a white jogging suit and sunglasses picking through bleached lavender stones at the base of the dune.

"You had a bad dream last night," Alex told her. He stooped to pick up a stone, dusted off the sand and dipped it into the water

245

so it sparkled. He handed it to Charlotte.

"It was that horrible nuclear war dream again. I hope it's not prophetic."

"I wouldn't worry about it, Charlotte," Alex chuckled. Whenever she referred to the prophetic he accused her of being grandiose. "It's your own anxiety. The wounded are aspects of yourself, but your unconscious is trying to tell you you're a survivor, Honey."

Charlotte kneeled on the wet sand and began building a cone-shaped mountain, a narrow wall around the base leaving a path for the water to drain when the wave came in. Alex stretched out on his back and moved his hands across the fine white hair that grew in a large triangle on his chest. Charlotte leaned over and kissed his nose.

"I have never doubted I was a survivor, Alex, not for one single minute. What do you think? I could have made sense of all that old madness without a huge dose of confidence? Even Aunt Rose said so. Years ago—it was just before Ivan was born, the day they launched the first moon rocket—remember? She said, Charlotte, you're going to survive. And she said I was like her in a way." Charlotte's eyes filled with tears. "Shit!" she said, sitting up and leaning on her knees.

Alex pulled her between his legs, her head onto his chest. "What are you crying about? Because you love your aunt? She's like a mother to you, Charlotte. You want *not* to care about Aunt Rose? She's old. Let's face it, she can't live forever. What are you so afraid of, Charlotte?" He meant what have you been so afraid of, ever since *then*.

They sat quietly and watched the water. Charlotte unhooked the straps of her black bathing suit and lifted her face to the sun. "How did Ivan seem this morning? Was he up when you left the house?"

"He seemed in a good mood. Maybe it'll last all day. But don't count on it. Anything can set him off these days. I hate the fact that he's an only child."

"It's not that he's an only child." She covered over the old argument between them—it was Charlotte who had refused to have a second. "It's normal adolescence. You miss your patients?" She

246

planted the stone he gave her in the sand, then dug it out and brushed it clean again.

"My patients? Not really. Well, maybe Sean. I have to be careful not to think he's me."

"What do you think of Paul? Do you like him?" Charlotte changed subjects nervously, uncertain of what she was trying to avoid.

"I do like him, yeah. But leave it to Hannah to fall in love with a Black man. It's funny how of everyone, you and Jacob are the only ones with kids. You think Hannah will marry him and have a kid?"

"It would be typical of Hannah to get married just when everyone else is divorcing." She thought of Vivian. "God, sometimes I miss Lynda. It's been so many years since she was home."

"I've never really understood it," Alex mused. "Why she stayed away so long. And hardly ever writes, and never visits. Maybe it's because she's the only one I don't know. But knowing how close you are, even with all your arguing—was she so unhappy as a girl?"

Charlotte looked out to sea, trying to call up the past. "She was the closest one to Uncle Buck. We all thought of her as being like him. But she fought with Aunt Rose more than anyone. Yes. I would say she was very unhappy as a girl. She always acted as if she had no importance in the family, as if she had no power at all. She once told me she lived a secret life, that none of us knew her. But later she said it wasn't true, that she had no secrets at all. I never knew which story was true. I remember lots of nights when she went out and no one really knew where she'd gone. But she always came in on time. She wasn't a rebel in that sense. She never once brought a boyfriend home, though. Not many girlfriends either. She kept her life completely to herself. If that's what she meant by a secret life, she had one."

"Did she sit on the fire escape with you, singing?"

"Oh no, never." Charlotte was shocked at the strangeness of the image. "She never would. I know she loved Hannah, took care of her a lot when she was little. And several times she was very good to me. But when I close my eyes and think back, I see

247

Lynda standing in the corner of a room watching everyone, especially Rose and Andre, looking at them with furious hate."

"I always felt protective of my mother," Alex said. "Even when she rejected me, or was mean to me, I felt like she was the child. Something about her touched me."

Charlotte reached over and touched his lips. "Lynda wasn't a soft person. She was a fierce person. Someone who went into a cave and disappeared, then burst out yelling at everyone, asserting her view of things. I miss her though. I miss that power she had in the family she never thought she had."

Charlotte buried the stone again, patted the sand down on top of it.

"You have any ideas for next year? What are you going to paint?"

That was the question she'd been leaping over, like a little girl playing hopscotch, avoiding the box with the stone. She turned over and buried her head in his belly, inhaled the mixed aromas of sweat, sea salt, his familiar flesh beneath it all— comforting, satisfying.

"Did you see that fishing boat anchored about a quarter mile out?" she asked him as he pulled her up. She hooked her straps and retrieved the stone before they began to walk up the beach.

He shaded his eyes and looked out to sea. The boat appeared immobile on the now gentle waves.

"I keep thinking Old Man Death's on it," Charlotte said, knowing it would annoy him. "He finally got Otharose, after snatching Uncle Buck and Andre. Now he's after someone else."

"Jesus," Alex pushed her away from him. "What does Clara say about your obsessive morbidity?"

"It's not morbidity, Alex. It's not even that I'm depressed. Okay. So it's not jolly, happy-go-lucky to think about death. But it's real. We're going to die, Alex, you know that? I've always known it because death was one of the first realities I understood. What's wrong with thinking about it? What's wrong with trying to make up some way of understanding it?"

"Because then you're unhappy and scared all the time," he answered. "Not to mention the fact that what you make up has a damn good chance of being completely false, a fact which has

248

never seemed to deflate your mania for mythmaking. You should have married a Jungian, Charlotte. I want to be involved with life. I always have. I don't want to wait around on some porch like my mother, killing myself with martinis."

Alex hadn't had a drink in over a year. She missed the way his lips softened, the loudness of his laugh, the way he kept telling her he loved her.

"I *am* involved with life. I just want to make up a story about death. So I'll know what to expect. It *is* Old Man Death out there, I bet. He's captain of that boat. That's what death is." She clapped her hands loudly. "A boat which comes to shore one day and takes you on a ride to somewhere you've never been before. Look, Alex! I can see him. See his hood and his jolly face? Look, he's pointing!"

"Jesus, Charlotte." He pushed her again.

"No, it's true," she insisted, running to catch up with him as he strode down the beach, taking long, hurried steps away from her.

"Alex," she pulled his arm. "Listen. All you have to do is go home and write a letter about how much you like being alive. Or write a letter to Sean. Or to Ivan. Really, Otharose told me. That's all you have to do. And when you're too tired to write letters any more, that means you're ready for the big boat ride."

Talking in the old images lifted her spirits. She felt something take life inside. Surely she wasn't returning to old obsessions, and yet for three years she'd felt parts of her closed, like musty rooms, their furniture covered with old sheets. Perhaps there was something left to retrieve.

Alex turned suddenly and picked her up in his arms. She screamed as if she were fifteen as he lurched into the water. When he was up to his knees he laughed out loud, into her face, up into the sky and he screamed at the top of his lungs, *I'm not ready, Motherfucker!* Then he dumped Charlotte head first into the sea.

She remained under water until she had no more air. She surfaced, breathed in and went under again. She continued this movement like a playful whale for some time, feeling strangely joyful and curious.

In 1925, when she was fifteen years old, Mathilda Cohen informed her parents that she wanted to become an artist. "How're you gonna eat?" her father responded. "Better find a rich man," echoed her mother. George defended her, and since he was his mother's favorite she grudgingly consented to allow her daughter to attend art school for a year. During that year, Mathilda produced twenty portraits of her parents, her brothers, and herself, nineteen of which she sold to various friends of the family, earning enough money to pay her fare to Los Angeles. The twentieth portrait was requested by the art school to be included in their permanent collection of works by alumni. It was a portrait of two young men—one disheveled, his face shadowed in dark blue, his shirt collar soiled and wrinkled; the other impeccably groomed, a neat blue tie striped down his white shirt to meet the triangular pocket of his vest, his rimless glasses resting on his small nose.

When Mathilda returned to New York, her dark red hair was platinum blond, and her name was Mrs. Lorin Cavendish. (She had married an actor who abandoned her one month after their wedding. She never saw him again except years later on television where she watched him portray first a deputy sheriff, then a bungling cop and, finally, an English butler on a series that ran for three years, from which, according to the newspaper column, Lorin Cavendish grew rich. By then, however, too much time had passed for there to be any question of alimony.) Mathilda sold a few paintings now and then, earned some money doing charcoal portraits in Washington Square Park on Sunday afternoons, and depended on the considerable generosity of her brother Buck.

But she could make ends meet if she had to, she insisted. She was a "working girl." During her short stay in California, Mathilda had learned to make hats, and soon after her return to New York, she opened a tiny store called "Chapeaux Mathilde." Some of the hats were practical, some elegant, some exotic. There were tiny pill boxes with matching veils, tailored Homburgs in navy blue or beige felt, and huge sombreros in reds, purples and kelly greens, velvet ribbons wrapped around their crowns, artificial flowers sewn to their sides.

The hats became more imaginative and elaborate as the years went by until no one would buy them. They were more sculptures than hats, "and who wants to wear a sculpture on their head?" Aunt Rose asked the day she found the dusty boxes in the back of the closet in the girls' old room and pulled out two hats. One was bright red straw, the wide, floppy brim abloom with yellow and white daisies made of silk. Threaded through the daisies was a dark green ribbon that hung in two narrow streamers down the back. The second was a beret of rust velvet with gold stitching and brass buttons fringing the side.

"What are those?" Charlotte demanded.

"They're Mathilda's hats," Aunt Rose shrugged and told the story.

Charlotte drifted slowly toward the area of the beach where the family was gathered, having remained in the water where Alex dumped her, thinking about his question—what would she paint? She felt seduced by a whirlpool of extreme receptivity, ideas and experiences belonging to another time and space. That was how she'd been feeling all morning about the wars around the world, as if the bodies were inside her. Now she felt grasped by the piece of family history she'd recently collected about Mathilda.

As the hats became more elaborate (the store had finally been closed when Charlotte was a year old) the portraits became plainer, less imaginative and more popular, bringing in a trickle of income to Mathilda until she died. Only her self-portraits, those thickly layered canvases Charlotte remembered, never sold and, after Mathilda's death, they were given to the Salvation Army. Only one remained which Aunt Rose had pulled out of the closet on that cleaning day and which, along with the hats, Charlotte had decided to take home with her.

"You actually want them?" Ivan had asked. At fourteen he couldn't imagine the sense of salvaging.

"She was my aunt. She was an artist. No wonder she went a little crazy."

Then she'd called over her shoulder to Rose who had taken a pile of old newspapers into the kitchen. "Mathilda had some letters from my parents when they were in Spain, or so Otharose once told me. What ever happened to them?"

Aunt Rose appeared in the doorway wiping her hands on a pink and white apron. "After all this time you're still making up stories?" Charlotte looked down at her toes, girlish and uncomfortable.

"What's so amazing about that?" Ivan asked to his mother's astonishment. He was trying on the brown velvet beret, posing in front of the mirror. "Mom wants to know as much as she can about her history. I wanna know too—just like I wanna know about you and Uncle Buck. I wished I hadn't missed him. And Uncle Andre. They all died. What shitty luck."

Ivan, Jennifer and Annie had been told that Andre died of an illness, the older people afraid of the power of suggestion during the storms of adolescence. Rose and Charlotte exchanged looks.

"What?" Ivan demanded, looking from his mother to Aunt Rose. "What's the secret?" The brown beret, slanted roguishly over one eyebrow, made Ivan look older, sexy. "You guys always have mysteries. It's not fair." He took off the beret and put on the red straw sombrero. He pranced across the room, swaying like a female model, hand on hip, his muscular torso moving gracefully in perfect imitation of a girl.

"Look at him," Aunt Rose accused. "Stop it, Ivan. Don't be crazy. And there's no mystery. It's history, family history. It's always full of confusion, ask your mother. You want to know, Ivan, why that is? Because hardly anyone ever tells the truth."

Charlotte raised her eyebrows which Ivan noticed instantly.

252

She gestured for him to keep quiet, but she was uncomfortable in the role of secret keeper. She decided to tell Ivan the truth about Andre and to go to the art school to see the portrait of Buck and George.

"What about those letters?" she'd repeated as she prepared to leave.

"Lynda took them when Andre died. She found them when she was going through the mess in that room. Children," Rose had snorted, removing her glasses and wiping her eyes with her apron. "What's the good." She'd begun replacing boxes in the closet. "I suppose by now she's thrown them away."

Poor Aunt Mathilda, Charlotte thought, envisioning dozens of paintings piled on Salvation Army counters, shoppers picking through them among old toasters and bent shoes. She began to swim fast, propelling herself by a hard, swift flutter kick. Now she felt as if she were caught on a hook reeled out by someone on that fishing vessel, and she didn't know what it had to do with her. Perhaps she would draw boats this summer, she thought.

She stood up and shook her hair out of her eyes. Marilyn and Michael had arrived. Jacob was digging the green and white umbrella into the sand. As Charlotte walked through the shallow water Ivan started down the beach to meet her. His thick legs were darkly tanned. His tight brown curls (from her side) and his neat, even features (from Alex's) combined to make his face the most beautiful Charlotte had ever seen. She tried to see him as others might, as ordinary. But his presence maintained for her a bewitching glare she could not dispel. She watched him dive into the choppy waves and felt, again, relief that the tide was lowering.

"Mom," he called, surfacing. "Come back in."

But she gestured a refusal, wanting to watch him from afar. The Chinese family was gathered on large blankets, eating. One white man, obviously a brother-in-law, spoke in comfortable Chinese to a small child and pointed to the fishing boat. It rocked on the water, its bare rigging a slanted black line against the blue of the sky. Charlotte shouted, "Be careful," to Ivan and turned away.

"I'm coming out anyway," he said, sounding disgruntled, and

swam in to join her.

Aunt Rose and Jenny were just arriving as Charlotte and Ivan approached the blankets.

"Grandma's tired," Jenny said, falling into a striped beach chair.

She put her clarinet, which she carried everywhere, under a towel in the shade. "Leave it there, in case I feel like playing."

"Here Mama," Jacob opened the other plastic chair, throwing his daughter a critical look. Rose sat down, sighing with effort. One of her combs had fallen to the edge of her hair and was about to drop into the sand. Jacob combed the curls back himself.

Annie ran over to the blanket from the water and reached into her knapsack. She brushed back her shoulder-length hair so that it looked like a sleek scarf, then shook her head swiftly so the hair fluffed up around her face. She rubbed a stick of lip gloss across her mouth.

"Is this a performance or something?" She noticed them all looking at her. Her father winked. Her mother giggled and said, "Girls." Jennifer ate a cookie.

"You're so beautiful," Charlotte explained, looking guiltily at Jennifer.

"You too can be gorgeous for seventy-five dollars a week at Bloomingdale's." Ivan reached into the cooler for a sandwich. Jennifer snapped open her book.

"I do not spend all my time at Bloomingdale's, for your information." Annie kicked Ivan lightly on the leg. "This bathing suit comes from Loman's."

"Where you can buy designer's clothes at cost," Ivan echoed the advertisement. "You buy them for the label, Annie. Admit it. You wouldn't buy a pair of jeans if they weren't Calvin Klein. Tell the truth. You wouldn't buy Jordache jeans if your life depended on it."

"Yes I would," Annie sneered. She fished for a sandwich. "I'd just cut the label off," she laughed.

"Oh brother," said Jennifer to the pages of her book.

"Well I have to deal with peer pressure." Annie glanced at her father, the sociologist, for approval.

"Peer pressure's just a defense for avoiding choice." Alex said.

"Why does this family always have to show off how much

254

they know," Ivan complained. "Boy, am I glad I'm not an intellectual." He flexed his triceps and glared at his mother.

"I didn't say a word," she objected. "It was your father. Tell *him*."

"Oh Jesus, Mom," said Ivan, jumping up and heading for the dune.

The day before, when Jacob's son Michael had climbed to the top of the large dune, another mother from down the beach had come over to tell them that last year a child got caught in a sand slide on that dune and was buried. By the time they dug him out he was dead. Everyone mocked her after she turned her back, except for Charlotte who made Michael come down over Jacob's objections.

"Ivan. . . . Don't," she shouted now.

"Mom. Give me one good reason why I can't climb that dune." She opened her mouth "No. One *good* reason, I mean. Not something like 'it's dangerous.' "

"Well, that's my reason, Ivan. The woman said someone was killed by a sand slide. It's possible, that's all. I don't want you to do it." She spoke quietly, not wanting to fight with him in front of the others.

"That's ridiculous! There is absolutely no way a sand slide could be so big that I would get buried. A little kid, maybe, Mom. But I'm as tall as a grownup." He had grown, in the last year, to be taller than his father and uncle.

"You may think it's ridiculous. But don't do it." She turned her back to him.

"Oh. Right. Just turn away. I thought you believed in talking things out." He spoke indignantly to the back of her head.

"I gave you a reason. You just don't agree with it. That's my reason—what the woman said yesterday. And if you do it, Michael will follow you."

"Can I, Dad?" said Michael, jumping up.

"I think it's okay," Jacob said sleepily, just as Marilyn said, "No, you can't."

"Oh, I think it's all right," Alex interfered, infuriating Charlotte. "Just be careful."

"And that's ridiculous about Michael. I'm four years older."

Ivan ignored his father's permission.

"We're not discussing Michael. And Alex, don't do that to me. I already said no." Charlotte didn't believe Ivan cared about climbing the sand dune. He'd been itching for a fight for the last twenty minutes, yet she had no idea why his mood had changed so dramatically. Was it that she had refused to come into the water? But surely she wasn't that important to him any more.

"Can I *please* climb the sand dune?"

"*No!*" she shouted so loud the people on the next blanket looked over in her direction.

"God, Mom!" And with that double epithet he stalked off down the beach, soon breaking into a jog. Annie ran after him. Aunt Rose chuckled.

"You live long enough, you get to see real justice," she said. "Communists. Capitalists. What do they know about justice. When a rebellious kid becomes a mother and has a rebellious kid, that's justice." She chuckled again. Charlotte pouted.

Hannah said, "Oh come on, Charlotte. He'll be okay. Listen," she told her family who had returned to various stages of hypnotic daze in the sun. "It's not peer pressure or simply choice." She pushed Jacob's thigh and stared at Alex. "We live in a society which is materially haywire. The pressure on these kids to consume is immense. Your daughter needs guidance about values, Jacob."

"I tell him that," ventured Marilyn.

Jacob ignored his wife and addressed his sister. "Your values aren't necessarily mine, in case you haven't noticed, Hannah."

"Mom said something." Jennifer leaned toward her father. "Did you hear her or was her voice carried away by the wind?" She moved her arm through the hot, still air.

"Don't be sarcastic with me, Jennifer. You still have a way to go before you achieve perfection." Jacob looked at his daughter's angry face and allowed his eyes to travel momentarily down her chubby thighs. For an instant, he grimaced. Jennifer stood up, pulled a sweatshirt over her head, and stormed away.

"Mean, Jacob. Plain mean," Hannah hissed and took off after her niece.

"You're too hard on her, Jacob, " said Rose. "You don't realize

256

it now, but you can lose them. Look at Lynda. Fifteen years almost and she's not home. Don't make the same mistake I did, son."

"This is different, Mama. This isn't Lynda. And please, don't interfere."

Rose raised her left eyebrow.

"She's very sensitive," Charlotte said. "Face it, Jacob. She reminds you of Andre. You won't protect her like this."

"I don't see her as Andre," Jacob took off his glasses, which left him nearly blind, and closed his eyes to the sun. "I see her as a self-indulgent, somewhat immature, very gifted and, I agree with you, far too sensitive young girl."

Anger drowned the accuracy of his perceptions in a flood of old resentments, jealousies, fears—a father of impenetrable authority, Charlotte realized suddenly, a disturbed brother who devoured attention the way he devoured food. The day so far, the entire summer, felt to Charlotte like an oozing mud slide of time, each minute layered with old fossils and dried, smooth bone.

"Far too sensitive," Jacob repeated as he turned onto his stomach to tan his back. Charlotte looked at Aunt Rose who smiled sadly.

Had she felt, then, like Jennifer as a girl when her precious Uncle Buck named her with an accuracy distorted by his disapproval? Had his nobility blinded her to the damage caused by his inability to see? Jacob relied on graphs and questionnaires rather than dialectical discussion in his assumption of his right to name things. His commitment was to descriptive accuracy rather than to abstract justice. Clever reversals in the content of their passions masking what was the same.

"You hurt her feelings," Marilyn told him as she adjusted the position of Jennifer's clarinet.

Jacob shot up and put his glasses back on. "Come on, Alex." He reached for the paddle-ball set. But Alex had fallen asleep, so Jacob engaged Paul who was too recent an arrival in the family circle to refuse. They walked down to the water and began to play.

"Sometimes I think I'm lucky not to have had a father for long," said Alex, who had only been pretending to be asleep, avoiding Jacob. "All the forty-year-old men I know are hung up on being different from their fathers."

257

"You think he's different from his father?" Aunt Rose shifted in her chair. "Alex, pass me a sandwich, please, and some iced tea, if you don't mind. You know what the old folks say about the tree growing close to the apples."

"It's the apples that don't fall far from the tree," said Charlotte.

"Same thing," said Rose, chewing on a piece of hard roll.

Charlotte picked up her drawing pad and put on her sun hat, the red straw one covered with flowers, made by Mathilda. "What do you think that boat's there for?" She pointed toward the water.

They all looked out for a moment. No one spoke.

"Maybe it's carrying illegal immigrants who are waiting to swim ashore tonight under the cover of darkness." The hook on the fishing line from the boat jerked in her flesh.

"Pirates, I think," said Michael. "They're diving for gold." Charlotte hugged him and considered his suggestion.

"How about it's out there fishing?" said Alex.

What might George have said? Charlotte was surprised at the question. She hadn't thought much about George since the experience with Leonard. She leaned over and kissed her husband. What she objected to, in all this talk of burying the past, was the idea that death was the equivalent. of disappearance. Many had died, but none disappeared. If they did, it was only temporary, a minor deception. And since they came back so often, she had decided that to ask why they did (was she crazy? morbid?) was the wrong question. The right question was, what did they want this time?

Charlotte brought a plastic chair to the edge of the water, adjusted her hat, dug her feet into the silky sand. The tide had pulled out a dozen yards or so. She saw Ivan and Annie in the distance, and felt relieved. She looked down at her blank pad. At a loss, she began to draw the horizon as she might have ten years before.

When she looked back at the tide, the water had pulled further out, exposing a wide stretch of dark mud which was covered with children building drip castles, adults with their arms crossed over their bellies, lounging in the clear, tiny waves. A blond, darkly tanned woman in a white bikini, her face half hidden by large sunglasses, her thighs and arms gleaming with oil, sat on a chair like Charlotte's, digging her well-manicured toes into the wet earth. It was the woman who had warned them about the sand slides on the dune. Eight members of the Chinese family wandered around in the mud, twisting their bodies like exotic dancers as they fished with their heels for clams which they tossed into large plastic garbage bags. At least six had been filled to the top and tied. They called to each other and laughed at the children as they imitated their elders, screwing their little bodies into the ground.

Charlotte felt a burning sensation on her shoulders. She had lost time. She was closing her drawing pad, considering a swim, when Paul walked up and sat down next to her in a shallow pool of warm sea.

"Nice hat," he said.

"Aunt Mathilda made it years ago," Charlotte answered. "Did Hannah tell you about Aunt Mathilda?"

"Oh, she told me about everyone—Buck, your parents, Andre, Lynda—even Otharose. She died, didn't she?"

It had been three years now since Charlotte had received the call from the nursing home that Otharose was near death. She and Aunt Rose rushed uptown together. She was lying in bed, under tight, smooth sheets. Her loosened, wiry hair, still more silver than white, seemed to float around her head like particles of shimmering dust, what they call stardust on a hot summer night. Long, brown fingers rested on white cotton. The planes of her angular, gaunt face caught the thin shaft of light that edged through the slats of half-closed Venetian blinds. She didn't look at them when they entered. She said, "Rose. Charlotte."

A young woman who was unknown to Charlotte sat by Otharose's bed. Her hair was completely covered with a yellow-and-black print scarf tied behind her neck. Her torso was draped in a dark red, knee-length caftan which she wore over tight pants.

"This is Lara, Rose's niece," Aunt Rose told Charlotte. And as she had been in the white room of the old grandmother years ago, Charlotte was thrown into the gap between Otharose's own life and what she knew of it.

Lara smiled and shook Charlotte's hand. "It won't be long now," she whispered bravely.

"Read to me, Sugar," Rose told Charlotte. A slim book of

259

poetry was lying at the foot of the bed, and Charlotte opened it to the middle. She read aloud for a while until she noticed Otharose's eyes were closed. Alarmed, she looked at Aunt Rose who leaned slightly forward and touched Otharose's hand.

"I'm still here," she giggled like a child who peeked out of a hiding place, thinking she had fooled everyone. "Go on, Sugar," she instructed, and Charlotte continued to read. But in the middle of a poem Otharose turned her face slightly toward Aunt Rose and said,

"We raised the same children. Took care of the same man."

Lara frowned. "Rest yourself, Ahnt Rose," she said.

Charlotte was startled by the pronunciation of "aunt." Otherwise the words might have been hers. Otharose, obviously satisfied with her last assertion, turned her face to the foot of the bed and said, "I'm ready now."

Charlotte smiled. If anyone could take power over this final lesson in humility, Otharose could. Then suddenly, the shock of an ending before she was ready (the trail of police into Uncle Buck's room, Vivian moving haphazardly around the kitchen, the smell of smoke), she heard Aunt Rose whisper, "It's over."

Charlotte bent her head onto the hard ankles of Otharose.

When Aunt Rose left the room to inform the doctors, Charlotte said to Lara, "I'm sorry we haven't known each other. We both loved her."

Lara smiled more warmly than she had before. "I always knew about you. I've heard stories about you all my life. I know all about your painting, your son, your letters to Old Man Death."

"My letters?"

"That's what Aunt Rose told me. You were always fascinated by her letters so you wrote one of your own. Pages and pages, she said. It was a kind of story, I think. About your parents."

Charlotte flushed with recognition. "Do you have any idea what became of her letters? Where they are?"

"She made me burn them yesterday," Lara said. "I wanted to keep them. I knew you'd want to see them. But she refused. She said they'd served their purpose and she didn't want any stories about her floating around for other people to misinterpret."

Charlotte thought of Aunt Mathilda's paintings, now lost, as

260

she stared at the familiar body, now called the remains, of Otharose. What after all remained? Letters burned. Paintings given to the Salvation Army. You would need a salvation army of another sort to preserve the words and images of all the old women. So much had been lost.

Lara let go of Otharose's hand, which she had been holding since right before she died. "She was always the one who could understand me," she whispered. "I loved her as much as my own mother. When I was a little girl I would sometimes sit on the bed and watch her get dressed. I used to read her things I had written while she pulled on her nylon stockings and put lipstick on. And she always listened as if she thought I was reading something special. When I was in college she encouraged me to write, even though my parents wanted me to be a teacher. Those were my poems you were reading." She reached for the book and put it into her bag.

She stood up, remaining next to the bed, and for some reason Charlotte did the same. (Boats disappearing into fog, hospitals bombed, the smell of smoke.) The two women were standing on either side of the bed watching tension drain from the dead face when the doctors and Aunt Rose returned.

"She died three years ago," Charlotte told Paul. "But not before she destroyed all those letters. Did Hannah tell you about the letters?"

"Oh yes," he said. He shifted his lean body into the mud and began digging a hole which filled up with water as he dug.

"I've thought a lot about those letters. And about the way she was hired as a maid and then treated like a sort of writer-in-residence. That must have been an interesting relationship, between her and Rose Cohen. I'd like to talk to your mother about it. You think she would mind?"

"My mother? Would my mother mind?" Charlotte repeated each word flatly, as though she were deciphering a foreign language.

"Oh, I mean your aunt," Paul laughed. "I mean Rose. I think of her as your mother. The thing is," he continued, unperturbed by Charlotte's flushed cheeks, "I mean if you all don't mind, I'd

261

like to write Rose Moore's story, Charlotte. Can I use the idea of letters to Ole Man Death?"

He pronounced it exactly as Otharose would, and the day before Charlotte heard him call Hannah George, Sugar, so she said, "Of course."

"Come on," he said, standing up and shaking mud off his thighs, "let's go for a swim."

She felt a sense of awe as she stood up beside him, although they were nearly the same height. He wrote stories that sounded like music. At a time in history when interracial mating was seen as a symptom of neurosis or contempt, he had fallen in love with a Jewish Communist. He unselfconsciously inquired if he could appropriate the idea which had grown at the center of her life, rooting its meaning into her hands, when she painted; her head, when she dreamed; her feet, when she stood. Well then, she thought as they pushed through the shallow water, walking forever it seemed, until it was deep enough to swim—she would paint boats.

The duties of the Commissar of Sleeping Arrangements were expanding by the day. Charlotte not only had to arrange everyone into bedrooms but listen to their complaints.

"It's not really that I mind sharing with Annie," Jennifer admitted after a long-winded objection to her aunt's putting them together. "But just because we're sisters doesn't mean we're comfortable roommates." Under the excuse of room arrangement, Jennifer confessed her resentments at length. "And it's not only Annie. I am a complete and total stranger in this family. No one understands me."

"Your mother does. I think I do. You remind us of the best of Andre, Sweetie. And you're strong too, like Lynda." She was holding on to Jennifer, frightened she would leave, as Lynda had.

"I'm not like any of you," Jennifer insisted. She did not appreciate the offering of unequivocal family membership. There was some boundary, unknown to Charlotte, more precious to Jennifer than the understanding she said she craved.

Charlotte gave her a room of her own, moving Aunt Rose in with Annie for a while.

"I'm taking over your responsibilities," she told Alex that night. "You're supposed to be Commissar of the Emotional Region." But Alex was on vacation from confession, interested in simple communications and even moral rectitude after a year of well-controlled countertransference and a professionally open mind. "Who asked you to be commissar of anything?" he teased. "Let chaos rule if you ask me."

263

Charlotte was warding off chaos of all kinds. Each time she neglected some crucial ordering she felt the mud slide of time move beneath her. Something was shifting, she was sure, and though she didn't mind change in itself, she did mind not knowing what to expect. Her sense of threat expressed itself in anxiety more chronic than any she'd felt since her months of involvement with Leonard. The only way she knew to manage this threat was to keep order. She limited herself to one glass of wine a day. She counted her daily calories to a mere 1,000, ordering and re-ordering her protein, her fats, her carbohydrates every morning before she went on a run.

One morning she and Hannah ran a leisurely two miles to the town under a cooling rain. Hannah, used to doing six miles at a stretch, ran up a steep hill and waited at the top for Charlotte. Going downhill, Charlotte's thighs loosened and she sped up enough to keep pace with her stronger cousin. Hannah's black curls had been cropped short that summer; she wore a rolled-up red bandanna across her forehead to keep the sweat out of her eyes.

"Want to go to Nicaragua with me?" she said out of the blue. "I'm going for the paper in January. But don't tell Mama yet. She'll worry me to death."

"You know I can't identify with most of what your paper writes," Charlotte said apologetically as they passed the small, white church that marked the last turn before the stretch to the tiny town.

"I'm not even sure you read the paper. We're not irresponsible fanatics, you know. You're not getting the golden truth from the *Times*. Jesus, Charlotte. Where were you raised." She softened her tone. "Besides, I need your help, Charlotte. Paul wants to get married. I don't know what to do. You seem to know yourself so well. Everything you find out—and paint or write about—like those Mara stories—teaches me something too."

"You're the only one who found anything useful in that old story. Besides me, of course. Everyone thought I was being neurotic, or childish. Living in the past."

"I loved it. I thought you were going to become a writer instead of a painter. Did you think about it?"

"Not really. I think it would have been too much like my—like George. Why did you care so much about my obsession?"

A look of shock passed over Hannah's face. "Your mother was dead, Charlotte. So you were always drawing all those big-eyed paintings of her. When I was a kid I thought you were trying to force her to see you. Well, I could never get my mother to see me either. I was kind of lost in the shuffle. Andre, Lynda, you, even Jacob, you were all so—well, visible. I always felt like I was jumping in front of her trying to make her see me. And how much I loved her, that I understood. It was my obsession too."

They passed the small fresh-water pond where, no matter how serious or compelling the conversation, they always sighed and said, "How beautiful." A familiar feeling of joy filled Charlotte and accelerated her running pace. Here she was with nothing to explain, no omniscient eyes to create in paint. Hannah saw. "More than any of us—," she said to Hannah, "you seem to be yourself. Not like—or defiantly unlike—any of them."

"I felt ignored. I had to find my own way, or maybe I was free to find my own way. Still, there's something missing in me that I find in you. And Paul. You could draw while we're there, Charlotte." She returned to her previous urgent tone. "You won't be short of subjects, I guarantee. And we could talk. Besides," she added, "the excitement would do you good."

Charlotte considered the possibility. "Is it dangerous?" She thought of Ivan.

"Not very. Oh, always a little. But we'd be as safe as anyone can be. I wouldn't be only writing. I'm leading a group of North American academics on a tour, trying to create resistance to an invasion. I don't think anyone on either side would want *them* hurt. Please come with me, Charlotte. I don't mean to be giving you a political lecture. It's just that you're the only sister I've got left, and we've hardly seen each other for years."

Charlotte surprised herself by saying, sincerely, that she would think about it.

They stopped at the glass doors to the post office and went inside. Hannah gave a list of names for General Delivery. There were some newspapers for her; a postcard for Jenny; two letters, obviously from patients, for Alex; and a letter from England.

265

Hannah and Charlotte reached for it at the same moment and held onto the envelope, reading the return address. It was from Lynda, addressed to Rose.

"Probably her usual sparse news." Charlotte anticipated disappointment as they broke into a slow run again, and for the two miles back, under a darkening sky and an increasing rain, Hannah talked about Paul.

When the rain stopped later that afternoon, some of them went fishing. Paul kept up a steady pace at his typewriter in an upstairs bedroom. Jennifer played the clarinet as Marilyn baked, humming to her daughter's music. Ivan fell asleep. After staring for hours at her three new sketches while trying to read a mystery, back and forth from the drawings which bothered her with their lack of force to the tan, crinkled pages of the old paperback, Charlotte abandoned the effort, announcing that she wanted to be near the ocean on a cloudy day. Aunt Rose said she would go too, so they drove down to the beach and, unburdened by family and the paraphernalia of a sunny day, they walked lightly over the dune to confront a turbulent fog-draped sea.

It didn't matter how often or rarely she saw it, how many centuries of poets had described or artists painted it, how completely, people said, its color and sound had been hounded into empty cliche. Each time she came over the dune and saw it again, she took a small breath of shock and pleasure — the pleasure riding into dull flesh on the velocity of the shock, the shock opening her cells to the liquefied swelling of pleasure. Every time she saw the ocean, Charlotte felt she had found her place.

Only one swimmer risked the high waves on that stormy day. There was no fishing boat to be seen. Where had it gone, Charlotte wondered. Docked at the horizon, too distant to see? Would it be back tomorrow for another day of searching for customers for the old man? She looked around as if the boat might suddenly appear from the deep, surfacing to meet her eye's need of it. And why had Aunt Rose insisted on accompanying her? She did not ordinarily go to the beach on what she called a lousy day.

It was the letter, Charlotte suspected. There was something important in the letter.

266

"You think you understand your life when you're young, and then your children grow up and tell you about their childhood. All of a sudden you see you had no idea what was going on. It's a gorgeous sea today." Aunt Rose looked out on the water rather than at Charlotte as she spoke.

Had Lynda decided to record all her grievances after all this time? Charlotte felt protective of her aunt.

High waves crashed against each other twenty feet out, joined, and changed direction as they rolled in. There must be terrific whirlpools out there, Charlotte thought, anxious at the sight of it, yet wishing she had the courage to dive in. She imagined herself years before, swimming as Alex watched. But then Alex turned into Leonard. She jerked herself out of internal whirlpools and paid attention to Rose. "What did the letter say?"

"It's not this one letter. For years, every once in a while she stops in the middle of her newsy chatter and tells me she's sorry we never understood each other. Sorry she always took her father's part against me. I don't remember us not understanding each other. I'll tell you what I remember. It was hard times. I had lots of kids and lots of worries. Andre of course was never an easy kid." She stopped to let the tears gather as she always did when she mentioned his name, brushing them off the bony plane of her cheek before they could fall. "I understood her as well as I understood any of you. Which maybe wasn't too much. Look Charlotte," she said as if Charlotte had disagreed, "it wasn't she took her father's part. It was that she was always like him. Daughters like their fathers aren't so easy for mothers. And the opposite too. Sons like their mothers give their fathers a hard time. I'm sure you see it in Alex and Ivan."

Charlotte had not seen it. She thought of Ivan as being very different from them both. What maternal failures of affection, or worse, perception, were visible to others, what nakedness did she expose in sublime humiliating unconsciousness for others to notice in embarrassment or glee? If Aunt Rose failed to remember that it wasn't only lots of kids and temperamental differences that had estranged her daughter from herself, could Charlotte be oblivious to the character of her own son? Now she remembered the other afternoon when they had argued about the dune. Alex

267

had told Ivan he could go, and Ivan had ignored him. Alex's face had paled with disappointment, but she had paid no attention at the time. Neither had Ivan.

"Ivan's the image of you, Charlotte. Just as you are more and more like your father. Not in every detail. I don't mean that. I mean the essence."

Charlotte jumped back from a crashing wave but Rose remained where she was. Water drenched her to the waist. "Come on, let's walk," she said.

"How am I like—George?" The old confusion rang in her head—portentous announcements, wedding bells, a death toll. She must mean because they were both artists, Charlotte thought.

"Yes, Charlotte. You're like George. No better answer to your old question than that."

"Oh, I don't think it's an answer. Not in some final sense." She was not ready to let go of her mystery. She had held its edges, modeled its lines, avoided solutions for too long. She had become attached to her putative fathers. An explanation after all this time would be like blinders on a horse, permitting greater efficiency of movement by restricting vision to a straight, mechanical line.

"I'll never know the final answer," she assured her aunt.

"You always had that *chutzpah*, just like George." Rose continued as if Charlotte had not spoken. "Even when you were a kid. Remember that day you got angry at Isaac for ignoring my new curtains? Oh boy, was he mad. Hah! He never thought one of you girls would defend me against him. You all thought he was such a god."

Charlotte was shocked at the resentment, the self-satisfied laugh. She put her arm through Rose's as they walked.

"I was so touched that day," Rose whispered, patting Charlotte's hand. "It was lots of things, I suppose. Maybe I liked colors and designs as much as you did, sort of got a thrill from something looking right. Like my doilies, and my cinnamon buns. Or maybe it was just you—coming to my defense."

She had not become a word-maker, like her father and uncle. She got a thrill from something looking right, like Rose. And if she had *chutzpah*, that highest of all compliments from Rose, it did not come, Charlotte saw, only from George, a dark design

268

of daringly shaped chromosomes. It came of course from Rose Cohen, even though she wasn't blood. (Charlotte remembered the first time she got her period, Rose's fingers offering the cotton pad, reaching toward her. She touched her thighs together, no blood yet.) Adopted mothers could bequeath, if not genes, features and muscular shape, still—something. *Chutzpah* was something. An inheritance.

She bent to pick up a pure white scallop shell. "So Aunt Rose. What did Lynda's letter say?"

"One of those letters where she tells me who she is." Rose spotted a matching shell and retrieved it for Charlotte before the next wave could slap it under its foam. "I never thought to tell my mother who I was. Anyway, she was dead before I knew. But my daughters tell me all the time. 'Mama, this is who I am!' " Rose thumped her chest. "So she tells me who she is. She's an independent woman. A writer. A woman, these are her exact words, for whom the world is more compelling than love. *Zolst laben und zai gezint.* You know that expression, Charlotte? She should live and be well."

Charlotte imagined Lynda's life—traveling all over the world, writing articles syndicated in a dozen countries, and one, a year ago, for which she won a coveted prize. It had been anthologized in several books of journalism, taught in universities. Rose had a copy of the prize announcement in a gold frame hanging on the kitchen wall. For the past two years, Lynda had lived in London, her home base she called it, implying all the other bases and outfields around which she roamed. Charlotte hadn't seen her since Andre's funeral, but she pictured her with dark hair blown around her face in a fashionable but casual cut. Most likely she was in good shape, like Hannah. Genes. She still had a big mouth, Charlotte presumed, which expressed itself not only in searing flights of journalistic precision but in ordinary conversation. "Jesus H. Christ," she would say to any government or man who attempted to tyrannize the disenfranchised, the weak, the oppressed. Uncle Buck would have been beside himself with pride. Had she ever come close to marrying? Had she wished for a baby? Who was she, besides her father's closest ally, her mother's rejected child? What had she run so far to escape? And how had she gotten so strong?

"She must be a wonderful woman. I wish she'd come home."

"You're about to get your wish. Next week, she says." Rose handed Charlotte the letter.

Nervously, Charlotte figured out the dates as she read. Today was Tuesday. She would arrive in about ten days, next Friday, with a very special surprise, Lynda said. But despite her many years of longing to see Lynda again, Charlotte was filled with resentment and fear.

When they arrived back at the house an additional car was parked in the driveway. A brown Chevrolet station wagon. Vivian's. She came bounding out to meet Charlotte followed by two of her four children—Matthew, long and lanky, blue eyes smiling behind thick round glasses, and Isaac, the youngest, named for Uncle Buck. Behind the children a tall woman appeared wearing khaki shorts and a dark blue sweatshirt that broadened her wide shoulders.

"This is Ruth," said Vivian, taking the tall woman's hand, looking at her with ardent eyes and softened mouth.

For a moment, Charlotte could think of nothing but room arrangements. Where would Ruth sleep? As she shook Ruth's hand, trying to appear casually hospitable, she saw Myron Shatsky amble out the light screen door. "Hello, Charlotte," he said softly, as he bent to kiss her on the cheek.

That night she lay next to Alex, her body a tight, ill-fitting armor. He kissed her, wanting to make love. She turned her cheek and her back. She pulled his hand around to her mouth and kissed it, apologizing. Ever since the family had convened at Jacob's house for their extended reunion, Charlotte had been experiencing a recurring pain in her eyes. In the middle of a conversation the faces before her would blur at the edges, or everything around her would seem covered with a watery mist. This visual distortion was accompanied by an ache beneath her lids that forced her to close her eyes, as if the light were too strong, or she'd been straining too hard to see. Aunt Rose asked her repeatedly if she needed reading glasses. Jennifer, who for days had been sunk in *The Magic Mountain,* still angry at her father, unavailable for beach trips or family dinners, wondered that morning if Aunt Charlotte realized

270

that cancer was the modern equivalent of tuberculosis—the disease of the sick at heart—and that faulty vision was one of the initial symptoms of a cancerous tumor in the brain. Charlotte knew who was sick at heart, and she promised herself, relieved as she heard Alex's deep breathing, to spend some time alone with her niece at the first opportunity.

How like Vivian, she thought, to spring this new shock on them all. She'd said nothing about a new lover, let alone a woman lover. Charlotte turned over uncomfortably, knowing her irritation was really jealousy and disturbing memories of her own. Her eyes ached at the idea of sleep. Her dreams of nuclear war had been replaced by recurring dreams about Leonard Genetti. She had long since stopped asking herself why he'd ceased loving her, was even grateful for whatever insufficiency or self-knowledge had restrained him from an offer to change their lives together, a change which, she felt sure, would have left her weakened, perhaps beyond repair. The question that chorused through her dreams in a dozen melodies, the same image in countless translations, was: what would she do with the part of herself he had jerked to the surface like a shocked fish?

There was something in Charlotte that swooned when out of control, more, when under the control of someone else. They had begun their affair with her standing completely still, a flesh and blood painting, while behind her literal back he created the terms of their passion. She had plunged into that desperate dependence as if she were swimming home. She recalled the powerless, prone Miss Sipinelli who still visited her sexual fantasies, though now in more sophisticated form, the lost time associated with her deepest concentration on a painting. All of it seemed connected, somehow, to the feelings she remembered, all too well, in bed with Leonard. It was not just the nature of sex nor, she felt sure, an instance of nearly outworn but still-tenacious female pathology. In her fantasies and her art, where she retained choice, that very submission to potential chaos (a force other than one's own consciousness) could release a unique energy. She felt as if she had moved down some road on wings rather than feet, as if, after months of a mile and a half, she suddenly ran four. By the power of that forceful submission, she felt slightly but irrevocably and healthfully rearranged.

And here she was, left with it—longing to escape the limits of self but unable to risk it, in sex and in her work. The adventure had proven itself unpredictable, after all, too much for her, a death and rebirth with the rebirth part uncertain—water for baptism and drowning, fire for purification and for death.

Leonard Genetti appeared in her dreams as an old man limping up dusty staircases, and she awoke feeling relieved. But the next night he was scaling a mountain (the Pyrenees, she knew. Dreams had no fear of a useful cliché.) And she followed him. At last he turned to her and pulled her to his chest. She remained there, inhaling his smell, losing time, solidity melting, caught in a whirlpool of deadly baptism from which she might not surface alive.

"**I**t's a new world, and I'm not sure I belong in it."

"The world changes, Aunt Rose. You belong to it as much as anyone." Charlotte sipped coffee, glad only Rose and herself were awake.

"But women? Lovers together? We always had them, but never in the open, like this." She pointed upstairs where, presumably, Vivian and Ruth were still asleep.

"Yes, Aunt Rose. It was always in the open in some circles. But now people feel they don't have to hide in ghettos, like before."

"Ghettos? You compare this to the oppression of Jews? Of Blacks? For God's sake, Charlotte."

"Of course I do. But let's not argue. The point is, this is Vivian. Whatever she does, we love her. Right?" Charlotte asked nervously.

"Of course right. What do you think? I would be rude? Ruth seems anyway like a nice woman. But first it's Hannah with Paul. So okay, that's something I always believed in. Color is nothing. Still, I'll confess to you, Charlotte, it's hard too. Their children —. But so okay. Now this? It's a new world. I know I can't change it. I'm just not sure I belong in it," she repeated as a group of early risers entered the kitchen.

They began to plan the day's activities, challenging each other to a tennis competition, figuring out who would make the mammoth lunch they would need for the beach. Myron asked Charlotte if she had any work up here she could show. "Only a few sketches," she told him, but she'd love to tell him her plans. "Later," he promised. "We'll walk on the beach." Charlotte and Hannah wondered about Lynda's surprise, confessed their ambivalence about the long-awaited return. Aunt Rose sniffed as if she didn't expect much, but she pored over recipe books, planning cakes.

The night before, Charlotte had dreamt of Leonard again and awakened with a hunger for him that caused her to embrace Alex furiously. She closed her aching eyes and shaded them with an open palm. "Do you need new glasses?" Rose asked for the fifth time that week. "Do you have a headache? Are you sick?" Charlotte shook her head and decided to go for a morning walk.

In the living room, she ran into Ruth, Vivian and Jennifer who offered to join her. They started out toward the bay.

The three older women talked about tides and sea creatures while Jennifer, deeply involved in her Thomas Mann, made references to the relative nature of time. "It must seem like an eternity between waves to these clams. Life is such a mystery," she sighed, fingering seaweed and snails.

"Not really," said Ruth, straightforward and interested. "It's mostly water. Somewhere between fire and ice."

Charlotte's affection was won, and she listened attentively as Ruth talked about her Irish Catholic girlhood in Jamaica, Queens. She castigated herself for jealousy when Ruth took Vivian's hand tenderly as they made their way over sharp-edged shells exposed by the low tide.

They walked out to the rusty, snail-encrusted lighthouse, out of use for years, and there, the water just up to their knees, they bounced and floated like contented babies in the dark, lukewarm bay. Having discovered that Jennifer was a musician and was reading *The Magic Mountain,* Ruth, who played the violin, engaged her in a discussion about the symphonic motifs in that novel while the two of them crouched lower and lower in the mud as the tide went out.

After a while, Charlotte and Vivian walked some yards away, Charlotte listening to news of Vivian's children. "Well, Matthew's fine, as you can see, adjusting perfectly. When he realized the nature of my relationship with Ruth he just said, 'Well Mom, if

274

you like her, it's fine with me.' But he's always been this little separate creature — as if he were born with some indestructible assurance of who he was. I've made plenty of mistakes with my kids. And David's terrible rages? Well, they've heard it all. But this one — ,'' she gestured back toward the house and Matthew, ''he rides every storm as if he's sure he'll survive. Isaac hasn't reacted at all yet, and Andy's another story. He's always been mad at me for being mad at his father. And he's mad at David too, which he can't express, so I get the anger meant for David as well. In the fall he goes to college where I hope he'll learn a little bit about his brother's distancing techniques.''

''And Nora? How is she?''

''It's hard for her too. If I'm a, well you know, a lesbian — which I don't feel like one single bit, then — .'' Vivian shrugged. ''But Nora's strong. And she can't help liking Ruth. I can tell.''

''Neither can I.'' Charlotte saw Vivian blush slightly. ''What's it like, Vivian?''

''It's like loving a man, only maybe a little bit warmer. The same problems — this one wants distance, that one wants to be close, push and pull, hurt and make up. The difference is with a woman it's a hell of a lot easier to talk. But Ruth's always been gay. I resisted her for a year, telling her I wasn't a l-l-l-lesbian. I couldn't even say the word. It's taken me almost twenty years, Charlotte, since the Party fell apart, to stop pursuing normality, what I thought was normality, with a fury. What I couldn't get from politics, I tried to get from love. The family. Order — a belief in something. I stayed in a God-awful marriage for years just to prove I was right that any deviation from the straight and narrow path was disaster. Or to put it another way, I was just plain scared. Then I met Ruth. It didn't matter that she was a woman — unless David's rages had ruined me for men. I just fell in love with someone intelligent and kind. She was so patient and respectful. And now — the sex is incredible, Charlotte. I think I'm in love for the very first time in my life.''

Charlotte stood still, the bay rippling around her knees, recalling vine-covered windows, soft cotton nightgowns and smooth, moon-lit thighs. When they walked back to the house and Ruth held Vivian's hand, Charlotte tried to appear casual. Toward the

275

end of the interrupted but persistent conversation about Thomas Mann, Jennifer, looking more relaxed than she had in a week, hugged Vivian, laying her cheek on her shoulder as if she were a small child being carried home after a hard day. "I think you two are wonderful." She imitated the voice of a young child. "I think I'll be a lesbian when I grow up."

From the warmth of Ruth's smile, Charlotte realized that her niece already was.

At the ocean that afternoon, Alex and Ivan, Jacob and Paul got involved in a touch football game that lasted for several hours. While the rest of the family tanned, talked and swam, those four scored touchdowns, blocked passes and shouted calls with the concentration of a Superbowl Sunday, millions of dollars riding on an afternoon. Isaac, thick-set and muscular like his father but still only five-foot-three, and Michael, only twelve, were the third, slightly superfluous members of the teams. Matthew leaned against the dune watching them intermittently when he looked up from his book on the Russian revolution. So far, he was the only one of the children to have inherited an interest in history, breathing life into his mother's neglected passion. Vivian had remained steadfastly cynical all these years, but when she wasn't handing her son reading lists, she was conveying to him the old beliefs: "Of course I don't know any more, but Charlotte's Uncle Buck would have said—."

Charlotte watched Matthew's expression change from dull attention, when he looked at the game, to brow-furrowed self-containment, when he looked at his page, and she felt ashamed. She wished her son were like that. At such moments, she realized she wanted for Ivan all the self-centered things woman-hating books accused mothers of wanting—that he remain cozy in her world, that he grow into a male image of herself, that he continue to love her best of all.

Ivan jumped to an amazing height in the air and picked the football out of flight. "Oh, awesome!" shouted Michael. "Nice catch!" Paul called, and even the enemy team, Jacob and Alex, whistled appreciation for the effortless dancer's leap. "Awright!" Ivan yelled, in praise of himself, and instantly Charlotte's desire for him to be something other than what he was evaporated. No

276

one could leap like that, thighs taut, back curved slightly inward with the grace of a quarter moon, long fingers stealing leather from the wind. Ivan had been a chubby toddler, but by the time he was ten it was clear — his body was his instrument. He was brilliant at any sport he tried. He could breakdance like a street kid. He imitated the movements of testifying Blacks so well he reached into Paul's childhood and revealed a part of the man none of them had seen. The night before, to the loud drumming of rock music on Annie's stereo tape deck, the two of them moon-walked all over the lawn, shoulders waving in rhythm with rippling hips.

She would always wish he could love her best forever, Charlotte thought, even as she felt stunned with admiration and relief when he leaped away from her, into the air.

Later, she took the promised walk with Myron. They discussed a possible musicians' strike in the fall, Charlotte's fear of showing her work, Myron's auditions for a larger orchestra, the endless battles for time to work, the complicated business of art which left little time for art itself. "Money and time. I think about that more than I think about my painting," Charlotte complained.

They exchanged news, moving effortlessly between mundane matters and secret yearnings, family gossip and half-formed insights about the nature of middle-age. When they headed back toward the others she noticed the fishing boat and felt the uncanny, irrational excitement return. They passed the Chinese family who were unpacking a huge feast at the water's edge. She anchored Myron to their family now that Andre was dead, she saw, and through their family to the world. She would have to keep an eye on him too, make sure he was okay.

"What are you thinking about?" he asked.

" About history," Charlotte said. "How we're in it, and it's in us. Look at Jennifer. Even Vivian. Look how relatively easy it is for them to be gay. What if Andre had been born twenty years later?"

"I know. I think about it all the time." He turned suddenly and hugged her so tightly he hurt her neck. When they stepped apart from each other to smile she saw that possessiveness in his eyes again — as if he knew her and wanted her but would never intrude on her direction, even if he thought she was heading down the wrong road. But Charlotte was not disturbed by Myron's desire, nor by her own. Some day, they might have this together, she thought. Or perhaps the existence of the feeling was enough, it's unspoken, unenacted power tying them more surely than actual sexual love would have done.

Later, escaping the crowded kitchen where everyone drank beer and vodka tonics—plenty of hands to get the dinner work done—Charlotte sat on a white lawn chair at the back of the house gazing at wild flowers and hills covered with green and lilac shrubs. She started thinking about Myron, giving into a sexual fantasy which she embellished and extended while she sipped wine, until she saw neither flowers nor shrubs but only herself, naked in Myron's arms. That image was replaced by thoughts of Lynda. She was hoping, she realized, for some transforming perspective from her cousin: she would tell stories of the family no one had known before—perhaps the letters to Mathilda—some secret knowledge of their childhood, long-forgotten by the others, which Charlotte had been too young to know. And she was afraid of Lynda's claim on her mother's heart, worried about her own closeness with Aunt Rose. She grimaced at her pettiness. Grow up, she admonished herself, turned her head and saw flowers again. The sky darkened a shade, and a delicate breeze began across the field. When she lost sight of her surroundings again, she was imagining sex between Vivian and Ruth. Hands on smooth buttocks moved up curving waists to full breasts. Ruth stroked Vivian until her thighs parted. She bent down to kiss and suck her—. Charlotte saw Andre's face, then Ivan's, then Vivian's thighs again. She grabbed her drink and took a long sip, having been to the end of the world, reaching back for the glazed and partial consciousness of normal social life.

"Mom!" Charlotte jerked to attention and turned to face an angry Ivan. "I've been calling you for ten minutes. Don't you ever listen to me! I'm going to the movies with the other kids. Matt's driving—Vivian said it was okay so don't say anything. We're going to see "Greystoke," the new Tarzan movie. Bye. I love you." A quick kiss grazed her cheek.

But the end of the world was where her best ideas came from,

278

almost at the horizon, about to fall off the edge. All week Charlotte had felt obsessed with the idea of extremity. But what extreme was she flirting with? Secure in all this domesticity, what risk was she planning to take?

"What about dinner?" she called to her son's back.

"Don't worry. We'll get something on the road," he yelled as he was joined by his cousins and friends.

"Take care of Michael," she warned. The six of them piled into the Chevrolet. Thank God Matthew, the calmest and clearest, was also the oldest, old enough to drive.

When they returned it was nearly midnight. "It was fantastic," Annie shouted as they burst into the kitchen where some of the adults sat around a recently cleared table, drinking coffee and tea.

"I hope there weren't any savage Africans," Hannah said, looking at Paul.

"Actually, there were a few," Matthew admitted. "They were about one level better than the old Tarzan movies." He shook his head in disappointment, his suddenly raised consciousness diminishing his pleasure.

"So what was it about?" Paul asked, generous. The discussion could continue now.

"It was seriously excellent." Isaac was relieved. "Oh my God, remember when he found his father in the cage of the horrible scientist!?"

Jennifer flung her canvas bag into the corner. "But Jane's still the understanding wife, representing social normalcy and convention," she complained, and her sister, loyal despite their temperamental differences said, "It's true." Annie sat down at the table with dampened enthusiasm, eyeing Jennifer for permission to rejoin the general acclaim.

"Oh come on, Jen." Matthew gently pushed her arm. "You know you loved it. I saw you crying and clapping." Jennifer smiled and relented. Immediately Annie began chattering again, describing scenes, the realism of the apes' costumes and gestures, the hypocrisy of the "so-called civilized English—I mean they were like totally cruel, Mom."

Marilyn sipped tea. Her dyed brown hair stiffly framed a

279

darkly tanned forehead. Tiny lines etched her lips so they looked chapped even though thickly covered with shining aloe gloss. Her eyes seemed tired to Charlotte, yet she always came alive in the presence of her daughters' energy, if only as a chorus of approvals. "Mmm, I know," she said now, as passive in public as an old-fashioned servant trained not to disagree. But Charlotte knew from discussions with Annie and Jennifer that, in private, away from the family, Marilyn expressed strong opinions about many things, had always enjoined her daughters to be assertive and self-reliant, contradicting her own behavior with whispered kitchen-secret words.

"But those apes," Matthew repeated. "They were amazing. I loved them. You couldn't help it."

And to everyone's astonished delight Ivan, right before their eyes, became a large, gentle ape. He whipped off his tee shirt and loped around the kitchen, his long arms stretching to reach the floor and help his simian stride. "Errrrrr, errrrrr hooooo, arh, arh," he crooned, lifting dark, pleading eyes to Charlotte as he circled her chair in small, graceful jumps. He was grabbing her arm, putting it on his head and, when it fell, grabbing it again as he crooned insistently at her, desperate to communicate some need she couldn't comprehend.

"What?" she laughed, eager to cooperate but unable to translate his monkey language into a clear message as to what she was supposed to do. The pain was starting in her eyes. "Hi, monkey. Hello sweet ape," she offered.

But Ivan was unsatisfied. His crooning became louder and more desperate. "Errrr, hoo, hoo," he insisted wildly, grabbing her arm again, as the other kids laughed and clapped, encouraging his performance to greater heights.

"He wants love! He wants love!" shouted Michael.

"That's what they do when they want love," Annie explained. "It's what Tarzan did when his ape mother died. He grabs her hand to try to make it caress him like she used to do when she was alive. And when the hand keeps falling off his head, he realizes she's really dead. Oh God. It was so sad!"

"Errr, hoo, hoo," cried Ivan, his head bobbing up and down like a buoy in the waves as he circled his mother's chair.

She reached out for his head and smoothed his curls, ran her finger across his forehead, forefinger down his still-pug nose. She petted him as if he were a needy dog. "I'm not dead, monkey," she assured her son. She played the game although she felt a strong need to leave them—their voices were too loud for midnight, their energy and demands. She stroked her son's head again then reached for her own aching eyes.

Satisfied at last, Ivan loped over to an empty chair and, never unbending his knees, a perfect ape, climbed on. There he sat, amid the applause of his family, errring and hooing and smiling, nodding his chin at his large, bony knees.

Alex was already in bed but not asleep. He turned over to hold her as she climbed in beside him in the dark. A wind rose outside their window lacing a calm swishing sound through their affectionate silence. Charlotte forced herself to imagine the terrible noises of the city in summer—the way she had to close all the windows and turn Bach up loud, a collected, organized, unemotional music so she could find quiet inside. Imagining that discomfort, she appreciated the sound of the wind and the silence behind it all the more. She relaxed in Alex's arms.

"That was nice when you and Ivan played ball today," she whispered. "He really adores you, you know."

"Mmmmm, Oh I don't think so. He does? Really?" He buried his mouth in her neck and giggled at his own eagerness.

The quietness of their marriage comforted Charlotte. But after all this time, they couldn't croon for love, only eye each other across a mysterious, impenetrable distance. Alex pressed her thigh with his own. "You want to make love?"

But she wanted him to fly across the distance, not ask her permission. She twisted uncomfortably in his arms. Hold me, she wanted to plead, save me. She was trapped between the clean, ironed sheets. The price of escape was to call out her oldest needs, and she was as silent as the silence behind the wind. Could she *errr* and *hooo* for him, who had cared for so long, who had loved her first when he watched her dive into a dangerous sea?

She kissed his neck, hoping to contradict her refusal, tempt his hands to ignore the stiffness of her back. What the hell did she want, she could hear him say to her thoughts. For him to provide her with quiet respect and overpowering demands all at once? To translate her turned back into a desire for love? You'll drive me crazy with your double binds, he would warn. She wanted him to croon for her, take her to the end of the world, spread her thighs with a womanly hand and still remain Alex, reminding her of earthly, orderly things.

What rearrangement did she expect after all this time? And if she got the changes she privately, safely courted (now he kissed her mouth and touched her breast) wouldn't she be afraid—if he suddenly released sweet boyish needs, old hungers for her to feed? (He slipped off his yellow underpants while she lifted her blue nightgown over her head.) Wouldn't he bolt in panic, rush away from her to some mountain where he would trudge to the summit until he felt brave again?

(She lay on her back, knees raised as he lowered himself into her.) But it was George and Leonard who climbed mountains, drawn by arrogance, heroism, defeat. The only way Alex would climb a mountain was if Charlotte got lost there. Then he would move heaven and earth to find her and he would, she knew. He'd drag her out of the forest or cave and nurse her back to health again. (He moved into her more deeply as he began to sigh and murmur her name. She answered "Alex, Alex"—a plea, an apology, a declaration. But she remained where she was, apart from him despite her best desire. She heard him call her, but she could not come.)

Charlotte sat at the kitchen table wondering where Lynda would sleep. On a yellow pad, she listed the names of every person in the house matched with the room they were currently using. Next week Vivian, Ruth and the children would be gone, but for the weekend, where would she put Lynda? She had to have some privacy after being away for so long. You couldn't just stick her on the living room couch.

"Mom! Are you going totally crazy? You're on vacation and you're always making lists!" Ivan shoved Charlotte's shoulder, only half in jest.

Charlotte shaded her eyes with her hand and put down her pencil. "But where will Lynda sleep?" she asked her son.

"Mom! Stop! She can have our room, okay. We'll sleep in the living room in sleeping bags. Relax." Charlotte felt soothed by his presence of mind. "Uh Mom," he switched to a quacking voice he used lately for teasing her, "we're talking serious obsessive compulsion here," his father's language.

"Leave the Commissar alone." Hannah patted Charlotte on the back. "She's working. Mama, you're baking for an army."

Rose made her way around the counters sniffing cinnamon rolls, dipping her finger into mixed chocolate, stirring satin coconut cream. "There *is* an army here in case you haven't noticed."

Jacob walked into the kitchen and kissed his mother's flour-speckled cheek. He sat down and pulled out his cards.

Charlotte watched him cut the deck into two equal halves

to shuffle, flipping the curve over and allowing the cards to fall swiftly into his palms. He repeated the movement several times, then laid out seven cards for Solitaire. Now, out of the disordered numbers and suits, he would try to recreate order—clubs, hearts, diamonds, spades in a neat pile from Ace to King. He could do it hundreds of times in a row, until someone was willing to join him for Poker or Hearts, a greater challenge. Then he would have to place his wits and his luck not only against the chance fall of the cards themselves, but against other people's behavior. "It's a survival lesson," was the way Jacob described the game to Jennifer, the only one of his children who had refused to take up her father's habit. "You play cards enough, you get to know people. For example, say you have a moonshot hand in Hearts—lots of high hearts and the Queen? And you don't shoot the moon? All that power unused? You're gonna lose big."

"You're always trying to shoot the moon and make other people lose," retorted Jennifer. "You win all the time, Daddy. It's no fun playing with you."

Hesitantly, he held out the cards to his daughter. "Come on, play with me." His tone seemed to promise he would lose. But Jennifer shook her head and returned to her book.

Charlotte watched Jacob lose at Solitaire, stymied by a buried ace of clubs. He clicked his tongue and began again.

"Takes Lynda coming, home to get some cake around here," he teased his mother.

"*If* she comes home," Rose grunted as she dried the baking pan she never traveled without.

"She's coming Aunt Rose. Tomorrow."

"So she says." Rose walked to the sink with a slight shuffle, her head bent forward a bit. Charlotte felt alarmed by the lines and creases around her eyes, down her cheeks, like delicate tracks of tiny birds at the shore. Aunt Rose was almost seventy-five. She hadn't seen her daughter in fifteen years, as long as Ivan was old.

"Mother." Marilyn was peeking in the oven door. "The rolls."

"She'll have plenty of stories," Paul said eagerly. He put his arm around Hannah's shoulder, taking a seat next to her at the table. He twisted his fingers through her curls. Hannah kissed him, then edged away. "Yes. It's a dangerous area of Lebanon she's been in. Did you read her piece on the invasion? She concentrated on the religious war. I completely disagree with her conclusions. It's the economic issues at the bottom of that war, just like every other war. I'm sorry, Paul—(now it was clear to Charlotte why Hannah had edged away from him)—Paul and I disagree about this—but the whole nationalist fetish—it's just another opiate. Just like religion, keeping people apart."

Paul folded his hands on the old wooden table.

"Oh, come on, Hannah," said Alex, who had been standing in the doorway. "That old language? It's dead as Marx himself. Of course it's the religious issue over there. Has been for thousands of years."

Jacob stopped shuffling his cards. "Look, Hannah. I've been studying society for twenty-five years—."

"Don't lecture me, Jacob Cohen. I may not have a Ph.D. But I've been studying as long as you," Hannah said.

"And don't *you* interrupt *me*."

"Well, don't condescend to me."

"You want to discuss, Hannah? Cause I'm just as happy playing cards."

"Go ahead, Jacob." Hannah exchanged a look with Charlotte. Andre, infuriated by Buck's formal professorial tones, pounding his fists on the table so hard he jostled the food off his plate, Andre's tortured impassioned eyes filled Charlotte's head. But Jacob had remained unperturbed. Charlotte had always thought it coldness, disinterest. Perhaps it had been the deepest kind of comfort instead.

Jacob leaned forward and pushed his glasses to the bridge of his nose. "Okay, since you give me permission, Hannah. I don't agree with you. We're controlled by complex forces. Psychological. Economic? Of course. Even spiritual, you should excuse the expression. Do you know there are anthropologists who believe much of human history has been determined by climate?" He counted each global force off on his fingers. "You can't reduce history to one cause. People have been trying ever since Heraclitus. 'All is fire.' Well, all isn't fire. And all isn't economics either. For Pete's sake, Hannah. Didn't you learn anything from our childhood?"

285

"I need help with this quick, somebody." Rose could not find a place for the hot baking pan. Myron held it while she cleared a space on the counter and was rewarded with a helping of frosting fed to him by Rose. "Alex. Jacob," she said. "Things aren't as complicated as you make out. We made mistakes in our youth, of course. And one of those mistakes was making truth too simple. And I know," she turned to Jacob, "you had a harder time than the others with friends in school, on the block, wanting to be a regular boy and always taunted by those stupid kids calling you a Commie, not knowing which side of their bread was buttered."

"Mama, we're not talking about my boyhood troubles. We're talking about Lebanon."

"Oh. Lebanon. Myron, enough stirring. Marilyn, start the icing for that one. Psychology. Religion. At bottom, it's goods. Who's got 'em and who wants 'em."

Paul laughed. He disagreed, Charlotte presumed, with the idea that all social conflict could be explained by the concept of class. But he didn't speak. Perhaps it seemed too obvious to him that links of culture and race could supercede class differences. Perhaps he was angry, or shy.

"What Mama is saying is a fundamental principle of Marxism," Hannah insisted, "which I happen to believe in."

"You're just like Mama," Jacob said.

Hannah blushed as Rose gave her an interested look. "You can't predict," she said, turning back to her cakes.

"Look," Hannah resumed. "The way property is divided is a foundation of social organization, am I right, Professor Cohen? If you follow any conflict, all injustice, even racism, Paul, even sexism, to its origin, you find the unequal distribution of wealth."

Everyone began shouting, supporting her, arguing. For a moment, Charlotte didn't distinguish words; she felt only the familiar rhythms around her, things spinning out of control. And yet there was order here, balance, the present neatly mirroring the past. She thought of her recent sketches. The boats were skillfully drawn, but they were lifeless, an accurate sum of the parts of a fishing boat. A list. There was no Old Man Death on her fishing boat, and the secret he had for her would not be revealed until (it was a risk of course) she gave him the chance to steer.

286

"Where the hell are you, Charlotte? What are you always thinking about?" Hannah pushed a doughnut in her direction, but Charlotte ignored it.

"I'm sorry. I was thinking about my painting. I'm not sure what I want to do."

"It's a little self-indulgent after a certain point, don't you think?" Jacob asked.

"Not if I'm going to paint." Charlotte swallowed anger.

Hannah said, "Painting is important. But there's the world, Charlotte. You have some responsibility to history."

"History?" She was amazed. "I'm always thinking about history. All my life. That's the whole point." Was she invisible then? Even to Hannah? She was shouting from under a mountain of sand.

"The place of an artist is to paint. That's her responsibility to history," said Paul. Charlotte looked at him gratefully.

"Nevertheless," Jacob raised his voice. "And you can listen to this, Jennifer. The world is a mess, and a thousand portraits or sonatas won't help that."

"And novels?" Charlotte asked. "Why don't you include Paul in your theory of the superfluousness of art?"

Jacob shifted position, picked up his deck of cards and shuffled. The shouting began again. Sub-arguments developed around the kitchen.

"Wait! Everyone shut up!" They looked at Matthew in surprise. "You can't discuss this way! Everyone's making speeches. You want to make speeches or you want to listen to each other?"

"Way to go, Matt!" from Ivan in the living room.

"Matthew!" said Vivian, proud but criticizing for the sake of form.

"Let him talk." Ruth had arrived in her bathing suit, ready for a morning swim.

"Well, I've heard the old stories all my life from Mom. And I've read a lot, trying to understand. I see my father. A decent man, building all those fabulous houses for people who can afford a hundred thousand dollars, and fifteen minutes away are industrial slums filled with bedraggled kids. No offense, Jacob. But there's a connection there. My father's a good man." He looked at Vivian

287

defiantly. "But he's bound by money. Well, by his class, I guess you'd say, as much as those poor kids. If everyone had an equal share, I don't think it would change everything. Like you said, Jacob, nothing explains everything. But I think it would change a lot."

Ivan and Jennifer stood in the kitchen doorway, impressed.

Ruth responded, no family baggage dragging her down, "I don't know, Matthew. Religion—that's pretty strong stuff. My family? To them Catholicism is everything. They'd die for the Church if they had to. Look what's happening in Ireland."

Paul nodded. "It's the poor and rich Catholics against the poor and rich Protestants."

"What's happening in Ireland is about economic control of the country, Ruth. Surely you see that?" Vivian and Hannah exchanged impatient looks, irritated by their lovers' positions.

Charlotte thought of her old mural. History and art. Politics and love. If she were to paint that way again, now, would she have the luxury of feeling connected to historical event? What portraits of historical figures would shadow the faces of her family? No, she could only imagine it one way. An enormous explosion of a nuclear bomb. In the corner, a madwoman, sweeping blood off the floor.

"But the individual is not just a collection of social forces." Alex was talking now. "There's more to it than that."

"Dad, please! Don't start on our buried desires. What Vivian and Matt are saying, and Aunt Hannah, it makes a lot of sense."

"May I please finish my point, Ivan?"

"No wait, I have something to say."

"Let him?" Charlotte asked.

"I mean," Ivan stammered, bounding the air with his hands, a perimeter for his attempt to focus. "Look, if you guys, you grownups, divided privileges among us, well—kids, unequally, we would start fighting right? The smart thing would be for all of us to fight you. But no, we'd fight with each other for the — scarce—goods." He edged onto the corner of his aunt's chair. "I'm just saying—I'm almost done, Dad."

"Oh, take no notice of me." Alex smiled.

"I'm just saying, it seems reasonable that it's the same thing in the world. People fight over a lot of things, but at the bottom level, it's about some people having power, money, stuff like that, and some people having less."

"*Men* fight about lots of things. *Men*. No one in there is bothering to mention the issue of gender." Jennifer had returned to the living room with Annie. Now she stalked into the kitchen, facing them all. "I've been reading," she announced. "Stuff none of you guys seems to know about. No one with any real intelligence relies on old-fashioned Marxism any more. Aunt Hannah, you should really read this feminist theory." She rushed back to the living room and returned with three large books which she placed on the table in front of Hannah. "It will change the way you think. It doesn't deny the central importance of economic relations, of nationalist wars for markets and all that. But it adds this crucial issue of gender — how women were the goods once, and how men had to control women's sexuality so they would know who their sons were. Their heirs." Hannah raised her eyebrows, interested. "So," continued Jennifer, "what's been the effect, after hundreds of years of the oppression of women, of treating them like property? Of getting the fear of death, which is universal, all mixed up with the body of the mother?"

"Now you lost me," muttered Aunt Rose. But they all watched, riveted by the visible energy of Jennifer thinking, a human brain in the process of growth.

"I don't know if I can put it into the right words. But everyone, everywhere, male and female, is reared by a mother. So everything they want in life, everything they feel about power and powerlessness, including when they realize they are going to die some day, all of it is related to this *woman*. Woman, not just parent. And that's the beginning of the idealization of women, and the contempt for her too, which is based on her position in the family, which is connected to all the economic factors of social life. Even Engels said that, Grandma." She turned to Rose.

"I always knew this kid was special." Charlotte looked hard at Jacob.

"I plan to look into this," he responded with real attention, leafing through one of Jennifer's books.

"You'll be amazed, Dad." She sat next to him, her chronic

289

tone of resentment replaced by one of lively interest. "It's amazing that most social scientists don't take this into account. It's out of—well, resistance." She turned to Alex. So she knew something about psychoanalysis too.

Rose uttered an exclamation of disgust and announced she was out of butter, perhaps, Charlotte thought with surprise, because she had ceased being able to follow the discussion. Nevertheless, she felt a rush of hope for Jennifer. The family was opinionated, capable of all kinds of lies, but, she realized with a surge of love, they talked. And sooner or later, they listened. Not because they thought it was *right,* like some families she'd seen, heeding the warnings of childrearing theory and obeying the rules of group therapy with grim affectations. But because they were truly interested. Jennifer was finding a passage for her father to read. Rose grumbled about butter again, and Matthew and Ivan offered to go to the store. She added a dozen more items to the list.

When the boys left, Alex said loudly, "As I was saying before this useful but lengthy interruption—that is, if anyone is interested?"

Amid encouraging mutters, he went on. "My point was going to be, however predictable you may think it, that the psyche of man, excuse me, of human beings, is a pattern of paradoxes. We want contradictory things. Everything we choose, or much of it, is sabotaged by the desire for its opposite. And one of the things human beings want to do—I know you're all going to jump on me—is suffer."

They all yelled, "Oh come on, Alex."

"Not this masochism shit again," said Hannah.

"Well," he shrugged. "I see it every day in my office. And the desire to suffer is connected to the desire to make other people suffer. Look." He lay both his hands flat on the table. "I loved my mother. None of you ever met her. She was—full of joyfulness, or she could be."

Charlotte watched amazed as Alex's eyes filled with tears.

"We would garden together. She showed me the difference between spices and flowers when I was about five. Then we would carry all the wonderful things into the house and make a salad. But, let me tell you, making that salad was like making a work of

art. When my mother created a salad—she was like a painter."
He colored as he looked up at Charlotte. "But, Charlotte knows
this. My mother had rages when I was little, especially when she
drank too much which was often. She used to completely lose
control of herself and—just strike out at anyone in her path.
Usually me, since my father was never around. Then she'd shout
at me, calling me all kinds of names. She'd even push me. Once
she threw a chair at me. Later, she'd cry and apologize and tell
me she was crazy and I was wonderful. But I always knew it would
happen again. When she did it—this is the point—I do not
remember feeling I hated her. I hated myself. I figured I must be
as horrible as she thought I was to make her—someone as
wonderful as her—so mad. When I went into therapy, it took me
years to work that through. To stop being willing to suffer so someone I loved wouldn't get mad at me."

At what cost to himself, then, had he remained silent during
the course of her affairs with Leonard?

"Oh, Alex," said Hannah and placed her hand on his arm.

"What I'm trying to say," he continued, "is that we all have
the need to create as well as destroy. The desire for pain and
ultimately death motivates us individually and therefore collectively. Sometimes it wins the struggle." He had gone too far before
he realized his direction. Rose stiffened and put her kitchen tools
down.

"Alex," cautioned Charlotte.

He got up and put his arm around Rose. "Can I say something
about this? I don't want to hurt you, but it's important."

"By me anyone can say anything. Anything they want as long
as they aren't tyrants." Her words reminded Charlotte of the time
in the old kitchen when she'd forbidden Leon to speak. It was
the afternoon Lynda had accused her mother of not loving her.
"And you, Alex, are anything but a tyrant. If I cry, I cry," she admonished her niece. She looked very old, tired, but not from
heavy burdens, and not from lack of sleep.

"What I'm saying," Alex remained standing with his arm
around Rose, "is that it's not enough to believe in the right things,
to come to the right conclusions. We're not only fighting evil in
the world—we're fighting against ourselves. Take Charlotte's

dreams of nuclear war. It's not only that she fears the earth's destruction, as we all do. She dreams because the idea of complete destruction touches off something in herself."

She may as well have been back on the beach with him, that first time she knew she loved him, so real and immediate was the memory of his eyes. She felt as if marriage and parenting formed a thick gauze veil, providing protection she craved but making her forget everything that was really important to her about him. She leaned across the table and took his face in her hands. She kissed his lips, sucking in drops of his saliva. The family circled around them, clapping.

"Smooch, smooch," Hannah teased. "We thought we were the lovers."

Charlotte released Alex and saw them all wander away to various chores, relieved to be done with the discussion. They had circled around her all summer, needing attention. Now she worried about Annie, back on the couch leafing through a dozen magazines, oblivious apparently to anything beyond the impending fashions of the fall. Charlotte wondered about this niece, how she could reach beneath Annie's superficial concerns.

She jerked her eyes back to the kitchen. Rose was stacking cakes on various platters. Myron stretched and announced his readiness for the beach. Jacob went off to play ball with the boys, Marilyn to her daughter.

"One thing you learn when you're Black," said Paul, a sudden announcement of confidence in them, of trust. "You know the difference between power and powerlessness. No mistaking those two things. Sometimes you can fight—against evil, or, as Alex says, against your own worst self. Sometimes all you can do is watch and keep a record and hope that some day someone might need to know what you've noted down. Or maybe you do it for no reason at all. And that's the big fear—it may be for no reason at all. Like a witness never called into court."

She had established herself as witness long ago, and now she had the funny power of the listener, the magnet of the family despite her adoptive status. (Paul had asked *her* permission to use the idea of letters to Old Man Death.) Yet, she was exhausted by the effort, wanted to leave them to whatever haphazard orbiting attracted each life. Was she, then, getting ready to leave them? Would they die without her watching them? Now that she knew, at last, that they needed her, would she abandon them to manage on their own? But they would continue. Was this what frightened her? Her replaceability?

Or did she finally not care as much if they perfectly loved her? She felt like a child, she realized, as part of her listened to Hannah and Paul argue about race and class. ("But we can't let the idea of race divide us," she insisted. Clearly Hannah loved this man. "It's history that divides us," he answered sadly. "That doesn't mean we can't explain our history to each other. Accept volunteers. Think of your namesake, Hannah George. He volunteered for the Spanish Civil War because he realized that history was also his own. I accept you as a volunteer.")

She felt like a child on the outskirts of history, powerless to affect events, whenever she separated her art from the world. Like George who never risked completing anything, she had, in the last years, hidden in her corner like a child clutching her drawings to her chest. It wasn't that she didn't know what she wanted to paint. She was afraid that no one—Jacob, Hannah, Alex, the world—would understand. That would be painful, she couldn't deny it. It would break her heart. How would she live with a broken heart, the disappointment as keen, as sharp, as a razor cut, the pain so pure she would hardly feel it at all, just look down amazed at the neat crevice in her body that poured out a narrow wave of blood.

"But how can you keep going?" she asked Paul, "recording and explaining when you know it might be for nothing?"

"Listen," he said. "When I was six years old I found a wallet in the hallway of my school. I went to school in Brooklyn—all the teachers were white then. I brought the wallet to my teacher. She looked at me harshly and said, 'What did you do with the money?' There was nothing in the wallet except cards. I was dumbfounded. I didn't answer. She asked me again."

Paul stopped speaking, unable to continue. "Jesus!" he said, surprising himself. "No. Let me finish. It's okay. She asked me again. 'What did you do with the money?' I knew she was asking me because I was Black. I knew she wouldn't ask a white child

293

the same question. I stood there shrugging and smiling because I was so scared and angry. I knew whatever I said she would only see a Black child returning an empty wallet." He paused. "But here's the point, I think. It wasn't just the false accusation that dumbfounded me. It was the contrast between that and how I had been taught to think about myself, from my mother I guess. She thought I was wonderful. I had been given a lot of love. Right then and there I realized it was a great luxury, the way my mother understood me. That I'd be very lucky if I ever found anyone to see me that way again." He looked at Hannah with soft eyes. "Why do you go to Central America again and again?"

Hannah shrugged. "I feel I have to see what's happening, I guess. Then I try to tell people what I see. There's so much suffering in the world. And I just — well, I care."

Charlotte watched Rose watching Hannah as if she were seeing her daughter for the first time. But perhaps Rose would forget, when she turned back to her stove, as Charlotte had repeatedly forgotten the strong, competent Hannah, seeing her chronically, falsely, as "the youngest child." Just as, except for an occasional flash, she could see Ivan only as "her son," depth of attachment creating distortion rather than clarity of line.

"When I think of even one life," Hannah said, "thwarted, ruined —."

Charlotte said, "Some people can't face how much they care because they feel impotent."

"Impotent?" Hannah looked confused. "Well, I never thought I was a general. Only a buck private. A tiny voice in the wind. I try not to think about it that way or I get obsessed with myself. I agree with you, Alex, you have to know yourself. I probably don't know myself as well as I should. But if you get obsessed with yourself, you deliver the world to evil without even a word."

"Without even a word." Paul smiled at Charlotte.

Alex rolled a tennis ball across the table to Paul. "Welcome to the family," he said.

They heard a car in the driveway. "The boys," said Rose who seemed reluctant to begin moving around the kitchen again. She dried her hands on her apron. "My butter. I better start the bread."

A few minutes passed and no one came in. "Maybe they need

help. I gave them such a list," said Rose. Everyone remained where they were, immobilized for a moment, reaching back for habitual roles so they could move again.

"I'll go," said Charlotte, and she went to the front door, which faced the driveway.

Standing against a dark blue Volvo, looking around at the miles of lavender and green brush, the shadowy hills, was a woman of medium height, her dark hair curling around her forehead and ears, her white shorts and tee shirt wrinkled, obviously from a long ride, her face strong-looking, welcoming. Next to her was a younger woman who looked remarkably like her except her hair was sleek black and straight, and her skin was a darker shade of tan.

Charlotte felt a narrow shaft of cool air open inside her as she stepped out into the yard.

"Hi Oscar," the woman said as she smiled.

The family embraced Lynda all at once, then separately. She was introduced to the newcomers, the children. The young woman was introduced to them only as "Leah." She sat silently on the grass while Lynda described the flight, the drive up from New York, and listened to descriptions of the feast waiting inside the house. Marilyn and Jacob brought coffee and a large cake into the yard and served everyone, even Rose who was silent and still, staring at Leah who stared uncomfortably, impatiently, at Lynda.

Ivan said, "I've heard about you all my life. I can't believe you're here." He smiled at Lynda like an adoring suitor.

Jennifer seemed shy, standing close to Charlotte.

Annie complimented the French cut of Lynda's white shorts.

"I have a pair like them you can have," said Leah in sharp, accented English.

"What a beautiful house," said Lynda, tearful, respectful eyes on her younger brother who had grown, obviously, into a benevolent patriarch. Jacob looked more boyish than Charlotte had seen him in years.

"It's your house for as long as you want to stay," said Marilyn.

Then there was nothing to fill the silence, and they all looked at Leah.

"This is my daughter. Your granddaughter," said Lynda, her eyes fastened on Rose's face. "Leah," she said again. They were all awkward and speechless, staring at Lynda. Rose gripped the back of a lawn chair with both hands as if it were a crutch, or a shield. More lies, held in place for a lifetime. The secret life Lynda

296

had wanted, to give her the importance she thought she lacked? False arrogance, or just revenge? Charlotte didn't know. The dimensions of Lynda's anger had been a secret, she realized that much as Alex began attempting to assuage discomfort, bringing up more chairs for people, and Rose, returning her daughter's stare, grumbled, "So where's her father? *Leah's*?"

Lynda sat down on the grass, an expression of defiance, Charlotte thought, in her eyes. But later Alex would describe her as looking like a scared child. Nineteen years before, she told them, she had been writing a series of articles for a French newspaper about the war in Vietnam. She became acquainted with a group of Vietnamese exiles in Paris, one of whom had been educated in the United States, became a professor of Political Science, and then, unable to tolerate the separation from his own country, he had returned to Europe to work as a journalist hoping at the right moment to return to his home. Two years before the right moment came, he met Lynda.

"His name was Le Duan Kien." Lynda twisted a wide silver ring as she began her story. Her tone seemed to beg Rose for something, but Rose remained stone faced, so Lynda reached for her daughter's hand. "He reminded me of the best in all the men I'd adored as a child—his passion for ordinary people, his dedication. Leah's father—" she encircled her daughter's shoulders with her arm, "had a kind of gentle restraint, completely different from the distance I'd known in men before. And since," she added bluntly, comforting Charlotte with memory of a Lynda she knew.

Leah Duan Kien was three years old when her father returned to Vietnam and, during the Tet Offensive, was killed in a bombing raid of a village the American government insisted was a military target. Over eight hundred people in addition to Le Duan Kien were killed that day. There had been a large protest demonstration in New York City and Charlotte remembered that she had been there, with Andre and Vivian and Alex (she had been pregnant with Ivan at the time) shouting and marching against the war, never imagining that someone they might have loved was a mass of torn flesh, reduced to an abstraction with the others in the body count. Lynda had spent that day demonstrating in the streets of Paris, knowing her husband was dead. The news

297

service had identified him immediately and called. Only the literal support of her friends' arms had kept her and Leah, whom she pressed to her chest, from falling to the ground as she blindly marched, her cries of pain blending in with the shouts of rage surrounding them.

"And you never told us anything. Even when you came home, when Andre died. You never said." The enormity of her daughter's rejection seemed to age Rose visibly as she moved from behind the chair to the front. She sat down heavily, her hand on her heart.

Jacob and Hannah moved to her side. Charlotte took the place behind the chair, her hands on Rose's shoulders.

"It takes some people a long time to grow up," Lynda said. "That's why I waited to introduce Leah properly. Because I wanted to say—I'm sorry." The words remained suspended in the air like dew on scorched desert ground, tantalizing, useless.

Rose looked confused, a woman trapped in a moment so barren of comfort or illusion one might, perhaps, die of the light. "We'll talk later, " she finally whispered, bending her lips to Lynda's dark curls. "Now, let me see my granddaughter if you don't mind."

Everyone turned to Leah who addressed each of them in turn, as if she were repeating her arrival, slightly awkward as she kissed the boys, unrestrained with the others. "All my life I have heard about you," she repeated many times. "I am so grateful to be here at last." The slight formality of her speech might have been the result of the dramatic events of the day, but it struck them as a sign of her sincerity. She seemed to be a person who would not claim such feeling casually, and they welcomed her home.

"A day early," said Rose.

"We thought we'd need to stay over a night in the city, after the flight," Lynda explained. She and Leah laughed. "But we couldn't wait." She winked at Ivan, hugged Jennifer, Michael and Annie again.

Much later, after eating, hauling suitcases from the car, opening presents, after they broke into small groups of twos and threes to exchange news and compare impressions, some of them decided to walk to the bay for a late-afternoon swim. The only

298

ones left, Charlotte saw with trepidation, were herself, Hannah, Lynda and Rose.

Rose and her daughters sat at the kitchen table, cups of hot coffee sentineled before them, chessmen waiting to be moved. Rose put a second spoonful of sugar into hers, although generally she didn't use sugar at all. Hannah, who had just finished a large piece of coconut cake, put a muffin in to toast. "Well, here we are," she winced.

"Here we are," Lynda repeated and sipped coffee, spilling some on her white blouse.

Rose said, "Where's Charlotte?" and all three of them turned to look.

Charlotte heard Rose say it as she walked past the kitchen window on her way to the beach.

Very few people remained at five o'clock. Two or three striped umbrellas tilted superfluously against a fading sun. The entire Chinese family was there, however, and as she walked past Charlotte smiled at a woman diapering a wriggling baby who sucked on a half-peeled orange that dripped onto her tiny chest. The tide was coming in quickly. Closer than ever to shore was the fishing boat, suddenly no dark silhouette, its neat wooden planks visible. Several men waved in the direction of the shore.

Charlotte walked into the ocean up to her knees. Waves crashed against her, wetting her to the shoulders. Despite the chill and her sweatshirt she walked in further. The fishing boat turned toward the sun, glistening against a platinum sky. Mechanically, in a kind of daze, she unbraided her hair just before a wave caught her unaware, throwing her onto the gravelly sand as she was carried back to shore. She stood up, shocked and shivering, but oddly pleased. Her long hair hung in dark twisted ringlets down her back.

She peeled off her soaked sweat shirt, wrung it out and threw it onto the sand. Then she dove under a wave, remaining submerged for as long as her breath would hold. Ordinarily, Charlotte rode the waves in, her body stretched taut as a surfboard, her hands pointed upward, fighting to avoid the underwater swirl, that momentary loss of control the children loved. But now she

299

let the waves throw her. She was flipped over, turned upside down by the increasingly rough tide. Each time she surfaced she breathed deeply, unsure if she felt fear or relief, and dove down again. The fifth or sixth time she was thrown onto the shore, her legs stinging from the sharp shells and stones, she heard screaming.

She crawled out of the path of the next wave and saw the Chinese family standing at the edge of the water waving and shouting as two men dove off the side of the fishing boat and began to swim in. One of them floated on his back, holding an enormous object in his arms.

Charlotte watched, transfixed, but felt as if she were viewing the inside of her brain. Her imaginary story, starring Old Man Death, seemed to push down one brain path, synapse linked to successive synapse, forming a solid bridge of brain mountain until it stopped right behind her eyes. From another direction came the ideas for paintings of boats, each boat picture looking more and more like a coffin and then turning back into a boat again. That ridge formed and stopped too, and a third one began—what she was seeing before her now. Two ordinary men swam in until their feet touched ground. They walked onto the beach laughing and greeting their enormous family who surrounded and welcomed them reaching out for the large watermelon that the floater handed over—a feast.

Death journals—black and white paint splashed across a shape that might have been a coffin or a boat. There was a hope beneath that image. Of some eternal reunion? Or, as Otharose had suggested to her over thirty years before, some ultimate power? All evaporated, illusion, mirage, at least for the moment, as the facts unfolded before her eyes.

"Where do you all come from?" Charlotte touched the shoulder of the white man in the family as he walked by her speaking easy Chinese to the young boy he carried in his arms.

"New York," he said. "We're all from New York. Those two guys have been fishing for days. No luck." He shrugged.

Charlotte chuckled, thinking of Alex. She picked up her soaked sweat shirt. She was freezing cold. It was not merely death she wanted to control. Power over what? she wondered as she ran up the dune.

300

"The day I heard of Le's death it was like losing Pop all over again." Lynda sat on an old sunken bed in an upstairs bedroom, hers and Leah's now that Vivian, Ruth and the children had gone, but everyone was changing places nightly it seemed. Charlotte had lost track. That morning her period had finally come. Her body was swollen with long awaited bloat, her breasts and belly heavy with liquid. She leaned back in her chair listening to Lynda, dizzy with a sense of excess — the long-awaited return, the menstrual blood flowing at last so that in several days her body and eyes would be normal again.

Lynda rested against an old down pillow and raised her muscular legs straight to the ceiling, bringing her head up to touch her knees, stretching her back. "And then —." She lay back and turned to face Charlotte who rocked in a frayed wicker chair combing her hair. "And then, I really had to figure a few things out."

"What did you figure out? What did you do?"

"What did I do? I kept working and taking care of my baby. I had lots of friends. A few lovers. When Leah got older I started traveling again, dragging her around the world with me. What I figured out? I figured out very little in a very long time. For all those years, until Leah was just about grown, I stayed angry at Mama."

Lynda sat up on the bed cross-legged, looking like a young girl herself. But when she pulled her hair straight back from her face, gathering the curls to the nape of her neck, she looked like Rose, the way Charlotte remembered her the night of her Sweet Sixteen. She finished combing, braiding and pinning her own hair.

"You look sort of like Mama, you know," Lynda said.

Charlotte turned her face. She didn't want the old rivalry to come between them.

"So. I started to say, I've had a pretty hard time in the men department." Lynda had sensed the discomfort. Charlotte turned back to her.

"I've always said I wanted someone to replace Le, but I think I've been kidding myself all along. I think I've been happy alone. Or not happy, safer maybe. And you, Charlotte? How did you come to terms with all those heroes we grew up around? Aaron, The Wise. Leon, The Strong. Buck, The Leader, The Noble, The Right."

"George, The Dead." They laughed. "They had everything covered. How did I come to terms with it? Are you kidding, Lynda? I didn't. I didn't come to terms with it. You mean like some therapists say, 'And now my dear, you have come to terms with the problem of death?' I've only had two serious lovers, Lynda. One was sudden, passionate, painful, the most intense sexual opening I've ever known and it almost destroyed me. Or what I know of me. Or what I count on. The other has been — well, the other has been Alex. Sometimes it's lonely and distant. Sometimes it's full of tenderness. Just like life. Mostly, it's been quiet."

"You always hated noise."

"Somehow," Charlotte caught a glimpse of her face in the mirror. She looked like a person listening. "Alex doesn't take me away from myself. But, does it sound selfish? My life hasn't been mainly about marriage. I think that's true for many women who've stuck it out with one man for years. My life has been about — myself. Being Ivan's mother, living with Alex all these years, is part of what I mean when I say 'myself.' I would certainly do anything for them. But I've always been reaching for something, Lynda. Maybe it sounds dramatic, but I've been trying to grasp something ever since I can remember. At first, I thought it was about who was my father. The wonder of two possible paternities! But George, the artist, was not only selfish but dead. And Buck — well Uncle Buck was impenetrable."

"Impenetrable," Lynda repeated. "Absolutely impenetrable. And absolutely kind. A maddening combination. Poor Andre."

"Poor Andre," said Charlotte who was thinking of Ivan as well, battering small fists on the bedroom door, protesting Alex's consistent discipline. And here was the reason she had allowed Alex his merciless tyranny — because of her own need to resurrect Buck. History, she thought. Nothing happened without the thing that happened before. It seemed an awesome, sorrowful thing suddenly, not comforting at all.

"Only this summer," — she felt she had to speak her thoughts or she might lose them again — "I realized I will never know which one of them was my father. I believe it was George when I think about things in a kind of orderly way. But then I'm confronted

302

by the way people need secrets, need lies." She returned her cousin's stare, not softening her accusation. "And I don't know. Perhaps it was Buck after all. Anyway, after *that* long obsession, I thought my whole life was about making art. But it isn't that either, though just like Ivan and Alex, painting is one of the closest things to my heart. But for me, it's a tool, one that I love and get very involved with sharpening, polishing, but still a tool. A way of trying to find out—what I'm trying to find out."

"And what is that?"

"I don't know exactly. It's been bothering me all summer. Something about those fishermen at the beach. And Otharose's letters." And Leonard, she added to herself. There was something she didn't understand about Leonard. "And," Lynda would be sure to think her crazy now," something about Aunt Mathilda's hat." She pulled it off the dresser, traced her fingers across the worn red straw and put it on her head.

"Oh!" Lynda jumped up and opened her suitcase which still remained packed after three days. "Speaking of Aunt Mathilda."

From underneath layers of cotton shirts, a folder thick with papers, a large, blue-plastic makeup kit, Lynda drew a thin packet of letters.

"I took these when Andre died." She remained on her knees peering into the suitcase. "I should have sent them to you, Charlotte. Years ago. I should have, but I never did."

"Why didn't you?" Charlotte's hands hung at her sides, stone-weighted. She looked at the letters, but she did not move.

Lynda stood up and turned her back to Charlotte. "Because— for the same reason I didn't tell anyone about Leah. For revenge."

"Revenge?" Charlotte's voice was a small whisper.

"Oh, maybe that's too grand a word. Talking like my father again. But yes, in a way, Charlotte. I hated you in a way. I felt you had taken my place with Mama. So I took something of yours. I hated Andre too, and I hated Mama. For not realizing I needed them."

"But you? You had Uncle Buck. You were his favorite."

"But Charlotte, you know what Pop was like. You've just been talking about it."

"He adored you."

"He adored me. But he didn't have the slightest idea who I was."

They were both silent. Lynda held the letters in her hand.

"I'm glad you came home," Charlotte said at last. "I hope you'll stay."

Lynda sat down on the edge of the bed. She looked knowingly at her younger cousin as though she were a daughter. Charlotte's blood stirred. She knew this look, this gaze both protective and harsh. Aunt Rose had looked this way the day before when Lynda described one of her more dangerous assignments. It was the perfectly unsentimental expression a woman growing older encounters in the mirror, an expression of recognition, respect and fear. When she saw Rose look at Lynda like that, Charlotte had turned her face from them to hide her longing. Now she lowered her eyes from Lynda's to the floor.

"I can't stay, Charlotte." Tears streamed down Lynda's cheeks, over her lips and chin. "It's too late to alter everything. I waited too long. Can you understand? My entire life has been based on this conviction—coming to terms with my mother's inability to love me. Or at least her difficulty in loving me."

Charlotte thought of all the stories she had heard from Rose in the last years. The woman had loved her daughters in a way that felt like disinterest to them. Something went awry in the translation from feeling to action. "She did love you," was all Charlotte said, stunned by all Rose had lost.

"At any rate, I can forgive her now. I forgive the mother of my childhood. She did the best she could under difficult circumstances. And I'm not a child now. I don't need her any more. But Rose Cohen in the flesh? When I'm around *her* I start feeling angry again. I have to watch my behavior every minute. I start—" her voice shook, "I start needing her again." Lynda sniffed, readjusted her position. "Anyway, I have a good life. I have a lot to do. I never thought I was an artist, but I always knew I had something to say about history. I got that much from my father. I'm going to Vietnam this fall to do a book. I'm leaving at the end of the week, Charlotte. I'm going home."

Now Charlotte began to cry. The package of letters lay on the bed next to Lynda.

"But here's the good news." Lynda pretended lightness. "Leah's staying. She's going to school in New York. She says she wants to know this part of her history. Keep in close touch with her, Charlotte."

"Of course. What would you think?"

"And these," she picked up the letters. "These are yours. They're from Mara to Mathilda, an unlikely pair of correspondents, I would have thought. There are only four of them, and only one is of any real interest to you. And even that one, Charlotte. Don't expect much. There are no headlines. I'm sorry I kept it from you all these years. Can you forgive me?"

"Will you stay here while I read them?"

Lynda nodded.

The first letter said simply that Mara had arrived and found George. The only thing that surprised Charlotte were the closing sentences, obviously a response to something Mathilda had written to them: *You shouldn't think that Rose and Buck see you as crazy. They love you very much. We will return as soon as we can.*

"It wasn't love she wanted," Charlotte said bitterly. "Apparently we didn't know all there was to know about Aunt Mathilda."

"We believed what we were told." Lynda's mouth twisted angrily, a criticism of Rose.

The second letter was about Spain. *The hopeless, noble, Loyalist cause,* said Mara, the realist. George had been slightly wounded. *He's not really a soldier, as we know,* were Mara's words. But the wound was minor, and Mara described her relief now that George was recuperating in the hospital where she worked.

Charlotte folded the old blue paper and inserted it into its envelope. She traced her mother's tiny script with her thumb. Then she opened the third letter and began to read.

Dear Mathilda,

I am so sorry to hear of your unhappiness. How ironic that you feel George is the only one who really knows you, who understands. Maybe some day the world will see your sensitivity, appreciate your work. What I see now is that he never understood me. No matter what personal reasons contributed to his coming here, he knows what he's really here for. He is brave. He cares

305

about the people here. He's full of love for their struggle. And so I can see the difference about the way he feels about Spain and the way he feels about me. I loved him with every ounce of my body. He seemed to touch me the way I needed to be touched. Or else he happened to need to touch me the way I needed to be touched. It all sounds so foolish now. I have come all this way, left my child, to discover there is not much between us. Please tell the others, Mathilda, that I don't want you to call me Mara any more. My name is Miriam. I don't know what will happen when I come home, but I have made a reservation for next week. George insists that he will stay and return to the front. I know you are all giving Charlotte a lot of love. Whatever happens I will always be devoted to you.

The last letter explained that the ship's departure had been delayed for several days and gave a new date and time. An old news clipping in a fifth envelope announced the bombing of the hospital and listed the casualities of the patients and staff. Mathilda had underlined the names *Dr. Miriam Friedman, George Cohen.*

They stood up. Charlotte paced the room in a circle, clutching the letters, then throwing them onto the bureau as she passed. Finally she stopped and looked at Lynda. She held out her arms, a gesture of futility, the only eulogy she could imagine to her aunt's art, her parents' lives. She stood there, her arms opened, her empty hands turned up to the sky, but Lynda thought it was a plea for embrace. They held onto each other, swaying in a slow dance. Charlotte touched Lynda's curls which were just like Hannah's and felt as if she were embracing them all—Mathilda, whose hat tilted precariously on Charlotte's head; Hannah George, the real soldier; Vivian, who was in love; Aunt Rose, the provider; Sybila, who had pulled Charlotte's work from her tight, frightened grasp and dragged it into the world; Otharose who battled Death; and Miriam herself—that young girl, Charlotte suddenly realized, who had never grown older than twenty-eight. If she were to come back now, if Charlotte's oldest wish were suddenly to come true, she would be one more person to take care of, to listen to. She held onto Lynda, the wanderer, the woman for whom the world was more compelling than love, and there was no part of her that was closed against her feeling. She was frightened that it would all rush out of her, an uncontrollable tide in a storm, that the fear, if not the storm, would make her mad.

"Lynda," she called. Lynda held on. And then Charlotte knew it was the fear she had to suffer and name.

That night, she felt haunted by the phrase, "suffer the fear." Why *suffer?* She had done nothing unusually wrong. She asked Paul who, as always, was awake long after the rest of them, writing in his notebooks at the kitchen table. He looked up the word in his dictionary of synonyms and antonyms.

"Suffer," he announced. "To suffer punishment; take the consequences; take one's medicine."

Then suffer meant to tolerate, she thought. Accept.

"Pay the piper," he continued. "Face the music; get one's gruel; get or catch it in the neck!" Paul read the increasingly baroque phrases as if they were a sermon and he the unlikely preacher, arguing against his own natural inclination to forgive.

"Stand the racket!" he shouted.

Charlotte laughed.

"What's funny about that?" Paul asked.

"Oh, it's too complicated to explain. It fits."

"Take the rap!" He was standing with the book in one arm, his other arm stretched before him, finger pointed at Charlotte as he read.

"Make one's bed and lie in it. Or sleep in the bed one has made. Be hoisted on one's own petard. Throw a stone in one's own garden. Be doubly punished, get it coming and going!"

He jumped onto a chair, taken over by the intensity of the language, his finger pointed at the ceiling as he read. "Sow the wind and reap the whirlwind!" he screamed. "Die on the scaffold; die with one's boots on!"

"What's all the screaming about!" They heard Hannah's voice and turned. She was standing in the kitchen doorway in her nightgown, her face slightly flushed and swollen, having been awakened from a deep sleep.

"Swing!" Paul demanded. "Dance upon nothing," he continued in a husky, vehement whisper.

"That sounds right," Charlotte said.

"Like I said the other day," he answered.

"Dance upon nothing," she chorused. "Amen."

"What are you two talking about?" Hannah insisted. She made her way to a chair and leaned her head on the the table. She looked up at Charlotte. "What's wrong with you? You look strange."

"Dance a jig!" Paul jumped down to the floor and danced a moonwalk that would have made Ivan drool. Charlotte applauded. She even copied his movements in her own odd version of the dance.

"Kick the air," he called to her as he rolled and slid across the floor, still reading from his book, "or the wind, or the clouds."

Or the sea, she thought, knowing full well where the sound of her naming waited, that large sea creature shocked to the surface by sex, teased to partial visibility by art and love, snorting and spouting its primal music beneath the noise of the world.

The sky was light with a full moon but the water was black, white foam rippling silver, like swift brush strokes made to look like lace. She pulled off her loose dress and left it on the shore. It was a high tide Ivan would love to risk. She unbraided her hair.

She had never been able to make out the words, her full actual name. Water filled her ears blurring specificity. She only knew that something was loud (waves rolling and crashing) and something else was a whisper, promising. Who am I, who am I, she had been shouting all these years. First, no one had thought the question interesting, what with the moral issues of revolution and government tyranny under constant debate, the practical issues of money and jobs escalating to crisis, Andre's problems always requiring attention.

So she had turned her attention to them. Portraits, murals,

stories, endless questions about their lives they pretended to find tiring. But they loved being listened to, watched, probed. By now they were as used to telling her their stories as they were to confronting the mirror in the morning, an assurance that they had survived the night. She somersaulted under water, her knees hugged to her chest, and floated that way for a while, surfacing, rolling down again. She straightened, returning to the surface. She swam.

And here she was, still calling out the old question so overused by men they found it ludicrous, redundant, selfish. Who am I, who am I, from the tiniest evidence of what I do with my days to the larger one of what I have done with my history? But she had not pondered that question for centuries, at least not in any record which had been left behind. She had not used up answers in billions of pages of philosophy, libraries full of experiment, confession and dream. Perhaps I am the "hero with a thousand faces," the greatest villain of all time, noble, perhaps, or merely ordinary; nothing but clay, or the son of god, a foot soldier, a general; only a genetic link in a design for millennia; a freak; a genius; or nothing at all.

Power over what? Her list of possible answers had only begun. The fear came. The suffering fear that it would all rush out before she had a chance to name it. She swam slowly, conserving strength. She was anxious in the wet darkness around her. Her shoulders shivered as she dove under again. Her breasts were thinly covered liquid in the black waves. Then for a moment she saw them, first Miriam, then George. Their eyes penetrated her face, the way she'd seen Lynda look at Leah, Rose at Lynda, the way she looked at Ivan (yes, she had known that look, how could she have forgotten?) wanting to possess him completely, take him back into herself so she could keep him safe, and knowing she could do no such thing. Spare him from death? He would die, he would die, the boy she had carried. She turned over a low wave and floated. She lay her hands on her belly, spread her legs where Ivan's head rested momentarily between her bloody thighs.

Miriam and George looked and looked. She felt her own face melt feature by feature, opening to them. She would give it back to them if she could, her eyes, her brain, her will. She would be

310

taken back to wherever they were, killing doubt, leaping out of history into complete obliteration, if necessary, as long as she was taken, held, named. "Leonard," she said.

But this was so heavy, this suffering quest, this insufferable burden of looking for names. People thought you were a fool, a coward, a child. You felt so alone. Charlotte sunk away from pain into serene comfort. Water covered her face, filled her lungs. When it moved over her, exposing her mouth to the night again, she shouted at the shock of air, she sucked in the night, she swallowed it. She twisted in the water and tried to see the shore.

She could see a line of lights, houses over the dune, but it seemed impossibly far away. She swam toward the lights, becoming more and more frightened as she kicked wildly, pulling her arms fiercely through the waves. She heard Andre's voice — "You're a survivor, Charlotte." Disappointed. Contemptuous. Dead On Arrival, he had said, always knowing too much. No one to cradle that innocent partial vision of the child. Had she wanted to see it whole? She would settle for any torn-off part of it now.

She focused on the lights, banished all voices from her head. She swam with all her strength. She called for help.

But her legs were unbearably tired. Her arms were heavy. She turned on her back to float. Cross currents beneath her vied for control, forming a cone, its watery walls pulling her down. Black silk waters swirled around the sides of the cone. Black silk waters in a perfect circle. Or black plastic, ridged, shining. Records, she said. How funny, like a dream joke, to see records in the sea.

And that was how it came to her. A record keeper. Superfluous perceptions and crucial notes. A dance upon nothing. A moon-walk on moon rock, odd floating movements. Kick the sea. She was a record keeper, an image maker, a woman for whom the confusing, partially heard noise of life was more compelling than anything else at all. She felt something thrown across her chest, flesh behind her flesh, and she was towed slowly, effortfully into shore.

On the cold sand she was wrapped in a blanket, her eyes were kissed. She had gone almost to the horizon that she had been unable to tolerate at the edge of her painting. Someone rocked her and, though its power came from near obliteration, that

311

rocking was deeper than sex, deeper even than love. For a moment, absurdly, she thought it was Rose, but when Charlotte opened her eyes and looked up, it was Hannah George who kept repeating her name.

Epilogue

Sybila, Vivian and Alex welcomed the guests — artists, critics and friends. The gallery was small, all that Sybila could afford with the capital from her sales, but it was hers. The crowd gathered at the wine and cheese table, then moved off in different directions to view the work. Charlotte's paintings surrounded them on the stark white, semicircular walls.

The ocean scenes were admired for their muted colors and sense of visual distance. The cityscapes were criticized for their intensity. In one, a frightened elderly woman sat on a bus, a group of boys looking down on her with threatening eyes. There was a portrait of a sultry girl wearing long earrings of multi-colored feathers, a large radio pressed close to her ear. Charlotte had painted Fifth Avenue, recreating the sandy light she'd loved as a girl. She had painted Korean fruit stands, a group of men on a crowded corner passing around a joint, a department store window decorated for Christmas, a slum. This series, collectively entitled "History," was climaxed with a painting called "Holocaust" — a lone, bedraggled woman in the lower right corner sweeping tides of blood off an armory floor.

There was a series of portraits, mostly of family and friends — Vivian and Ruth wading in the bay; Jennifer reading; Annie dressed to kill, the tips of her hair died pink to match her layered dress. (This one looked more like a photograph from a fashion magazine than a painting, one critic complained.) There was a stark portrait of Alex, no background but the unpainted canvas.

"Powerful," a man said.

"Too powerful, uncomfortable," responded his friend.

There were two black and white drawings of Ivan, centered like small jewels in elaborate frames.

One dark, silver-shadowed portrait of Paul survived that summer at the beach. It was entitled "Moonwalk."

In a narrow, rectangular watercolor, Myron sat on top of a tombstone playing his flute. "Is she kidding with this one?" Vivian heard a writer say. "Yes, she is," Vivian told him. "It's a joke."

The most abstract painting was a multiple portrait, a suggestion of five faces overlapping each other. The faces looked like flat planes, only a delicate black line indicating an eye in one, a mouth in another. It was titled "For Sybila."

Finally, there was a series of boats, dark with thick purple and black. Scarce white lines indicated a hull, a broken mast. An Asian man was standing in one, lying down in the next, as if he were dead. These were the favorites of those who came to buy. One collector offered several thousand dollars for the series.

"Mom's a success," Ivan whispered to Alex as they ambled around the room, sipping white wine. "It's a good show," Alex agreed as Ivan ate an entire plate of tiny hors d'oeuvres. "Ivan!" Alex nudged him. "They're for the guests." "I'm starving," Ivan said and threw four olives into his mouth.

At the end of the gallery, close to the door, were two portraits, one of Rose Moore, the most realistic of all the paintings in an old-fashioned Renaissance style, and one of Aunt Rose. Jacob and Marilyn, Myron, Vivian and Leah stood before it for a long time.

"I wish I'd known her longer," Leah said. "I'll never forgive my mother for keeping me away so long."

"It's almost too much like Mama to take." Tears gathered in Jacob's eyes. Rose was young in the painting, her dark braid coiled neatly at the nape of her neck.

"You were as good to her as any son could be," Marilyn said, putting her arm around Michael and pulling him to her side.

"The only thing I don't understand," Jacob said, "is that old tacky hat Charlotte liked to wear last summer. Why'd she put it on Mama? Mama never wore hats."

The reviews were mixed, though everyone liked the portrait of

314

Aunt Rose in Mathilda's hat. "A mysterious image from the creative depths," said one. Charlotte received them in the mail from Alex at the small hotel in Managua where she was staying with Hannah and Paul. She was drawing constantly and corresponding regularly with Lynda in Vietnam, comparing historical notes. The day she received the news of the show she found a letter from Lynda which ended: "And Charlotte, I understand how much you miss Alex and Ivan. But they'll be okay. Don't worry so much. You've always been too emotional. Concentrate on what you're doing. You don't have all the time in the world, you know."

Charlotte stuffed Lynda's letter, along with the others, into her canvas bag and rushed into the street to meet Hannah and Paul at a political rally. She passed a line of soldiers, many of them younger than Ivan. There were American warships in Nicaraguan waters. She heard the sound of spy planes overhead. She wished she could be like Hannah, her belief tempered by necessity, her focus on what was actual, protecting her from bitterness and hasty dreams. But Charlotte feared the sight of the boys carrying rifles. She hated her country for making necessary the military efficiency of which the young soldiers were clearly so proud. She wished to see them clumsy. She wished they would be sent home. She was criticizing herself for sentimentality when she spotted Hannah George and Paul, stretching their necks, looking for her. She felt a wave of a different fear when she saw them—she might lose them too. It was beyond her contol. Everything she loved might be destroyed, her shouted protest not heard at all.

For a moment, she longed for that melting she had known in the night sea. Perhaps some day, if she lived long enough, she would be able to risk the sea again, swim better and survive. She longed for Ivan and Alex, wished it were four weeks hence when she would be on her way back to them. But she had not come with Hannah out of friendship alone, nor out of some romantic illusion that she could change her life into the one her parents had led. She had not volunteered, as Paul had put it, though she had nothing but admiration for Hannah, who had. She moved through the crowd. Charlotte was looking—she knew it now— for perspective. A side face when a direct portrait would no longer do. She had to try to keep penetrating the layers or succumb to the

315

threatening pain in her eyes. She would draw this country, its houses, its children, its guns, but when she returned home she would put Ivan's eyes in the soldier's face. She held onto the small pad and felt her fingers move with the power that had come to her as a child, demanding first her attention, then her devotion, then her dedication. This was the power that enabled her to ascertain direction, to love more wisely, to move from one place to the next—her hand on the pencil or brush, her tool on the page. Her work.

Hannah saw her, nudged Paul. They both waved. Charlotte glanced at the soldiers to her right and left and, beginning a quick drawing of a zealous young face as she passed (she ran her fingers through her short, easily managed hair), she crossed the street feeling that she might face squarely and with relatively few illusions the second half of her life.